The

Ladies of Longbourn

The acclaimed Pride and Prejudice sequel series

The Pemberley Chronicles:
Book 4

DEVISED AND COMPILED BY

Rebecca Ann Collins

SOURCEBOOKS LANDMARK™
AN IMPRINT OF SOURCEBOOKS, INC.®
NAPERVILLE, ILLINOIS

By the Same Author

The Pemberley Chronicles
The Women of Pemberley
Netherfield Park Revisited
Mr Darcy's Daughter
My Cousin Caroline
Postscript from Pemberley
Recollections of Rosings
A Woman of Influence
The Legacy of Pemberley

Published by Sourcebooks Landmark, an imprint of Sourcebooks, Inc.
P.O. Box 4410, Naperville, Illinois 60567-4410
(630) 961-3900
FAX: (630) 961-2168
www.sourcebooks.com

Originally printed and bound in Australia by SNAP Printing, Sydney, NSW, 2000.
Reprinted in 2002 and 2003.

Library of Congress Cataloging-in-Publication Data

Collins, Rebecca Ann.
  The ladies of Longbourn : a companion volume to Jane Austen's Pride and prejudice / devised and compiled by Rebecca Ann Collins.
    p. cm.
  ISBN-13: 978-1-4022-1219-2
  ISBN-10: 1-4022-1219-4
  1. England—Social life and customs—19th century—Fiction. 2. Domestic fiction. I. Austen, Jane, 1775-1817. Pride and prejudice. II. Title.
  PR9619.4.C65L33 2008
  823'.92—dc22
                                2008022771

Printed and bound in the United States of America
DR 10 9 8 7 6 5 4 3 2 1

Dedicated with love to my son,

without whose help and encouragement

none of this would have been possible.

An Introduction . . .

To those who have already read *The Pemberley Chronicles* and other Pemberley stories, an introduction is hardly necessary.

The characters "borrowed" from Jane Austen and those that Rebecca Ann Collins has created have all come some way since the days of *Pride and Prejudice*. In such a period during which England has undergone a dynamic transformation in industrial, political, and social terms, it would have been incredible that these men and women would have remained like petrified statues, untouched by the turbulence that swirled around them.

Nor is it possible to accept that they continue to be engaged only in matters of romance, gossip, and intrigue, while the forces that shaped Victorian England, reflected in the work of the Brontës and Charles Dickens, passed them by. That would be unrealistic and unfair to the intelligent and compassionate characters that Jane Austen created and certainly not believable of the men and women devised by Ms Collins.

In *The Ladies of Longbourn*, the myth of the conventional Victorian marriage is explored, revealing that women, however well brought up, were not immune from making serious errors of judgment that jeopardized their chances of happiness. That women must and did always accept a bland, passive role in return for material security is neither acceptable nor true.

How young Anne-Marie Bingley confronts and overcomes the trauma of such a situation, and its effect upon her family and friends, is seen against the background of a society where the pressures are increasing upon individuals and their families. It is a difficult and complex period, when old standards are being questioned and individual integrity is tested. It is, nevertheless, an era when certain basic values of decency and decorum may yet be applied to the conduct of men and women, whose worth may not be judged by wealth or beauty alone.

Jane Austen may not have been altogether comfortable in the world that was mid-Victorian England, but her characters would have had the stamina and wit to deal with its challenges. Ms Collins certainly believes this to be true and, while the original Austen characters provide the framework of accepted values in this story, those of the next generation such as Jonathan Bingley and his daughter Anne-Marie make their own choices and must live with them. The importance that Jane Austen placed upon personal responsibility is endorsed and reflected throughout as the characters are observed with both humor and affection.

Many of these characters will be familiar to readers of the earlier Pemberley novels, but inevitably, there are new faces and names. For those who need an aide-mémoire, a list of the main characters is provided in the Appendix.

Sydney 2000

Prologue

October 1862

WHEN JANE BINGLEY HEARD THE news, delivered by express post from Harwood House, she was at first so numb with shock that she could not move for several minutes from the chair in which she was seated.

Afterwards, she rose and went to find Mr Bingley and tell him that John Bradshaw, the husband of their granddaughter Anne-Marie, was dead of a sudden seizure, the result of a completely unforeseen heart condition, which had caused him to collapse unconscious in the vestry after Evensong on Sunday.

It appeared from the letter, written hastily and despatched by Anne-Marie's friend Eliza Harwood, that only the verger, Mr Thatcher, had been with him at the time and despite his best efforts to render what assistance he could, poor Mr Bradshaw had passed away before the doctor could even be summoned. Mr Bingley, when he had recovered from the shock, had ordered that the carriage be brought round immediately and they had set off for Pemberley to take the news to Darcy and Elizabeth.

On arriving at Pemberley, they were spared the need to break the bad news, by virtue of the fact that a message sent by Anne-Marie's father, Jonathan Bingley, via the electric telegraph, had reached Pemberley barely half an hour earlier. Elizabeth was at the entrance to greet her sister as she alighted. It was clear from Elizabeth's countenance that she knew already.

Now, there was need only to speak of the terrible sadness of it all. Mr Bradshaw was still a young man, being not yet thirty, and though not a particularly inspiring preacher, he got on well enough with everyone, and of course, here was Anne-Marie, married no more than fifteen months, a young widow.

Then, there was the need to prepare for the funeral. Mr Darcy had said his manager would attend to all the arrangements and they could travel down together. Jane was particularly happy about that. She liked having Lizzie beside her on these difficult occasions.

The letter had said the funeral would be at the parish church in Harwood Park; both the Bingleys and Darcys had houses in town, and preparations were soon in train to leave for London on the morrow.

When the Bingleys were leaving Pemberley, Elizabeth said softly, "It is difficult to believe that Mr Bradshaw is dead; they were dining with us at Portman Square only last month, together with Caroline and Fitzwilliam. We were such a merry party, too, were we not, Darcy?"

Her husband agreed, "Yes, indeed, and Bradshaw looked perfectly well."

They were all a little uncomfortable in the face of the sudden departure of someone they'd had little time to get to know and so could not mourn with any real conviction, except as the husband of Anne-Marie, for whom they all had great affection and sympathy.

At Harwood Park, where, in a small churchyard amidst many old graves, an assorted collection of relatives, acquaintances, and parishioners had gathered to bid farewell to the Reverend John Bradshaw, many could only sigh and wonder at the suddenness of his death. Jane still seemed stunned by it all. Her granddaughter Anne-Marie, veiled and clothed in deepest mourning, her small, pale face moist with tears, clung to her grandmother, accepting her comforting embrace even though Jane had no words of consolation for her.

Afterwards, there had been a very simple gathering at Harwood House, where Mr and Mrs Harwood mingled with the mourners, but Anne-Marie retired upstairs until it was time to leave. Then she said her farewells and kissed, embraced, and thanked them all before leaving with her father, his wife, and their family in a closed carriage, bound for Netherfield Park in Hertfordshire, some twenty-five miles away.

Returning to Derbyshire, other members of the family were staying overnight in Oxford, at a favourite hostelry not far from St John's College.

When the ladies withdrew after dinner, Jane, who had remained silent for most of the meal, approached her sister.

"Lizzie, this has been a time for funerals, has it not? There was our sister Mary, then the Prince Consort, and now poor Mr Bradshaw."

Elizabeth nodded; she knew Jane was feeling very depressed.

"Yes indeed, Jane, though I am quite confident that if our sister Mary could speak at this moment, she would surely point out that 'these things are sent to try us' and they usually come in threes."

Elizabeth was not being flippant or facetious, merely noting their late sister Mary Bennet's propensity to produce an aphorism for every occasion, whether happy or catastrophic, thereby reducing everything to a level of banality above which it was virtually impossible to rise. Jane, however, was not amused.

"Oh, Lizzie, how could you say such a thing! Do be serious; I was thinking of our poor young Anne-Marie and how this wretched business has blighted her life," she cried.

"So was I," said Elizabeth. "It must be a dreadful blow, but as for blighting her life, look at it this way, Jane. She is still young, not yet twenty-three, still very beautiful, and well provided for by her father. No doubt she will inherit something from her husband as well. With no young children, she will have very little to trouble her, and when she has recovered from this terrible shock, I am quite certain she will not remain a widow for very long."

Jane was aghast. "Lizzie, how can you say that, with poor Mr Bradshaw barely cold in his grave? Anne-Marie will be very cross with you."

"I am sure she would, so I shall not be saying any such thing to her," replied Elizabeth, adding, "of course she must mourn her husband. I mean only to reassure you, dear Jane, that life has certainly not ended for young Anne-Marie. I am confident there will be a better future for her."

Entering the room at that moment, Elizabeth's daughter, Cassandra Gardiner, heard her mother's words and, on being applied to for an opinion, agreed with alacrity.

"If you really want my opinion, Mama, Anne-Marie was wasted on Mr Bradshaw. Neither Richard nor I could ever understand why she married him and in such haste, too," and seeing her Aunt Jane's outraged expression, Cassandra added, "Oh I know he was good and kind and all that sort of thing, but dear me, Aunt Jane, he was quite the dullest person I have ever encountered. When they came to visit after their wedding last year, he had nothing at all to say unless it was about church reform. Poor Anne-Marie did all the talking. Mr Bradshaw insisted on walking miles to visit all the village churches in the district and wanted to attend everything from matins to Evensong, and he would drag poor Anne-Marie along, even when you could see she was longing to stay and chat with the rest of us."

"And he made some boring sermons," said Elizabeth with a sigh. "When they came to Pemberley after they had become engaged, Darcy and I could not believe they were really going to be married. Darcy still believes that Anne-Marie would never have accepted him if she'd had the opportunity to meet more people, especially more eligible and intelligent young men. He would agree with Cassy that Anne-Marie was much too good for Mr Bradshaw and so, I am sure, would Colonel Fitzwilliam. He was at Pemberley at the time, and I remember his astonishment as Mr Bradshaw got up from the table after breakfast and hurried poor Annie, as he used to call her, off to church. She went quite cheerfully, I will admit, but Fitzwilliam was amazed and said as much.

"'Upon my word,'" began Lizzie, who was a good mimic and could do Colonel Fitzwilliam very well. "'Upon my word, Darcy, I cannot imagine he is in love with her if he just keeps dragging her off to church so often.' Whereupon Darcy said, 'It appears to be his only interest. Church reform is his pet topic; I have heard him speak of little else.'"

"And did Mr Darcy not regard Mr Bradshaw as a fit and proper husband for Anne-Marie?" Jane asked, anxiously.

"Oh he was certainly fit and very proper, too, Jane," replied her sister, smiling, "but I do not believe he was interesting or energetic enough for her. She is so full of vitality and energy, feels everything so deeply, while he...I cannot honestly say I could pick a single subject upon which I have heard him speak with anything approaching passion."

"What, not even church reform?" asked Cassy, with a wicked smile, to which her mother replied with a doleful look.

"No, not even church reform. It was a subject he addressed at length and with some conviction, but in such measured tones that it was difficult to listen to him for more than a few minutes, which, if he meant to enthuse us, must surely have defeated his purpose altogether."

Jane, still shocked, did recall on being prompted by Lizzie that Mr Bingley had fallen asleep during one of Mr Bradshaw's sermons, much to her embarrassment. "Poor Bingley," she said. "He was mortified."

She was promptly assured that no one would have blamed her dear husband for the completely understandable lapse.

Cassy said she had frequently wondered what had prompted the marriage, and Richard had been of the opinion that after her mother's death, Anne-Marie must have been so deeply hurt and troubled by what she clearly regarded as her mother's betrayal of their family that she had sought the safety of a marriage with a good, dull man, who would never dream of doing anything similar.

Jane agreed that in all her letters as well as in conversations, Anne-Marie would only refer to Mr Bradshaw as "dear Mr Bradshaw" and would always tell them how very good and kind he was.

"I do not doubt, Aunt Jane, that he was a good man, but one cannot live out one's life with a person whose only claim to fame is 'goodness.' Doubtless he will have saved her soul, but surely one needs some warmth, some rapport, some shared love of music or reading to nourish the soul, which must learn to enjoy and delight in God's gifts, before it comes to be saved." Cassy, in full flight, had not noticed her father and Bingley as they entered the room until Darcy said, "That was a fair sermon in itself, Cassy."

She smiled, knowing he was teasing her, but Jane applied to Mr Darcy for a judgment upon his daughter's opinion.

"Let us ask your father if he agrees," she said, whereupon Darcy smiled a wry, crooked little smile and declared,

"If Cassy was speaking of the late Mr Bradshaw, I have to admit that I am in complete agreement with her. Neither Lizzie nor I could ever get much more than exhortations to virtuous living from the man. I am in no doubt at all of his worthy intentions, but for a young man—he was not yet thirty—he was an amazingly dull fellow." Turning to his wife, he added with a smile, "Not quite as tedious as your late cousin Mr Collins, Lizzie, but close, very close."

Jane pressed him further, "And do you believe, Mr Darcy, that Anne-Marie was mistaken when she married him? Was she deceived, do you think?"

"Mistaken? Probably. Deceived? No indeed, Anne-Marie is an intelligent young woman. She may have been mistaken when she decided that Mr Bradshaw was the right man for her, but I would not accept that she was deceived by him. Bradshaw seemed incapable of deception. He was honest—transparently so—and dull; he had few remarkable qualities, but honesty was, I am sure, one of them. No, Jane, my belief coincides to a very great extent with Cassy's. I think, though I cannot know this for certain, that Anne-Marie was so disturbed by her mother's irrational behaviour and by the terrible events that led to her death that she accepted Bradshaw, believing that marriage to him offered a safe, secure life without risk of betrayal or hurt," he said, and his sombre voice reflected his sadness.

It had been only a year or two ago that Darcy had, in conversation with his wife, expressed the hope that Anne-Marie would widen her horizons beyond her nursing career, hoping her friendship with Anna Faulkner would engage her mind and encourage an appreciation of the arts.

"Do you believe she never loved him then?" asked Jane, sadly.

Darcy found it hard to answer her.

"I am not privy to her thoughts, but I do know that she always spoke of him with respect and affection. But whether her feelings were deeply engaged, I cannot judge," he replied.

"I saw no sign of it," said Cassy, firmly.

"No indeed," Elizabeth agreed, "yet, they always seemed content. I cannot believe she was unhappy."

As her husband Richard Gardiner came in to join them, Cassy spoke.

"Not unless you believe that the absence of deeply felt love in a marriage constitutes an absence of happiness," said Cassy, of whose happiness there was never any doubt. "For my part, such a situation would have been intolerable."

Cassy had once declared she would never marry except for the very deepest love, and no one who knew them doubted that she had kept her word. Recalling her own determination that she would rather remain unwed than marry without an assurance of deep and sincere affection, Elizabeth could only express the hope that Anne-Marie would find that life had more to offer her in the future.

❦

The return of Mr and Mrs Bingley to Netherfield with their widowed daughter was certain to cause comment in the village and on the estate, but knowing the esteem in which the family was held, Mrs Perrot, the housekeeper, was quite confident it would be uniformly sympathetic.

Ever since the news had arrived by electric telegraph late on Sunday night, the house had been in turmoil, with the master plainly shocked and Mrs Bingley, who was usually so calm, in floods of tears.

"Poor Anne-Marie, poor dear Anne-Marie," she had said over and over again. "Oh, Mrs Perrot, it is just not fair!"

Mrs Perrot, who had lost a husband in the war and a son killed in an accident on the railways, agreed that life sometimes just wasn't fair.

Mrs Perrot and the manager, Mr Bowles, had had a little discussion and decided that no special fuss would be made when Mrs Bradshaw arrived at Netherfield House. "It's best we let the young lady rest a while," Bowles had suggested and she had agreed. He would convey the sympathies of the entire staff and, if Mrs Perrot wished, she could add her own, he had said. So it was resolved and the maids and footmen were urged to restrain themselves, lest they cause Mrs Bradshaw even more distress.

But, when the carriage drew up at the front steps and Mr Bingley alighted and helped first his wife and then his daughter out, their resolutions counted for naught. As the slight figure in deep mourning, her face still veiled, came up the steps, sobbing maids and tearful menservants scattered. Recalling the bright morning a mere fifteen months ago on which she had left the house as a bride, they were overcome with sadness.

Anne-Marie entered the hall and, having accepted the condolences of both Mr Bowles and Mrs Perrot, went quietly upstairs, following the maid who was to look after her at Netherfield. Jenny Dawkins's mother had worked at Netherfield many years ago, before the Bingleys moved to Leicestershire, and Jenny had returned as a chambermaid when Jonathan Bingley bought the property three years ago. She had been honoured to be chosen by Mr Bowles and Mrs Perrot to attend on Miss Anne-Marie when she first came to Netherfield House. Thereafter, Jenny had attended her whenever she visited, and a warm friendship had grown between them.

Jenny had remained very quiet, warned by Mrs Perrot not to "blub" and upset Mrs Bradshaw, but once they were in her room and Anne-Marie removed her bonnet and veil and turned to her maid, Jenny could hold out no longer. It all came out in a great rush of tears and words, as she ran to her mistress. "Oh, ma'am, I am so sorry," she cried, and as they embraced and wept, it seemed as if Anne-Marie was doing the comforting and it was Jenny who was bereaved.

Jonathan Bingley had been concerned for his daughter. She had been silent for most of the journey, and he was not surprised when she did not come downstairs to dinner.

"Jenny did take a tray upstairs to her, sir, but Mrs Bradshaw had hardly touched the food," said Mrs Perrot, when asked.

Anna, who had finished her dinner, rose and moved to leave the room.

"I shall go to her," she said, and Jonathan reached out and touched her hand, thanking her, reassuring her of his confidence.

He recalled how it had been three years ago, when his first wife Amelia-Jane had been killed in a dreadful accident on her way to Bath. Anna had been invaluable with the girls.

Anne-Marie, though barely twenty at the time, had borne the shock of the news well, with Anna's help, and had helped her two younger sisters, Teresa and Cathy, to cope with their loss. This time, the loss was her own, and there was little her young sisters could do or say that would help her.

Anna, however, was different, Jonathan thought.

He was sure she would find the right words. Her strength of understanding and sensitivity to the feelings of others had enabled her to bring harmony and purpose into their lives at Netherfield Park at a time of considerable confusion, even despair. He knew he could never thank her enough for the delight she had brought him in their marriage, with her warm, affectionate nature and passionate heart.

He had no doubt that Anna would help his daughter cope with her present misfortune. For herself, Anna was not altogether confident that she could.

❧

Anne-Marie had spent only a small part of her adult life at home with her parents, since at seventeen, inspired by the example of Miss Florence Nightingale, she had decided to train as a nurse. Tired of her mother's superficial social round and the inconsequential comings and goings at Rosings Park, where they had lived while her father managed the estates of Lady Catherine de Bourgh, Anne-Marie had determined to do something useful with her life.

Abandoning the clothes and jewellery with which her mother had decked her for many years, she had taken to dressing with abstemious simplicity and had taken work at the military hospital in the grounds of Harwood Park, where for many years she had lived at the invitation of her friend and cousin Eliza Harwood. It was there she had met the hospital chaplain, John Bradshaw, who ministered to the same broken men she worked so hard to heal. She had found much to admire in his work in the spiritual ministry to dispirited men and had shared his concern for them and their families. As a close friend of the Harwoods, Bradshaw had been a frequent visitor to their house, and both Eliza and her husband were very pleased when Anne-Marie had announced that they were engaged to be married.

Anna remembered well the day her letter had arrived. Jonathan Bingley had been in his study and had raced upstairs at great speed to find her, unable to comprehend how it had come about.

"Why, Anna, we hardly know him at all," he had said, clearly perturbed by the news. Anna had been very surprised herself, but concealed her feelings well as she let him explain his reservations.

"Had you any knowledge of this?" he had asked, and when she confessed to being totally ignorant of the matter, he had been extremely concerned.

"It is not like Anne-Marie to be so secretive. She is by nature open and frank in all things. When she was little, far more than Charles or Tess, she would seek me out and tell me everything she had been doing and then, during those terrible weeks before her mother's death, it was she, above anyone, who tried to alert me to Amelia-Jane's troubled state of mind.

"Why has she not said a word to me about this—this Bradshaw fellow? I know nothing of the man," he complained, clearly unhappy.

There was little Anna could say to reassure him, having no knowledge at all of Mr Bradshaw, except that he was a conscientious hospital chaplain. Of his character, background, and other interests, they were in complete ignorance.

Later, when Anne-Marie and Mr Bradshaw had visited Netherfield, together with their friends, the Harwoods, who were plainly delighted with the match, her father's disquiet had appeared to ease somewhat, if only because he had a good deal of respect for the Harwoods and knew that Eliza was Anne-Marie's close friend.

"It is unlikely," he told Anna afterwards, "that they would have seemed so pleased about the engagement if they had not been sure it was well founded. After all, they know both Anne-Marie and Bradshaw and are best placed to judge."

Anna had agreed, but after Mr Bradshaw had spent a few days at Netherfield, during which his conversation had seemed limited to just one or two topics of an ecclesiastical nature, and the only music he was familiar with were hymns and anthems, she had admitted to herself that she was beginning to worry. With so little in common, what, she wondered, would they talk about when they were not at the hospital or in church?

Writing to Emma Wilson, her sister-in-law and confidante, Anna had said,

Dearest Emma,

I am unable to ignore a feeling of unease about this match, as if all is not as it seems. Yet, Anne-Marie seems so content, it is difficult to believe that a mistake has been made. Reverend Bradshaw is himself most attentive to his bride to be, whom he calls "Annie," which Jonathan reminded me was the name of the little ladies' maid, Annie Ashton, who was killed in the same accident as Amelia-Jane. He wonders if Mr Bradshaw's use of the pet name may upset Anne-Marie, but in truth, she appears not to mind at all.

Though confused and a little apprehensive, Anna had said nothing to Anne-Marie. Experience had taught her tact and, together with her natural reluctance to pry into the affairs of others, she had restrained any desire to query, confident that in time she would come to know Mr Bradshaw better and discover why Anne-Marie had chosen to marry him. Anna was certain there would be a good reason. Anne-Marie was not some silly young woman, nor was Mr Bradshaw the likely subject of a thoughtless infatuation; it was just that she could not see it, she told herself.

She continued her letter to Emma,

I can understand the attraction in his case—apart from her beauty, her intelligence, good nature, and strong sense of Christian charity would be obvious advantages to a man in his position. She will make an excellent clergyman's wife, but, Emma, dear, I wish I knew why Anne-Marie has accepted him. We know nothing of him beyond the obvious, and in his conversation, he reveals very little of himself. Perhaps, he is reserved, as many clergymen are, and it may be that after they are married, he might be less so, and his excellent qualities of mind and character would become clear to us all. For Anne-Marie's sake and for the peace of mind of my dear husband, I pray this is true. Jonathan is filled with misgivings, and if it were possible, he would speak with her, but this is impossible since we are at all times accompanied by either the Harwoods or Mr Bradshaw himself.

He is courteous and very well spoken; if only he were even a little more interesting, I might be satisfied and say no more!

Despite her hopes, however, Anna had not succeeded in discovering why young Anne-Marie Bingley had decided, with no prompting from anyone in her family, that it was time to be married and then chosen to wed Mr John Bradshaw. All they knew was the couple had worked together at the military hospital, where he was chaplain, and Mr Bradshaw had served in the war with John Harwood. That both Mr and Mrs Harwood held him in high esteem was at least some source of satisfaction, but it had not explained Anne-Marie's attachment to him. Neither her father nor Anna had discussed it with her, although both had some reservations about the match, which they had expressed chiefly to one another.

Anna wrote to Emma Wilson,

At least, Eliza Harwood can be counted on to ensure that Anne-Marie is fully aware of everything she herself knows about the man to whom she has become engaged, and if Mr Harwood and he served in the Crimea together, there is probably not a great deal the two men do not know about each other. Surely, he cannot have been of questionable character and be appointed a chaplain; he must be a good and respectable man.

In her reply, Emma had seemed to concur, and in the year that followed, nothing had come to light to change their opinion.

꧁꧂

When Anna Bingley entered Anne-Marie's bedroom, she found her alone, still seated in the chair she had drawn up to the window, from where she could look out at the park. This was her favourite room, her very own room in her father's house; Anna recalled how much care had been taken to furnish it with taste and style, making it ready for her, when following her mother's death,

Anne-Marie had come home to Netherfield for the first time. It had been, for the most part, a happy homecoming.

Here she was again, coming home after another funeral—her husband's.

As Anna closed the door, Anne-Marie rose from her chair and Anna went to her, embracing her, holding her close. As Anne-Marie's tears flowed and her sobbing increased, Anna could not help wondering at the violence of her grief. While she had expected and indeed welcomed Anne-Marie's expressions of sorrow as being natural and necessary, Anna was quite surprised by their intensity, which seemed to her to be not commensurate with the restrained nature of the couple's attachment.

There had always appeared to be a high degree of reserve in their relationship, even in the privacy of their family, a quality one might have interpreted as part of the natural decorum of a clergyman and his wife. Yet, on occasions, the lack of any warmth and ardour had caused Anna to wonder whether, in spite of Anne-Marie's apparent contentment, there was some impediment to their happiness of which she was unaware. Apart from her own experience of marriage, in which she was deeply happy, Anna knew other couples, who when newly wed, had seemed far less able to conceal their feelings than Mr Bradshaw and his bride.

This was why Anna was so astonished by the extraordinary severity of Anne-Marie's outpouring of grief. As her body shook with sobs, Anna held her, trying to find a moment at which she could intervene, to speak some consoling words, but for fully five minutes there was not a word exchanged.

Finally, fearful that she may suffer some injury as a result of her exertions, and not wanting to encourage her to any further extremity, Anna took Anne-Marie to the bed and attempted to help her lie against the pillows.

"There, let me help you out of this gown and into something more comfortable," she said, picking up a wrap which the maid had laid out for her. At those words, Anne-Marie sat up abruptly and having borrowed a handkerchief to dry her eyes and blow her nose, she said in a perfectly ordinary voice, "Thank you, Anna, but if you will send for Jenny, I think I should like to take a bath and go to bed."

Taken aback by this sudden change of mood, Anna asked, "Would you like me to stay with you or perhaps come back after you have had your bath?" But it seemed this would not be necessary.

"No, Anna, you must be very tired yourself. You have been very kind and it has been a long day. I think I can cope. If you send Jenny to me, I shall be all right," she said, very firmly.

Anna could not make it out at all and was becoming increasingly concerned about young Anne-Marie's state of mind. Having found Jenny and sent her upstairs to her mistress, she rejoined her husband, who had waited for her in the drawing room. Anna did not wish to trouble him with her own disquieting thoughts. Fortunately, Jonathan was himself so tired that she found he was in no hurry to question her about Anne-Marie. Once she had reassured him his daughter wanted only to bathe and go to bed, he was satisfied that she was being well cared for. It had been, for them all, a most exhausting day.

Anna kept her thoughts to herself until she had time later in the week, with her husband having left for Longbourn soon after breakfast, to write again to Emma Wilson. They had met briefly after Mr Bradshaw's funeral, and it was Anna's turn to write.

With Emma, she could be as open and forthright as she wished to be, for between them there had grown an association of affection and trust, which meant a great deal to both women. That their husbands were close and loyal friends, political colleagues as well as brothers-in-law, served only to enhance the value of their own friendship. Their letters to each other were always as candid and honest as the depth and intimacy of their friendship would allow.

When Emma Wilson received her sister-in-law's letter, she was extremely puzzled. Anna seemed quite unlike her usual calm, collected self; indeed she seemed so discomposed in concluding the letter that her handwriting appeared unusually hurried and unclear, as if her hand was shaking. Yet, at the start of the letter, the words and hand were both quite distinct. Emma turned back to the beginning.

Anna wrote,

> *Dearest Emma,*
>
> *It is not only because I owe you a letter that I sit down to write, but because I truly have need of a trusted friend to whom I may unburden myself. I cannot, so soon after the shock of Mr Bradshaw's untimely death and the pain of the funeral, impose upon my dear husband more anxieties,*

greater even than he has borne to date. Yet, I can no longer keep my misgivings to myself, so you, my dear sister, must forgive this intrusion of my troubles into your oasis of peace at Standish Park. I have some time to myself this morning, with Jonathan gone to Longbourn and Anne-Marie still abed with a cold, while Teresa and Cathy are gone with Mrs Perrot to church.

My concerns are about Anne-Marie, who has been with us this last week, since the funeral. Naturally, I had expected to help her cope with her grief, and believing I knew her well enough, I sought to comfort her, only to be faced with an outpouring of sorrow so extreme as to completely confound me. I wondered, had I laboured all these months under some misapprehension? Had there been some great passion between them, which I had failed to recognise? I was afraid lest anything I said offended her and yet I understood her not at all. It was most confusing.

However, infinitely more disquieting was the suddenness with which she stopped weeping, blew her nose, dried her tears, and declared that she was well and no longer needed my company, much less my counsel. Emma, if I believed this to be true, I would not be concerned; but it is difficult to accept that the young woman whose lamentation I had just heard had within a few minutes pulled herself together and decided she needed only a bath before bed.

The following morning and every morning thereafter, she has risen early and gone to church, alone or with her maid Jenny, returning only after the family has finished breakfast. During the day, she retires to her room or to the library, where she spends most of her time reading or gazing out of the windows. This I have from Mrs Perrot in whom Jenny has confided. She is most concerned about Anne-Marie. At night, she dines early, eating a mere morsel of food, and retires to her room, where if Jonathan or I intrude upon her, even to say goodnight or ask after her health, she is immediately in floods of tears. Only with young Jenny, her maid, is she able to converse without weeping.

Now Emma, you are probably going to tell me that Anne-Marie has just been widowed and at twenty-three she is young enough to behave as she does in such distressing circumstances. You would be right, and I would be the first to acknowledge it, if I thought that the explanation fitted the circumstances. Unfortunately, dear Emma, I cannot. Nothing that I have known or observed of Anne-Marie and Mr Bradshaw leads me to believe that their feelings were commensurate with the intensity and violence of her present grief.

Emma, I think if I were to give you one instance, you might better understand my concern. Some months ago, Anne-Marie and Mr Bradshaw were spending a week with us, as were Caroline Fitzwilliam and her young daughter, Amy. On the Sunday, Frank Grantley, who had recently become engaged to Amy, arrived, announced that he had been invited by my father to visit St Alban's Abbey and Cathedral, and urged all of us to accompany them. It being a perfectly splendid day, with no sign of rain, it was suggested that we take a picnic and so it was arranged.

Now, as you know, Emma, my father's enthusiasm for these historic places is quite fanatical, and together with the verger he took us through every significant part of the old place, from the Norman tower to the site of the martyr's tomb!

Both couples followed us through the ruins of the abbey and the great cathedral, but the contrast between them could not have been greater. While Frank was keenly interested and Amy listened eagerly to every description, there was no mistaking the fact that their chief fascination was with each other. Indeed, it was quite touching, and not a little amusing, to watch how much care he took to explain details of church architecture and practice to her and even console her, when she seemed distressed at the rather gruesome story of St Alban's martyrdom, as told by the verger. Not only was their fondness for one another quite obvious, it was clear that neither wished to conceal it, although they behaved with decorum at all times.

With Mr Bradshaw and Anne-Marie, there was no such closeness. His interest was all upon the architecture and antiquity of St Alban's Cathedral and the historic abbey. Indeed, he would be fixed upon the proportions of the tower or the nave or the detail of the carved oak doors, asking so many studious questions of the verger or my father, while she wandered away, seemingly disinterested, into the presbytery or the cloisters. A stranger might well have taken them to be indifferent acquaintances rather than husband and wife. It was quite remarkable, except none of us seemed to want to remark upon it.

Later, as we enjoyed a picnic in the adjacent meadow, Anne-Marie sat with Jonathan and myself and talked of the blueness of the sky or the beauty of the flowers, while Mr Bradshaw continued his interrogation of my father about St Alban's. The other pair of lovers took advantage of the opportunity to walk in the woods and disappeared accordingly.

On the way home and afterwards, I could see no sign of the warmth and affection one expects of couples newly wed between Anne-Marie and Mr Bradshaw. Which is why I am truly unable to fathom the intensity of Anne-Marie's grief. Can you help me, dear Emma? Is there something I have failed to see?

At this point, the writer appeared to have been interrupted, for the letter was broken off and was not resumed for, it appeared, quite a while.

As it turned out, it was several hours before Anna could take up her pen again. Unbeknownst to any of her family, it seemed she had faced a crisis, which had come upon her so swiftly and with so little warning, she'd had no time to call upon anyone for help, except young Jenny Dawkins.

Her description of the frightening episode quite bewildered Emma, as she read of Anna being interrupted in her sitting room by Jenny Dawkins, who had rushed in, wringing her hands and claiming that Anne-Marie had collapsed upon the floor of her room. Anna had rushed to her bedroom and found Anne-Marie slumped on the rug beside her bed. With Jenny's help, she had been revived and helped into a reclining chair. As the colour returned to Anne-Marie's face, which had been frighteningly pale, Anna had sent Jenny downstairs to bring up some tea and toast. Then, taking advantage of her maid's absence, Anna had pleaded with Anne-Marie.

"My dear Anne-Marie, you can, if you wish, tell me to mind my business, but your father and I are worried and anxious about you. We love you and want to help you through this dreadful time, if you will only let us. I can see you are unhappy and grieving; will you not talk to me about it?"

At first, Anne-Marie had merely looked away, shaking her head, but as Anna persisted, "Are you sure, my dear? This is not like you. We have shared sad times before, and I know it must be very difficult, but I would like very much to help, if you wish it," the tears had begun again, but this time the words came, too, and soon it had all poured out.

Haltingly, painfully, it was told, a strange tale of John Bradshaw's approach to her some months after her mother's death and Eliza Harwood's active encouragement of it.

"She reminded me that he was a good, kind, Christian man, who could be trusted to look after me and would remain faithful to me." But, when Anne-Marie, while acknowledging all this, had said she did not love Mr Bradshaw, Eliza had reassured her that one should not always look for love and romance, for as she had said, "Love is not everything, and Romance, well it is a fleeting, fanciful thing. Trust, loyalty, and goodness above all are far more important to a marriage," she had said, adding that marriage to Mr Bradshaw would mean that "you will always be near me, my dear friend, for if Mr Harwood does as he plans and offers your Mr Bradshaw the living at Harwood Park when it falls vacant next year, you will want for nothing, for we shall be neighbours, forever!"

When Anna, who was already shocked by Anne-Marie's revelations, asked, "And what did you say, Anne-Marie?" she replied, "I said most firmly, that I could not, however good Mr Bradshaw might be and even more because of it; I could not possibly agree to marry him, knowing I did not love him. But Eliza was very persuasive."

Anne-Marie admitted that her friend's kindness to her in the recent past had weighed upon her mind and she had not wanted to lose her friendship.

"I wondered also, what would become of me, were I to remain unwed."

Anna was astounded. "My dear Anne-Marie, surely you did not imagine that your father would not have made the best possible provision for you? There was no need for you to feel under any obligation to the Harwoods, however hospitable they had been to you, not to the extent of taking Eliza Harwood's advice on the man you marry!" she said, and to her great relief, Anne-Marie agreed.

"I know that now, but at the time I think I was so depressed by all that had happened with Mama, I felt I needed the security of her approval," she confessed and added, "but there was also Mr Bradshaw to consider; he had waited patiently for my answer, for many months, as he promised he would. I began to feel guilty about refusing him after all that time. Besides, we worked very well together at the hospital."

Anna shook her head, unable to comprehend the situation.

"And do you mean to tell me that you accepted him and later married him, knowing you did not love him? Did he know how you felt?"

At this, Anne-Marie began to sob again, and Anna had to hold her until she was quiet and able to speak coherently.

It appeared, from the story Anne-Marie told, that Eliza Harwood had agreed to acquaint Mr Bradshaw with her young friend's answer and returned with the astonishing response that Mr Bradshaw accepted that she was not in love with him, but he so loved and admired her qualities, he had remained steadfast and had not changed his mind. By this time, it appeared Anne-Marie seemed to have allowed herself to be persuaded that this unselfish love was more to be valued than any romantic passion and accepted him, confident of the rightness of her choice.

Trying to explain the situation to Emma Wilson, Anna had returned to continue her letter, some hours later, her hand still unsteady from the shock.

Now, her conscience is stricken as she contemplates his sudden death, seeing it as some form of divine punishment upon her for having entered into a marriage without love. She believes she is being punished for having falsely vowed to love him, when she knew she did not.

Emma, she has told me that while she never denied her husband his rights, she felt no passion, no love, and no pleasure in the consummation of their marriage.

So depressed has she been, she claims, she has often wished from the bottom of her heart that she would catch some disease as she tended her patients in the hospital and die!

And yet, to us and to her friends at Harwood Park, she maintained a pretence of being a contented wife. Poor Anne-Marie, how wretched must she have felt, alone, unable to confide in anyone; dear Emma, one is almost persuaded that his death has been for her, at least, a merciful release from a nightmare. However, she blames herself, for she alone made her choice, and her contrition is all absorbing, making her grief excessively painful to bear.

There is also the added sorrow of the loss of trust in her friend Eliza, whom she will not blame but quite clearly does not trust anymore. Indeed, I am inclined to believe that this is an even greater source of grief to Anne-Marie than the death of Mr Bradshaw.

I have done my best to console her, but she refuses to be comforted, believing she must suffer for having wronged her husband and deceived her family. She claims Charles, her brother, warned her she would be miserable with Bradshaw, but she had declared that she loved him, which was completely false. Now, she wonders how she is to face her brother with the truth. It will not be easy to persuade her that she is not entirely to blame. How shall we restore her trust?

Dearest Emma, I cannot still believe all I have seen and heard today. How am I to help her and how much of this must I tell Jonathan? He is her father and should know it all, but she will not let me speak to him of it, at least not just yet.

My dear sister, if it were not that I could trust you implicitly and tell you everything, I think I should have been quite ill myself with anxiety. Please do not speak of this to James, at any rate, not until I have Anne-Marie's permission to tell Jonathan.

I must conclude now, for Jonathan will soon be returning from Longbourn.

Dear Emma, please write as soon as you can spare the time. I need your understanding and wise counsel.

Your loving sister-etc.

When she had read Anna's letter through a second time, Emma Wilson knew exactly what she had to do. Her husband James was at Westminster; with the busy autumn session of the Parliament drawing to a close, he was not expected back at Standish Park until the end of the week. Her daughter Victoria, recently engaged, was with her Aunt Sophie and her husband, who were touring France. That left her two sons, Charles and Colin, who could surely be trusted to the care of their tutor and the rest of the staff at Standish Park.

Having decided upon a course of action, Emma wasted little time, despatching a man to send a message by electric telegraph to James, in which she explained that Anna and Jonathan needed her help and she was travelling to Netherfield Park with Stephanie, her maid Lucy, and a man-servant. She expected to return at the week's end, she said, with her niece Anne-Marie and her maid.

She knew that James, reading between the lines, would understand that a crisis of some sort had developed and she was needed at Netherfield. He would make no objection, she was certain, but in case he arrived home earlier than she did, she left him Anna's letter in a sealed cover with a note attached in her own hand, by way of explanation. So strong was her belief in his understanding, so sure her faith in his love, that she made her arrangements and left for Hertfordshire, having no qualms at all.

They would have to break journey en route, and she arranged to send an express to Anna, advising of their imminent arrival.

The news was greeted with great pleasure and even greater relief at Netherfield Park, for Anna knew that Emma Wilson was a favourite among Jonathan's daughters and she was confident her arrival would help Anne-Marie as nothing else could. Anne-Marie adored her aunt and upheld her as an example to all women. Anna had no doubt that Emma must have a plan to invite her niece to return with her to Standish Park.

When she told Jonathan the news, he threw up his hands and sighed, as if a great burden had rolled off his shoulders.

"Thank God!" he said, taking her hand in his, needing the comfort of her touch. "Emma is one person who will be able to match Anne-Marie's anguish. Even though it was many years ago, none of us has forgotten the pain and hurt she suffered and from which she has emerged without bitterness. If anyone can help Anne-Marie through this sorrow, she can."

Anna was happy to have been the bearer of good news, but even as he spoke, without the benefit of the whole truth concerning his daughter's marriage, believing only that she was still mourning the death of her husband, Anna wondered how he might respond, were he to discover all of the facts. She knew she would have to tell him one day soon, but for the moment, she was certain it should not even be attempted. She loved him dearly and wanted to ease his anxiety. It was sufficient for her to see the relief in his eyes, knowing that his sister would soon be here, confident that she would know, more than he would, how Anne-Marie might be comforted.

When the little party from Standish Park arrived the following day, they were received with so much warmth and affection that Emma knew she had been right to come at once. Her brother and Anna, both of whom looked drawn and tired, clasped her close and thanked her for coming. When she entered the saloon, there was Anne-Marie, still in deep mourning, but trying to smile, while tears still stained her pale cheeks.

Emma, whose love for her brother's children was unqualified, took her niece in her arms, and as they stood together quietly, the rest of the family left the room and followed Mrs Perrot to the back parlour, where refreshments awaited the travellers after their long journey.

End of Prologue

THE LADIES OF LONGBOURN

Part One

1863

S PRING TOOK ITS TIME COMING to Hertfordshire that year. January and February had been cold and wet, providing little encourage- ment for anyone to venture out, unless it was absolutely essential to do so. Teresa and Cathy had been invited to their grandparents' home, Ashford Park in Leicestershire, and would not be back for some weeks. Anna Bingley went regularly, sometimes with her husband, to visit her parents at Haye Park and to Longbourn, to see her aunt, Charlotte Collins.

The Faulkners always welcomed their visits. In addition to the obvious pleasure of seeing their daughter and grandson, Dr Faulkner had found in his son- in-law a man after his own heart. Modest, amiable, and good humoured, with strong principles and a genuine desire to help those around him, be they his friends and relations or the men and women who lived and worked on his estates, Jonathan Bingley had pleased and surprised his father-in-law with the strength of his conviction that fairness was an essential ingredient of a civilised society.

As one who cared with equal solicitude for all his patients, rich and poor alike, Dr Faulkner was singularly impressed with a landowner who had been a parliamentarian and yet could put the interests of his tenants and labourers above profit, in an age that saw men grow greedier by the day. He was well satisfied that his daughter had married such a man as she could both love and respect.

As for Mrs Faulkner, so completely overwhelmed was she by the idea of her daughter being the mistress of both Netherfield Park and Longbourn, which Jonathan Bingley had inherited in its entirety after the death of his aunt Miss Mary Bennet, that she asked for little more than an occasional invitation to dine at Netherfield. With the arrival of their grandson Nicholas, her cup of joy was filled to overflowing.

Following the death of Mary Bennet, Charlotte Collins had continued to live at Longbourn, where on Anna's initiative and with Jonathan Bingley's encouragement, a School of Fine Arts for Young Ladies had been established. As the excellence of Anna Bingley's teaching of Art and Music and her aunt's reputation as a firm and scrupulous mistress in charge became more widely known, several new enrolments had resulted and there had been many more enquiries this year, from all over the district, as the daughters of the middle class sought artistic accomplishment. Mrs Collins believed they ought to consider taking on another teacher, in addition to Mrs Lucy Sutton, a widow who had moved to Meryton from London with her children, and was doing well teaching the younger pupils. Plans were afoot to resume after Easter for the new term, and Mrs Collins and her staff were busy making preparations to receive their new pupils.

Jonathan Bingley, having just returned from Longbourn, was divesting himself of his coat in the hall, when Anna came downstairs with their son Nicholas, who flung himself into his father's arms with the excessive enthusiasm of most energetic two-year-olds. Stopping to hoist his son onto his shoulders, Jonathan joined his wife on the stairs and, as he did so, noticed the letter in her hand. Recognising immediately Anne-Marie's handwriting and the notepaper from Standish Park, he asked "Does Anne-Marie write to say she is coming home?"

Anna nodded, smiling. She knew how much he had missed his daughter, who had been away in Kent since before Christmas.

"Yes indeed, we are to expect them on Thursday. I believe, Emma, James, and their youngest boy will stay with us a week. Young Charles is back at school, and Victoria and Stephanie are in London, making preparations for the wedding," she said, glancing at the letter, as she told him the news.

"That is excellent news, excellent," said her husband, fairly beaming with pleasure, "and how does she write? Is she cheerful? Has she been well all Winter?" he asked and Anna laughed, "Oh, Jonathan, you know we would have been informed if she had been unwell. Of course she is well and what is even better, she seems well on the way to recovering her spirits, too. She writes of her determination to get back to work."

Then seeing the look of alarm that crossed his face, she said quickly, "Not at the hospital at Harwood Park, no, but she has a plan in mind for a children's hospital in Meryton. She says she has discussed it with Emma and James and is keen to get to work on her plans. I gather from her letter that she has accompanied Emma on some of her charity work in the back streets of London and has been moved by the plight of the children there. They get little medical attention and many die of neglect," said Anna, adding grimly, "It really is a scandal, Jonathan."

Her husband agreed that it was.

"Yes indeed, my dear, I am ashamed to admit that governments in England, and here I do not exempt my own party, have repeatedly shirked their responsibilities in this regard. Ever since 1848, decent people have demanded that the government take action to improve the health of ordinary folk, but despite the passage of the Public Health Act, very little progress has been made. Unfortunately, our governments prefer to leave it to the local boards of health and the religious charities to run health services. These bodies are usually far more concerned with other matters than the health of the poor. Both James and I have always believed the government must do more," he declared.

By this time, young Nicholas had become bored and impatient. He had hoped his father would play with him, but since that was not forthcoming, he demanded to be set down, so he could climb the stairs alone and demonstrate his independence. Conversation had to be suspended while his parents indulged him and praised his efforts. He was a lively child and was not often refused attention when he sought it.

Later, after his nurse had taken Nicholas away to the nursery, Jonathan returned to his daughter's letter. He wanted to know what more she had written and what impression Anna had formed of her state of mind.

He was still desperately anxious for her.

In the long Winter months during which Anne-Marie had remained with her Aunt Emma Wilson at Standish Park, Anna had had the unhappy task of acquainting her husband with the whole truth about his daughter's marriage and the reasons for her anguish, which had been kept from him.

At first, he had been stunned by the enormity of it all. He could not believe that the Harwoods, who had been her special friends, had thought it right to persuade her into such a marriage. It seemed to him a heartless and unconscionable thing to have done. He was angry, too, that he had never been consulted.

"What right did they have to take upon themselves the duty of advising her upon such an intimate and important matter? Surely, if any one had responsibility, it was I? Anne-Marie should have been encouraged to confide in us before accepting Bradshaw. I cannot concede that the Harwoods had any greater claim to advise her on such matters. I should, at least, have tried to make her see that it was a decision fraught with danger for both of them. To make a mistake in love and acknowledge it is one thing; but to coldly agree to enter into a marriage without love is quite another matter. I am not surprised she has suffered terribly; she is too sensitive, too softhearted to accept such an arrangement and feel no remorse," he said and, hearing the anguish in his voice, Anna knew his resentment would not abate easily.

❧

Shortly after Christmas, Jonathan had received a letter from his mother, Mrs Jane Bingley, which set him thinking. Jane had reported, that in the opinion of her sister Elizabeth and Mr Darcy, the Harwoods had probably been motivated by the thought of securing a suitable wife for their good friend Mr Bradshaw and saw Anne-Marie, with her dedication to the sick and suffering, as the ideal person.

Jane had written,

Your Aunt Lizzie believes that this intention was probably behind their promotion of the match, by which they hoped to advantage their friend and, at the same time, ensure that Anne-Marie was settled near them. I do know that Eliza Harwood has always been very attached to Anne-Marie. I think it likely that the Harwoods, perhaps with the best of intentions, attempted to secure the interests of both their friends, for I cannot believe that Eliza would knowingly encourage Anne-Marie to do something that was detrimental to her own happiness. It must also be admitted that seen from a purely practical point of view, Mr Bradshaw was a respectable man, of good character and with a good living; though we could, of course, argue that he was not good enough for our Anne-Marie.

Mrs Harwood's mother, Emily Courtney, has told Aunt Lizzie that Eliza is desolated, not only by the death of Mr Bradshaw, but also by the inevitable separation from her very dear friend and cousin that has resulted from this tragedy. Eliza does not make friends easily, Emily says, and Anne-Marie's friendship was very precious to her.

Jane Bingley, still inclined to seek the most favourable motivation for any action, was clearly unaware of the more harrowing details of the situation in which Anne-Marie had found herself after her marriage to Bradshaw and the extent to which her friends had influenced her decision.

Despite his mother's rather charitable explanation, Jonathan was yet to be convinced that there had not been some devious plan by the Harwoods to contrive a good match for their friend Mr Bradshaw, who appeared to have little or no fortune apart from his living at Harwood Park, which would secure his future in the church. The Harwoods, well aware of Anne-Marie's circumstances and those of her family, may well have seen an advantage to their friend in her connections, especially with the Darcys at Pemberley, and acted to bring about the match, despite Anne-Marie's reservations. He knew little of Eliza Harwood and even less of her husband John, except that they had been his daughter's dear friends. Now, he was not so sure.

Set beside Anna's revelations of the anguish his daughter had clearly suffered, Jonathan found it hard to credit the Harwoods with noble intentions.

Anna, aware of his feelings of outrage, had spent many hours encouraging him to believe that Anne-Marie would not be permanently scarred by what had happened. Emma Wilson's letters had helped convince her that there was hope, but her husband was less easily persuaded that his daughter would fully recover her spirits.

Now she was coming home, he was delighted and yet apprehensive.

"Do you suppose, my dear, that she has come to terms with the experience, or has she perhaps tried merely to thrust it out of her mind, hoping to stifle it?" he asked his wife, as he returned to the subject.

Anna was unsure, but promised that during the week the Wilsons were to spend at Netherfield, she would, in her conversations with Emma, attempt to discover the truth. She knew well the source of his anxiety and hoped, with his sister's help, to ease his mind.

"I intend to ask Emma; I know she will advise us how best to deal with any future problems," she promised and then, as if to distract him from gloomier reflections, changed the subject to a matter that had concerned her Aunt Charlotte for some time.

Mrs Collins had asked if it would be possible to have some alterations made to the back parlour at Longbourn, to accommodate a waiting room for mothers who accompanied their young children and had to wait until their lessons were done.

"It would be a place where they could read, knit, or embroider without feeling they were in the way," Charlotte had said.

"Do you suppose, my dear, that such an alteration may be made without destroying the character and proportions of the house?" asked Anna.

"It would be very useful, if it could be done. I thought it might be possible to extend the back parlour into the area of the old kitchen garden, without altering the lines of the house at all. Any extension would be well concealed by the shrubbery," Anna suggested.

Seeing Jonathan's eyes light up with interest, she hoped her plan to distract him had succeeded. Anna was determined that her husband should not become mired in melancholy recriminations about Anne-Marie's unfortunate marriage. Her own experience had taught her that misfortune is frequently compounded by prolonged contemplation of the circumstances surrounding it and the apportionment of guilt. It was not in her husband's nature to be vengeful; it was an indication of the depth of his grief that the subject continued to occupy his mind.

Mention of possible alterations at Longbourn had certainly helped redirect his thoughts. She noted with satisfaction that he had paid careful attention to her suggestion; indeed, he rose instantly and walked about the room, talking animatedly of improvements he had planned to make at Longbourn, sometime in the future. He had intended to speak to Charlotte Collins about extending the pantry, he revealed, and had thought about adding extra storage behind the scullery. There were the servants' rooms, too, which he had long felt were in need of refurbishment. If they were to make alterations to the back parlour, why not have it all done at once? he argued reasonably.

After some discussion, he decided they would hire an architect; Mr Wilson would recommend one he was sure. They'd had some excellent work done at Standish Park, he recalled and turning to his wife, said, "Anna, my love, I think your aunt's request has provided us with an excellent scheme. We know how much pleasure we had redecorating this place; if you could involve Anne-Marie in planning the changes at Longbourn and I consulted James about an architect, we could have the whole thing going within the month and Anne-Marie will surely have no time to mope and become depressed again."

Anna thought it was a good idea, but before they could resolve the question, Nicholas had returned to say goodnight and all was mayhem again. There was no denying the delight that his young son had brought into Jonathan's life. Anna was particularly diverted by his father's willingness to let the child demand his attention at will. Not that Nicholas was spoilt; they would never allow that, but he was loved to distraction by both his parents and knew it.

～❦～

Two days later, on a fine Spring morning, they had the pleasure of receiving the Wilsons, James and Emma, who arrived with their younger son Colin and Anne-Marie.

Seeing her again, so remarkably changed from the wretched young woman who had gone away some four months ago, both Jonathan and Anna were quite astonished. She was thinner and yet seemed healthier. Her complexion was brighter; she smiled as she alighted from the carriage; and her entire demeanour was wholly changed. She looked her age again, for one thing. Soberly dressed, not in dreadful black bombazine, but in a silk gown of deep blue, her blue bonnet trimmed with lilac ribbons, she seemed transformed.

Anna hardly knew what to say as she greeted and embraced her, while her father was completely speechless, except to say over and over again how glad he was that she was home at last. Anna could have sworn he was very close to tears. Fortunately, young Nicholas came to the rescue and, hurling himself into Anne-Marie's arms, kissed her face with great enthusiasm, to the laughter of the entire household and the obvious delight of his victim, who seemed quite pleased with his greeting.

She picked him up in her arms and then feigned immediate fatigue. "Nicholas, how you are grown in just a few months! You are almost too heavy for me now," she protested and they could all see how pleased she was that the child had lavished so much affection upon her. When she set him down, he took hold of her hand and playfully dragged her towards the entrance, just as a cool breeze blew in from the park and the little group at the foot of the steps pulled their capes closer around them.

Anna said, "Shall we go in? I think Mrs Perrot has tea waiting," which was the cue for everyone to move indoors and into the saloon, where a good fire and refreshments would occupy them for a while.

Jonathan and Anna could hardly believe their eyes. Anne-Marie was not merely looking better; she was talking quite normally, even cheerfully. There was scarcely a trace of the mournful young widow, except for the simple sobriety of her gown and the quiet tones of her voice. Nicholas, unwilling to part from his beloved sister, had seated himself on the floor beside her chair and the two appeared to be engaged in the sort of childish conversation that most adults cannot comprehend.

Anne-Marie appeared perfectly at ease, as he prattled away and, when his nurse arrived to take him upstairs, she protested that there was no need, insisting they were getting on very well together.

"I promise I will not keep him very long from his bath, Nurse. I shall bring him upstairs myself," she declared, and returned to entertaining her young companion, with obvious pleasure.

And then, she greeted Mrs Perrot when she returned to replenish the tea table, even remembering to ask after her ailing sister; Anna was completely bemused by this amazing alteration in Anne-Marie's mood and manner. Noting that her husband and Mr Wilson were engaged in a discussion, Anna met her sister-in-law's eye and with a glance indicated her wish to see her alone.

Emma soon detached herself from the group and they went upstairs together. As they reached the privacy of her sitting room, Anna could contain herself no longer.

"My dear Emma, by what miraculous means have you wrought this transformation? I can barely recognise the young woman who left Netherfield last Autumn, in such a state that we despaired of her ever recovering from her melancholy," she said, and Emma nodded, recalling the bleak desolation of those early days.

"It has not been easy, Anna; it was no miraculous transformation either, I assure you, more the consequence of much soul searching and long hours of talking, listening, and trying to understand how Anne-Marie might free herself from the burden of guilt and misery that she carried.

"I have spent many hours listening to her and, Anna, it was such a bleak, unhappy tale, it made me feel that what I had been through in my own life, with my first husband, paled into insignificance by comparison."

Anna, who knew well what unhappiness Emma had suffered in almost ten years of marriage to an uncaring, arrogant husband, suffering that had ended only with his death, could not accept this to be true. "I cannot believe that, Emma; you were married to David for ten long years!"

"Yes, but at least I married him believing in my heart that we loved each other passionately, and for the first few years, I kept believing that he loved me and would change. It was my fervent hope, because, Anna, I did love him, else I would never have accepted him. I was young and made a serious error of judgment, but then, very soon, I had my two dear daughters and I think I would have put up with anything for the blessing of having them," she explained.

"With Anne-Marie, it was quite different. She was miserable because she chose deliberately to enter into a marriage with a man she did not love for reasons that do not make sense to her anymore and she has nothing to show for it. With her husband gone, she has no children, no loving family, no home of her own, and worst of all, no happy memories of him. All she had was a nightmare of a marriage made for all the wrong reasons, and while there are many men and women whose hearts are stern enough to countenance such a cold, hard arrangement, Anne-Marie is not one of them."

"But why did she agree, Emma?" asked Anna, "She had so much to look forward to, I cannot understand it, nor can her father."

"She claims that at first she had believed, with some persuasion from Eliza Harwood, that the obvious goodness and decency of Mr Bradshaw was sufficient. She believed she would come to love him, but when this did not follow, she tried to deceive herself and pretend that though she did not love him, she knew him to be a good man and that would help her overcome her abhorrence of the whole situation, but it did not. Each day and every night made matters worse between them."

Anna had listened as her sister-in-law told the story, silenced by the appalling truth and her own feelings of revulsion.

"Emma, was he ever...did he ever...?" She struggled to find words to ask an obvious question. Emma shook her head.

"Abuse her or mistreat her? No, she says he was always patient and gentle with her; even when she reviled him for having inveigled her into the marriage, when she had told him honestly and openly, that she did not love him and indeed, it seems to compound her feelings of guilt that she could not accuse him of anything more than keeping scrupulously to his side of the bargain and asking no more of her than she had agreed to give. But to Anne-Marie, it became a nightmare."

Anna was aghast. Her own marriage, deeply happy and satisfying as it was, made it almost impossible for her to contemplate such a travesty as Emma had described.

"Oh, Emma, what a wretched plight to be in. Poor Anne-Marie, I do not know how she bore it; and Mr Bradshaw, having agreed to it in the first instance, what an insupportable situation did he create for himself?"

When Emma replied, the serious tone of her voice was unmistakable. "There is no way of knowing how much longer she would have borne it, Anna. From all I have heard from her own lips, I think we must be thankful that Mr Bradshaw's death came when it did, by natural causes for which no one can be blamed, and so released his unhappy and reluctant wife from a truly impossible marriage, which brought neither party any joy. Had it continued much longer, we may well have had a tragedy on our hands for I do believe Anne-Marie would either have become dangerously ill or she would have been driven in her desperation to take her own life!"

Anna gasped in disbelief. "No, Emma, never that!" she cried. "Nothing could be so bad as to make her do such a terrible thing." But Emma was adamant; she had spoken with Anne-Marie for many hours, and through all their earlier conversations had run a thread of despair so dark, as to make it plain what the end might have been. She was certain that it was certainly not out of the question.

"Believe me, it was not far from her thoughts on many occasions. Anna, I would prefer that we did not speak to Jonathan of this, not just yet at any rate, until Anne-Marie has settled in at Netherfield. I do not mean that you should keep secrets from him, but it would be best for both of them that this dreadful fear does not come between them at this time. I know this to be Anne-Marie's wish, too."

Anna agreed at once, seeing the sense of her sister-in-law's words. "Anne-Marie needs to return to her place in her family, with you and Jonathan and the girls, and I can see that Nicholas is going to be a great help," Emma said, and smiling, rose to embrace her young sister-in-law, whose eyes had filled with tears. She was grateful for the knowledge; it would help her care for Anne-Marie and she appreciated, above all, Emma's wisdom and humanity.

As Anna dried her eyes, Emma said, "I think we should go downstairs. They will wonder what is keeping us." She led the way and Anna, following her downstairs, wondered how she was ever going to tell her husband how close they had come to tragedy.

When they reached the hall, they found that Anne-Marie had persuaded Jonathan to let her take Colin and Nicholas around the park in the little pony cart. The rest of the party, watching from the windows of the saloon, were amazed at her energy as she drove them, cheerfully joining in their laughter.

Turning to his sister, Jonathan spoke from the heart, "Emma, I have no words to thank you. You have performed a miracle, bringing her back to us so changed and restored to health. What can I say except thank you and God bless you?"

Emma Wilson smiled and took her brother's arm as they stood together. There was between them a close and affectionate understanding.

"I have done what I could," she said quietly, "but Jonathan, she is not completely healed. There remains some hurt and guilt, which will break out from time to time, so do be patient with her. She has suffered a great deal for such a young woman. But I am quite sure you and Anna will take good care of her. She loves you both dearly; indeed her greatest regret was that she had caused you so much distress. As you can see, she adores young Nicholas, so that is a very good start."

She spoke seriously and, as they were alone, frankly.

"I have explained to Anna that we tried to help Anne-Marie come to terms with what happened in her marriage and I think, when you have had time to hear it all, you will also understand how to help her.

"But, my own opinion is, she is now quite determined to heal herself and will make every effort to do so. She knows she has made a mistake by letting herself be persuaded into a loveless marriage, against her better judgment. Her attempts at deception only compounded the error and she has endured much pain as a consequence. But now, she has understanding and wants to make amends. We must pray that she will have the strength to go on as she has started and make a complete recovery."

The return indoors of Anne-Marie and the children with James Wilson, who had been out on the lawn watching them make a circuit of the park, ended their conversation, but not before they noted the glow on her cheeks and the brightness of her eyes, reflecting the pleasure and excitement of the children.

Soon afterwards, the visitors were shown upstairs to their rooms to rest a while, before dressing for dinner. Anna, accompanying Anne-Marie to her room, was a little apprehensive; recalling the last time they were together and the repercussions of that scene, she was uneasy, wondering whether Anne-Marie would remember, too, and how she would respond. The room had been cleaned and aired for her return, with fresh linen, flowers, and a new framed sketch of Hatfield House over the fireplace. To her surprise, Anne-Marie noticed it almost at once and, going over to the picture, exclaimed at the fine work before recognising the artist's signature and turning to Anna to congratulate her. Anna was delighted at her response.

"It was your father's choice; he thought you would welcome a change from the old Dutch harbour that used to hang there," said Anna, and Anne-Marie smiled, "He was quite right. That was such a dull picture, I could never see anything in it. This is beautiful; what fine work you do, Anna. I wish I had your talent," she said, with such warmth and sincerity that Anna felt tears sting her eyes.

"My dear Anne-Marie, you have a great deal of talent and skill, far more than I would ever claim," she said, taking her hands in hers.

"What is more, you have used your skills to do so much good, caring for those wounded men, helping to heal them; I could never have done that, and I have always admired and valued those who could. Your father knows of your desire to campaign for a children's hospital here in Meryton; it is a goal with which he is totally in sympathy. We will both help you in every way we can."

Anne-Marie's eyes shone, with excitement.

"Will you?" she asked.

"Indeed we will. We agree with you that it is sorely needed; indeed your father believes it to be long overdue," said Anna.

"That is wonderful news, Anna. I must tell my Aunt Emma and Mr Wilson; they have been advising me on the best way to secure the support of the community and the local council. With Papa's help, it would be far easier," she said, and Anna could see how much it meant to her.

When her maid Jenny arrived to help her mistress bathe and dress for dinner, Anna left to go to her room, feeling a good deal more confident than she had been before. She looked forward to acquainting her husband with the situation.

At dinner that night, the subject of the hospital was raised again, when Anna introduced it. No sooner had she mentioned it, than Anne-Marie began eagerly to speak of her hopes and the ways and means of winning the support of community leaders and councillors. She sounded eager and her voice was keen as she pressed her argument.

Even the Wilsons were surprised at the passion in her voice. Her father, forewarned by Anna, was delighted by her keenness and a welcome lightness in her tone, which he had sorely missed.

"Papa," she said, as they waited for the table to be cleared, "I was remarking to Aunt Emma, how much simpler it would have been if you had stood for re-election to the Commons; you might have pressed our case for the children's hospital," and Jonathan, taken aback by her lighthearted, almost teasing tone, was tongue-tied for a moment.

When he did respond, however, it was with his usual modesty. "Anne-Marie, your optimism presupposes that I would have won the seat in Hertfordshire, which has always returned Conservative members to Parliament. The incumbent, Sir Paul Elliott, owns vast tracts of land in the county and is a very influential Tory. It is unlikely that, had I stood against him, I would have succeeded. I think your Uncle James will agree with me," he said.

As Anne-Marie turned to her uncle for his opinion, James Wilson smiled and addressed his brother-in-law's argument. "I agree that Sir Paul has been invincible in Hertfordshire, but you would have stood a much better chance against his younger son, Mr Colin Elliott, recently returned from the colonies and set to replace his father in the Commons. He has little knowledge of the county and, having been away in the colonies working for the East India Company for several years, I would wager he has far less knowledge of the issues that concern the people here. You would have had a definite advantage, Jonathan. However, that is all in the past and Anne-Marie, if you want your children's hospital, young Mr Elliott is the man you must convince."

"And it will not be easy; remember, he is a Tory," said Emma, "and they have rarely agreed to spend public money on schools or hospitals."

Anne-Marie shrugged her shoulders, apparently untroubled by this intelligence. "He may be a Tory, but surely he is also a human being. He cannot fail to understand that a hospital in the area will mean fewer children will die of curable diseases," she said simply and Anna, catching Jonathan's eye, smiled. They had both heard the genuine excitement and energy in her voice; it sounded very much like the Anne-Marie they used to know, before her marriage to Bradshaw.

James Wilson encouraged her, "You are quite right, Anne-Marie; Mr Elliott may be far more receptive to new ideas than his father was and, indeed, if the Tories ever want to get back into government, they would have to be. The people demand it."

"Then you think, we have a chance of persuading him of the value of a children's hospital?" Anne-Marie asked, keen to be reassured that this was the case.

James smiled, "You may well do; I have not had the pleasure of meeting Mr Colin Elliott, myself, he is new to Westminster; but I have colleagues in the Parliament who have, and they have found him to be a pleasant enough fellow; young for the job, mind you, he is not much more than thirty-two or thereabouts, but then, that may be an advantage; you may find he is easier to convince than his father used to be."

Then he laughed and added, "He is better educated, too, being a Cambridge man." Jonathan joined in the laughter, lightening considerably the atmosphere around the table.

"Sir Paul Elliott never once voted to extend the voting rights or reduce the working hours of the ordinary man," James Wilson reminded them, "but, it is quite possible his son may be less of a Tory and more of a Liberal. I note that Mr Gladstone is making liberalism fashionable these days." Then turning to his niece, he spoke more seriously, "In matters such as these, my dear Anne-Marie, if you succeed in getting the support of the local member, you have won a significant battle. When you have also convinced the council and the Church, you can claim to have won the war."

As the ladies rose and withdrew to the drawing room, Anne-Marie continued speaking eagerly of her hopes and plans. "Tomorrow, I think, I shall visit the Rector at the church and tell him about our scheme," she said, with a level of determination that convinced Anna she was well on her way to recovery.

That night, as they retired to their room, Anna saw that her husband seemed free of anxiety for the first time in many weeks.

Jonathan Bingley's strong sense of responsibility, no less than his love of his daughter, had cost him several sleepless nights. Even the enormous confidence he reposed in his sister Emma had not allowed him to relax when Anne-Marie was away at Standish Park, and he worried constantly about her. Since her departure for Kent, each day had been spent in waiting for letters with news of some improvement in her condition, and while Emma was a good correspondent, keeping them well informed, any delay would cause renewed anxiety and concern. Jonathan had blamed himself for some part of Anne-Marie's predicament, and while Anna had spent many hours persuading him that the contrary was true, he had been difficult to convince.

On this day, however, for the first time, he felt there had been a significant change for the better.

Anna sensed the relief in him and as they went to bed, she asked, "Am I right in thinking that you are happier tonight, my love?" and he turned to her, grateful for her sensitivity and held her close, not as he had done often in the weeks past, for reassurance and comfort, but in a long and contented embrace, reminding her of how it had been before. "Indeed I am, dearest," he said. "Even though I know it is but a small step on a very long and painful road, I am delighted to see her take it. She seems to have regained a sense of purpose and energy, as she had when she at seventeen, inspired by Miss Nightingale, decided she wanted to work in the hospitals and train as a nurse. Her mother was against it and warned her of dire consequences, but she would not be swayed.

"Abandoning all the comforts and fine clothes she enjoyed at Rosings, she went to work at the hospital in Harwood Park. We were astonished at her dedication and capacity for hard work. It was terrible work, but she loved it. She never found the time to pursue any other interests, whether in the Arts or some other field," he explained, a little sadly, as Anna listened, understanding more clearly how deeply he had been concerned. "I have often regretted that she had denied herself what most other young women in her situation would have taken for granted. She attended few parties or balls; there was no time to spare for Art or Music lessons, and certainly no grand tours to Europe, not because she did not have the means, because I stood ready to afford her every opportunity, but she had neither the time nor the interest, so single-minded was she about her wounded soldiers."

Seeing the deepening frown on his wife's brow as she listened, he was suddenly apologetic, "I should not burden you with all this, my dear; you have borne enough of my anxiety already, and given me much comfort, but it has been such a relief to me tonight to see Anne-Marie so much improved. I am sorry if I have seemed preoccupied."

Anna interrupted him gently, seeking to reassure her husband. "Hush, Jonathan, you have nothing to regret. Every one of us knows how deeply you have cared for Anne-Marie and as for myself, I would consider it a poor return for my love if you thought you could not speak to me of your anxieties regarding any matter, and particularly if it concerned the children. I share your relief today, as I have shared your anguish these past weeks and months; but dearest, we must not celebrate too early. Emma warns that there is still a long journey ahead." He was grateful for her understanding and her excellent good sense.

"How right you are, my love, I know there is still much to be done," he said, as he snuffed out the candle, "but of one thing, at least, we can be certain, she will not have much time to mope or become depressed again; my fears on that score were, I am happy to say, quite groundless."

❦

The following morning, breakfast had not long been over when Anne-Marie announced that she was ready to walk down to the church in the village to see the Rector and invited anyone who wished for some exercise to accompany her. She was dressed for walking and Anna, exchanging glances with her sister-in-law, realised that she should avail herself of the opportunity for private conversation that the walk would allow. Rising hastily from the table, she said, "If you will wait but a few minutes, Anne-Marie, I should be happy to join you. I need only to fetch my hat and some sheets of music, which I have been copying for the choir."

As they walked towards the village, Anna wondered whether her young companion recalled, that as a new rector at Netherfield, Mr Griffin had been somewhat smitten when Anne-Marie had been home for Christmas some years ago. He had been very persistent in his pursuit of her, hoping to involve her in his choir and other church activities. Then, out of the kindness of her heart, Anne-Marie had been happy to help with some things, especially in the charitable services to the poor and aged, while carefully avoiding any intimacy. But now, Anna wondered how, after her disastrous marriage to one clergyman, Anne-Marie would cope with the obvious devotion of another.

Mr Griffin's ardour may have been dampened by her marriage to Mr Bradshaw, but Anna was sure that it could quite easily be fanned to flame again, with the slightest encouragement. But Anne-Marie seemed untroubled, speaking of the Rector in practical, sensible terms.

"I understand," she said, as they walked towards the village, "that it is very important to have the local council and the church officials on one's side in these matters. My uncle, James Wilson, assures me that such support is even more essential than the pleas of the people themselves, who of course, have no vote and so no power. I know little of the council; I shall need Papa to help me there, but I do not anticipate any problems with the Rector, Mr Griffin. He seems a devout Christian and a charitable man; I am sure he will understand the need for a children's hospital," she declared, with a new confidence that quite surprised her companion.

Anna did try, tactfully, to introduce the topic of Mr Griffin's previous interest in her. "Do you recall how keen he was to have you sing in his choir?" she asked, with a tinge of humour in her voice.

To her astonishment, Anne-Marie laughed and said lightly, "Of course I do, and I said no, because then I had neither the time nor the inclination, Anna, but if he will lend his support to our campaign for the hospital, I shall be quite happy to sing in his choir."

"You will?" Anna was puzzled.

"Certainly. I know I have never had my voice trained, like Aunt Emma has, but, if you will help me, Anna, I am sure I could join in a few of the hymns and psalms. Do you not think so?" she asked, and Anna, even though she was totally amazed, had the presence of mind to agree.

"Oh yes, of course you could. I can certainly teach you; they are quite simple and not difficult to learn," she said reassuringly.

"That will suit me well. I did try at Harwood Park, just to please Mr Bradshaw, but it was of no use at all. He insisted on choosing some very difficult anthems in four parts and I was absolutely hopeless. It was another disaster. Poor Mr Bradshaw, he must have thought I was a failure at absolutely everything," she said sadly.

Anna froze.

It was the first time Anne-Marie had mentioned her late husband since her return to Netherfield Park. Anna did not know what would follow. Tears perhaps? She reached out instinctively and took her hand.

"My dear Anne-Marie, you must never think that. You are not in any sense a failure. No one, least of all Mr Bradshaw, who saw all the good work you did at the Harwood Park hospital, could have thought it. You made an error of judgment and you have had the courage to acknowledge it. You will feel depressed and downhearted from time to time, my dear, but you are not a failure, never."

Anne-Marie said nothing for a few minutes, but she pressed Anna's hand as she held it in hers. Then suddenly, stopping to face her she said, "Thank you, my dear Anna. I shall never forget your kindness to me on so many occasions. I know I must fight the desire to wallow in guilt. Aunt Emma told me it was a form of self-indulgence, just as destructive as self-pity." Then, as if to explain, she added, "I believe her, because I know she has suffered, too, far more than I have. She told me about her first husband, David, and how she had to struggle to retain her sanity for the sake of her children. She must have been so brave."

Then, turning to face Anna again, she said, "But Anna, when I see how you have helped Papa recover from his own unhappiness, I am so grateful. Once, before you were engaged, I asked him about his feelings for you and he told me you were the most enlightened woman he had ever met," and smiling, she teased Anna, "He confessed that he loved you deeply, but was unsure if it was returned. I can see now that it is, in full measure, and you are both blessed with enviable felicity. I know I am doubly fortunate to have both you and Papa as well as my dear Aunt Emma to help me at this time."

Both women were moved to tears as they embraced, standing in the shade of a grove of trees beside the road to the village.

Looking across to the woods that lay to the right of them, forming the outer boundary of Netherfield Park, they had noticed a figure trudging towards them along a path that crossed the fields. It was only when he stood before them, hatless, bowing, and smiling as he mopped his brow, that they realised it was Mr Griffin. In one hand he held his hat, while the other clutched a parcel tied up with string; though its shape was indeterminate, the aroma that emanated from it suggested that it was a cheese of some sort, probably a gift from a generous parishioner. If he was at all embarrassed, Mr Griffin did not show it.

"Ah, my dear Mrs Bingley and Mrs Bradshaw, how fortunate I am to meet you," he said after both ladies had acknowledged his greetings. "Are you, by some chance, on your way to church?" he enquired, hopefully, to which Anna muttered something about music for the choir, but Anne-Marie, smiling amiably, said, "Indeed we are, Mr Griffin, however, it was not to pray for ourselves but to seek your support for a good cause." A big, happy smile lit up his usually doleful face and he seemed ready, Anna thought, to leap in the air for joy, as Anne-Marie went on, "We must not stand idly here, keeping you from your duties; shall we walk on?"

Clearly flattered, Mr Griffin smiled even more broadly. "Ah, my dear Mrs Bradshaw, your consideration does you credit, but you are not keeping me from my work; indeed I was just returning to the Rectory, having visited an errant member of my flock. The sheep who stray are as dear to the shepherd as those who do not," he declared.

"Of course, now I have met you ladies, I must hear your concerns, too. Indeed, I am eager to hear them. If you will do me the honour of accompanying me to the Rectory, we might talk about it over a cup of tea," he suggested brightly. The ladies agreed and they walked on.

⊱⊰

Anna, who had remained silent, except for a few words of greeting, later recounted the whole of their encounter to her sister-in-law, whom she sought out after their return to Netherfield House, while Anne-Marie, a little fatigued after their walk, retired to her room to rest.

"Emma, believe me, I was absolutely amazed at the calm, collected manner in which Anne-Marie handled it all. Here was poor Mr Griffin, all smiles and grovelling before her, but she was so poised and self-possessed, I could scarcely believe it. She took all those silly aphorisms of his, about his flock and the good shepherd, without even a flicker of a smile. I have to confess, I giggled when he referred to his errant parishioners as straying sheep, but not Anne-Marie; she went right on listening and talking, and soon she had him eating out of her hand!"

Emma laughed merrily at the vision,

"Like a sheep, how very appropriate! But Anna, tell me, was she able to talk seriously to him about the hospital?"

"Indeed, she was and she used the argument so well, that the children were dying of dreadful diseases, which could have been cured. She said it was our Christian duty to save them and help them live; he was drawn right in and agreed with her completely.

"'Of course,' he declared, 'Jesus bade them (the disciples, that is) to suffer the little children to come unto him, and he commanded them to go forth and heal the sick and ease their suffering, so it is our duty to do likewise as good disciples.'

"He was not proposing to work any miracles, you will be relieved to hear, Emma, but he certainly had no difficulty supporting us in a campaign for a children's hospital, and it was all Anne-Marie's doing! It was an astonishing performance; I have never seen anything like it before."

Emma Wilson smiled at her young sister-in-law's astonishment.

Anna was clearly unfamiliar with the persuasive powers of the lobbyist. As the wife of a Member of Parliament, Emma was well aware of them.

"It must be her background and observation, the value of commitment to a cause, the ability to argue and persuade, it's all there; she has seen her father and uncles practise it and she knows how to use it to advantage, to advance a good cause. She has used it in her work at the hospital, and now she is using it again. Anna, I am so very happy to hear this; it means she is well on the way to recovery. Jonathan will be pleased," said Emma, well satisfied with what she had heard.

Anna had some reservations. "But, what of poor Mr Griffin? Is he not likely, if he becomes too involved with her campaign for the hospital, and I am sure he intends to, he sees it as a crusade, I think; will he not be in danger of falling in love with her?" she asked anxiously. "He is not a very sensible young man, I do not think."

This time, though she was still smiling, Emma's voice was quite serious, "Anna, I doubt if his earlier passion, having once been extinguished by her marriage to Mr Bradshaw, will be stirred into life again." When Anna seemed unconvinced, Emma persisted, "If he does show any such signs, I think we may be confident that Anne-Marie will deal with it. In any event, she is now in very safe hands; with you and her father to turn to for counsel and support, she will not be alone," she said sagely.

Anna smiled and though she said little, she was not as sanguine as her sister-in-law about the prospect. She had no great confidence in the common sense of Mr Griffin, having seen him in action before.

She hoped fervently that Anne-Marie would be spared any further aggravation, especially if it were to involve the Rector, whose good intentions, she feared, however sincere, may well be driven by his susceptible heart, rather than his zeal to emulate the Good Shepherd.

At the end of a week filled with many pleasant hours of companionship, entertainment, and illuminating discussion, as well as a good deal of fun, the Wilsons left to return to Kent, after affectionate and sometimes tearful farewells. Jonathan, Anna, and especially young Anne-Marie let them go, but only after they promised faithfully to write often and everyone declared they were looking forward to seeing each other again at Victoria Wilson's wedding in June.

Anna had been wary and watchful, lest talk of her cousin's forthcoming wedding should cause Anne-Marie some understandable distress. But, to Anna's immense relief, she showed not the slightest discomposure, asking to be remembered to both her cousins, Victoria and Stephanie, and promising to be on hand to help them on the wedding day.

It was a further welcome sign of her improving spirits and her increasing confidence, of which Anna saw more evidence with each passing day, and to his great joy, so did Jonathan.

The Wilsons, whose present happiness had appeared to rise from the ashes of Emma's marriage to David Wilson, whose cruelty and dissolute behaviour had ended only with his shame and suicide, exemplified for Jonathan and Anna the kind of marriage that one dreamed of and hoped for but scarcely expected, in reality, to achieve. Only where there was the deepest love, the finest judgment, and the strongest understanding could one hope to encounter such felicity and contentment. Jonathan and Anna, though more recently wed and still deeply in love, craved in their hearts the same estimable qualities they recognised in James and Emma's marriage.

Both couples had long been intimate friends and shared many fine ideals and hopes. They loved and respected one another more sincerely than most sisters and brothers did and their children followed suit.

Whenever the two families spent time together, they always parted reluctantly, and yet, each seemed to leave with the other some portion of their shared delight to temper the sadness of separation.

On this occasion, the sadness was further assuaged by the arrival, a few days later, of Teresa and Cathy returning from Ashford Park, accompanied by their governess and their brother Charles, who was to spend a week or two at Netherfield, before proceeding to London to take up an appointment as an assistant in a medical practice. To both Anna and Jonathan, Charles's return was doubly pleasing, since they had not seen him since Christmas. His relationship with his father by now completely restored, he was warmly welcomed. Having had the benefit of being spoilt by their brother for the space of two days, as they journeyed from Leicestershire via Cambridge, where he had proudly shown them around his college, his two younger sisters were prepared to part with him to their parents, while the household staff, with whom he was universally popular, planned to celebrate his return with an appropriately festive dinner.

For Anne-Marie, however, her brother's arrival was not an undiluted pleasure. Though he greeted her with affection and remarked upon her improved appearance, she was aware that there were between them unresolved matters. She had confessed to Emma that Charles, on hearing of her engagement to Bradshaw, had arrived at Harwood Park and strongly discouraged her from marrying him, declaring at one point, "The man's a cold fish, Anne-Marie; he speaks only of church matters, and he will never make you happy."

But Anne-Marie, resentful of her brother's interference, had turned stubborn and protested that she loved Mr Bradshaw and was determined to marry him. Charles had said no more, but it had been clear that he was unhappy, and when Bradshaw had died suddenly, he had appeared shocked, but had seemed unable to sound genuinely sorry.

Now, Anne-Marie realised that Charles knew little of the harrowing detail of her marriage and would have to be told the truth, by her. She could not let him continue to believe, that she was a grieving widow, mourning the loss of a beloved husband, while both her father and Anna knew otherwise. How this was to be accomplished, she knew not, but that it had to be done, she knew for certain.

Anna learned of her determination almost by chance through Charles, who sought her out one warm afternoon, when Jonathan had taken all three of his daughters to visit their grandmother, Mrs Collins, at Longbourn. Charles had spent several hours with his sister on the previous day, when she had asked if he would drive her to St Alban's. She had claimed that she wished to see again some feature of the cathedral they had visited on a previous occasion and discuss with her brother the campaign she was planning for the children's hospital. On their return, Anne-Marie had been tired and spent the rest of the evening in her room, while Charles had disappeared into the library.

On the following day, Charles resisted his younger sisters' invitation to accompany them on their morning walk and, when the girls left with their father for Longbourn, went upstairs to find Anna.

She saw at once that he was troubled, and it did not take her long to discover the reason for his disquiet.

Writing some time later to Emma Wilson, Anna recounted the manner in which Charles Bingley had revealed to her his full knowledge of the dismal circumstances of his sister's marriage to Mr Bradshaw.

My dearest Emma, she wrote,

You are still the only person with whom I am able to discuss these matters frankly and openly, especially since I am reluctant to curtail by this means the happiness my dear husband has enjoyed since Anne-Marie's return to Netherfield. When Charles arrived a few days ago, I sensed a certain reserve between him and his sister, which I found to be extraordinary, since they are usually very fond of one another. I do not mean to suggest that there was any anger or hostility, but it was clear to me they were not at ease with each other.

A day or two later, at Anne-Marie's request, he drove her to St Alban's, where they spent most of the day and, on their return, both appeared out of sorts. At dinner, Anne-Marie ate very little, said even less, and then excused herself and retired to bed, while Charles was almost morose. I was afraid they may have quarrelled, but was reluctant to pry. On the day following, Jonathan took all three girls over to Longbourn to visit their grandmother, and I had decided to do some work on some of the sketches I'd made on our last visit to Pemberley, when Charles appeared. Emma, from the very first moment I saw him, I knew he was seriously upset. There was none of his familiar lighthearted banter; he showed no interest in my work, which is unusual in itself, for he is always polite about such things. His face was pale and he seemed agitated, which caused me to ask if he was unwell. My simple question seemed to be sufficient provocation to open the floodgates of his injured feelings. It all poured out. He demanded to know how much Jonathan and I had known of Anne-Marie's marriage troubles, when we had become aware of her predicament, and why he had not been told the truth. When I explained, as calmly as I could, that we had had no inkling of the real situation, save for some vague uneasiness I had felt on my very first meeting with Mr Bradshaw, he revealed that he had known nothing until the previous day and now, he knew it all!

He had heard it from Anne-Marie herself, on their visit to St Alban's, which she had, quite clearly, arranged for the purpose of speaking privately to him. You will recall that we discussed the matter of his appeal to her, on hearing of their engagement, not to marry Mr Bradshaw, pointing out several reasons why he considered him unsuitable.

At the time, Anne-Marie had claimed she loved him and ignored her brother's entreaties. It appears however, that she now feels deep remorse at having deceived her brother and does not wish him to believe she is grieving at the death of a beloved husband.

Emma, she has told him everything, all she had hidden from us and from him for many months.

To say Charles was shocked is an understatement. Having suppressed his anger for her sake, he was near to exploding with outrage at the actions of the Harwoods in promoting the match. He claims he once had a high opinion of them, believing them to be dear friends of his sister, whose concern for her when she had been ill was commendable. However, he regards their recent behaviour as a complete betrayal of trust; indeed his indignation is so great he was threatening to travel to Harwood Park and confront them. He was dissuaded only when I pointed out that such an action would only further add to his sister's unhappiness and seriously displease his father.

To quote his words, "Had I known at the time or even suspected the truth, I swear to you I would have stood up in church and objected to the marriage. I ask you, Anna, how could she promise to love, honour, and obey him, when she knew and he knew she did not and could not love him? It's outrageous!"

Emma, he was so agitated, there were tears in his eyes as he spoke, and I had to urge him to calm himself. So consumed is he with resentment, he could not understand why she felt any guilt, believing she was persuaded into the marriage by the Harwoods, seeking preferment for their friend, Mr B, through Anne-Marie's family connections. He declared quite confidently that they must have known through Eliza's parents, the Courtneys, that Mr Darcy's estate included more than one well-endowed living, and as Anne-Marie's husband, Mr Bradshaw might have hoped to benefit from Darcy's patronage.

Even as she recounted it, Anna recalled with some trepidation the rage of young Charles Bingley. She had never seen such anger. Having let him give vent to his feelings, she had urged him to abandon attempts to confront the Harwoods. "Surely, Charles, you must know that such action would achieve little or nothing for Anne-Marie? Instead, will you not help us to cherish and sustain your sister as she tries to recover her spirits? I believe she has already taken the first steps, and your love and support will be crucial."

"Anna, I will do anything, anything at all to help her. Give me any instruction and it shall be done," he promised. "Poor Anne-Marie, she devotes years of her life to heal others, and this is her reward? A contemptible arrangement by which she is persuaded to marry a man wholly beneath her in every way, a man for whom she says she had no love. Just think, Anna, what it must have been like for a young woman to endure. After all, she had no idea he was going to die fifteen months later; he could quite well have lived to be seventy!" After a while, he had become calmer, promising to talk to his sister and offer his help with her campaign for the children's hospital.

"It is very dear to her heart; I know she will welcome your support," Anna had said, quietly.

Interrupted by her son, demanding his mother's attention, Anna put aside her letter and went downstairs with Nicholas, who was eager to be out in the garden.

Following him down the steps, she saw Anne-Marie and her brother in earnest and seemingly amiable conversation at the far end of the lawn. Seeing Anna, they came towards her. Smiling and walking arm in arm with Charles, Anne-Marie revealed that her brother had promised her his complete support for her campaign to get a children's hospital for the area.

"You see, Anna, Charles has a wonderful opportunity to help us. Once he is in London, he will put together the kind of evidence that only a practising physician can provide," she said. "What is even better, when we have gathered all the material we need, he is going to help me prepare a proper case and present it to our new Member of Parliament, Mr Colin Elliott."

There was no mistaking her delight, and even he seemed calmer and more content. Having declared her unreserved approval and added her own offer of help, Anna took them to see the new Conservatory. As they talked of Winter roses and exotic orchids, she was relieved to note there was no longer any tension between them. Helped by the untiring efforts of young Nicholas, both Anne-Marie and Charles were soon smiling.

On her return to the house, Anna completed her letter to Emma Wilson and despatched it to the post, happy to reassure her sister-in-law.

> *I am indeed happy to conclude with some good news. I know you will be relieved to hear that Charles is calmer now, having decided to take a more rewarding path, helping his sister with her beloved children's hospital scheme.*
>
> *It has made us very happy.*
> *Your loving sister, Anna.*

When her husband returned to Netherfield, Anna gave him the news and, while he shared her sense of relief, he did warn her against building up Anne-Marie's expectations. "Do remember, dearest, that whatever their hopes, they must obtain the support of the council and our new MP, Mr Colin Elliott, which may prove more difficult than we imagine. He is, after all, a Tory from a notably Conservative background. His father and grandfather have fierce reputations for their harsh treatment of tenants and farm labourers during the enclosures of small holdings and commons in the district. Of course, as a result, Sir Paul Elliott and his family prospered mightily, but many poor families turned out of their farms and cottages were deprived of everything—their livelihood, their homes, and the sources of food for their families. The gamekeepers brutally enforced the game laws and magistrates, usually friends or relations of the Elliotts and other similar landowners, hanged, jailed, and transported men and women for poaching fish or rabbit to feed their children."

His voice was sombre and even Anna recalled that her father had told them of many children who had died of malnutrition, while their mothers were close to starving, having been thrown off the land.

When she told him, Jonathan nodded, unsurprised. "Indeed, your father is right; it seemed that neither Sir Paul Elliott nor his father believed the welfare of the poor was their responsibility," he said, adding a cautious warning, "So you see, my dear, for Anne-Marie's sake and the sake of the children she wishes to help, we must hope that Mr Colin Elliott is less hard-hearted than they were."

Early in the Summer, a Mr Lockwood, an architect highly recommended by James Wilson for his excellent work at Standish Park, arrived at Netherfield. He was escorted by Jonathan to Longbourn, where he discussed the proposed "improvements" with him and Mrs Collins, before returning to Netherfield House. He spent some hours making notes and sketches, as he talked endlessly to Jonathan, Anna, and Anne-Marie of the various ways in which the work might be accomplished. At the end of the day, he went away and returned with more ideas and sketches. When the scope of the work and its design had been decided to their general satisfaction and costs agreed, Mr Lockwood returned to London, promising to be back within the month with a draughtsman who would persevere with the plans and supervise the building, which was to start no later than July.

In June, the family journeyed to Standish Park for the wedding of Victoria Wilson, the Wilson's eldest daughter. Young Teresa Bingley, who had been invited to be one of the bridesmaids, was very nervous and while Anna kept watch over her, for it was Teresa's first big social occasion, she was far more concerned about Anne-Marie. She was reassured, however, when Charles, who had arrived from London, undertook to escort his sister; Anna knew she was in good hands.

"I knew thereafter that I could stop worrying about her and enjoy the wedding," she said to Jonathan, noting that even young Teresa seemed to be quite at ease as she carried out her bridesmaid's duties. Later, she was seen in animated conversation with one of the groom's party. The accomplished and handsome Miss Victoria Wilson was marrying a Mr Edward Fairfax, son of a distinguished family from Hampshire.

Not reliant for their reputation upon their estates alone, the Fairfaxes were all well educated and some were professional men, involved in the law, politics, and the church. The groom, Mr Edward Fairfax, was a lawyer and a Member of

Parliament, having entered the Commons in 1859. His younger brothers, Henry, a diplomat with a secret desire to be a writer, and Frederick, who confessed to Teresa that he was a mere draughtsman with ambitions to be an artist, were both pleasant and personable gentlemen. Frederick's apologetic admission that he "drew for a living," because, he said, "a fellow has to earn a crust" fascinated Teresa, who confessed that she had been "unable to draw at all" until Anna taught her.

She was clearly interested in his work and asked several intelligent questions, which the gentleman found quite astonishing. There were, he declared, very few young ladies of his acquaintance, who had shown any interest at all in the sort of drawing he did.

"Indeed, Miss Bingley, the only drawings they wish to see are of themselves," he declared. "And do you never oblige them?" asked Teresa, in a somewhat playful tone, to which he responded lightly, "Only when I can credibly reproduce their features; else I might find myself under attack for taking liberties with their looks!"

Teresa laughed. "Then you would be safest if you restricted yourself to architraves and flying buttresses, Mr Fairfax," she advised and he agreed at once, smiling and promising to heed her wise counsel in the future.

As the wedding celebrations drew to a close, they went their separate ways and Teresa, returning on the morrow with her family to Netherfield, did not recount her conversation with Mr Frederick Fairfax to anyone, although in a record she made in her diary, she did allow that he was an "amiable and amusing young man who drew for a living!"

In fact, what with Cathy and Teresa being pressed into service to help their sister with her campaign for the children's hospital and the excitement of their father's purchase of a Victoria—an open carriage, mainly for the use of the ladies of Netherfield and Longbourn, young Mr Frederick Fairfax was almost completely forgotten.

That was until a fine morning in late June, when a carriage drove up to the entrance of Netherfield House and Mr Lockwood alighted. As he came up the steps, Teresa, carrying a basket of flowers, which she was about to arrange in the parlour, met him in the hall. Greeting her, Mr Lockwood announced that he was here with his draughtsman to see Mr Bingley about the improvements to the buildings at Longbourn.

Having sent a servant to fetch her father, Teresa looked out and saw a young man struggling to extract some unwieldy equipment from the carriage. As he put his burden down, straightened up, and dusted down his coat, she recognised him.

"Oh look, it's Frederick Fairfax!" she cried and went out and down the steps towards him.

"Mr Fairfax, what are you doing here?"

On hearing her voice, he spun around, a look of complete amazement upon his face, and exclaimed, "Miss Bingley! I do beg your pardon; I had no idea this was your home. Is this Longbourn, where we are to undertake some improvements?"

Teresa smiled, "Certainly not, this is Netherfield Park and yes, it is my home. My father, Mr Jonathan Bingley, is also the owner of Longbourn, which is about three miles from here. Do you work for Mr Lockwood?" she asked.

He did not appear at all abashed. "I do; I am a draughtsman. You will recall I told you when we met at my brother's wedding that I drew for a living. Well, here I am, at your service, or rather, at your father's service," he said with a mock bow.

Teresa was very amused. "This is such a coincidence. My sisters will be astonished. Well, you had better come in and we can ask Jack to help you with that heavy equipment."

Anne-Marie, coming downstairs, saw them in the hall, and was so surprised, she forgot her usually exemplary manners and stared at Mr Fairfax and her sister, uncomprehending, until Teresa reminded her who he was.

"Anne-Marie, this is Mr Frederick Fairfax. You remember him at the wedding; he is Vicky's brother-in-law," and as recognition dawned, "Well, he is a draughtsman and he's here with the architect, Mr Lockwood, who's with Papa in the library."

Now joined by Anna Bingley who had come out of the library, hearing voices in the hall, Anne-Marie apologised, and greetings were properly exchanged. Young Mr Fairfax then excused himself and went into the library, leaving the ladies shaking their heads at the extraordinary correspondence of circumstances that had brought him to Netherfield.

While Frederick Fairfax was not to any extent a particularly remarkable or handsome young man, not being blessed with the very fine features and figure that distinguished his elder brother Edward, he had a naturally amiable disposition, excellent manners, and a pleasing sense of humour that stood him in good stead. Over the next few months, there developed between him and all the ladies at Netherfield and Longbourn a pleasant and happy association, for he was obliging, cheerful, and polite to them all. Teresa, who had always been by nature a somewhat solitary young woman, found him both interesting and amiable. So began a firm friendship between them, which flourished through the Summer, while plans were drawn, builders hired, and work began at Longbourn.

Anna, often with Anne-Marie or Teresa, went to Longbourn almost daily to ensure that their planned improvements were being carried out as required. Charlotte Collins, whose suggestion for a minor alteration to the back parlour had started all this activity, could only marvel at the speed and efficiency with which the work proceeded.

Teresa, whose friendship with the draughtsman survived the stresses of the Summer, enjoyed most of all watching the way in which the skeletal drawings on sheets of paper were translated into bricks and mortar. Frederick Fairfax was a patient teacher and she was a keen student, showing a remarkable under-standing and appreciation of the work.

As the Summer drew to a close, Anna's early disquiet about the wisdom of their seemingly innocent friendship soon gave way to sanguine acceptance, for neither Mr Fairfax nor Teresa had behaved in any way other than with perfect decorum.

Only once did Anna notice anything deeper than simple friendship between them and, even then, it was a matter of such lightness and innocence that she hardly gave it a second thought.

The work at Longbourn being completed, Mr Lockwood and his popular young draughtsman were preparing to leave. They had originally taken rooms at the inn in Meryton, but when work began in earnest, Jonathan at Mrs Collins's suggestion had invited them to use a vacant suite of rooms in the house at Longbourn, a generous gesture that was appreciated, since it saved them time and money.

On the day before their departure, they were asked to dine at Netherfield and, on his arrival, Mr Fairfax was seen to hand over a small, flat, neatly wrapped package to Teresa, which she opened quite innocently, making no attempt at concealment. Inside were two pencil drawings, portraits, one of Teresa and Cathy seated together on the terrace and another of Teresa alone, so skilfully rendered as to capture perfectly and with great delicacy, the features and general air of both subjects.

Plainly delighted, Teresa thanked him warmly and promised they would soon be framed and hung for all to admire. While everyone praised his work, Frederick Fairfax modestly claimed that all he had wanted to do was to show that he could draw something more than building plans.

"I was a little tired of architraves and flying buttresses," he quipped, with a glance at Teresa, and it was generally agreed that his aim had been amply and charmingly achieved.

After dinner, Anna and the girls had slipped upstairs and, at her instigation, returned with one of her drawings of St Alban's Cathedral, inscribed from all of them, with thanks, "to a modest gentleman." When Mr Fairfax expressed his gratitude and delight at the fine work, but admitted that he had never visited the great cathedral, it was Anna who invited him to return and rectify the gap in his experience.

"My father would tell you what a wonderful experience it is to stand in one of our oldest cathedrals, even though it is sadly fallen into disrepair," she said and noted with approval that he seemed genuinely interested. "Should you come back to Hertfordshire in the Autumn or even in Spring, you should make the journey to St Alban's and see it for yourself," she suggested, and was surprised when her husband pointed out that Mr Fairfax had already been commissioned to look at some of the farmhouses and labourers' cottages that needed renovation.

Mr Lockwood, Frederick's employer, spoke up. "Indeed, ma'am, Mr Bingley has done us the great honour of asking my firm to look at some of the old cottages on his estates, with a view to improving them, and as I am engaged to work on another estate in the Midlands for some months, I have instructed Mr Fairfax to do the preliminary work. He will certainly be back before the year is out."

Pleased by the general approbation that greeted the news, Frederick Fairfax was still smiling when he left for London, promising to take up Jonathan's invitation to call on them when he was next in the area.

❧

For Anne-Marie Bradshaw, the Summer had not brought much satisfaction. Her plans for a children's hospital had begun well, with a good deal of enthusiasm from many of the ordinary people she had spoken with, but with the men she had to convince, she was having no success at all. For a start, she had not persuaded any of the councillors she had approached to support her, except one who was a friend of the family.

Her brother Charles, busy establishing himself in his new partnership in East London, had written.

> *My dear Anne-Marie,*
>
> *Ever since I have been in London, we have been run off our feet, simply trying to keep up with all our pitiful patients, men, women, and children, many of whom are terribly undernourished as well as sick and all of whom are in the direst of circumstances.*
>
> *My Aunt Emma has brought us several of her "special cases," mainly young children with a plethora of complaints, almost all of which are eminently preventable with a modicum of regulation. Sanitation, clean water, and better nourishment would make an enormous difference to their lives. It is a disgrace that neither the government nor the local councils appear to want to enforce laws ensuring basic health standards in the very heart of London.*

Unhappily, for his sister's cause, he had not as yet fulfilled his promise to provide the evidence she could use to convince her recalcitrant councillors of the need for a hospital. She had recently written, begging him to hasten in his efforts, and when she received no immediate reply, she was most unhappy.

Driving back from Longbourn one afternoon, Anna had noticed that her companion was unusually silent. An attempt to discover the reason for her depressed state of mind provoked a complaint.

"I am at a loss to know what I should do next, Anna. I feel so discouraged. What must one do to persuade these men, with their families so comfortable in their safe, clean homes, that the children of the poor deserve a hospital where they may be treated when they are ill? I wish Charles would write. I know he is not a regular correspondent and he is very busy, but I do need him to send me the information I can use to persuade people that we must have a hospital," said Anne-Marie, sounding quite despondent.

They were approaching Netherfield House. Anna urged her not to despair, pleading that a little patience would be appropriate in the case of her brother, who had only recently started work in London, when they noticed a curricle with a very handsome pair of horses, drawn up at the side of the house.

"Someone quite grand is visiting Papa," said Anne-Marie.

Neither of them had seen the vehicle before.

"I wonder who it can be. We know nobody who drives around in one of those. What a fine pair of horses…" Anna mused aloud, as they turned into the drive and pulled up at the entrance.

As they walked up the steps and into the hall, Jonathan Bingley came out of the saloon and greeting them, said, "Ah, there you are, my dears; you've arrived just in time to meet a very important visitor," then, seeing a small frown on Anne-Marie's face, and thinking she was about to plead that she was too tired to meet the visitor, he spoke more quietly, "Our new Member of Parliament, Mr Colin Elliott is here, and I was about to order some tea."

Anne-Marie's frown disappeared in a trice and as Anna and Jonathan exchanged glances, she smiled brightly and declared, "Mr Elliott? How very opportune; Papa, I must meet him."

Anna, happy to see such a swift reversal of mood, turned to Mrs Perrot and asked for tea and cakes to be served, while she and Anne-Marie accompanied Jonathan as he returned to the saloon and their guest.

The gentleman, who was standing at the windows looking out upon the park, turned as they entered and came to meet them, as his host presented his wife and eldest daughter.

Colin Elliott was slim and tall, though not as tall as Jonathan Bingley, good-looking, with dark hair and a pleasing smile that creased up his face and reached his eyes as he greeted them graciously, professing himself to be singularly honoured. He had intended to call on Mr Bingley, he said, acknowledging his standing in the county and his reputation as a distinguished parliamentarian, but he was aware also of the excellent work done by the ladies of Netherfield and Longbourn in the community and was delighted to meet them.

When they were seated and taking tea, he addressed Anna, "I understand, Mrs Bingley, that you are mainly responsible for starting the School of Fine Arts for Ladies at Longbourn; my aunt Mrs Boucher with whom I am staying, has spoken of you. Her daughters Margaret and Alison are your students, I think. As I have already told Mr Bingley, they have nothing but praise for you."

Anna was both surprised and pleased at this information. It gave her a convenient opening for conversation, and she assured him that she was ably assisted at the school by her aunt Mrs Collins, "who does most of the difficult work, leaving all the pleasant and interesting things to me."

Turning to Anne-Marie, Mr Elliott, who had been made aware by Mr Bingley that his daughter was recently widowed, was discretion itself, saying, "And Mrs Bradshaw, I am astonished to hear that you are not only a trained nurse, but have spent a great deal of time attending upon our sick and wounded soldiers. Let me say how very proud and honoured I am to meet you."

Anne-Marie, unable to resist the opportunity afforded her by his words, thanked him and responded that she was truly honoured and pleased to be meeting him as their new Member of Parliament, and she hoped he would be able to help her. When he seemed delighted, if a little puzzled at her words, she declared her interest.

As Anna and Jonathan looked on in some surprise, Anne-Marie set about explaining the very important matter of the proposed hospital for children. Mr Elliott, seeing as she spoke, her face alight with enthusiasm for her cause, her eyes bright, her words purposeful and keen, could not fail to be impressed.

Anne-Marie was by anyone's standards a lovely woman. Her recent bereavement and consequent distress had caused her to lose some of her youthful vivacity, but Mr Elliott saw only a remarkably handsome young woman, her complexion gilded by a long Summer in the country, making an eloquent plea for a cause dear to her heart.

He was clearly quite moved and assured her that it was indeed a most worthy cause and her interest in it did her credit.

Not content with his response, she proceeded to press him for an acknowledgement that a hospital for children was needed in the area.

"Your interest and support would be immensely significant, Mr Elliott. It would make the difference between success and failure," she pleaded.

When Jonathan and Anna, anxious that their guest should not feel besieged, intervened to suggest that perhaps Mr Elliott had only just entered Parliament and might want to wait a while before becoming too involved in this matter, he assured them this was not the case at all.

"Please do not be concerned on that score, Mr Bingley; I certainly wish to know more about it. I had no idea of the extent of the problem we have with childhood diseases. I am sorry, but I have been away in India for some time and I am not as familiar as I should be with conditions in England. It is essential that I learn all I can so I may press for the right policies and, if Mrs Bradshaw wishes to acquaint me with the facts, I shall be most grateful," he said and turning to Anne-Marie, added, "Pray, do go on, Mrs Bradshaw. This is clearly a matter on which I am very ill-informed."

Anne-Marie did not require any further persuasion. Later, when he was leaving, having accepted an invitation to dine with them on Saturday, it was clear to Anna that, while their new MP was interested in the children's hospital, he was even more fascinated by its charming advocate.

Throughout Autumn, Anne-Marie poured most of her energies into gathering information to put before the Council, whose approval was essential, if her dream of a hospital was to be realised. Her brother had arrived with information on the large numbers of deaths he was seeing, of young children from croup and whooping cough in a small part of East London, which when presented to Mr Elliott, worried him greatly. Charles did well, impressing upon their new Member how vital it was that these afflictions were diagnosed and treated early, if the victims were to have a chance of survival.

"Only in a hospital or a clinic can the poor receive decent care. Without it, they will most likely die; the children certainly will, after several ineffective remedies have been tried, only because their parents are too poor to afford a doctor. I see them every day," he had declared.

Colin Elliott had been sufficiently concerned to ask if he could visit the practice in East London and see for himself, a request to which Charles Bingley was happy to agree, glad to have secured his interest, at least.

A pleasant interlude in their busy lives was provided by a visit from their cousin Caroline Fitzwilliam and her youngest daughter, Rachel. Since her father Mr Gardiner's illness, Caroline had taken over running much of his business together with her brother Robert. On this occasion, she was on her way to London to meet with his lawyers. She expected to be joined in town by Robert and Mr Darcy, who was a partner in the business. Her husband, Colonel Fitzwilliam, was unable to attend, being kept busy with harvest home on the farm.

En route to London, she had accepted a long-standing invitation from the Bingleys to spend some time at Netherfield Park. She brought them happy news of the forthcoming wedding of her daughter Amy to Mr Frank Grantley, nephew of Mr Darcy.

"They plan to wed in the Spring at the church at Pemberley; Lizzie and Mr Darcy have most kindly offered to host the wedding breakfast, afterwards," she said, adding, "Of course, we look forward to seeing all of you there."

Caroline was a popular guest, lively and interesting with plenty of stories to tell. She was generous with her advice and praise for Anne-Marie in her campaign for her children's hospital. She had the benefit of many years of active campaigning for several political and social causes, both in Derbyshire in her local community and at Westminster, when her husband was a member of the Commons. Her recollections of the long and difficult struggles leading to the passage of the great Reform Bills of that period, which had abolished rotten boroughs, extended voting rights, and improved conditions of work for women and children, made gripping anecdotes and were recounted in detail to Anne-Marie's delight. She regarded Caroline Fitzwilliam as the very epitome of what an enlightened woman should be.

"I think Cousin Caroline is a wonderful example of someone whose desire to help people is so strong that it overwhelms all obstacles," she had declared to her father, who had to agree.

"She has certainly come a very long way from her quiet, comfortable life in the village of Lambton," said Jonathan. "She knew little of politics before they were engaged, but I know from Colonel Fitzwilliam that she enjoys the excitement of campaigning for her causes and is very popular with the people of the dales, because she has worked tirelessly for them, long after he retired from the Commons."

Anne-Marie was disappointed that Caroline had not been able to meet with Mr Elliott, who was away at Westminster. She was confident that he could not fail to be impressed by a woman as energetic and vivacious as Mrs Fitzwilliam.

"Papa, I do wish Mr Elliott had been able to meet Cousin Caroline; it would prove to him that women can be just as interested as men in politics and ought be able to vote in elections," she said ruefully, after Caroline had left for London. Her father was cautious. "Anne-Marie, you are not seriously suggesting that you can convert a conservative like Mr Elliott to supporting Votes for Women, are you?"

"I am. My Uncle James says it must come and probably sooner than we think. But my purpose is not to convert him; rather I would hope that he would come to his own understanding of its value, as he has about the need for the children's hospital. Cousin Caroline would be a fine example of what a determined woman of conviction can achieve."

"And am I now hearing another determined woman of conviction?" asked Jonathan, wondering whether his daughter had considered what such a commitment would involve. Anne-Marie smiled. "Indeed you are, Papa," she replied with a subtle smile. Her father, while he had some reservations, was happy to see her so engaged and excited by a worthy cause.

Some days later, Mr and Mrs Bingley together with Anne-Marie travelled to London themselves, where Jonathan Bingley and James Wilson were due to attend a meeting of their party at Westminster.

James had indicated in a letter to Jonathan that matters arising out of the American Civil War, which had been raging for over two years in the former colonies, were causing problems within the government.

Some members of the government are surreptitiously supportive of the Southern Confederate cause, mainly because of pressure from the English textile manufacturers, who wish to ensure that they have a continuing source of cheap raw cotton produced by slave labour,

he wrote and as Jonathan read it out, the ladies had been horrified and Anne-Marie had expressed her revulsion. "Is there no limit to their greed, Papa?" she asked bitterly. "Have they no humanity at all?"

"Apparently not," said her father, adding that many of the more principled members of Parliament had insisted that the British government express its support for the North and President Lincoln's bid to free the slaves. Charles, who had joined them in London, pointed out that the old Tories were quite opposed to Abraham Lincoln and the whole idea of freedom for the slaves. "They contend that Lincoln is an upstart Republican, who ought not be supported at all," he said, with a wry smile and neither Anna nor Anne-Marie knew whether to take him at his word. They could scarcely believe it to be true.

They dined, later that week, with the Wilsons at their London residence in Grosvenor Street. On arriving, Anne-Marie was pleasantly surprised to find that her brother Charles had brought Colin Elliott along to the party and he appeared to be quite at ease in the company.

Here was an excellent opportunity for him to meet their cousin Caroline.

She was eager to discover how they would get on and what they thought of one another. The introductions being made, Mr Elliott was soon enjoying a quite lively conversation with Caroline and Charles. Caroline was complaining at the condition of the Thames. She had been very shocked to see the river in its present sorry state.

"When we were children, we lived in London at Gracechurch Street and, often on Sundays, we would go to Richmond, where we had friends who had a house overlooking the river. I have such delightful memories of the place and the river that I almost wept when I saw it yesterday, all choked with rubbish. As for the streets, I cannot ever remember them being so dirty," she said.

"It is the dreadful price we have paid for the industrial and commercial success we boast about," said Charles Bingley, a hint of sarcasm in his tone, and Mr Elliott agreed, but added that sometimes he wondered whether the price demanded was not too high.

"I realise it is heresy to question the value of progress," he said, with a self-deprecating grimace. "I may well be drummed out of my party, if I make much of it, but I do wonder at the untrammelled march of industry in Britain. Do we have to sacrifice everything for commercial success?"

"Of course not," replied Caroline, in a spirited voice, which caught the attention of a few other guests standing nearby. "I am glad to hear you question it, Mr Elliott, and if the Tories do threaten you, I am sure the Reformists will welcome you with open arms."

He laughed, a little embarrassed at having drawn attention to himself, but he had spent much of the day with Charles, and his response to what he had seen at the practice and on the streets of London had been one of disbelief. Anne-Marie was delighted. Joining them, she heard him express his horror at the state of the dwellings in which hundreds of London's poor lived. Returning from India, where there was much poverty, he had not expected to find these levels of hardship and destitution in what he remembered as a prosperous and modern England.

Mr Elliott had heard something of the Fitzwilliams from Charles Bingley and so was prepared for Caroline's frankness. She was curious to discover more about this handsome and personable, yet modestly soft-spoken gentleman. Having heard he was a Tory MP, son of the diehard Sir Paul Elliott, whose name her husband could scarcely mention without flying into a rage, Caroline was intrigued to find him speaking with some degree of concern and even compassion for the poor.

The sights he had witnessed in the East End and in the grimy hovels that lined the rutted streets where Charles Bingley's patients lived had engendered strong feelings of abhorrence. He declared that it was a travesty that the people whose hard work contributed to the immense wealth of Britain were expected to live in such appalling conditions.

"What is much worse, their children are condemned to grow up, those that survive, in unimaginable circumstances, while their parents' work enriches those who are already rich beyond their wildest dreams," he complained bitterly.

"When did you return to England, Mr Elliott?" Caroline asked.

"Not much more than a year ago," he replied and she persisted, "You were in India during the Mutiny, then?" and her eyes were wide with astonishment, recalling the unspeakable horrors that had been committed by both sides of that dreadful conflict. How much of that, she wondered, had he seen and how had it affected him?

Colin Elliott shook his head, "No, ma'am, I was, by sheer chance, spared that awful debacle. Early in the Spring of '57, I had asked for leave of absence, in order that I might travel to England for my brother's wedding," he explained. "At the time I left India, there were rumours of trouble brewing in the Meerut district, but by the time I arrived home, the Mutiny was in full swing, with attacks on Delhi and the upper Ganges region. Chilling tales were told and retold by all and sundry, and after my brother's wedding, I felt no inclination to return. My father, who was looking to retire soon, used the imminent election to try to keep me here, but when the government abolished the East India Company, I was asked by the Colonial Office to return to India with the new administrators, who were civil servants, of course, and assist with the transition."

Mr Elliott paused to accept a drink from a footman, and the ladies who had been listening with bated breath, expecting to hear hair-raising tales of his exploits, relaxed for a moment.

Anne-Marie noted with approval that he had not sought in any way to make a hero of himself, choosing instead to point out that much of the responsibility for the Mutiny could have been sheeted home to the poor administration and mismanagement of the colony by the company, which had failed to understand the traditions of the Indian people.

"The East India Company had no inkling that they were dealing with people who were part of an ancient traditional culture, averse to being pushed to accept Western ways. They treated the native people with scant respect," he said.

Charles did not let this go unchallenged. "Elliott, you are surely not suggesting that all that carnage was the result of poor administration?"

"Indeed no, Bingley, I am not. But the resentment had built up over years. If some attention had been paid to the grievances of the Indian people, and in particular the sepoys, if we had a less inept administration, which was directly accountable to Whitehall, the bloodbath would not have been so terrible nor so widespread. I am not alone in holding this opinion; the East India Company cared nothing for the people and everything for profit and the people, both British and Indian, paid the price," he declared, sounding more radical than any of the Whigs and Liberals in the room.

"I take it you have no intention of returning to India?" asked Caroline.

"No, ma'am, I have done my time in the colonies; I am committed to effecting some change and reform in England," he declared, with a degree of determination and firmness that left no one in any doubt of his intentions.

Caroline, her eyebrows raised in mock astonishment, teased him, "What? A reforming Tory? Now there is a most unusual combination. Do you not agree, Mr Wilson?"

James Wilson, very much the elder statesman in this gathering, laughed, but only gently, and said, "Oh, I don't know about that. They're not all diehards, Mrs Fitzwilliam. I must remind you that it was Lord Shaftesbury who was responsible for the Mines Act by which the underground employment of women and children was forbidden; and it is he who is still fighting to stop the chimney sweeps sending babes with brushes up the smoke stacks.

"Now they are significant reforms, with which he persisted in spite of entrenched opposition from the Lords. If Mr Elliott wants to be a Reformer, he should look to our side of the house for support," he said, and to make it quite clear that he bore him no ill will, James made a point of addressing Colin Elliott directly.

"I know you have made some important speeches in the Commons already, Mr Elliott, on Health and Education; if you intend to pursue these matters, I can promise you our support," he said, and Mr Elliott expressed his gratitude, acknowledging the experience and influence of his host. At dinner, seated next to Anne-Marie, Colin Elliott was quizzed once more about his time in India. Anne-Marie was eager to know more about a country of which she had very little knowledge and he was happy to satisfy her curiosity.

"You were fortunate, indeed, not to have witnessed the horrors of the Mutiny, Mr Elliott," she said and he replied quickly, "Indeed I was, Mrs Bradshaw, and in my own defence, I have to say that I did not participate in the gruesome national pastime of those days of retelling, in great detail, accounts of murder and mayhem, some so excessive that they bore scant relation to reality, as I discovered on my return to the subcontinent the following year."

"Did you not mind having to go back there?" she asked. He shrugged his shoulders. "No, there was an important job to be done, and I suppose it was easier to go, knowing I would soon be home again for good. I returned to England just in time to see Lord Derby's government voted out of office and Palmerston back in power. I have recently discovered, Mrs Bradshaw, that your father had a great deal to do with the negotiations that brought about that particular catastrophe."

The tone of his voice and the half smile on his face made it plain he was teasing her, but Anne-Marie pretended not to notice.

"Oh dear," she said, "I am sorry; that must have been very inconvenient for you." He had to laugh. "Not as inconvenient as it was for my father, I assure you. He was furious. He had just been through the business of winning an election only to find himself back in opposition! It hardened his resolve to retire from the Commons, which gave me my opportunity, of course. So in the end, it might even be said, if I were to be very magnanimous, that your papa did me a favour! How's that for a nice piece of sophistry?"

This time, she stopped pretending and giggled at his logic. He appeared to enjoy amusing her and was unprepared for her next question, which was a serious one.

"And, do you mind being in opposition?" she asked.

"Yes I do, because I should like to get things done. I know that as a new boy on the backbench, I do not have much influence, but at least it would have been less frustrating. It is impossible to get anyone to listen, especially if you are trying to change a policy or make a new one; I've been trying to get them interested in schools and housing . . ."

"…And hospitals?" she prompted.

"Exactly. I have really tried hard, but no one wants to listen."

He sounded suddenly, despondent, and apologetic. She relented and said in a kind voice, "I am sure you have and I am quite confident we will succeed. Papa and my Uncle James have always said that in politics, it is the timing that counts; you must wait for the right moment and then everything falls into place."

She went on, as he listened, somewhat surprised, "My heroine Florence Nightingale did exactly that. No one was interested in the welfare of wounded soldiers when they were dying like flies in the Crimea, not from their wounds alone, but from cholera and typhoid, and the conditions were appalling. Then, when the nation demanded action, they asked for her help and you know the rest. She asked for and got everything she needed to reform the military medical service. It was the right moment," she explained and once more Colin Elliott was astonished at her wisdom and sound common sense. She could not be more than four or five and twenty at most, he thought and was about to respond to her comments, when someone laughing across the table distracted their attention and the moment was lost.

There was, no longer, in Anne-Marie's mind, any doubt about Mr Elliott's support for her children's hospital. Even though, he was, as he pointed out, not a member of the Liberal-Whig alliance, which was in government, he promised to do his best again when he returned to Westminster to press her concerns upon those members with influence, who could get something done.

As they moved to the drawing room for coffee, she said, "I cannot believe that Members of Parliament do not understand that it is in their interest to ensure that their constituents are looked after." She was baffled by the lack of interest shown by most MPs.

Colin Elliott explained gently, "Mrs Bradshaw, I share your frustration and distress but not your surprise; Members of Parliament tend to count the votes in the causes they support. Most are unwilling to advocate the expenditure of much money unless they can see political advantage in it."

Anne-Marie was instantly up in arms. "I am quite sure that was not true of my papa, and I am absolutely certain it is not the case with my uncle, Mr Wilson." As Colin Elliott listened, she defended Mr James Wilson.

"Why, I know that he has frequently supported causes like the abolition of slavery and better working conditions for women and children, at the risk of losing votes," she said, outraged by the suggestion, and Mr Elliott was immediately apologetic.

"My dear Mrs Bradshaw, I do beg your pardon," he said, trying desperately to correct his indiscretion. "I am certain, too, that neither Mr Bingley nor Mr Wilson, both distinguished Members of Parliament, could ever be so accused. Please believe me, I had not intended to cast any aspersions upon either of them. I was only speaking generally and did not make myself clear; forgive me."

His contrition was so sincere and his manner so gentlemanlike, that she would have found it difficult not to pardon him, but it had let him see how deeply she felt and how swiftly she could be moved to defend those she loved. It did not, in any way, reduce her in his estimation. Quite the contrary.

For her part, Anne-Marie seemed to pay little attention to any other aspect of their association, except that which could be directed towards what was now their common goal, her precious children's hospital.

They parted without rancour; he was too gentlemanly and she too kind-hearted for that. They spoke amicably of meeting again in a fortnight when he returned to Hertfordshire at the recess, by which time, he expressed the strongest hope that they may have some good news.

"I shall do my very best, Mrs Bradshaw," he promised, solemnly. "If need be, I shall speak with my father, I promise," he said, as he kissed her hand before bidding the rest of the party goodnight.

As he went out into the night, the ladies of the party were all agreed that Mr Elliott was a very agreeable gentleman indeed.

They returned on the morrow to Netherfield, and Anna and Jonathan noticed that Anne-Marie seemed more than usually cheerful. She was clearly more confident now of achieving her goal and talked avidly of plans to be made and funds sought for the hospital.

"Has Mr Elliott spoken with his father yet, regarding his support for the hospital?" Jonathan asked.

"I do not know for sure, Papa, but I think he intends to. But does it really signify? He is the Member now, not Sir Paul. He surely does not require his father's permission to lend his support to each and every project in the area?"

Her father smiled but said nothing, not wishing to disillusion her. Sir Paul Elliott was one of the most domineering Tories in the Parliament.

She shrugged her slight shoulders and said, "Ah well, we shall see if he has the fortitude to persevere, like Lord Shaftesbury and the little chimney sweeps." She sounded very determined indeed, and Anna could not help feeling some sympathy for Mr Elliott. Anne-Marie was very single-minded. If he disappointed her, he would probably get short shrift, she thought.

Late that night, on her way to her own bedroom, she looked in on Anne-Marie. She had been tired when they returned and had begged to be excused from coming down to dinner, claiming she wanted no more than a bath and some tea, which Jenny had been requested to provide. When Anna opened the door of Anna-Marie's room and looked in, she was fast asleep.

Finding her husband reading in bed, Anna leaned over and took his book out of his hand; she had urged him on many occasions not to ruin his eyesight by reading in poor light. He surrendered the book without complaint, but kept hold of her hand, making her sit beside him on the bed. They enjoyed a remarkable degree of intimate understanding. When she asked, "Do you think Colin Elliott is in some danger, dearest?" he understood her drift immediately.

"He may well be, I doubt that Anne-Marie is, though. She sounds and looks well in control of her feelings," he replied and was about to draw her closer, when she resisted him gently, and said, "Are you sure? I do wonder sometimes, whether she is as controlled as we think she is or just a very good actress. At the moment, it seems that nothing will deflect her from her purpose, but it cannot be denied that Mr Elliott is far more personable than poor John Bradshaw was and, for all her wisdom, Anne-Marie is young and impressionable; she may well end up falling in love with him. Caroline has hinted to me that she thought he appears to be rather partial to her already."

Despite her earnest tone, Jonathan was not inclined to take her concerns seriously tonight, teasing her with the warning that Caroline Fitzwilliam was herself an arch romantic and prone to such fantasies.

"Colin Elliott strikes me as a sensible fellow," said Jonathan, trying to convince his wife there was no cause for concern. "Since I informed him, before they met, that Anne-Marie had been recently widowed, I have noticed that he is very respectful of her feelings."

"But dearest, that is because he believes her to be grieving for her husband," Anna interrupted, adding that her own observation, while it had confirmed her good opinion of him, had also noted signs of interest and a distinct partiality towards Anne-Marie.

"He is very particular not to take any liberties and is never familiar in any way, yet, I cannot help feeling that he is attracted to her and quite clearly admires her. When she is in the room, he hardly leaves her side."

This time, her husband, pointed out that Anne-Marie was a beautiful young woman and it would be surprising if she did not attract some admiration; then clearly seeking to divert her, he said, "Trust me, my love, I am confident neither of them will do anything imprudent or foolish, not sufficient to warrant your anxiety anyway; whereas, your poor neglected husband would give his entire fortune to be the subject of your undivided attention at the moment."

She had to laugh, but it was a strategy that never failed and she turned willingly into his arms.

The sudden departure of Charlotte Collins's maid, Harriet Greene, for her home in Nottinghamshire threw the entire household at Longbourn into confusion. Well taught and remarkably well-spoken, Harriet, who had been with Charlotte for many years, was a most efficient and well-organised woman, who had assisted not only with the running of the household, but had also kept the accounts and handled the correspondence for the School of Fine Arts. Without her, it was unlikely that Mrs Collins would manage at all well. However, when the letter had come saying that Harriet's mother was gravely ill, she had to go and no one suggested otherwise.

Anna drove over to Longbourn with Anne-Marie and Teresa to see what might be done to assist Charlotte. Offers of a maid from Netherfield to help out and Teresa to keep her company were appreciated, but Anne-Marie could see that her grandmother was apprehensive. She had come to depend a great deal upon Harriet, surrendering the running of the house to her and consulting her on many other matters.

"Anna, I do not believe my grandmother is going to cope," Anne-Marie said on the way home. "I know Tessie will be company for her, but it is not very fair to her either; she is going to be very bored."

Anna was inclined to agree, but pointed out that there was little they could do in the present circumstances. Jonathan, when he was told, agreed that it was not fair to Teresa to send her away to Longbourn on her own and wondered whether Cathy would like to join her sister, a plan that did not appeal at all to young Catherine. Nothing very satisfactory was suggested and a decision was postponed for the morrow, when Jonathan hoped to ride over to Longbourn himself. But on the morning after, they had hardly finished breakfast when an urgent message arrived from Longbourn.

The manservant who brought it said little, except that the doctor had been sent for and everyone assumed that Charlotte was ill. On opening the note, however, which was not in Charlotte's hand, it was revealed that Teresa had been taken ill in the night. Within minutes, Anne-Marie had raced out of the room and upstairs to pack some clothes and a nursing kit, without which she went nowhere, while Anna asked for the small carriage to be brought round at once.

"I knew we should not have left her on her own; my grandmother is kind enough, but she is not the most cheerful company for a young girl, is she?" Anne-Marie said and Anna could not disagree. She was immensely grateful to Anne-Marie for her readiness to step in and assist. The note had suggested that Lucy Sutton could help, which did not meet with Anne-Marie's approval at all.

"It would not be satisfactory at all to have Lucy Sutton in there," she declared. "I do not think Papa would approve either; she's a complete outsider and she may gossip with the servants and once she settles in, who knows when she will depart?" she grumbled, and even Anna, who had not seen the danger of Mrs Sutton becoming a permanent resident at Longbourn, had to acknowledge it was a possibility.

"There is that," she said, "and I do agree that your father would look askance at the prospect."

"Indeed, which is why I think, Anna, that I should move to Longbourn at once and stay until Harriet returns," said Anne-Marie, making it seem as if she had decided it all well in advance and nothing would shake her resolve.

"Anne-Marie, are you quite sure? I know you want to be with Tess, but once she is sufficiently recovered, would you not both wish to return home?" Anna asked.

"Of course I would wish it, but I must also see that Mrs Collins is comfortable and, above all, that she is not importuned and put upon by outsiders who may have other than the purest of motives," she replied.

Even as she spoke, Anna frowned and asked what it was that had made her uneasy about the prospect of Lucy Sutton staying at Longbourn. Anne-Marie looked uncomfortable, reluctant to speak in the hearing of the driver, indicating in a whisper that she would tell her when they were at Longbourn, but not in her grandmother's presence. Perplexed, Anna could hardly wait for the short journey to be over; she could not imagine why Anne-Marie would be so intensely suspicious of Mrs Sutton. Anna had found her quiet and obliging at all times and she knew Charlotte liked her very much. Indeed it was at her instigation that Mrs Sutton had been engaged to teach the younger pupils at the school.

When they arrived at Longbourn, however, they were both surprised that it was not Charlotte, but Lucy Sutton, who came out to greet them. Disconcerted, Anne-Marie barely acknowledged her, as she rushed indoors and upstairs to Teresa's room, and Anna hoped that her obvious anxiety for her sister would excuse her brusque manner.

Mrs Sutton was all smiles and explained to Anna that she had come in that morning to prepare for her lessons with her three young pupils, who were expected later in the day, and on finding Teresa ill and Mrs Collins "in a state," she had set aside her own business and got to work to ensure that the two ladies were attended to.

"I could have done more, but Mrs Collins would not permit it. She insisted that I write that note and send it forthwith to you," she explained to Anna, who thanked her and assured her that she had done the right thing.

Later, having reassured Charlotte that Teresa would be well looked after, Anna went upstairs and, finding Anne-Marie sitting with her sister, who was asleep, insisted on being given the reason for her suspicions.

Anne-Marie shook her head and sighed, "Because, Anna, she is not who she says she is."

Astonished, Anna asked, "Whatever do you mean?"

"She is not a widow. Her husband was a soldier; he lives in London."

Aghast, Anna said, "How do you know this?"

"Because he has a brother at the hospital at Harwood Park and he used to visit him," she said, "I knew him as John Sutton."

As Anna listened, increasingly bewildered, she continued, "The brother, Joseph, had no family to go to; he'd get very depressed and Mr Bradshaw used to talk to him to comfort him. He discovered that John Sutton's wife had deserted him, disappeared one day, taking their three children with her. They thought she'd gone to her mother, somewhere in the Midlands."

"What if he discovers she is here in Meryton?" asked Anna.

Anne-Marie looked alarmed. "If he does, he will probably come straight down and take them away," she said, adding, "He may not be able to force his will upon her, but he will certainly take the children. His brother believed he was very angry about losing them and spoke constantly of going off in search of them."

"Good heavens!" Anna exclaimed, and asked, "How long have you known of this?" Anne-Marie looked a little uncertain and then replied, "I have known half the story for quite some time, well before Mr Bradshaw's death; but, I did not know, until recently, that Lucy Sutton was the woman in question.

"I was visiting my grandmother one afternoon, and Mrs Sutton was just leaving after her lessons, when Harriet informed me that the poor woman had been widowed during the war in the Crimea. She said her husband, John Sutton, had been killed at Sebastopol. Poor Mrs Sutton had no family and no fortune, Harriet told me. She was very sympathetic. She saw Lucy Sutton as a victim of circumstances who was bravely struggling on, supplementing her meagre income with what she earned by teaching music at the school."

"Was there anything in particular that made you suspicious?" Anna asked.

"When she told me the names of the children, especially the little girl, Marigold, I knew it was the same family. Lucy is John Sutton's wife."

"And you said nothing to anyone?" asked Anna.

"I did not, because I had no wish to become embroiled in her affairs. I had no knowledge of her motives; she may have had reasons I did not know. Perhaps he was a harsh man and ill-treated her or the children. I did make some enquiries though."

"How?" Anna was curious to find out.

"I wrote to a friend, a nurse I knew well at the hospital, and asked her to verify some things, such as casualty lists at Sebastopol. Her information has confirmed my suspicions. John Sutton certainly did not die at Sebastopol. He served in the war and returned to England unscathed."

"And what do you mean to do?" asked Anna.

Anne-Marie shrugged her shoulders, "Nothing; I have no desire to persecute Mrs Sutton or her children, but I shall not stand by and let her deceive and take advantage of my grandmother's kind nature, nor will I permit her to become entangled with any other member of my family, while she pretends to be other than she is. She has taken us all in, Anna, and abused our hospitality," she said, sounding decidedly more aggrieved than before.

"What do you mean entangled with members of your family?" asked Anna, now thoroughly perplexed.

"Ah well, I noticed her when my brother Charles was here. He met her when he visited Longbourn and then again, when we were walking to Meryton and back. He was pleasant and attentive to her, as he always is with women. But she, having discovered he was a physician, made every effort to engage his attention, especially as we walked to Meryton, when she all but ignored me and talked assiduously to my dear brother, drinking in every word that fell from his lips."

At this, Anna could not contain her laughter. "Anne-Marie, my dear, surely you are exaggerating. I cannot believe that Charles would have been taken in by her; he is a man of the world, and he must have known other women who did the same."

"Indeed, I did not suggest that he was taken in, but she was certainly trying her very best to draw him in. I had no doubt of that: her smiles, her deferential manner, her constant exclamations at everything he said, as if he were the Oracle; it was unmistakable, Anna. Which is why I am very wary of permitting her to become too familiar with Longbourn and my grandmother. I certainly would not approve of her coming to live here, for however short a period," she declared, very firmly.

"Do you believe she has designs on your brother, then?" Anna asked and it was difficult for her to treat this as seriously as Anne-Marie did; there was an element of laughter in her voice.

But Anne-Marie was not going to be diverted from her outrage. "I most certainly do. However, it is not just Charles. I do not believe that he would become seriously involved with her; she is older than him for a start and there are the children, but Anna, just think, if he were to be inveigled into some liaison with her, without realising that she is still married and clearly in hiding from her husband, would it not be disastrous for his own reputation? Do you not see how such a scandal could ruin his career and damage Papa and all of us?"

Now, Anna did see and, realising how anxious she had been, asked,

"My dear Anne-Marie, why did you not tell me or your father? You could have trusted us to be discreet, surely?" Anne-Marie shook her head.

"I cannot explain; I do not know myself, except I honestly did not wish to harm Mrs Sutton in any way, just to keep her from harming my family, that was all."

Teresa, roused from her sleep, sat up in bed and Anna was prevented from pursuing the subject. She went to call for the maid, who soon arrived with tea for the invalid, who claimed, to their great relief, that she was already feeling much better.

Later, when their father arrived, Anne-Marie convinced him that Tess should not be moved and she should stay at Longbourn to care for her.

Dr Faulkner had promised to call in again to see his patient and pronounce on her condition. Jonathan, though anxious about the health of his rather frail young daughter, who had a very special place in his affections, allowed himself to be persuaded.

Anne-Marie had decided and Anna was sure she would not be denied; that was clear.

"I shall thoroughly enjoy being busy again," she said, urging her father and Anna not to suffer any anxiety on her account. "With Harriet away, I shall have plenty to do helping my aunt. Tessie, when she is stronger, can come downstairs and sit in the parlour and amuse us, while we carry on with our chores. So you must not worry. We shall all be quite agreeably occupied."

Mrs Collins was moved almost to tears by her granddaughter's solicitude and begged Jonathan to let them stay with her.

Returning to Netherfield with her husband, Anna was in an agony of uncertainty. Should she tell him about Lucy Sutton's strange behaviour, she wondered. If she did not and later, some scandal befell the family, would he not blame her for her silence?

After much thought, she decided she could not speak, at least until she had consulted Anne-Marie. She hoped they would get an opportunity to speak privately soon.

Unfortunately, the weather began to close in a few days after their visit to Longbourn and Dr Faulkner, having seen his patient, came to Netherfield to declare that he was absolutely against any attempt to move Teresa.

"I cannot take the risk of her catching a chill or even a bad cold," he explained to Anna and Jonathan. "Miss Teresa is a delicate young lady and, if she were to get pneumonia, there could be serious complications and she might not recover quickly. I think it best that she remain at Longbourn, where I am close at hand in the event of an emergency. Mrs Collins had indicated that she is happy for her to stay on as long as need be and Mrs Bradshaw is a wonderful nurse."

So it was settled.

Both girls stayed on at Longbourn and, as Tess recovered, Anne-Marie found more things to interest them in the old place. Mr Bennet's library, which was now a music room as well, was full of memories of the family that had lived for many years at Longbourn. There were dozens of books, in both the classical and modern style, learned and lighthearted, for Mr Bennet had been an avid reader, spending many hours in his library, where he had found sanctuary from domestic tribulation.

Anne-Marie selected a few and took them upstairs, where she and Tess would read to each other, sampling everything from the satires of Pope to the political writings of Cobbett and the poems of Wordsworth.

Anna and Jonathan, who came to visit, found them very comfortably settled in and Tess well on the way to a complete recovery.

They learned that Charlotte had lately received a letter from Harriet requesting that she be allowed to extend her stay with her mother by a fortnight, until she was fully recovered. Charlotte had no words to express her appreciation of her two dear granddaughters.

"I cannot tell you how good they have been to me," she said. "Anne-Marie has been a veritable tower of strength; I truly do not know how I would have coped without her, and my dear Tessie, she is an angel. She never complains and takes all the potions and pills that Dr Faulkner prescribes without a murmur! She reminds me so much of dear Jane Bennet, when she was a young girl, so sweet and kind, with never a harsh word for anyone." Clearly, Mrs Collins was completely happy with her present situation and the Bingleys departed, confident that all was well at Longbourn.

Teresa grew stronger and was soon able to sit out in the garden, while her sister and grandmother pruned and weeded away to their hearts' content. In the last year, she had grown closer to her older sister, whom she admired and loved dearly. As for Anne-Marie, with her grandmother gladly surrendering her authority to her, she was virtually the Mistress of Longbourn and found she was enjoying herself very much indeed.

❧

One mild morning, in the third week of their stay at Longbourn, Anne-Marie was reading to Tess, who was reclining upon a wicker couch in the shade of an old elm that stood to one side of the lawn. Indeed, she had noticed that with the combined soporific effect of balmy weather and the plangent quality of the poetry of Keats, her sister was finding it difficult to stay awake. Seeing her dozing off again, Anne-Marie put down her book and decided to take a turn in the shrubbery. She had not had much time to spend on her own during the last two weeks and resolved to take some exercise while she let her thoughts wander.

She had not been occupied thus for very long, when the sound of horse's hoofs on gravel reached her. Walking towards the lawn, she was expecting to see her father, who frequently rode round to see them when he was inspecting the estate. To her complete surprise, she saw alighting from his horse, Mr Colin Elliott.

It was clear from his smile and cheerful demeanour that he was very happy to see her. He explained that he had been to Netherfield to call on them and, on being informed by her father that she and Teresa were staying at Longbourn for a while, he'd ridden over to see them.

"Mrs Bradshaw, I am happy to see you. I hope you are well and I trust your sister is quite recovered now," he said, and Anne-Marie assured him that she was very well, adding, "And Tessie is much better too; indeed, we are still at Longbourn only because my grandmother Mrs Collins is without her companion Harriet and we are reluctant to leave her bereft of all company."

Colin Elliott looked most impressed.

"That is uncommonly kind of you, Mrs Bradshaw. I know of few other young ladies who would give up so much time for such a purpose. For my part, I am delighted to find you here. I have brought you a report from your brother on the plight of hundreds of orphans in the city, who live on the streets and often die on the streets. They have no schooling and no medical attention at all," he said, clearly concerned.

"I've read your brother's report; it contains some powerful evidence, which may well help your case for a children's hospital," he said, his countenance suddenly grave. Anne-Marie was pleased indeed and thanked him with all her heart. She was very relieved to learn that her brother had not forgotten her cause.

Charlotte, coming out and seeing Mr Elliott, invited him to take tea with them, while Teresa, waking from her sleep, went indoors to help her grandmother.

Left together, Anne-Marie and Mr Elliott spent only a very few minutes in what might have seemed an awkward silence, before they both started to speak at once and having thus broken the silence with laughter, their conversation flowed happily thereafter.

Colin Elliott proved to be a diverting guest, relating stories of his experiences in the Parliament. His irreverent tales of drowsy old Tories snoring in the middle of the Prime Minister's speech and recalcitrant Lords who would filibuster until dawn to deny a bill passage, kept the ladies entertained. Neither their father nor their Uncle Wilson had revealed this side of Parliamentary life to them.

"I never knew they had this much fun," said Teresa.

After a pleasant hour of refreshment and conversation, he rose to leave, but before he did, suggested that he could bring his curricle round if the mild weather held, and perhaps they could take Miss Teresa for a drive.

Before anyone could say anything, Teresa's delight was so enthusiastically expressed that it was settled immediately and he took his leave, promising to see them on the morrow.

Charlotte Collins was particularly impressed by his generosity and personal charm. "There are not many young men of his consequence who would be content to spend his time with us. Most of them, these days, seem to want to be racing around town, being seen with people in high places," she said, as they retired upstairs.

"Is Mr Elliott a very important person?" Teresa asked, "Because he certainly does not behave like one."

Anne-Marie laughed at her sister's naiveté, but Mrs Collins answered her seriously.

"That is principally because he gives himself no high and mighty airs," she declared, "but I understand from Dr Faulkner that he is the younger son of one of the wealthiest men in the county, Sir Paul Elliott. Their family is a distinguished one, and while the elder son is likely to inherit the lion share of the estate, I dare say Mr Colin Elliott will not be left without a reasonable fortune."

Anne-Marie smiled, thinking as she listened to her grandmother's words that, at least, Mr Elliott would not lack support at Longbourn. His pleasing manners had clearly won him an influential friend in the family.

On the following day, he returned in his curricle, and taking advantage of the fine Spring sunshine, they drove from Longbourn in the direction of Hatfield, stopping once or twice to alight and enjoy the prospect of meadows filled with Spring flowers.

Teresa wished to pick some and Anne-Marie noted, with approval, how gently Mr Elliott helped her out and led her down the bank and into the meadow where she gathered wild flowers until her arms would hold no more.

Waiting for her, Anne-Marie thanked him. "Mr Elliott, please let me say how much I appreciate this kindness to my sister. Tessie is rather shy and may not express her thanks in such a way as to convey her true feelings, but I know she is very grateful, and so indeed, am I. It is very thoughtful of you to do this," she said.

At first, he looked rather uncomfortable at her words and moved quickly to deny that there was any need for gratitude.

"Mrs Bradshaw, please do not think that I expected gratitude for this, it is such a trifling thing; I have been happy to be of service. I have greatly enjoyed the drive myself as well as your company and that of your sister, so there is no need for you to feel any gratitude at all. The pleasure has been entirely mine."

But his companion was adamant. "But it is not a trifling thing, Mr Elliott, here you are spending time with us when you could be doing many other things; I wish you to know how much we appreciate it."

Colin Elliott wished he, too, could speak of his feelings, but Teresa was returning and he went to help her up the bank and very carefully into the vehicle; there was no opportunity to say more until they reached Longbourn.

As Teresa went indoors to put her flowers in water, he said, "The pleasure is mine, Mrs Bradshaw; I can see your sister is very precious to you," and he saw the tears in her eyes as she said, "She certainly is; we almost lost her at birth, she was so tiny and frail. My grandmother Mrs Bingley says they did not know for days if she would survive. Each time she falls ill, we panic, afraid she will not recover. I would much rather we were back at Netherfield now; it would hasten her recovery. The house is more comfortable, having been recently refurbished, and our rooms are warmer, looking out on the sunniest aspect in the park."

Colin Elliott looked puzzled. "Well, why then are you...?" he began, and Anne-Marie intervened quickly to prevent him asking the obvious question. "We must still ensure that my grandmother is not left on her own, until Harriet Greene returns next week," she explained, keeping her voice low.

Mr Elliott understood, but still thought there could be a way. "Is there no friend or relative who could stay a week or two with Mrs Collins?" he asked and was told that this had been considered and no one suitable had been found.

An idea occurred to him and he was about to speak, when there was a sound of a light vehicle arriving and Anna Bingley appeared, greeting them all with great affection. Seeing her, Mr Elliott decided that it might be best to acquaint her with his plan before suggesting it to Anne-Marie or Mrs Collins. When, after delivering a basket of fruit to her aunt and taking tea with the ladies, Anna rose to leave, he accompanied her to her carriage and helped her in. He began tentatively, unwilling to appear presumptuous, "Mrs Bingley, forgive me if this seems like impertinence on my part, but I gathered from my conversation with Mrs Bradshaw, that it would be better for Miss Teresa if she could return to Netherfield."

Anna was taken aback and would certainly have considered his intervention impertinence, but seeing the concern reflected in his face, she did not. Instead, she explained, "Indeed, the house is warmer and there are more people to attend upon her; she would certainly regain her strength and her spirits quicker with her family around her. But both Teresa and Anne-Marie will not leave their grandmother alone with only two servants at Longbourn. They fear that she will become depressed on her own and be taken ill. I have to confess we have not, as yet, found a way to resolve the matter."

Colin Elliott nodded. "I gathered as much, and it occurred to me that I may have a solution to your problem," he said.

Anna was more than a little surprised, but succeeded in concealing her astonishment as she listened, curious to discover what he had in mind.

"Mrs Bingley, in a village a mile or two west of Meryton, on the boundary of my father's estate, lives a Mrs Banks, a lady who used to be my sister's governess many years ago. She is a very respectable, well-educated woman, a widow who lives now with her son and daughter-in-law. If you and Mrs Collins agree, she may be persuaded to come to Longbourn and help Mrs Collins until her companion returns."

Seeing the still puzzled expression on Anna's face, he added, "I can vouch for her character; she was almost one of the family and left our employ only after my sister was married. She is a very kind, honest, good sort of woman and I am sure she will suit Mrs Collins. But more importantly, she will enable Mrs

Bradshaw to take her sister home and speed up her recovery. Do you think she may be useful to you?"

It had taken Anna some time to fully absorb and appreciate the implications of his words. That he had been sufficiently concerned about Teresa's health and had decided to put forward a plan that would help in a very practical way to solve their problem had taken her totally by surprise. Hitherto, she had regarded him as a gentleman of intelligence, amiable, with pleasing manners and a sense of public duty. Her husband had also recognised these qualities and commended him to her, "even though he is a Tory!"

But now, he had revealed a far deeper sense of personal concern, a desire to help where he could. She was surprised, but pleasantly so. It must say something for his character, she thought, as well as his regard for their family. Realising suddenly that he was waiting for her response, she said, with some enthusiasm, "Mr Elliott, if, as you say, she is an honest and kind woman and can keep my aunt company, her usefulness will be unarguable. I have lent Mrs Collins a maid who will attend to the household tasks; indeed, your Mrs Banks, if she will come, sounds like just the person we need."

He looked genuinely pleased and she added, "Mr Elliott, it is very kind of you to do this for us. I have no doubt that it will be very good for Teresa to return home. Your generosity and compassion are truly appreciated." Begging her not to thank him, he promised to see Mrs Banks that very evening and have an answer for her tomorrow.

As he left her and returned to his curricle, Anna was still wondering at this new side of Mr Elliott that had been revealed. She could not as yet make out the reason behind it; perhaps he was just a genuinely compassionate man, who seeing their predicament with her aunt, was moved to help. There was also the possibility, she had to admit to herself, that his feelings were more deeply engaged than she had imagined. She had observed how he regarded Anne-Marie with a mixture of admiration and something more than ordinary friendliness and, though the lady herself gave no sign of noticing it, Anna was sure there was deeper affection there.

~❦~

The following week saw Mrs Banks, a pleasant, friendly woman, comfortably settled at Longbourn and the two sisters return at last to Netherfield and the comfort and care of their loving family. Writing to her sister-in-law, Anna spoke of their relief.

Dearest Emma,

I do not have to tell you of our happiness and relief at having Tessie back at home. While I was sure that Anne-Marie could care for her, I could not help worrying that it was taking her longer than usual to regain her strength and her spirits.

There was also some anxiety about her accommodation at Longbourn, where her room was much less well appointed and colder than at Netherfield and was probably impeding her recovery.

Which is why I am so grateful to Mr Elliott for his intervention, helping to obtain the services of Mrs Banks, his sister's former governess. She is a remarkably friendly and capable woman and my aunt Mrs Collins is already wondering how she ever got on without her. Indeed, Jonathan has suggested that she should be invited to stay on, if she is willing, even after Harriet returns.

At the end of the same week, Mr Frederick Fairfax, the architect's assistant, returned as promised, with all his drawings and plans for the improvement of the cottages on the Netherfield estate.

This time, he was accommodated at Netherfield, in one of the best-maintained cottages on the estate, only a short fifteen-minute walk from the main house, where he was invited to take his meals with the family.

This he did, gratefully, save for breakfast. He was, he claimed, an early riser, who liked to walk a mile or two before breakfast and was well able to get his own porridge or toast.

"My dear mother, a great believer in self sufficiency, taught us all to cook," he declared.

"And do all your brothers cook their own breakfasts?" asked Anna.

"No, ma'am, but my sisters can and do cook very well. I was forced to learn or they would bully me unmercifully, being older than I was," he replied. They laughed, enjoying his company, especially Teresa, whose recovery seemed to have sped up considerably with the sunshine, the loving care of her family, and coincidentally, the arrival of Mr Fairfax.

Meanwhile, Colin Elliott was endeavouring to discover more about Mrs Bradshaw and the nature of his own feelings towards her. It had not been simple or easy.

He had found, during the past fortnight when he had been away from Hertfordshire, that he had greatly missed her. Indeed, she had rarely been out of his thoughts. Yet, unlike most young women he knew, Anne-Marie had no mastery of the performing Arts. She hardly played the piano and did not sing with any distinction, often declaring that she could only sing in the church choir, because all the other good voices masked her own. She neither drew nor painted, and yet, she fascinated him.

He had told himself it was because he knew few women of such keen intelligence and independent views; but he had then been disturbed to find that, in his quieter moments, it had been her lovely face and graceful figure, rather than her opinions, that seemed to dominate his thoughts. Indeed, if he were to be honest with himself, he would have to admit that these feelings had little to do with her fine social conscience and humanity, nor was he particularly concerned that her political loyalties were rather more radical than her father's or his own.

Having accepted the fact that she seemed to occupy his mind during most of his waking hours, he finally conceded that he was rapidly becoming bewitched by her. Her beauty and charm now appeared to him to be enhanced, while her character had acquired a peerless quality that placed her well above any other woman he had known.

Having contemplated all of this over a reasonable period of time, Colin Elliott had begun to wonder whether the lady was, even to the smallest extent, aware of his feelings. Of her affections, he was uncertain.

When they had met in the garden at Longbourn, after his absence at Westminster, he had been quite unable to conceal his pleasure at seeing her again, yet wondered if she had even noticed. If she had, she had given no indication of it and though she had greeted him with warmth and friendliness, he could not detect even a flicker of additional interest on her part, except, of course, when he mentioned the hospital or the activities of the Parliament. Of the latter, there was always plenty of interesting news, but of the former, he was beginning to despair.

Unfortunately, he had not had an opportunity to broach the subject of the hospital with his father and so had very little to report.

Throughout the following week, and especially when they moved Teresa and Anne-Marie back to Netherfield, he had tried desperately to discern some change in her attitude to him with no success.

She had thanked him warmly and sincerely for his help, appeared most grateful for his compassion, but nothing more. Colin Elliott was convinced he was getting nowhere.

Called away for a few days to his father's estate, he returned vowing to discover if she had missed him at all. Having called first at Longbourn, to inquire after Mrs Banks and Mrs Collins and found them very satisfactorily settled, he rode over to Netherfield. There, he found all three ladies at home, though Mr Bingley had gone up to London on business. When Anna invited him to stay to dinner, he accepted with alacrity. As they sat taking tea on the lawn, they were joined by another young man, one he had met on a previous occasion, but in different circumstances, a Mr Frederick Fairfax. Mr Fairfax had brought along his sketch pad and while he scribbled and scratched incessantly, Teresa who seemed most interested in his work, sat beside him and looked on, occasionally pointing out some feature of the drawing.

When Anna was called away to console young Nicholas, Colin Elliot found himself alone with Anne-Marie, seated at some distance from the other two, who seemed intent upon their task. Expecting to be asked about his efforts to secure his father's support for the hospital, he had prepared an answer, something plausible, which he hoped she would believe. But the need did not arise, for Anne-Marie was deeply involved in a book she was reading. It was a novel by Emily Brontë, a young woman whose authorship had been originally concealed by a male pen name. Anne-Marie had acquired a copy of *Wuthering Heights*, the only novel Miss Brontë had written, and confessed to Mr Elliott that it had absorbed her totally. There was no mistaking her enthusiasm.

"There is so much energy and passion in the characters and the writing, yet when one recalls that Miss Brontë lived out most of her short life in a parsonage at Haworth, on the edge of the Yorkshire moors, one has to wonder at the power of her imagination," she said.

Colin Elliott was unfamiliar with the novel, but in view of his companion's recommendation, he determined that he would obtain a copy and read it forthwith.

Meanwhile, he was content to listen to her read him particular passages and discuss their meaning.

So engrossed were they, that they did not notice that Frederick Fairfax had completed his sketch. Teresa brought it over and held it up; it was a sketch of two figures seated together, poring over a book, their faces obscured, hers by a beribboned hat, and his, because his head was bent close to hers, looking at the page.

In attitude and stance, however, they were unmistakably Anne-Marie and Mr Elliott, and the sketch lent them an air of familiar intimacy that was quite remarkable. Colin Elliott held his breath, somewhat embarrassed and apprehensive, afraid that she may be offended or, worse, regard it as impertinence and probably destroy it. He found it very appealing and would have liked to ask the artist for it, but, unwilling to be the first to comment, he said nothing.

Anne-Marie took the drawing from her sister and having regarded it for a few minutes, smiled and said lightly, "That is very good, Mr Fairfax; if you will sign it for me, I think I might have it framed."

Mr Elliott's relief was palpable. It meant she was not offended. He smiled and plucked up the courage to look more closely at the picture and commented that he thought Fairfax had not got the detail of Mrs Bradshaw's hat quite right, which remark brought laughter all round.

At that very moment, Anna returned and, seeing the drawing as well as the looks on their faces, she knew—indeed she was certain—for the first time that there was, or at least there was soon going to be, much more than an ordinary friendship between Anne-Marie and Colin Elliott.

To her, the signs were unmistakable.

꧁꧂

At dinner, the conversation returned to India, more specifically the Mutiny and the horrors thereof. This time, Frederick Fairfax mentioned his uncle at the Colonial Office, who had gone to work in India after the Mutiny, he told them. Teresa then volunteered the information that Mr Elliott had spent several years out there. Mr Fairfax was interested.

"Did you really, Mr Elliott? Was it awful? Why did you leave? My uncle, who quite enjoys the place, says the horrible things that happened during the Mutiny have driven thousands of English people away…"

Anne-Marie, who had already noticed the expression on Mr Elliott's face, an expression that spoke to her of distress, was unwilling to have the pleasant ambience of their dinner table destroyed by recollections of evil and mayhem and decided to intervene in the conversation.

Colin Elliott had started to speak; plainly reluctant, he stuttered, "Well, it was not really the Mutiny at all…in fact, I was in England at the time—" he began, when to his complete surprise and subsequent delight, Mrs Bradshaw interrupted him, "Mr Elliott is far too modest to tell you himself, Mr Fairfax, but the truth is his party wanted him to stand for Parliament and take over the mantle of his father, Sir Paul Elliott. That is why he left India. Is that not so, Mr Elliott?"

Stunned by her diplomacy and profoundly grateful, he agreed instantly, "Yes, that is correct. My father was anxious to retire and I could hardly refuse such a secure seat in the Commons."

This information so impressed Mr Fairfax, that he raised his eyebrows and changed the subject altogether and Anna, intercepting Anne-Marie's glance, smiled to herself.

Later, when they were gathered in the drawing room taking coffee, Frederick Fairfax brought out his drawings to show them how he planned to improve the cottages on the home farm at Netherfield. While Anna, Teresa, and Cathy were poring over them, gathered around a table in the corner of the room, Anne-Marie offered Colin Elliott more coffee.

He accepted; it gave him the opportunity, as they moved away from the others, to say in a low voice, "Mrs Bradshaw, please let me thank you for preserving me from another recital of the horrors of the Indian Mutiny; I am afraid I was hopelessly stranded and without your intervention I would not have escaped."

She laughed, a genuinely happy, lilting laugh, like he had not heard from her before, and said, "I was quite certain you had no wish to go through all that again. Mr Fairfax is probably too young or has had too little experience of life to realise that those who have known that kind of agony have little desire to retell it in all its particulars on every occasion.

"I recall your distress when you first told us of it; it was plain to me, that even though you were not present to see the atrocities, hearing of them had been sufficiently harrowing to cause you much pain. I do not blame you for wanting to put it behind you, and I certainly did not wish to have you go through it all over again at dinner tonight."

She spoke honestly, without sentimentality or drama and yet, once again, Colin Elliott was lost for words. This time, because he was so delighted by her admission of understanding and sympathy for him that he knew not how to respond, fearful of saying too much or too little.

He wanted desperately to let her know how much her words had pleased him, yet feared that too effusive a declaration may alarm her and spoil everything.

In the end, he thanked her simply and sincerely with all his heart and, looking into her eyes as he spoke, he felt...he wondered if perhaps...no indeed, he was absolutely certain that he had seen in them a response that gave him a glimmer of hope.

END OF PART ONE

THE LADIES OF LONGBOURN

Part Two

THE WEATHER BEING WARM AND dry for much of the season, a considerable amount of work was accomplished on the cottages of the Netherfield Estate. Frederick Fairfax had worked hard on the plans, which had met with Mr Bingley's approval before Mr Lockwood was recalled and the builders hired to begin the work. It was completed to the satisfaction of his employer and the occupants, who were perfectly happy to put up with the temporary inconvenience to have their dwellings so much improved.

Jonathan Bingley was a conscientious landlord and, with his wife and daughters to support him, his management of the estates at Longbourn and Netherfield was exemplary. Here were no displaced and impoverished farmhands and tenants without a piece of land to cultivate or a roof over their heads. They were still free to use some of the fields and all of the commons and woodlands. While several of the younger men had travelled into the big towns to look for more lucrative work, many returned disillusioned to the farms and orchards.

Like his father Charles Bingley and his uncle Mr Darcy, whose fine estates of Ashford Park and Pemberley owed nothing to the ruthless practices of greedy landholders, Jonathan had sought always to engender trust and loyalty between himself and the men and women who lived and worked on his land. The maintenance and improvement of their cottages, the provision of many traditional amenities as well as a new hall for the church school, had all been initiated by him and in return he had received their loyalty in good measure.

So satisfied was he with the work on the cottages that Messrs Lockwood and Fairfax were reengaged and asked to produce a plan for a modest hospital for children. There was as yet no approval from the council and certainly no money, but Jonathan believed that if they had a plan and a site, the rest might well follow.

Just outside the boundaries of the Longbourn Estate, in a place called Bell's Field, stood a derelict chapel, which may have been, some centuries ago, before the destruction of the monasteries, part of a Catholic convent. It was surrounded by some acres of farmland, woods, and meadow, most of which had lain neglected and overrun by weeds for decades.

Aware of Anne-Marie's desire to establish a hospital for the children of the area and persuaded by his wife of the importance of providing his daughter with something worthwhile to occupy her time, Jonathan Bingley had contacted the agents for the owners of the property and found them very willing to sell and at a most reasonable price.

"Their father was killed at Balaclava and they could not afford to do anything useful with it and agreed that it was a shame to leave it to the brambles and weeds," he explained, as they discussed their plans.

"When I told them we had in mind a hospital for the children of this area, they were overjoyed. Their father, who was himself a physician, would have approved, they said, and wished our scheme every success. They asked only that the two graves that lie behind the old church be respected."

When Anne-Marie heard the news, she was ecstatic and wanted to be taken immediately to the site.

"After years of neglect, it is not in the best condition," her father warned, "and you may be disappointed."

But, she would not be dissuaded.

"I could not care if it had a thicket of thorn bush and brambles as high as the sky, so long as we had a piece of land and permission to build a hospital. Oh Papa, you are wonderful!" she cried and flung her arms around her father's neck.

Unfortunately, he had to dampen her enthusiasm by reminding her that they did not have approval yet, and it was by no means a certainty. However, he was hopeful. "When Mr Elliott was here last week, I intimated that we may soon have a site and he has promised to speak with his father about the matter of approval. Sir Paul has considerable influence on the council and could be of assistance in this regard."

Even Anna was surprised at this news and, as they climbed into the carriage and drove to Bell's Field, where they alighted and gazed at the forlorn little church, she hoped with all her heart that Colin Elliott would not disappoint them. Clearly, Anne-Marie was very hopeful, and her enthusiasm was undiminished by the appearance of the neglected site. "We could have it cleared and made ready in a week," she declared, and once again, Jonathan had to warn that they could do little more than clear away the brambles, without the approval of the council.

"I have asked Mr Lockwood and Frederick Fairfax to look at the place and draw me a modest plan," he said, and before she could cry out in delight, he added, "Only because I believe that with a site and a plan and some pushing from Sir Paul Elliott, we may stand a better chance with the council."

But she would not let any of his reservations dull her bliss, so filled was her mind with the picture of what had been a dream for almost a year. She could scarcely believe it was about to become a reality. Turning to Anna and her father, she said, "I should like to keep the chapel, Papa; restore it and use it as part of the hospital."

Anna thought it would be a good idea too, but Jonathan was cautious. "It has been neglected and exposed to the weather for so many years that Lockwood would need to get his builder to look at it. It may not be safe, if the timber has rotted away. But, if he says it is, I can see no reason why it could not be retained and refurbished; we shall have to see."

"Could we look?" Anne-Marie asked, her eyes shining with excitement.

At that point, he had to refuse. "Oh no, my dear, it would be foolish to venture in while it is in this neglected state. I think we must wait until the place has been cleared and the rubbish burned."

Seeing her disappointment, Anna added a word of caution also: "Your father is right, Anne-Marie, there could be rats . . ."

"Not rats!" Anne-Marie's desire to explore evaporated at the mention of rats. Brambles she could face, but she drew the line at rats. Reluctantly she agreed and they returned to their vehicle, even as she turned to look longingly at the place which now held her dreams.

Passing the turn-off to Longbourn, they decided to call on Mrs Collins, whose spirits had been greatly restored now that Harriet had returned.

Mrs Banks came regularly to sit with her and read to her, for though she was as active as she ever was, Charlotte's eyesight was not as good as it had been. The two women had become good companions.

"Ever since we lost dear Mary, I have missed having someone to read to me," she had said to Anna, "Harriet is too busy and Mrs Sutton does not speak the words as clearly, though she does try. Mrs Banks is very good indeed."

On this mild afternoon, as they approached the usually quiet house, they could hear a great commotion, and as they drew up at the entrance, Mrs Sutton came running out in floods of tears, crying out "No, no, please, no!"

So astonished were they, that for a few seconds they were unable to decide what to do. But, as Mrs Sutton recognised the occupants of the carriage, she ran back into the house and, by the time the ladies had alighted and gone indoors, she had fled upstairs.

Anna found her aunt in the parlour looking quite anxious and bewildered, while Anne-Marie followed Mrs Sutton upstairs, only to find she had locked herself in a spare bedroom and could be heard weeping uncontrollably within.

Unable to get in and unwilling to force an entry, she came downstairs and found Harriet Greene. "Harriet, what on earth is the matter? Why is Lucy Sutton in such a state?" she asked.

"Mrs Sutton has had some bad news, ma'am," Harriet replied.

"Is this to do with her husband, Mr John Sutton? Has he discovered her?" Anne-Marie asked.

Harriet held back for only a moment and then decided that it was best that the truth be told.

"I think so, ma'am. I believe Mrs Sutton received a letter from him last week and when she did not reply, he sent another; only this time, he is threatening to come down and take the children back to London."

Anna had come out of the parlour and joined them. Hearing Harriet's words, she asked, "Harriet, how long have you known about this business of Mrs Sutton's husband?"

Harriet looked anxious; she was an honest woman and knew that the family trusted her implicitly. She would not lie. "Not very long, ma'am. Mrs Sutton spoke to me, in confidence, soon after I returned from Nottingham," she explained.

"Mrs Sutton was very upset, ma'am; she said a man had been asking questions about her in Meryton and she was afraid. She feared he was a private detective. She told me then that her husband was not dead; he had returned from the war, and she said he was stark raving mad, ma'am. He would drink a lot and swear and shout and beat her and threaten the children. She could not bear it any longer and ran away, when he was fallen asleep, dead drunk, she said. The way she told it, I felt truly sorry for her, ma'am," said Harriet, looking pretty miserable herself, as she recounted the events for them.

"Mrs Sutton begged me not to tell Mrs Collins or yourselves, fearing she might be put out of her cottage and lose her work here, teaching the children. Her two little girls, they are so terrified, ma'am, it breaks your heart to see them."

Both women were speechless for several minutes. Then Anna asked, "And what happened today?"

"She has had a letter, ma'am, saying he will come for the children. She came to ask me if we could hide the two girls here. The boy is at boarding school, and his father cannot get to him there; besides the lad is old enough to stand up to him, she says, but she is mad with fear for her two little girls, the poor woman, she will surely lose her mind if they are taken from her, ma'am." Harriet was almost in tears herself.

Anne-Marie asked quickly, "Where are the girls now?"

"They are upstairs, ma'am, and Mrs Sutton is very afraid. I told her I could not allow them to stay and she had to ask Mrs Collins, and then Mrs Collins said she could not say yes unless Mr Bingley agreed. Mrs Sutton was only weeping quietly until she heard the sound of the carriage, and I believe she did not stop to think; she was afraid he had followed her down here. She ran out and back again, when she saw it was yourselves."

Jonathan Bingley had come into the room, having waited a while in the hall. He had heard some but not all of Harriet's story, but it had been enough to convince him of the seriousness of the situation. He asked Harriet Greene a few more questions, sufficient to enable him to understand the predicament in which they had been placed.

Turning to his wife, he said quietly, "My dear, we have no choice but to protect Mrs Sutton and her daughters from whatever danger threatens them. We must convey them to Netherfield. They cannot stay here; should Sutton discover them, he will surely arrive and harass Mrs Collins and the rest of the household.

It would be a most unsatisfactory situation. At least, at Netherfield, they will be out of his reach."

Having first cautioned Harriet, that she must on no account reveal their whereabouts, he asked her to go upstairs and get the girls and their mother ready to depart for Netherfield. "Tell them they need have no concerns about their things; we can send someone round to the cottage to collect them tomorrow," he said and added, "You can assure them they will be quite safe at Netherfield."

Addressing his daughter, he said, "Anne-Marie, you can tell Mrs Sutton that I shall send for my solicitor tomorrow and he will advise what can be done to afford them some legal protection."

Meanwhile, Anna went to reassure her Aunt Charlotte, who was, by now, distressed and eager to discover what was going to happen.

"I had no idea at all, Anna, none at all," she protested, "Lucy Sutton told me she was a widow and I believed her. I am truly shocked. I thought she was a good, quiet woman."

Anna tried to reassure her, "My dear aunt, please do not concern yourself; I am sure she still remains a good woman. If what she has told Harriet is true, she has run away from a drunken, cruel husband to protect her children. She probably pretended to be a widow in order to avoid too many questions; you know what village gossip is like."

This explanation seemed to put a whole new complexion on the matter, for Charlotte. She could feel sympathy for any woman who found her children threatened. "Poor Mrs Sutton, what will she do?" she asked, and Anna explained that they were being conveyed to Netherfield. Mrs Collins was clearly relieved. "Oh good, I know they will be safe with you," she said.

Minutes later, Harriet returned with Lucy Sutton, who looked shamefaced and unhappy, while her two girls seemed cowed and afraid as if memories of their father's violent temper had come flooding back.

Anne-Marie could bear it no longer; she went to them and embraced them, assuring them that they would all be perfectly safe at Netherfield.

Jonathan sent them on their way with Anna and decided to wait with Anne-Marie for the return of their carriage.

He had let Anna go with them to Netherfield so she could help them settle in after their ordeal. On the morrow, he hoped a magistrate might be found to afford them protection.

Before Harriet took Mrs Collins upstairs, Jonathan reassured them, "I shall send Mr Bowles round to you tomorrow; should Sutton or anyone else arrive, he will deal with them. You will not be harassed."

As they waited for the carriage to return, it grew late, and Jonathan could see that Anne-Marie was very tired. On the way home, she began, suddenly, to weep.

"Papa, I feel so terrible," she said, through her tears, and he, believing she was distressed by what had transpired in the hours before, tried to comfort her, but she wept even more. "You don't understand, Papa; I knew all the time. I had seen her husband, John Sutton, at the hospital last year and when I met her and heard she had claimed to be a widow, I thought she was lying because she was guilty of something terrible and I condemned her. Papa, I just condemned her; I feel so dreadful now."

Astonished at this recital, Jonathan said nothing, as she continued, "I feel I have behaved so badly, I who should feel sympathy and concern for a woman who is unhappily married, I who knew what it was to have to pretend to be what one is not, how could I have been so presumptuous as to condemn her without ever asking to hear her side of the story? Papa, how could I have been so wicked?" she asked, still weeping, plainly unable to control her anguish.

Jonathan let her weep, knowing she needed to relieve her pent-up feelings of guilt, but then spoke gently though firmly, "My dear Anne-Marie, you are the last person who could be wicked to anyone. I know you well; you are tender-hearted, even with complete strangers, caring for them as if they were your own. Pray, my dear, do not judge yourself so harshly. No doubt, you misunderstood Mrs Sutton's motives only because you were ignorant of her circumstances. But, you did no real harm and now you have an opportunity to do some good. When they are at Netherfield, you can help them, especially the two children; they must surely be in great need of comfort and reassurance," he said.

She looked up at him, confident of his understanding and affection.

"Thank you, Papa, I shall try, but what will they do? How are they to be protected?" she asked.

"When Mr Hart, my solicitor, has spoken with Mrs Sutton and ascertained the whole of her situation, he will advise the best course of action. Meanwhile, she and her daughters will remain at Netherfield under my protection. Should Sutton turn up on my property, I can have him arrested for trespass and brought before the magistrate."

Certain her father would do everything in his power, Anne-Marie was content to wait until they were back at Netherfield, where they found Mrs Sutton and her daughters had been shown their rooms and were, even now, safely ensconced therein. One of the maids had been sent to assist them, and tea had been taken up to them.

When Anna came downstairs she reported that their guests were a sad, fearful little group, who had pleaded to be excused from coming down to join the family at dinner.

"They are very tired and the girls have frightening memories of a violent father. Poor Mrs Sutton can hardly think, so terrified is she of losing them to him. I've asked Mrs Perrot to have their dinner served upstairs. I do hope they will feel better tomorrow," she said.

On hearing this, Anne-Marie went directly upstairs and found them all huddled together in the large bed in Mrs Sutton's room. They looked so apprehensive and pathetic, she went to them and put her arms around them and as they hid their faces in her gown, Marigold and Lucinda began to weep, while their mother stood by, looking totally helpless and wretched.

Anne-Marie had to fight back her tears. In her own heart, she was so miserable that the tears she shed were partly for her own relief. She had been badly shaken on discovering how utterly wrong she had been about Lucy Sutton. Not only had she misjudged the woman on very little evidence, she had also deliberately spoken ill of her, voicing what had turned out to be unfounded suspicions, ascribing the basest of motives to a helpless woman who had only been trying to protect her children.

Realising the gravity of her mistake, she was deeply sorry and her contrition was both genuine and painful.

She tried to make amends, "Mrs Sutton, Lucy, please do not be afraid; you are perfectly safe here, and my father has assured me that tomorrow he will summon his solicitor, who will advise on some resolution to your problem."

Lucy Sutton, clearly grateful, clung to her hand and, still tearful, revealed that she had feared that her husband would return and remove her children. She had been traced to Meryton by a hired private detective, she said, and then the letters had begun to arrive, threatening her, ordering her to return to London with the girls or else . . .

"I could not go back, Mrs Bradshaw, not with my two girls. They have been happy and safe here; I could not let them go back to that squalor and fear, with no schooling, no money, and no hope of a decent life. It would be a sin; I would rather die than do it," she declared.

Anne-Marie was alarmed. "Hush, Lucy, there is no need for that. You will only put more fear in their hearts," she said and, having sat with them a while until they were quieter, she left them as the servants brought in their dinner. As she went downstairs to join the others, she wondered at the extent of Mrs Sutton's suffering and thought bitterly, "And how could I have condemned her so? I, who should have been understanding and helpful to such a woman?"

Later that night, she talked long and seriously with Anna, who had come to her room before retiring. Jonathan had told her of Anne-Marie's outburst of guilt in the carriage. Anna understood her distress yet urged her not to dwell upon her sense of shame.

"But, Anna, how could I have been so blinded by prejudice as not to even question my own judgment?" she asked and Anna replied,

"You were mistaken. I know you must feel unhappy, but think, Anne-Marie, it is far better now to turn your mind to helping them deal with this nightmare, especially the two girls. Think how much you can do to help them; that is far more important than pursuing your own guilt."

She was still not content. "But how was I so utterly unfair? I am not normally overbearing and censorious."

"Of course, you are not. I know that," said Anna.

"Yet, there was I, prepared to expose and condemn her, with no evidence of wrongdoing. Oh, I shall never live this down."

Anna smiled. "Not in your own estimation, perhaps, but in truth, the damage has not been great. I am sure when you have set out to help them, you will cease to be as severe upon yourself as you are now."

Summoned by an express sent by Mr Bingley, the solicitor, Mr Hart, arrived at Netherfield, together with his clerk, a learned young man, very thin, and bespectacled but with a great many volumes of law books in his case. Mr Hart was a man well versed in the law and its applications, and Jonathan Bingley was sure he would give Mrs Sutton sound advice.

For over two hours, he was closeted in the library with Mrs Sutton, her elder daughter, Marigold, and Anna, before Jonathan was called in to hear what he had proposed. Mr Hart laid the facts out in painful detail.

"Marriages," he declared in a grave voice, "be they happy or miserable, are very difficult to dissolve." He described, for their benefit, "the three routes available, under the Act of 1857, to a party who may wish to divorce or be separated from a partner."

In appropriately solemn tones, he went on, "There is a *vinculo matrimonii*, which allows for an annulment in the appropriate circumstances, which does not apply in this case; then there is divorce *a mensa et a thoro*, under which, in cases of adultery, extreme cruelty, or gross physical violence, a separation may be permitted. However," he warned, in a most severe voice, "if that is chosen, there can be no remarriage. The third route involves an application to Parliament. This is a real divorce and the partners may then remarry, but I must warn, it is an extremely expensive and dilatory route to take."

Mrs Sutton could scarcely wait for him to finish, to point out that she had no wish at all to marry again and wished only to be allowed to live separately and bring up her children in peace, free from abuse and harassment.

"In which case, ma'am," Mr Hart intoned sombrely, "I should recommend the second course, which is also the least expensive. However, you will need reliable witnesses to the acts of cruelty."

To Anna's surprise, Marigold Sutton, not quite eleven years old, having sat through the ordeal holding her mother's hand, spoke up and declared that she had frequently witnessed the violence visited upon her mother and brother by their father, and promised she would swear to it before a magistrate if need be.

When Anna, who had been deeply shocked, later told her husband of this, her eyes filled with tears again at the memory.

"To hear a child, for that is what Marigold is, say with so much feeling that she would give sworn testimony against her father was so appalling, I could not believe I was hearing right," she said. Jonathan comforted her and told her that it was certain proof that the children were better for being separated from their violent father. He told her also that Mr Hart, before departing, had hinted that there appeared to be sufficient evidence to obtain a separation order on the grounds of cruelty and physical violence.

"It is certainly fortunate that she is not seeking to remarry, since that would have been a good deal more difficult and expensive," said he.

Anna commented that any woman who had suffered as Mrs Sutton had done, in one marriage, was unlikely to be eager and willing to rush into another.

When Anne-Marie was told of Mr Hart's advice to Lucy Sutton, she expressed her satisfaction but asked what was to be done in the meanwhile to secure the safety of Mrs Sutton and her children. Anna, who had already discussed the matter with her husband, replied, "They would have to remain under your father's protection, if only to spare them the indignity of harassment, until the separation is granted. I have suggested that they should be allowed the use of the vacant cottage at Abbotsford, which lies within the estate and is close enough to afford her and her girls some security, since it is situated in close proximity to the home of Mr Bowles," she explained, adding, "Mr Bowles has been over to Longbourn today and there has been no sign of Mr Sutton or the private detective, which is good news."

Anne-Marie was pleased. She had some good news of her own to add: "I have been talking with young Marigold; she is very interested in the children's hospital and wishes to help. She says when she is older she would very much wish to train as a nurse!"

Anna was delighted. "That is excellent news; it will mean that the girl will have something to occupy her and, if she is to help you, Mrs Sutton will not have to worry about her at all," she said and Anne-Marie agreed. "She is hard-working and sensible, too, which is a great start. Both girls have offered to help me make posters for our campaign."

It was clear that Anne-Marie had taken Anna's advice seriously and was throwing herself enthusiastically into the task of helping the two girls recover from the shock and fear of the past week. Mrs Sutton would be most grateful, too. It meant she could continue to teach at Longbourn, knowing her girls were safely occupied.

Anna felt deeply for her; being happily married herself, it was most depressing to encounter the pain and bitterness of broken marriage that afflicted Lucy Sutton and her children. She felt a deep sense of gratitude to her own husband, as well a strong desire to help those less fortunate who had been hurt. The knowledge that her husband shared this sense of responsibility gave her great satisfaction.

❦

The removal of the Suttons from Netherfield House to the cottage at Abbotsford coincided with the return of Charles Bingley and Colin Elliot to the district. The two men had met several times in London and appeared to have become firm friends, despite the fact that their political loyalties were to opposite sides of the house. They were dining at Netherfield House when this was commented upon and Charles laughed heartily, declaring that he had hopes "by one means or another, of making a Reformist of Elliott, even if I have to perform some surgical operation upon him!"

Amidst much laughter, his friend retorted that he hoped this operation would not be too painful. "It would need to be performed upon the heart, would it not?" asked Anne-Marie, obviously intending her remark to be taken lightly. But Anna noted that Mr Elliott glanced at her quickly and looked surprised, even hurt, by the taunt.

She spoke quickly, hoping to assuage his distress. "Come now, that is unfair. I do not think there is anything lacking in the quality of Mr Elliott's heart, which I know is not only compassionate, but is well disposed towards Reform already," she said, to which Elliott replied gratefully, "Indeed, ma'am, I thank you for your kind defence of my heart. Should you care to ask any of my colleagues in the Tory Party, or indeed my own father, you will learn that most of them believe I lean too far towards the Liberals."

"Indeed?" said Jonathan Bingley, sensing the need to steer the conversation into safer waters, "On what particular matters?"

"Well, sir, I suppose it would be mainly on matters relating to Parliamentary reform. I support the principles that Mr Bright and Mr Gladstone wish to enshrine in a new Reform Bill; I am astonished to hear it will be defeated by the Whigs who will vote it down."

"Those infernal Adullamites," said Jonathan, clearly irritated. "Mr Elliott, there are men in our party of whom I sometimes despair."

"If it were introduced, would you vote to pass it?" asked Anna.

"Certainly, Mrs Bingley," Elliott replied.

"Even if it meant crossing the floor?" interjected Anne-Marie, who had remained silent since her unhappy remark.

"Even so, Mrs Bradshaw. I know it will do my political career no good at all, but it is a matter of principle; I could not vote in the Commons to deny ordinary working men the right to vote for their Member of Parliament."

In a gentler tone, Anne-Marie asked, "Then surely, you would not oppose giving women the vote?"

Elliott, though taken aback somewhat, answered her directly, "No indeed, I would not, though I confess I am unaware of any such proposition in the Parliament at this time."

"I meant as a matter of principle, Mr Elliott," she persisted, a subtle inflection in her voice, leaving no doubt as to her meaning.

"Absolutely not, Mrs Bradshaw; it is my strong conviction that all adult citizens should have the right to vote; I can find no argument to justify denying it to one section of our community, solely on the grounds that they are not men!" he said, and everyone laughed including Anne-Marie. Charles rubbed it in, teasing his friend, pointing out that it was easy to support a proposition when there was no possibility of it being introduced into the Parliament in the foreseeable future.

But this time, to Elliott's surprise, Anne-Marie came to his defence, "If Mr Elliott says he will support it in the future, we must believe him, Charles. Indeed that makes him a good deal more of a Reformist than many of the Whigs sitting in the Parliament today, does it not, Papa?"

Jonathan smiled and agreed, adding that he was not at all surprised to hear Mr Elliott's views. "In my conversations with him, I have found him to be far more enlightened in his opinions than most Tories I have known. Indeed, I have wondered what Sir Paul Elliott may have to say when he hears his speeches in the Commons."

As the company broke into laughter and the port was placed upon the table, the ladies rose and withdrew.

The talk around the table ranged from the American Civil War to the urgent need for reform of rural councils.

"Most of them are dominated by large landholders and the country gentry, who have no time for democracy," said Charles, and Elliott agreed; his own father kept a pretty tight rein on the local councils in Hertfordshire, where he had the largest land holdings of all. He was well aware that rural councils in England were still in need of reform.

Happily, they discovered they were all in agreement about the American Civil War. President Lincoln had to be supported in his struggle to free the slaves and preserve the Union.

When the gentlemen rejoined the ladies in the drawing room, Anna was making tea while Anne-Marie poured out the coffee. She had had early hopes of discovering the extent of Sir Paul Elliott's support for their hospital, but the matter had not come up at all during dinner, and she had not been sitting near enough to Mr Elliott to introduce the subject, without drawing too much attention to it. She was impatient to know, however, and had decided to approach Colin Elliott at some time during the evening.

There was another matter, too, that she was very keen to mention. An opportunity presented itself when he came to her with his empty coffee cup, which she refilled. When he thanked her, she moved away from the table with him and said quickly,

"Mr Elliott, I do apologise; I hope I did not offend you. My remark about surgery on the heart was meant in jest. I was not intending to suggest that you were deficient in compassion or sensibility," she said and was relieved to see him smile.

"I knew you were not, Mrs Bradshaw, and I took no offence, I assure you. But, I would not wish you to misunderstand my situation; while I am a member of the party, I am often unable to support some of the extreme views of my fellow Tories in Parliament. My father knew this when he asked me to stand for election to his seat. I made it quite clear that there were some issues on which I would not follow the party line."

She nodded and went on, "And may I ask, what was his response to the proposal to establish a children's hospital?"

She expected some evasive answer, for it was clear to her that he had no good news to impart, else he would have spoken earlier. But to her surprise, he made no such attempt, saying frankly, "Mrs Bradshaw, I have to confess that in this enterprise, I have had no success at all. My father is completely uninterested in such matters; he regards the health of the poor as a concern for charitable organisations, which should be left entirely to the local council or the church."

Even though she had expected it, the answer was deeply disappointing, "I am amazed," she said. "Is he not a man of humanity? Has he no compassion? What arguments did you use with him?"

Colin Elliott looked decidedly downcast. "All of the usual arguments about responsibility and compassion, social conscience and the rest; regrettably none of these has any resonance with my father. Indeed, Mrs Bradshaw, I was mortified; I mean if I cannot secure support for such a noble cause as a children's hospital, what use am I to my constituency? I said as much to my father and left the house having declared that I was seriously considering resignation from the Commons."

Anne-Marie was aghast. "Mr Elliott, you will do no such thing!" she said, and he saw her eyes flash with anger as she spoke. "Why, that would be such a waste; there is much to be done and much you can accomplish for your constituents, with their support. It is not the consent of your father you need; it is the support of the people you represent and they will support you, if you convince them of the value of our project for their community," she explained, speaking with a degree of warmth and zeal that he had not seen in her before.

"And how do you think this may be accomplished?" he asked.

"In the same way that my cousin Caroline Fitzwilliam and her friends won support for a school and a hospital in their part of Derbyshire," she replied. "We shall apply to the council, of course, but we shall also take the matter to the people directly. If you help us do this, help us explain to the ordinary people how important it is for them to have a hospital here for their children, I am certain we will succeed. It is the only way."

Colin Elliott was transfixed by her passionate advocacy and offered his help whenever she needed it.

"Of course I will help you in any way I can. What do you propose to do?" he asked.

"Well, I think, tomorrow, I shall call on the man who produces our local newspaper, the *Herald*. He is a Mr Tillyard; do you know him?"

Colin Elliott said yes, he knew Stephen Tillyard very well.

"We were at school and Cambridge together. There is a family connection, too; our mothers were cousins."

Anne-Marie was delighted. "Well, there you are then; we shall take my brother Charles along, and you can both persuade him to support our campaign in his paper."

Mr Elliott was impressed by her energy and her grasp of the issues involved in their scheme. He had a few questions, though.

"What about funds?" he asked, "We shall probably need several hundred pounds, maybe more, if we get no help from the council."

Anne-Marie seemed untroubled. "Once we have approval, we shall find the money. We must get over the first hurdle," she declared and, seeing her brother approaching, she drew him towards them and left the two men together to discuss the matter, while she went to help Anna with their guests.

Anna noticed the change in her. Despite her earlier disappointment, Anne-Marie was smiling as if all her hopes had been fulfilled.

❦

Their visit, on the following afternoon, to Mr Stephen Tillyard at his office proved more successful than any of them had expected.

All three men seemed to get on very well together, Mr Tillyard being especially helpful and supportive of their scheme. However, while pledging support for the children's hospital, he declared that what his paper needed was a good story.

"Now, if we had something that would grip the attention of our good citizens and get them talking and worrying about the health of their children, demanding a hospital in the area, your battle would be easily won. Councils are becoming sensitive to the demands of their electors. A good story would stir them to action."

Charles Bingley laughed and said, "Do you mean, like a good epidemic of whooping cough or influenza?"

"Exactly, but not with too many deaths, please. We cannot have them getting too depressed or they'll forget about the hospital and sink into a slough of despondency!" he quipped.

Charles stopped laughing. "Seriously, Tillyard, if what I saw in London last Winter is any indication, you may well have your story before long. Influenza is everywhere, the lack of sanitation, the overcrowding, poor public health services, it's a certainty that many people will suffer from completely preventable diseases and the children are always the first to die," he said and his tone did not admit of any levity.

Anne-Marie, seeing that Tillyard was moved, intervened with a plea, "Mr Tillyard, could we not persuade you to write one little article, perhaps warning of the flu in London and its possible danger to our community? It would help to mention the fact that we have no public hospital in the district."

Tillyard, obviously convinced by the weight of the facts Charles had produced, as well as the appeal of his sister's lovely dark eyes, seemed to consider the matter for only a few moments, before agreeing to include a few paragraphs in next week's issue.

They left soon afterwards, promising to provide him with all the information he needed, but as he reminded them, "It's not more information I need, Colin; it's a really good story!"

⊱⊰

A few days later, Anne-Marie was persuaded by her father to visit one of the improved cottages on the estate.

"Mr Fairfax and the builders have worked very hard; I would like very much to have your opinion on the quality of the work," he had said.

Taking young Marigold Sutton with her for company, Anne-Marie set out to visit the Martins. They were a family well known to her; both husband and son had worked up at the house and, according to Anna, their youngest daughter, Elsie, had shown a remarkable talent for drawing everything from farm animals to wild birds and woodland creatures. Anna had a small collection of her pictures pinned up on a screen in the upstairs sitting room.

On approaching the cottage, Marigold remarked on how neat and tidy it looked, and Anne-Marie assured her that was exactly how they were.

"All the Martins are perfectionists, from their grandfather down to little Elsie. They work hard and try to do everything right," she said, as they reached the house.

Expecting to hear sounds of a happy family gathered inside their newly improved dwelling, they were surprised to hear instead, the incessant crying of a sick child and on entering, saw the family gathered around a little girl's bed, looking very anxious indeed. Little Elsie lay on her bed, her eyes red and her face hot with fever, while Mrs Martin tried unsuccessfully to hide her tears, as she tried to soothe the child, who was clearly in pain.

Recalling all the lessons of her excellent training, Anne-Marie took young Marigold outside at once and said, "Marigold, I cannot be certain, but little Elsie appears to be very sick with a fever and it may be catching, so you must not go in there. Wait here for me."

Going back in, she looked again at the child and was soon convinced she needed urgent medical attention. She asked a few questions and when the answers confirmed her fears, she stepped outside and asked Marigold to return as quickly as she could to Netherfield House and find Dr Bingley. "Tell him he must come at once; Elsie is very sick. Now, do not go back to your house; you must stay away from your sister Lucinda until you have changed and bathed, and your clothes must be washed in boiling water and carbolic soap. We do not want little Lucy falling ill, do we? Now hurry, Marigold; it's very urgent."

The girl raced away across the field and towards the road leading to Netherfield House. As she hurried along, she was overtaken by Mr Elliott, proceeding in the same direction. He was on his way to call on the Bingleys. He stopped and, recognising her as Mrs Sutton's daughter, asked if anything was the matter. When she explained her errand, he picked her up and sat her down in his curricle.

"You'll be there much sooner this way. It is very important that you find Dr Bingley as soon as possible," he said as they drove on.

Charles Bingley was reading in the parlour when they entered and broke the grave news.

"Did you see the child?" he asked.

"No, sir," Marigold replied, "Mrs Bradshaw said I was to wait outside; she thought it might be catching."

Charles shook his head. "Good Lord, I hope it is not scarlet fever." He gave the girl instructions for her safety and that of her younger sister, called for his carriage to be brought round, and raced upstairs for his bag.

When Colin Elliott offered to accompany him, he said, "No, you would just be in the way and probably get the wretched contagion yourself; I may have to remove the child from the house."

"Where would you put her?" asked Elliott.

"Good God, I don't know. We shall have to think of something. She cannot be left with the others, especially the infants," he replied.

Anna Bingley, coming in from the garden and seeing their troubled faces, asked what was wrong.

"Oh, everything," said Charles in an aggravated voice. "We may well have an epidemic of influenza or even scarlet fever on our hands! Anne-Marie has sent word from the Martins' place that one of the children is very ill. We will probably need to isolate the child, but where?"

Anna groaned, "Oh, if only we had a hospital," and at her words, Colin Elliott leapt up as if he had been bitten. "That's it! Stephen Tillyard wanted a good story, one that would get the people talking and demanding a hospital; well, he has it now! Charles, while you proceed to the Martins, I shall go on to

Tillyard's office and tell him what has occurred; if he can run the story, it may be just what we need to get the council's support."

He was gone in a moment, driving briskly towards Meryton, while Charles Bingley climbed into his carriage and drove down to the Martins. He took somewhat longer because he had to take the road around the fields, but when he got there, he did not take long to agree with his sister. Little Elsie Martin was very ill indeed and, while it was not immediately possible to tell, he feared very much it was influenza.

He had seen too many similar cases in the city. His first instinct was to isolate the child. Where? That was the problem. All of the improved cottages were occupied and even the barns were full after a good harvest. He was certain there would be more cases soon. It was Anne-Marie who suggested the church hall.

"It is far enough away from the main village and yet near enough for the mothers to come in and look after their children. It is secure and we need have no fears of infecting anyone, if Mr Griffin can be persuaded to stay away."

Charles agreed and, while he gave instructions to Mrs Martin and the rest of the children about some simple precautions they could take to avoid the contagion, Anne-Marie set out on foot across the fields to reach the church, which was almost a mile away. She arrived in time to find Mr Griffin about to leave to visit a parishioner. He was plainly delighted to see her. "Mrs Bradshaw," he began, "it is so good to see you," but she had no time for niceties, pouring out the story of little Elsie Martin, knowing full well, he would take pity on them. The Martins were exemplary members of his "flock" as he liked to call them and Mr Griffin would not turn his back upon them.

"I know I am asking a great deal of you, Mr Griffin, but we badly need a safe place where the children may be isolated and cared for, without infecting the others in the village."

At first, he seemed taken aback. The very idea of having several sick children in the church hall alarmed him. Then he heard her say that she and her brother Charles would be there for most of the time and he seemed to change his mind.

Whether he sensed her desperation and felt some compassion for her and the sick children or whether he was attracted by the thought that she, whom he admired so much, would be there for much of the time, will never be known.

Whatever it was that moved him, he did agree and with more eagerness than reluctance, it must be said.

"If you are sure it will be all right, Mrs Bradshaw, and your father Mr Bingley will have no objection?"

Anne-Marie assured him it would indeed be all right. "My father will have no objection at all, Mr Griffin. I promise you will have no trouble on that score," she said and when he intoned some words about caring for his flock, she said, with genuine feeling, "God bless you, Mr Griffin," and was soon hurrying back to the Martins.

There she found her brother and Mrs Martin ready to move Elsie, who was by now complaining of a headache. Within the next hour, all their preparations were made.

Mr Griffin had opened up the church hall and a few of the men from the village had come around to help with moving in some bedding and lighting a fire, while Mr Griffin himself brought round a couple of chairs and a table from the Rectory.

Charles, having provided what medication and advice he had to hand, hoping to ease the child's discomfort, left to consult Anna's father, Dr Faulkner, whose experience was invaluable.

Meanwhile, Colin Elliot had reached the office of Mr Tillyard and, finding him struggling to put together the next issue of his newspaper with nothing more exciting than the visit of the bishop for his front page, Elliot called out, "Tillyard, hold the front page, you have your story," and proceeded to relate the story of little Elsie Martin and the very real fear of an epidemic of influenza in the village.

"Now, if we had had a proper hospital, with a place to isolate infectious patients and treat them away from their siblings and friends, it would have been possible to prevent it spreading through the community," he declared and seeing that Tillyard was interested, Colin Elliot provided him with a lurid account of what Charles Bingley had had to deal with in East London in the Winter.

"It could quite easily happen here, if nothing is done. How many more children are to be infected? How many must die?" he asked dramatically and he had no doubt at all that Tillyard was impressed. He promised to give the story prominence in the paper.

When he returned to Netherfield to inquire after Elsie Martin, Anna met him and told him that two more children, neighbours of the Martins, had been taken ill. "Anne-Marie is at her wits end, collecting old linen and blankets, because they will all have to be burned, of course, once this is over. I think she and Charles intend to spend the night at the church hall. Cook is busy preparing some food to be sent over later," she explained, as she asked to be excused because she had a great many things to do. He immediately offered to help.

"I could take things across to the church hall in my carriage," he said and as he spoke, Anne-Marie coming down the stairs, her arms full of linen and pillows, heard him.

"Thank you, Mr Elliott, I think we could do with another pair of hands, especially clean ones; so if you would step into the scullery please and scrub your hands and come over here, you can help me take these over to the church hall," she said.

As they worked that night, he could not but marvel at her energy and fearlessness. It was only when the three children had all been bedded down and given their last potions for the night that she sat down to rest.

He remarked that she must be tired, but she only laughed and reminded him that she was a trained nurse who had tended hundreds of sick and wounded soldiers returning from the war.

He wanted very much to say how much he admired her for the work she had done. He had heard, he said, from her brother that she had worked at the military hospital at Harwood Park for some years.

When he saw her bite her lip at the mention of Harwood Park, he thought he had upset her, by reminding her of the wounded men. He stopped abruptly and apologised, even though he was unsure what he had said to distress her.

"Mrs Bradshaw, I am sorry, I should not have run on so, please forgive me," he said, but it was only a momentary slip; soon she was herself again and Colin Elliott never knew, that it was not the memory of the wounded men, more the recollection of personal misery, that had assailed her at that moment.

But, as she had learned to do and successfully did on many occasions, Anne-Marie used the present to heal the past and rose, saying it was time to go back in and relieve Mrs Martin, who was watching over the children as they tossed and slept fitfully through the night.

A few other women had come in from the village and a nurse from Meryton was sent for to help. Mr Griffin had put his kitchen at their disposal and one of the women had prepared hot soup and tea, while the Rector himself, flitted in and out, saying prayers and offering words of comfort, well-intentioned but mostly ineffectual.

Charles looked weary and in need of sleep, but would not leave until Dr Faulkner came to relieve him and then only because his sister insisted that he return to Netherfield House for a bath and some dinner.

Colin Elliott waited on, reluctant to leave, even when there was little he could do. "At least let me stay until Charles returns," he said. "You may need the carriage, if we have an emergency."

Anne-Marie was glad of his company. Later, she returned to find him propped up against an old pew at the back of the hall, fast asleep, his cravat askew, his coat dusty. Looking at him, she smiled, feeling for the very first time a tug of affection upon her heart. It was a feeling born of gratitude perhaps, and some admiration for his tenacity and compassion, which she now knew to be genuine.

At first, when he had agreed to support the campaign for the hospital, she had thought he was doing what politicians did best, winning votes by espousing a good cause for his constituents. Yet, she had suffered no qualms about using his support, if it meant they could get the hospital built.

But over the weeks and months and especially in the last few days, she had begun to believe that he was sincerely committed to the cause and would even go as far as alienating his own father to support it. She recalled his words, as they had parted on that night after dinner at Netherfield: "I give you my word, Mrs Bradshaw, I shall not give up on this. I know how important it is to you and to this community and as your Member, I intend to fight for it."

At the time, she had thought they were fine words and had wondered whether they would come to anything; now she believed they were sincerely spoken. Colin Elliott was clearly willing to do his best to help achieve what had now become their common goal.

Anne-Marie was particularly remorseful about the flippant remark she had made about surgery on his heart and was grateful for the magnanimity he had shown in taking no offence. Later, Anna had taken her to task for the hurtful implications of her words, and Anne-Marie had been pleased to assure her that she had apologised and the matter was settled amicably between them.

"Mr Elliott is a very gentlemanly man, Anne-Marie, and your father regards him well. He is also from a family of consequence and influence in the county. It would have been unfortunate, if there had been a falling-out between you, as a result of some thoughtless remark. I am happy it is settled."

"Dear Anna," she thought, "how right you are. He is indeed a very gentlemanly man; else, he would not so easily have forgiven me for my apparent impertinence."

Mrs Martin came in with some tea for Anne-Marie, and her footsteps roused the sleeper who, seeing them, jumped to his feet in some embarrassment. In the half-light of the hall, he could not make out the time on his watch and they followed him as he stumbled out into the open. It was cold and the hot drinks were welcome.

The first tentative strands of dawn light appeared in the sky, and a few early birds had begun tuning up for their morning chorus. He ran his fingers through his hair and made some show of dusting off his coat and tying his cravat, before gratefully accepting tea in a plain rectory china cup. Having returned his cup, he thanked Mrs Martin, then addressed Anne-Marie, "Mrs Bradshaw, plainly you have had no sleep at all; will you not let me drive you home, so you can get some rest?" he asked and when she hesitated, added, "If you intend to be constantly with these children, it would be best that you get some food and rest, else you may well fall ill, too."

She was touched by his concern for her and had to agree with the logic of his argument.

When two more women arrived to relieve those who had been with their children all night, Anne-Marie decided she would take his advice and return to Netherfield. He helped her into the carriage and drove slowly down to the main road and then on towards Netherfield House.

It was that perfectly peaceful time between darkness and dawn, usually lasting no more than a few minutes, when one is reluctant to speak above a whisper. A fine mist lay over the fields and meadows and, in the distance, the rising head of Oakham Mount was just being touched by the late rising sun.

After admiring the loveliness of the scene, they fell silent and remained so for most of the journey; it was a comfortable silence, not a strained or disconcerting one, and neither felt any pressure to break it.

When they were still some distance from Netherfield, however, he slowed the horses down to a trot and turning to her said, "Mrs Bradshaw, may I say how much I have admired what you and your brother have done here; I cannot recall another occasion on which I have seen such dedication and hard work."

Anne-Marie smiled and, in spite of her weariness and lack of sleep, he was struck by the singular sweetness of her face.

"What else could we do, Mr Elliott? These people and their children are part of our responsibility. They, no less than the members of our immediate families, depend upon us for their livelihood and welfare. My father and grand-father have always held this to be the case, and Charles and I know of no other way to live. They have shared our joys and our sorrows; it would be unthinkable to use their labour for profit, as we do, and turn our backs on them in hard times. Do you not agree?" she asked, but in a quiet, gentle voice, not being at all didactic or argumentative.

He did and said so immediately, wanting her to understand that in expressing his appreciation, he had accepted the correctitude of the way her family dealt with their tenants.

"I most certainly do and, believe me, I envy your family's reputation for enlightened management of your properties; unfortunately, I have only to be ashamed of mine. Even though I have never been personally involved in running my father's estates, I almost choke at having to accept that my family's fortunes are the result of some pretty shameful practices in the past. Even today, my father's tenants fear him more than respect him, and in Africa and Australia, where he has vast tracts of land, the record is even worse."

Anne-Marie shook her head and looking at him directly said, "Mr Elliott, I am aware of those matters of which you speak, but you cannot be held responsible for the sins of your father and grandfather. In your own right, I think you have clearly shown yourself to be a man of principle and compassion, and I can only applaud that. Keep to that path and you will soon feel none of that shame and guilt; it is theirs, not yours, and your own actions will help you cast off its burden."

"Do you really believe that?" he seemed incredulous.

"Indeed, I do. We can all do what we can to right past wrongs and if, as I am sure you will, you do your part, you will soon discover that Mr Colin Elliott will be regarded as a man in his own right and not just as the son of Sir Paul Elliott, the unyielding businessman. People who know you will value you for yourself, not for your connections."

"You are very kind; I fear I cannot believe that I will escape the opprobrium of their actions," he said.

But she was absolutely certain.

"Mr Elliott, you can and you must, else you will spend your days bewailing your family's guilt and doing nothing to alleviate it. I mean no disrespect to your father, but his uncaring attitude towards the children's hospital is an example; there is an opportunity, which he has turned down and you have picked up. If you persevere with it and help us achieve what we have set out to do, no one will remember your father's intransigence; they will not, however, forget his son's tenacity and diligence in the service of his community. These are both very valuable attributes for a good local member."

By this time, they had slowed down almost to a walk and the sun had crept up on them, slowly filling the late Autumn sky with golden light. Colin Elliott wanted to say much more but, despite the lightness in his heart, he decided this was not the time to speak. Instead he simply picked up her hand and kissed it, before saying in a quiet voice, "I thank you, Mrs Bradshaw, from the bottom of my heart," and as they drove on, more briskly now, they met Charles Bingley on his way back to the church hall.

He slowed down as they waved to him and asked after the children. Anne-Marie leaned out to assure him that all was still well and Dr Faulkner was with them.

It was still quite early in the morning and Charles was not an early riser. Neither his sister nor Mr Elliott made mention of this fact, but they could not fail to grasp the significance of it, as he drove on.

⁕

In the course of the next week, five more children were taken ill and sadly, despite the best efforts of Drs Faulkner and Bingley and all of the hard work done by Anne-Marie and her team of mothers, who never left the children unattended for a moment, two of them, a boy aged two and a girl of five, whose parents had not recognised the seriousness of her condition, succumbed to the fever. They had tried everything they knew, but these two had been too frail and had slipped from their grasp.

Anne-Marie was devastated. Nothing, not even the gratitude of the parents who thanked her for all her hard work, could assuage her sorrow. Anna was afraid she would relapse into her previous mood of depression and tried to advise her not to attend the funerals. She was sure the sight of the little coffins would exacerbate her grief.

But, determined to support the families in death as in life, she went, as did Jonathan, Charles and Colin Elliott and many others in the neighbourhood.

In the days following, the newspapers told the story in vivid, touching words and, at the end of the week, the Council, stung by the anger of the community and the opprobrium heaped upon them by the press and public, reversed its decision. It may also have been influenced by the trenchant criticism voiced at the Council meeting by the new local member, who had angrily demanded to know how many more of the children had to die, before the Council could be persuaded to change its mind?

However, this was not generally known when the decision was announced that the Council had agreed to the establishment of a hospital for children on a piece of private land at Bell's Field, with private money. The Council would not fund it because the Council could not control it, they said, pointing out that public funds may not be diverted to private projects, however meritorious.

Stephen Tillyard, who'd been with Mr Elliott when the decision was announced, rushed away to write it up for his paper. He had already suggested that a public trust be set up to collect funds for the hospital, promising a generous donation from his newspaper. Colin Elliott, thinking this was a capital idea, pledged that he, too, would donate money and hoped other landowners and businessmen would follow suit.

Leaving Tillyard at his office, Elliott drove on to Netherfield House to take the news to the Bingleys. Their exultation was a joy to witness, but unhappily, his was short-lived. He had barely sat down in the parlour and accepted a glass of sherry, when a messenger, who had gone first to his house and been sent on to Netherfield, brought an express from his brother. On opening it, Elliott discovered that his father had died that morning of a stroke and he was summoned home to Hoxton Park.

He had only a few minutes to tell them and accept their condolences, before it was time to leave. Seeing him go, his countenance suddenly grave, they wondered whether he had fully comprehended the implications for him, of his father's death. It was likely, Jonathan observed, that he would not realise its full import until much later.

Jonathan and Anna, Charles and Anne-Marie attended the funeral before Charles Bingley returned to his practice in London. The grateful families of the five children in the village who had survived the fever went, too. News had got around, based on whispers from the Council clerks and, of course, a prominent article in the *Herald*, which told of the part played by their local MP in winning the Council's agreement for the children's hospital. Although nobody said a word to him, everyone knew what he had achieved and their admiration knew no bounds.

Eager to show their gratitude and demonstrate their enthusiasm, they began work at Bell's Field even before Mr Elliott returned to Meryton. With Mr Bingley's permission, the site was cleared of brambles and Mr Griffin was persuaded to assist with the restoration of the old graves.

When the fallen headstones were cleaned and set upright, it was discovered that they had stood over the bones of an entire family called Harlow, who had lived in the area several centuries ago, as the church register showed. A special ceremony was held and the entire village turned out for the blessing of the restored graves; it had to be said also that Mr Griffin and his little choir excelled themselves. A Mr Harlow, who still lived in Meryton, came too, having discovered the graves were those of his ancestors, of whose existence he had known nothing at all.

Colin Elliott, returning some weeks later after the completion of the formalities following his father's death, was delighted with the progress made at Bell's Field. When they met at the Church on Sunday, Anna Bingley invited him to join them at dinner, an invitation that was accepted with pleasure.

So much had happened and so much more was known than before that the occasion promised to be a lively one. For a start, he was to discover that his role in changing the Council's decision was, by now, well known, since his friend, the editor of the *Herald*, had made it very clear that the local Member had won the day for the community. This had only served to confirm the rumours of his fiery speech in the Council, which Anne-Marie had heard word for word from the wife of Mr Briggs, the Council clerk, who had taken it all down, of course.

Mrs Briggs had been effusive in her praise of him. "It was all Mr Elliott's doing, ma'am; they say he asked to be allowed to address the council and spoke out like no other gentleman has done before," she had said, "My Joe thought he was marvellous."

"They thought you were wonderful, Mr Elliott. Congratulations," said Anna, and he was overcome with embarrassment, especially when young Cathy Bingley declared innocently, "and so did Anne-Marie!" at which the lady named seemed to disappear under the table, scrabbling around for her napkin and taking quite some time to recover it.

Jonathan Bingley saved the day, when he turned the conversation to the more mundane business of money, commending Colin Elliott and Tillyard on their idea of a public trust for the hospital.

"We have already had several amounts pledged," he said, "sums both large and small. Mr Griffin's church group has been working hard and the people on the estates and in the town are all being very generous."

Colin Elliott nodded. "That is good news, Mr Bingley, but unless we can get the funds together more expeditiously, we will not be ready by next Winter, when Charles tells me we can expect an epidemic of influenza."

"Each member of my family is donating a hundred pounds," said Jonathan, "and Anne-Marie has decided that she will donate the whole of the sum she inherited from the late Mr Bradshaw, a sum of 500 pounds, to the hospital trust."

As he finished speaking, Mr Elliott looked up and said very quietly, "Mr Bingley, you have all been more than generous. It is now my turn, as the local Member, to make a contribution."

He looked directly at them as they sat around the table.

"I do not think you will blame me if I say that I shudder at the very thought of going back to the Council for funds, to flint-hearted businessmen like Ludgate and Stamp, whose indifference to the suffering of the poor must be seen to be believed," he said, and Anne-Marie understood the mortification he would have suffered, having to plead with such men for permission to build the hospital.

"How would they understand the needs of poor children, living as they do in considerable comfort?" she asked.

"How indeed, Mrs Bradshaw? It was a point I had to make most forcibly to obtain permission to build." He went on, "I have therefore decided, and indeed I have had all the paperwork completed for the transfer, before I came here today, I have decided to donate the total proceeds of the sale of my shares in some of my father's businesses to the hospital trust."

When there were gasps and raised eyebrows around the table, he said quickly, "Please, do not imagine that I am attempting to make some grand political gesture; nothing could be further from my thoughts. I find that I have inherited most of my father's business interests, while my brother gets all the property, save for a town house in Knightsbridge, which was a gift to me from my late mother when I returned to India."

He proceeded to explain. "Some of these businesses are not the sort of enterprise I wish to be associated with, much less profit from. There is, for instance, a gold mine in Africa using native labour and paying them a pittance, in which my father had shares. I have instructed my agents to sell my shares and place the money in trust to provide income for the hospital. I have not as yet ascertained how much will accrue to the trust, but I expect to know before Christmas. There are other similar enterprises, the sale of which I expect to negotiate very soon."

There was no need for words. He could see clearly the appreciation on their faces. Presently, Jonathan spoke, "Mr Elliott, this is most generous, but . . ."

Colin Elliott held up his hand, "It is what I wish to do, Mr Bingley. You must all know that my father and grandfather did very well from their landholdings in Hertfordshire, sometimes at the expense of the local people. I am hoping to give some of that wealth back to the people, by this means," he said.

Noting the smiles of approval on the faces of the ladies, he continued, "I wonder if I may ask just one favour. Should you not agree, it will make no difference; the money is not conditional upon your agreement. It is that I would wish, I would very much like to have the hospital carry a small plaque, which states that it is dedicated to the memory of my mother, Lady Dorothy Elliott. That is, if your family has no objection."

There was almost an explosion of disbelief.

"Objection? Mr Elliott, why on earth would we object?" asked Jonathan, and Anna said, "Why, that would be a very appropriate memorial to your late mother. My father says she did a great deal of work for charity."

"Indeed she did, Mrs Bingley, and was often berated for it by my father. She would use her own money to help the maids buy wedding clothes and linen. He would scold her for giving them ideas above their station," he said and Anne-Marie, unaccountably, felt tears sting her eyes.

Glancing at him, she found him looking intently at her and she looked away quickly, a little confused by her own feelings.

Later, when they were all gathered in the drawing room after tea, Anna was called away to young Nicholas, and Jonathan sat down with a book. Colin Elliot took the opportunity to tell Anne-Marie how happy he was that they had finally succeeded in starting work on the hospital. He was especially pleased, he said, to help her achieve her dream. He may well have said more, but Anne-Marie stopped him, gently.

"Please, Mr Elliott, I appreciate very much what you have done, but do not spoil it by saying you did it to please me or for any purpose, other than to save the lives of the children in our community. They have died, year after year, of curable conditions such as croup and influenza, only because they had no one to look after them and no place to attend for treatment. Two of them, God bless their souls, died only a few weeks ago. I would not have you think I am unappreciative of your wish to please me, but it would mean more to me than almost anything else, were you to say that you thought solely of the children."

Colin Elliott was momentarily silenced by the quiet passion in her voice. He knew that while it was important to him to have her good opinion, it was far more important that she should believe in his sincerity. When he spoke, his voice was low and earnest. "I would gladly say it, Mrs Bradshaw, but if I did, I would not be speaking the whole truth, for while I share your beliefs and hopes for the hospital, I had hoped also to earn your approval, especially in the context of a discussion we had some weeks ago, as we returned to Netherfield from the church hall. Perhaps you have forgotten it?" he said, tentatively.

Anne-Marie smiled, "Mr Elliott, let me assure you, I have not forgotten our talk and, indeed, let me say how very greatly I admire what you have done. The value of your gift to the trust is enhanced by the nobility of your motives and if in doing it, you also sought my approval, then let me say, you have it in full measure. I know no other person, apart from my dear father, who has been as generous as you have."

Colin Elliott was smiling, as he said later to his friend Tillyard, "like some callow schoolboy with an unexpected prize!"

He longed, above all, to tell her then that he had fallen in love with her, but unfortunately, a glance around the room made it clear that this was neither the time nor the place.

Her father was ensconced in his chair with his book; her sisters were playing "Beggar my neighbour," punctuated with screams of delight or outrage; and when Anna returned, she was greeted by her husband with a request for music, which she was happy to provide.

It was no time for a declaration of love.

⁓✲⁓

It was a quiet Christmas at Netherfield that year. The annual Netherfield Ball had been cancelled and at the usual Boxing Day celebrations for the tenants, farmhands, and their families, the atmosphere was somewhat less than festive. Not only was the weather uniformly bleak, but the families grieving for their children could not participate and the memory of their deaths cast a pall over the village.

Anna was not able to do very much to encourage them, being very close to the birth of their second child. It was left to Anne-Marie and her sisters to liven them up.

The Bingleys were on their own.

Anna's parents had gone to their elder daughter in Hampshire, while Charles had elected to stay in London with friends. Anne-Marie had received his letter a few days before Christmas.

He wrote,

> The weather is too terrible to even contemplate travelling; if this weather improves, I hope to see you all at the New Year, with all your Christmas presents intact! Colin Elliott has been here; he has taken up residence in his smart town house in Knightsbridge. I met him in Bond Street buying an expensive gift, for whom he would not reveal, the sly fox, and he said he may go down to Hertfordshire in the New Year. I took the liberty of asking him to dine with us at Netherfield, since I hoped to be there myself, and he accepted, with some alacrity. So, you may wish to prepare for an extra guest.
>
> Speaking of Elliott, in the opinion of our general acquaintance here, he is become a very wealthy man since the death of his father. I believe he has inherited all Sir Paul's business interests including a very substantial shipping line, conveying merchandise between Europe and the Eastern colonies, a very profitable enterprise I am assured.

But to see him, you would not know it; he is still the same modest fellow and lives a rather simple life. I called on him at home the other day and, while the house is furnished in excellent style, it is far from being gaudy or opulent and he keeps only a manservant, a parlour maid, a butler, and a cook, who are, amusingly, all of the one family! I suppose, they get on well together.

This is very unlike the usual Tory toffs, of course. I said as much, just to tease him, and he said he had never liked that type of thing.

He talked a great deal about this hospital of yours. I have never seen him so enthusiastic. He thinks the world of Father and Anna, of course, and I would wager London to a brick, he will leave the Tories one of these days. It just wants the right issue. The extension of the franchise may well do it!

My dear sister, do have a care; because he thinks you are the next most wonderful thing to an angel!

Anne-Marie smiled as she read on…

When he talked of the hospital and the sick children, he spoke mainly of you! It was as if your poor brother did nothing at all, you were the angel of mercy! I think I shall watch him closely in the future!

Anne-Marie had read her brother's letter through when it arrived and since then, for fear of leaving it where it may be picked up and read by her sisters, she had carried it around in the pocket of her gown, moving it from one to another each day and rereading it from time to time.

As the New Year approached, Anne-Marie wondered whether the weather would improve enough to persuade Charles to make the journey to Netherfield. She looked forward to his arrival; she wanted very much to ask him some questions pertaining to his letter. She had grown away from her younger sisters, who had themselves grown closer together over the past year. She missed her brother and wished with all her heart that he would come.

Early on New Year's Eve, having had no further communication from Charles, Anne-Marie had almost given up hope of her brother arriving. Sitting by the window in her room, she was reading. She had completed Emily Brontë's *Wuthering Heights*, which had absorbed her totally and had proceeded to the work of the other sister—Charlotte, whose novel *Jane Eyre* was very popular, too. Anne-Marie had got some way through the book and was beginning to tire of Jane's docile role in Mr Rochester's household, when a vehicle was heard coming up the drive. On looking out of the window, she glimpsed a gentleman's coat, as the visitor alighted from the carriage and was admitted to the house.

She was sure it was not her brother.

Minutes later, her youngest sister Cathy came running up the stairs. "Anne-Marie, Mr Elliott is here and you will not believe the size of the basket of fruit and flowers he has brought from the hothouses at Hoxton Park," she said, excitedly hopping from one foot to the other.

Anne-Marie glanced at herself in the mirror and patted her hair, but, reluctant to rush, now she knew who their visitor was, she dawdled a while, much to the chagrin of her sister, who was impatient to be gone.

"And there are gifts for everyone; Jack has gone out to the carriage to fetch them in," Cathy added.

Anne-Marie reddened a little at this news, recalling the line in her brother's letter about meeting Mr Elliott buying gifts in Bond Street.

Finally, when she could no longer bear Cathy's pleading, they went downstairs.

Colin Elliott was in the saloon with Mr and Mrs Bingley and, as Anne-Marie entered the room, he rose and came to greet her.

There was something different about him, she thought at once; he looked more at ease, more confident than before. Yet in his manner, he was as courteous and amiable as ever. After the first seasonal greetings were duly exchanged, they sat down and partook of refreshments that were brought in and placed upon a low table in front of them.

On another table stood the magnificent basket of fruit and flowers and beside it a small pile of prettily wrapped gifts. As the servants brought more refreshments, Colin Elliott rose and rather tentatively asked if he may present them with what he called "a few small tokens of my esteem, in the spirit of the festive season."

"Mr Elliott, you are very kind," said Anna as she accepted her gift and Jonathan was pleasantly surprised to discover that he had not been forgotten, for there was a box of fine cigars for him.

Anne-Marie took time opening hers, while her sisters exclaimed at seeing theirs. Each had received a finely wrought silver pin in the shape of their name letter and while they admired their gifts, Anne-Marie's was to arouse cries of envy, for hers was a delicately carved brooch set with a tiny pearl, where the two letters of her name intertwined.

Her face warm with the memory of Charles's words . . ."He was buying an expensive present for someone, he would not say who, the sly fox . . ." she thanked him and tried to cover her confusion by showing it around to the others.

Outside, the weather had worsened. It had started to snow and the arrival of her brother in the midst of this caused a great fuss, as the servants rushed to get his trunks in out of the wet. This gave her some time to recover her composure, as the rest of the family had gone into the hall to welcome Charles, who was making much of the perils of his journey in this atrocious weather.

Taking advantage of the bustle around them, Colin Elliott said, in a voice kept deliberately low, "I hope, Mrs Bradshaw, that you have not been offended by my gift."

Seeing his anxious expression, she answered quickly, "Indeed no, Mr Elliott, why would I be offended? It is a beautiful piece and a most generous gift, as are those you have given my sisters. I appreciate it and thank you very much for it."

"I am glad," he said, clearly relieved. "I purchased them in a rush of enthusiasm and the Christmas spirit, I suppose, but having done so, I became fearful that you may think it impertinent and presumptuous of me."

She smiled. "Perhaps it was not impertinent but a little presumptuous, but it is no matter; you are forgiven, because I am quite sure that was not your intention."

"It most certainly was not, I can assure you—" he began and at this point exactly, Charles, having divested himself of his greatcoat, hat, and scarf and greeted the rest of his family, entered the room and enveloped his beloved sister in an enormous embrace, before proceeding to greet Colin Elliott and welcome him to Netherfield.

Thereafter, there was never much time for private conversation; all the talk was of Charles's adventures and the dreadful doings in London.

"The place is quite mad; there are thousands of people milling around the streets, no matter how bad the weather," he declared, "and the government is in dire straits with Palmerston no match for Bismarck." Jonathan and Mr Elliott were inclined to agree.

The rest of the day was spent with the ladies discussing preparations for the dinner party, while the gentlemen were involved in deep discussions on everything from the state of the nation to the nature of the Universe!

"There are very real rumblings among the middle classes in the city, who supported the Whigs upon the promise of electoral reform," said Charles. "They are tired of waiting for Palmerston to keep his word."

Colin Elliott agreed, adding, "Palmerston is far more interested in European diplomacy than in Parliamentary reform in England. He appears to want Britain involved in every little scrap on the continent, all this fuss about Denmark. Do you honestly believe he will go to war with Germany over it?" he asked.

"Of course not, it's just bravado, nothing more," said Jonathan, who had reached the unhappy position of wishing that the government he had worked hard to get into office would do more to justify his belief than wave the flag abroad, with increasing degrees of belligerence.

The dinner party, to which the Faulkners and a few of their other neighbours had been invited, was a great success, for everyone except Mr Elliott. He had hoped to get some time in private with Anne-Marie; for the more he saw of her, the more he was convinced he was in love with her. He had missed her terribly when he had been in London and wanted to discover if, perhaps, she had missed him, just a little. But, alas, no such thing had been even remotely possible, for she was so beset with duties, looking after their guests, since Mrs Bingley, feeling poorly, had to retire early. He promised himself that he would find time on the morrow to speak with her. He had another matter on his mind as well, which needed settling.

After a late breakfast, on the following day, Mr Elliott sought out Mr and Mrs Bingley and Anne-Marie in the sitting room. He revealed that he had disposed of his father's shares in the African gold mines and the American cotton and fruit plantations and had invested the money, so a steady stream of income would accrue to the hospital trust. In addition, he had also received the proceeds of the sale of a textile mill in Leeds, another of his father's ventures in which he wanted no part. He presented Mr Bingley with a cheque for the hospital fund, saying, "That will pay for the work we must complete to get the place ready for the first patients later in the year. The proceeds of the overseas shares will provide us with funds to equip the hospital and clinic; Charles has promised to help us plan our needs and appoint our staff. We shall require the services of a good doctor and trained nurses."

Anne-Marie was amazed.

"Are you sure about this, Mr Elliott? It is an extremely generous gift. You are giving away a good deal of your inheritance," she said.

"Mrs Bradshaw, believe me, I have never been more certain of anything in my life. I hope you will accept it in the spirit in which it is given."

"Have you considered the consequences to your own financial situation?" asked Jonathan.

Colin Elliott assured him that he had.

"Mr Bingley, I have quite sufficient for me to live very comfortably. I do not have a country estate, but I have my apartment in Knightsbridge and the place I lease here is reasonable. These investments are neither essential to me, nor do they give me any satisfaction," he said.

Feeling the need to explain further, he added, "My father believed that investments were for making money alone; they had no moral dimension. I'm afraid I cannot accept that argument. I get no pleasure from money earned through the exploitation and suffering of other human beings, in this case, the native people of Africa and the black slaves of the United States. I cannot change or influence these overseas enterprises, whose rapacious practices I abhor, but at least, by selling my shares and giving the proceeds to charity, I am dissociating myself from them," he said and none of those listening could doubt the sincerity of his words.

Jonathan spoke for them all, "Mr Elliott, I thank you for your generosity especially on behalf of all those children and their parents who will benefit from your gift to this community."

At this, Colin Elliott looked exceedingly happy and shook Jonathan's hand warmly and, turning to Anna, took hers and kissed it and then having started, he had to go on, so he kissed Anne-Marie's as well, and thanked them all most sincerely for permitting him to become involved in what was largely their charitable project.

Jonathan Bingley suggested a glass of sherry to celebrate.

※

That night, when Anne-Marie went to say goodnight to her sisters, Teresa said, "Mr Elliott is a very generous man, is he not, Anne-Marie?"

She had absolutely no hesitation in saying, "Indeed he is, very generous."

"And he is very gentlemanly and kind, too?" Teresa added.

Anne-Marie, wondering where this was leading, had to agree.

"He certainly is," she said.

"And handsome?" Teresa's voice had a degree of archness that aroused her sister's suspicions and this time she was not so accommodating.

"Do you think so?"

"I do," said Teresa, "do you not?"

Confused, Anne-Marie stumbled. "Well, I had not thought about it."

Teresa smiled, a subtle little smile. "Perhaps you should give it a little thought, my dear sister, because he is in love with you, I think."

At this, Anne-Marie appeared more outraged than Teresa's words appeared to warrant.

"Sssh, Tessie, you are not to say that. You will start people gossiping; if the servants hear you, what will they…?

Teresa laughed, "The servants? Why they have been having wagers about how soon you two will become engaged," she declared and Anne-Marie was visibly shaken. "In that case, Teresa, you must refrain from adding your voice to theirs; you must not encourage the rumours."

This time it was Teresa's turn to feel hurt and misunderstood. "I am sorry, but it seems so obvious to all of us; we think he really loves you. Do you not like him at all?"

Taken aback by this approach, her sister replied, "I do like him because he is, as you have said, a good and generous man, but that has nothing to do with being in love with him."

"Does it not?" Teresa seemed astonished at this admission.

"No, and I have discovered that for myself, when I married Mr Bradshaw, who was a decent, good man, but God must forgive me, because try as I might, I never could love him and our marriage was a nightmare!"

Teresa, wide-eyed and troubled, saw the tears in her sister's eyes and instinctively put her arms around her and held her, while she sobbed.

"Oh, Tessie, I am determined that I will never make the same mistake again. Nor must you, my dear sister. I am quite determined that I shall marry only for the deepest love or remain single for the rest of my life." There was no mistaking the anguish in her voice and young Teresa, deeply affected by her sister's sorrow, said no more.

In the early hours of the following day, Anna Bingley was brought to bed with her second child. There having been little warning that it would happen so early in the month, the household was thrown into some confusion and every other matter was set aside, while doctors and midwives were roused from their beds and fetched to Netherfield House.

Colin Elliott, who had prepared himself to speak with Anne-Marie that day, hoping to discover something of her feelings towards him, was awakened very early by the sounds of horses and carriage wheels on the gravel drive and footsteps of people with hushed voices coming and going up and down the stairs. Having guessed what was afoot and not wanting to be in the way, he had risen while it was still dark, dressed quietly, and gone downstairs only to find the entire kitchen staff in a huddle at the bottom of the stairs.

Seeing his embarrassment, Mrs Perrot took pity upon him, put him in the sitting room, and brought him some tea.

"Is everything all right?" he asked tentatively, to which she replied, "Yes, sir, the doctor is with Mrs Bingley now—" but before she could finish her sentence, the door opened and Anne-Marie rushed in.

"Mrs Perrot," she cried, her voice rising with excitement, "It's a boy! He is beautiful, but poor Mrs Bingley is very tired and weak." She hugged the house-keeper, not seeing Mr Elliott, sitting by the fire, with his tea.

Mrs Perrot left to tell the rest of the staff the news and as Mr Elliott stood up, Anne-Marie caught sight of him and gave a little gasp of surprise.

"Mr Elliott!" she said as he put down his cup.

"Mrs Bradshaw, I am sorry if I startled you. I heard a lot of comings and goings and I came downstairs," he said, trying to explain his presence in the room, but she smiled and said, "Please do finish your tea, Mr Elliott; I did not see you when I first came in."

But he felt he was in their way and was keen to be gone.

"I think I should be leaving; you are all going to be very busy and you will not want me in the way, I am sure. Please convey my congratulations and best wishes to both your father and Mrs Bingley. I trust the little boy and his mother will both be doing well, soon," he said.

"I certainly shall," said Anne-Marie and then asked, "Will you not have some breakfast before you leave?"

"Thank you, it's very kind of you, but I must be gone. I do hope I will see you again, soon," he said, and she smiled as she said, "Of course," and in a moment, he had kissed her hand and was gone.

In Meryton, Colin Elliott went directly to the offices of the *Herald*, where he found his friend Stephen Tillyard asleep in his chair. The paper had gone out an hour ago. It was the best time of day for a tired newspaperman. When Elliott walked in, Tillyard opened his eyes and, seeing who it was, closed them again.

"What are you doing here?" he asked sleepily, "I thought you were at Netherfield House, wooing the beautiful Mrs Bradshaw. Did she turn you down or are you here to announce your engagement in the *Herald*?"

Colin Elliott snapped, "Neither, you idiot; wake up, Tillyard, I need some breakfast, I am starving!"

"Do they not serve breakfast at Netherfield anymore? No, don't tell me, you fled before the household was awake, you were too scared to propose! Elliott, if you do not ask the lady, you will never discover if she will have you." Tillyard was enjoying his friend's discomfiture, but his friend had lost patience with him.

"Oh, damn you, Tillyard, it's none of those things. Mrs Jonathan Bingley was delivered of a child very early this morning, and I left because I did not wish to be in the way."

Finally, Tillyard looked interested. "Was it a boy or a girl?" he asked.

Puzzled at his sudden interest, Elliott looked surprised, but answered, "A boy, I believe. I heard Mrs Bradshaw tell the housekeeper the news. Unhappily, I think Mrs Bingley is rather weak . . ." Then realising suddenly that he was telling a newspaperman, he broke off.

"Tillyard, don't you dare print any of this. No, not if you value your life! Not till you get Mr Bingley's permission," he warned, and Tillyard promised he would print nothing until he had obtained Mr Bingley's consent.

"The Bingleys are a very well-respected, public-spirited family in these parts; there would be a natural interest in matters relating to them. Mrs Anna Bingley is much loved and admired. She is a talented woman, with a lot of personal style, in the European mode, as I am sure you have noticed; people would want to wish her and her child well," he said, as he rose and pulled on his coat. Closing the door behind them, they went out to get some breakfast at the inn across the road.

News of the birth of Jonathan and Anna's second son, Simon, was delivered to Jane and Charles Bingley at Ashford Park in Leicestershire that very day, via the electric telegraph. No sooner had she heard, than Jane had to set out for Pemberley to acquaint her sister Elizabeth and Mr Darcy with the news. The Darcys were pleasantly surprised to see them, having dined with them but a few days ago. But they were always welcome at Pemberley and on this, a cold January day when it looked very bleak out of doors, it was a special pleasure.

Elizabeth was, as always, pleased to see them and when Jane, a little tearful, told of the birth of her latest grandson, both Darcy and Elizabeth understood exactly why she had ventured out on this day.

The occasion, said Darcy, called for a little celebration and while the drinks were being brought in, Elizabeth urged them to stay to dinner.

"We're expecting the Fitzwilliams, too, so it will be nice, very much like old times," she said and sent for her housekeeper to advise her of their extra dinner guests.

The Bingleys accepted, of course. Though Bingley and Darcy had not gone into active politics in the way Fitzwilliam and Jonathan Bingley had done, they remained interested. Colonel Fitzwilliam and Caroline still kept up with all the goings on in Parliament and, whenever the families met, they could be counted upon to have some of the latest news, scandal, and rumour from Westminster, and lively conversation was assured. Elizabeth was sure that this evening would be no exception.

Jane had received a letter from her daughter Emma, whose letters were always full of news. As they took refreshments in the saloon, where the footman had stoked up a fine blaze, Jane brought out her letter and read it to them.

My dear Mama, she wrote,

> *We had hoped to be able to make the journey to Ashford Park and to Pemberley, as well, after Christmas, but at this most inappropriate time, there is much talk at Westminster of war. It is difficult to believe that such a thing is possible. James says it is all to do with Lord Palmerston having encouraged the Danes to defy Bismarck, with vague promises of support. Now that they are under grave threat, Palmerston finds that Britain has no heart for it or rather no army able to stand up to Chancellor Bismarck.*
>
> *James does not believe that the government will send troops to defend the Danes, but he says it is not the right time to leave London. Everything*

is too uncertain and should we have a spell of bad weather, a blizzard, or a heavy snowfall, as we did two years ago when everyone was snowed in for days, he may not get back to London in time for the party meeting.

We are both very sad, and Charles and Colin are disappointed that they will not be there for the fireworks. Perhaps when this is over...

Emma's letter stimulated an energetic discussion about the wisdom of Lord Palmerston's foreign policy. Fitzwilliam, an admirer of the Prime Minister, defended his strategy, but Darcy and Bingley thought it foolhardy and, worse, would end in humiliation for Britain, when Bismarck called their bluff.

"You cannot believe that he plans to go to war, Fitzwilliam," said Darcy. "Clearly he has encouraged the unfortunate Danes to stand up to Bismarck, knowing all the while, that if the Chancellor chooses, he can walk all over them and Britain can do nothing to stop him. It is thoroughly reprehensible." Fitzwilliam would not agree and Elizabeth and Jane, who wanted to talk of things other than politics, decided to leave them to argue the point.

As they went upstairs, Jane intimated to her sister that there was a section of Emma's letter she had kept to herself. Now, she wanted her to see it and Elizabeth was very curious. It was not like Jane to be so secretive.

When they reached the privacy of Elizabeth's room, Jane handed her the letter and pointed to the last page, "Lizzie, read it and tell me what you make of it," she said.

Emma had written that her husband James Wilson had recently invited Mr Colin Elliott MP to dine with them at Grosvenor Street.

He is, you may recall, Mama, the new Member in the seat formerly occupied by his father, Sir Paul Elliott. Having been away in the colonies, he has recently returned to England. I gather he has already called on Jonathan at Netherfield and is well regarded by him.

Although he is a Tory, I understand he is not as intractable as his father was and James seems to like him well enough. Indeed, he has it—he says on very good authority—that young Mr Elliott may one day be persuaded to join the Reform Group in the Commons.

For my part, I have to say he was extremely charming and has the most pleasing manners of any young MP I have met. None of the arrogant cockiness that marks so many of them. And, he does seem genuinely keen to do something for the people he is supposed to represent. But, more importantly, Mama, he spoke endlessly and with great enthusiasm of the Bingleys, Jonathan and Anna, of course, for whom he has great respect and Anne-Marie. She has, for some time now, been wishing to establish a children's hospital for the area and, as the local MP, it seems Mr Elliott has become involved in this charitable scheme.

I am aware, from Anna's letters, that she and Jonathan have been supporting their efforts and so I believe has the local rector, Mr Griffin, but to listen to Mr Elliott, you may be forgiven for thinking that Anne-Marie was doing it all on her own. He was so impressed with her generosity, her hard work and her energy, I was left in no doubt that he thought very highly of our dear niece.

Later, after he had departed, I asked James if he thought Mr Elliott had been inordinately keen to speak of Anne-Marie.

"Not inordinately, perhaps, but certainly remarkably so," he replied, pretending he had noticed nothing unusual, but I soon got it out of him that he had heard a great deal about Mrs Bradshaw's scheme for a hospital and, if one were of a suspicious frame of mind, one might assume that Mr Colin Elliott was in some danger of falling in love with the lady!

Now, Mama, you and Aunt Lizzie will soon have an opportunity to judge for yourselves, because Mr Elliott has been invited to Derbyshire by the Tates, whom he met recently in London, (James says Anthony Tate, like a good newspaperman, can scent a crossing of the floor coming on!) at exactly the same time as Anne-Marie is to travel thither herself to stay with the Fitzwilliams at Matlock. I shall be very surprised if their paths did not cross. I know the Tates will want to introduce Colin Elliott to Mr Darcy and Aunt Lizzie and if you should meet, I should very much like to know your opinion of the gentleman.

When Elizabeth read and returned the letter, she looked a little bewildered and said in a cautious voice, "Now Jane, you are the great romantic in our family; tell me what does this signify? Do you believe Mr Elliott, whom I have never met, is really in love with Anne-Marie, and will she countenance his interest?"

Jane looked anxious and troubled; she was clearly concerned about her granddaughter, "I really do not know, Lizzie; she has not confided in me, though

I expect I shall learn something of it from Teresa when she visits me in May. Meanwhile, I worry about Anne-Marie because I know she suffered terribly and wish to protect her from any injudicious decision."

"Do you fear she may marry again in haste?" Elizabeth asked, but her sister shook her head.

"No, Lizzie, I am more concerned that she may not consider some one like Mr Elliott seriously. You know how difficult Anne-Marie can be when she is set upon an idea; she does put me in mind of you, sometimes, Lizzie," said Jane and her sister laughed merrily.

"Poor Anne-Marie," said Elizabeth. "I doubt she can ever have been as recalcitrant as I was; do you recall our mother's wrath, when I refused Mr Collins? No indeed, Anne-Marie accepted her clergyman and look what became of that marriage."

Jane nodded, remembering well. "You are right, Lizzie, but I do hope she does marry again and happily, this time. I cannot bear to think of her growing old alone."

This time, Elizabeth laughed and berated her sister

"Come now, Jane, must you have us all neatly wed and settled? Will you not admit that a woman can be happy without a husband and family, on condition, of course, that she was not left in a state of poverty?"

Her sister looked askance; happily married for many years, she and Bingley were certainly examples of conjugal felicity, but she had the good sense to know that marriage alone was worthless without esteem and love.

"Oh no, Lizzie, that is not fair. While I certainly believe that a happy marriage with a good man is the best situation a woman can achieve, I do not and never have advocated matrimony for common or mercenary reasons. Why, I cannot imagine how anyone could contemplate such intimacy without the deepest affection and respect. I certainly could not, nor would I wish it on anyone of mine."

Having settled that question, they were about to go downstairs, when they were joined by Caroline Fitzwilliam, who revealed that a Mr Colin Elliott was indeed expected in the neighbourhood soon.

Rebecca Tate had invited the Fitzwilliams over to meet him, she said; there was to be a dinner party on Saturday week.

"Fitzy is looking forward to it; he believes the gentleman is available for conversion to the Reform Group," she declared.

"And is he?" asked Elizabeth, to which Caroline replied with a laugh, "I could not say, Lizzie, the subject did not come up when I met him at the Wilsons' in London, but I found him to be a most impressive young man, intelligent, charming, and very much in love with our Anne-Marie."

At this, Jane and Elizabeth exchanged glances and protested in one voice, expressing complete consternation. "Caroline, you cannot possibly know that!"

But Caroline, whose own love story would have outdone even the most passionate romantic novel, was unrepentant. "Indeed, I can. It was quite clear to me just watching him observing her and so could you, if you saw them together," she said.

"And do you believe Anne-Marie is aware of his interest?" asked Jane.

"And does she reciprocate it?" prompted Elizabeth.

Caroline was more circumspect, "I could not be certain; Anne-Marie is remarkably good at concealing her true feelings. But I am sure they have moved on since then and when they meet again as they surely will, when they are both here, I am sure we shall know."

Both Jane and Elizabeth wondered how this was to be arranged, but their cousin was confident. "Leave it to me. Anne-Marie is eager to find out as much as possible about the hospital at Littleford. When they are both in the area, it will be the most natural thing in the world that I should have a dinner party to which you are all invited along with the Tates and Mr Elliott. Would that not be a good scheme?"

It was generally agreed that it would and, having sworn each other to secrecy, they went downstairs to join the gentlemen.

Colin Elliott arrived at the house of Mr and Mrs Tate, bearing dismal news from Westminster. Even Anthony Tate, who owned newspapers with reporters in London and all over Europe, did not have a great deal of information on the situation. Mr Elliott confirmed their fears that Chancellor Bismarck, who had long been spoiling for a war to enable him to consolidate his united Germany, was on the verge of invading the Danish-ruled Duchies of Schleswig and Holstein.

"This is by no means unexpected, Mr Tate," he said as he took tea with his hosts. "Bismarck has been threatening the Danes ever since the death of King

Frederick last year, but that he should seek to invade with impunity has shocked many in Westminster. Worse still, it is quite clear that Britain intends to do nothing. Despite their belligerent rhetoric, Palmerston and Russell never intended that we should go to war for Denmark. The Chancellor has called their bluff."

Anthony Tate agreed.

"The entire policy has been a disaster," he said. "It's Palmerston's fault. He was once a great Prime Minister; today he is an embarrassment!"

When the gentlemen met again that evening with Colonel Fitzwilliam and others of the Tate's friends and neighbours, Colin Elliott was scathing in his criticism of Lord Palmerston and his government. Fitzwilliam alone defended Palmerston and, stopping only to refill their glasses, they continued their lively debate.

Earlier in the day, Caroline had driven out to the inn at Lambton to meet Anne-Marie Bradshaw and her maid, who had arrived on the coach.

Having welcomed her visitor warmly, Caroline conveyed them to her home, where Anne-Marie rested and bathed before preparing to attend the dinner party at the Tates'. Though a little tired from her journey, Anne-Marie was excited at the thought of meeting the Tates, whom she knew to be very influential in local politics in the Midlands and extraordinarily supportive of their community. Her father had claimed he owed much of his success in politics to the support of Mr and Mrs Tate.

Caroline explained, "The good work Rebecca has done pleading our cause in the newspapers and the Council, together with the work of her husband, Anthony, has enabled us to achieve much for our community; without them we would have been hard put to it to gather the funds for the school, let alone the hospital."

This was exactly what Anne-Marie wanted to hear.

"Convincing the Council is the hardest task of all" she confessed, sounding a little diffident, but Caroline was optimistic.

"Becky will teach you how to win a round with your Council. She has a vast amount of experience and is very determined," she said, as they journeyed towards the Tates' house. "I know they will welcome you and you will surely like them," she added. She did not mention that Mr Elliott was to be present also.

Meanwhile, Anthony Tate, always an eloquent advocate of a good cause, was taking on Colonel Fitzwilliam, whose support for Palmerston was being sorely tested.

"You do realise, Fitzwilliam," he said, "that thanks to Palmerston's bungling diplomacy, Britain will never again be taken seriously by the Prussians or the Danes."

"Or anyone else in Europe," interjected Elliott.

Fitzwilliam refused to give in, "Come now, Tate, I do not believe this is going to cause us permanent damage, do you?"

He was trying desperately to find a way out of an exceedingly difficult situation and was not succeeding.

Fortuitously, it was at this point, that Caroline Fitzwilliam and her young companion were announced. Anne-Marie, very beautiful in a gown of lavender blue silk, which complemented her dark hair and brilliant complexion, entered the room feeling rather nervous in the midst of the large party assembled there. Apart from the Fitzwilliams she knew nobody and searched in vain for a familiar face, until her eyes lighted upon someone she knew well, she smiled.

It would be entirely correct to say that instantly, Colin Elliott lost interest in Bismarck, Lord Palmerston and the fate of the Danish Duchies. He was not to know that the brilliance of the lady's smile was, for the most part, a consequence of the relief she had felt at seeing in the crowd of unfamiliar persons, someone she regarded as a friend.

Persuaded by Caroline that she must wear some jewellery, Anne-Marie had borrowed a simple necklace and earrings, which enhanced her elegant appearance. Mr Elliott noticed the difference and appreciated the sparkle it gave her.

Enchanted, he moved forward to greet first Caroline and then Anne-Marie, and said what a wonderful surprise it was to see her there.

"I had no idea that you were even in this part of the country, Mrs Bradshaw, much less that you were to be at this gathering. May I say what a great pleasure it is to see you and looking so well, too?" he said, and was content to hear her acknowledge that she had been equally surprised and pleased to find him among the guests.

"I know no one here apart from the Fitzwilliams and I was quite daunted by the prospect of spending an entire evening trying to converse sensibly with people I knew not at all," she said. And then with a teasing smile, she asked, "Now, shall I tell you why I am here or will you go first?"

Unaccustomed to being teased, Colin Elliott almost missed his cue, then recovering his composure, he smiled and explained that he was the guest of Mr and Mrs Tate, to whom he had been introduced by her uncle Mr James Wilson. As they moved towards a large window overlooking the rose garden, he said, "I had not known that your families were related until Mrs Tate revealed that her daughter is married to your cousin Mr Julian Darcy. I believe they are away in London."

Anne-Marie sympathised with his confusion and explained, "I suppose there was never any occasion to explain, but yes, my cousin Julian is married to Josie Tate and they are come recently to live at Pemberley. Julian is a dedicated scientist; he would rather live permanently in his beloved Cambridge, I am sure, but since their son was born Josie has not been very well and needed help with young Anthony."

As they talked, she told him of the work being done by Caroline and her sister Emily at the hospital at Littleford.

"I thought it would be useful for me to discover the problems of running such a hospital. When Caroline invited me to visit, I was very grateful for the opportunity and I intend to learn everything I can."

"So, it is not pleasure alone but a labour of love that brings you here?" he asked with a smile and she answered him just as lightly.

"Surely, Mr Elliott, it is the best sort of labour there is and as such, may bring pleasure as well. Do you not agree?"

It was a proposition with which he found himself in complete agreement. So much so, that he had, even before he knew it, offered himself as a participant in the said labour, asking if it could be arranged for him to visit the hospital at Littleford as well.

"It would be powerful evidence should it be necessary to argue the value of our scheme at Bell's Field," he said and with such a cogent argument available, Anne-Marie could see no reason to refuse his request.

"I shall certainly ask Mrs Emily Courtney. She is responsible for such matters now and I cannot believe she will refuse."

She had begun to tell him of the circumstances in which Emily Courtney had become involved in the establishment of the hospital at Littleford, when dinner was announced. They repaired to the dining room and discovered that were to sit next to each other at table and supposed it to be a happy coincidence. They were unaware that Caroline was plotting a romantic conspiracy; having taken Rebecca Tate into her confidence, she had influenced the seating arrangements.

"My dear Becky, I have no doubt at all. Call me a romantic if you will, but regard this couple and tell me whether you do not agree that they are in love— even if they do not know it," she had said.

Rebecca had smiled indulgently; everyone knew what a hopeless romantic Caroline was. On this occasion, however, Becky was inclined to agree. Mr Elliott certainly looked smitten, more so than Mrs Bradshaw, whose calm lovely countenance rarely betrayed her deeper feelings.

Happily married and of an affectionate and generous disposition, Caroline was happiest helping others to find true felicity, whether they needed it or not. Her care and concern extended from the poor and needy to her friends and family. Anyone who was bereft, whether of money, friends or food, became the beneficiary of her generous heart. The prospect of bringing together two people, who might be happily partnered was irresistible and she was already planning how she might achieve this end.

Unbeknownst to her, however, Colin Elliott was making plans too. During dinner he had discovered more about Mrs Emily Courtney, the wife of the rector of Kympton. Chiefly in order to avert any possible embarrass-ment to Mrs Courtney, Anne-Marie had revealed though not in very great detail the tragic love story of Emily and her first husband, Paul Antoine, whose death from tuberculosis had climaxed a catastrophic year for the fami-lies at Pemberley. The Darcys and Fitzwilliams had lost young sons, both killed in an horrific riding accident.

"My father believes the responsibility of helping to establish and run the hospital, caring for all those children and the enormous satisfaction of knowing how much she was loved and appreciated in this community kept Emily sane when Paul died and helped her heal herself," she had said. "Now, she is an inspiration to us all. She does a great deal for the people of the district and there is very little she does not know about running a children's hospital."

Clearly Anne-Marie admired Mrs Courtney immensely and Colin Elliott responded that he looked forward to meeting her too.

After they had parted, Anne-Marie to return home to Matlock with the Fitzwilliams, Elliott had retired to his room and penned a letter to Mr Bingley, in which he suggested that Mrs Bradshaw might be, if she could be persuaded, placed in charge of the children's hospital at Bells Field.

Pointing out that as a trained nurse, her qualifications were impeccable, he further affirmed that it would give the hospital exemplary credentials, so that the Council would no longer be able to cavil and criticise.

Before sending his letter to the post, after breakfast on the morrow, Elliott consulted Mrs Tate. He was keen to get her opinion on his proposition.

Becky Tate, who was privy to Caroline's hopes for the couple, knew exactly what to say.

"Why Mr Elliott, that is an excellent scheme. Anne-Marie is a trained nurse and did a great deal of wonderful work with the unfortunate men returning from the war, when she was at Harwood Park," she said and then, in a more confidential tone added, "No doubt you know she is only recently widowed—poor girl. For many months her family were unsure she would ever recover her health. But as you see, she did, thanks mainly to the efforts of her aunt—Emma Wilson. I believe your plan could be very beneficial to her; it would give her something to look forward to."

Colin Elliott had no knowledge of the details of Mr Bradshaw's death, except he had heard it had been very sudden. Hearing Mrs Tate's words, he was somewhat puzzled at not having seen any signs of deep emotional distress in the lady, even though she had been quite recently widowed, when he had first made her acquaintance. If what Mrs Tate had said was true, and he had no reason to doubt her word, he could not explain it at all. Perhaps, it was time to confide in her brother, he thought, and determined he would speak with Charles Bingley on his return to London.

For the present, however, he put away those thoughts and seized upon an opportunity provided by an invitation to a soirée and supper with the Fitzwilliams. This extremely talented family was able to produce a complete program of music, from gentle airs and lyrics sung by the younger children to a superb performance of a Mozart serenade by a chamber music ensemble, all of which attained an enviably high standard of excellence.

As the guests were congratulating Fitzwilliam, Caroline, and all the young performers, refreshments were served and Mr Elliott, who had placed himself within reach of Anne-Marie at the back of the room, approached her and suggested they get some coffee. He noticed that she did not look as pale tonight as on the previous occasion and her eyes sparkled as she asked, "Did you enjoy the music?" to which he replied, "Yes indeed, very much."

"Do you play?" he asked, and she sighed as she confessed that she did not play with any distinction.

"Sadly, I never took the time to learn properly; I became too involved in nursing, but I do enjoy a good performance. Whenever I hear Anna or Mrs Wilson's daughters, I confess I am filled with regret and envy." When he appeared surprised, she went on, "I should have loved to have been able to play. I know I cannot sing; only poor Mr Griffin believes I can sing!" she said, with a crooked little smile.

At this, they both laughed and commented upon the simple optimism of Mr Griffin.

"He strikes me as being one of the true believers; like Bunyan's pilgrim he will struggle valiantly and never give up on anything," said Elliott, and Anne-Marie smiled her agreement but forbore to say anything. She'd had experience in the past of Mr Griffin's dogged persistence, too.

When they were serious again, he invited her to attend a function to be held at Hatfield House, where the joint choirs of three parishes were to sing Mr Handel's great oratorio, *The Messiah*.

"I know it is probably too ambitious for the parish choirs and I cannot guarantee a great performance, but if you were to attend, perhaps we might at least assist each other to appreciate the great man's music," he said and added quickly, "I should be very happy if your father and Mrs Bingley could come, too." Anne-Marie replied that she would be delighted to attend, and thanked him for inviting her.

"Once, when I used to live at Harwood Park, we went to hear an opera by Mr Handel. I cannot recall the name of it, but it was set in Roman times and it had a most wonderful solo, sung by a splendid soprano; it was divine. When we were returning home I said, if I had died just at that moment, I think I would have felt I was in heaven."

Mr Elliott thought that a most charming response and said so, but she shook her head. "Do you think so? They just thought I was being childish."

"They?" he asked, innocently, unaware of the abyss at his feet.

"My friends the Harwoods and my late husband, Mr Bradshaw, of course."

Her voice was suddenly dull and he knew the exquisite moment had been shattered, like a precious glass, into a thousand sharp pieces. She was silent and uncomfortable.

Colin Elliott felt a pang of regret, wishing he had never spoken, never asked and aroused what was perhaps a painful memory, but there was nothing he could do or say just now. His companion said nothing more that was of any consequence and sometime later, complaining of a slight headache, asked to be excused, thanked him for his company, and went upstairs to her room.

Some of the guests were leaving and Elliott thought it was time to go, too. As he thanked the host and hostess, they expressed their thanks and their disappointment that Mr and Mrs Darcy had been unable to attend. Mrs Darcy had a slight cold, Caroline explained.

"You shall meet them, Elliott; I know you will find both Darcy and Elizabeth excellent company," Fitzwilliam promised, as they agreed to meet again to enjoy some fishing in the stream that ran through his property.

Colin Elliott, despite the disquiet he felt about his final conversation with Mrs Bradshaw, was generally satisfied with the evening, which had brought unexpected pleasure. He looked forward with some anticipation to their next meeting.

❦

Some days later, Mr Elliott returned as arranged to the Fitzwilliams' property. Colonel Fitzwilliam met him and took him on a tour of the farm, of which he was clearly very proud. Having admired the house and its beautiful views which rose from the river to the rugged heights of the Peaks, they went indoors, and Elliott expected that the ladies would soon join them, until Fitzwilliam took him into the sitting room, poured out two glasses of sherry, and said, "Caroline has taken Anne-Marie down to Kympton to see her sister, Emily Courtney, who is in charge of the hospital at Littleford."

Colin Elliott had to struggle to hide his disappointment. He had hoped very much to see Anne-Marie, assuming that she was staying with the Fitzwilliams. After what had been a pleasant evening, he had spent a somewhat sleepless night, wondering whether he was right in believing that there was between them a mutual attachment, which may in time lead to something more. He had hoped at this meeting to discover something of her feelings, perhaps.

But alas, it was not to be, at least not on this occasion.

He had to be content with a political discussion with Fitzwilliam, who was sounding him out about his allegiance to the Tories. He had as good as admitted that he was unhappy with the party, but had wondered what alternative existed.

"What does one do, Fitzwilliam? I absolutely abhor the slothful smugness of my own party, yet I cannot see an alternative in the government. Palmerston has just made Britain look foolish and unreliable, while Russell, who I believed to be genuinely committed to Parliamentary Reform, seems paralysed without Palmerston's approval," he complained, "I had hoped to see bills brought forward in this session of Parliament, but nothing has transpired. I find it difficult to believe they are serious about reform."

He was clearly irritated and Fitzwilliam was sympathetic. A long-term supporter of Palmerston, he attempted to recover the damaged reputation of the man who had dominated British politics for several decades, excusing his current shortcomings and lauding his earlier triumphs. Elliott did not appear very impressed.

Fitzwilliam tried another tack. What, he asked, would Elliott say to a proposition that enabled him to cross the floor and declare himself an Independent private member, who would retain his independence, but agree to work with the Reform Group on special issues. "How would that suit you?" he asked, and Colin Elliott's eyes lit up.

"That would suit me very well; I should very much like the freedom from the party whip," he said, "but, is it possible?"

"I cannot see why not," said Fitzwilliam, quite delighted at this outcome. "I shall send word to James Wilson and ask him to call on you in London. It seems, Elliott, that we can do business."

Later, it being such a fine day, Fitzwilliam offered to drive his guest down to the village, from where it was a mere five miles to Pemberley.

"How would you like to visit?" he asked.

Colin Elliott's expression brightened. "I should like that very much, if you are sure we will not be intruding upon the family," he said and was assured that they would not.

"The grounds are splendid and the interior of the house has been recently improved without in any way destroying its essential character. My cousin Darcy is obsessed with the place and in Elizabeth he has a wife who has grown to love it as much as he does."

His companion muttered something about it being a fortunate man, who finds a wife who shares his interests and matches his obsessions, only to have it endorsed in total by Fitzwilliam.

"You are absolutely right, Elliott, I cannot imagine how I would have coped without my Caroline's support and yet, poor Jonathan Bingley suffered from the very opposite condition."

Mr Elliott looked bewildered. "I had thought," he said "that Mrs Bingley was totally supportive of him. In the time I have known them, which has not been long, I admit, I have not heard a single discordant note between them."

Fitzwilliam laughed, recognizing his mistake.

"Oh, I am sorry. Elliott, I did not mean the present Mrs Bingley; no indeed, Anna is a wonderful woman and Jonathan is a most fortunate man to have married her. I was referring to his first wife, Anne-Marie's mother. Amelia-Jane Collins she was, whom Bingley courted and married so quickly he did not have time to discover, that apart from a very pretty face and a fetching figure, she had very little to recommend her, especially as a wife for a promising member of Parliament."

Colin Elliott listened as he went on.

"She was at first very pleased to be seen around London and at Westminster, but the novelty wore off and she lost interest in politics. Caroline believes that she was never interested in the work Bingley did, nor did she try to understand it. Their marriage was in a parlous state; no one blames Jonathan, as he was extraordinarily patient and loyal," he said. "She took no part in his political work at all and, in the end, became involved with a strange couple from Bath, who were using her for their selfish purposes and was persuaded to leave him."

Colin Elliott was beginning to feel rather uncomfortable; he wondered if he should be listening to all this private information, but, at the same time, he realised that if he wanted to understand Anne-Marie better, he had to know more of her life before their short acquaintance. Already he thought he could see why she often seemed withdrawn and occasionally even wary of people.

He listened without comment, as Fitzwilliam continued.

"It was a disastrous decision; they left London on a stormy night and their vehicle went off the road somewhere near Maidenhead. They were all killed in a dreadful accident. The family was devastated."

Colin Elliott was shocked; he had known that Anna was Jonathan Bingley's second wife, but having been away from Britain for much of that time, had not heard of the circumstances of the first Mrs Bingley's death. He was not now surprised that no one had spoken of it to him; it must be a particularly painful subject.

"Poor Mr Bingley, what a dreadful blow!" he said, "and the children, they must have been desolated."

"Indeed they were, but Anne-Marie held them together. She was superb. The family rallied round, of course. Jane, Jonathan's mother, took the younger girls to stay at Ashford Park for a while, but Anne-Marie was quite heroic. Later, there was Anna, too, but Jonathan knows he owes his daughter a great deal. She is a remarkably strong and determined young woman." Colonel Fitzwilliam was unstinting with his praise.

Colin Elliott agreed at once, but did not trust himself to say too much lest he should give himself away.

They had reached the village of Lambton and, having stopped at the inn for some refreshment, proceeded up the road towards Pemberley. As they drove through a beautiful wood, towards the crest of a gently rising mount, Colin Elliott could not help exclaiming at the wealth of natural beauty that surrounded them. The large park, with its fine woods and ample meadows, stretched for many miles until they reached the highest point where, as the woods fell away, they caught sight of the handsome stone mansion that was Pemberley House.

Mr Elliott did not know it, nor did Fitzwilliam, but they had stopped to admire the excellent prospect at the very spot where Elizabeth Bennet, as she then was, had first sighted her future home. Mr Elliott was warm in his praise for the house, its situation, and the surrounding grounds. As they moved on to descend the hill, he was a little nervous at the prospect of meeting the owners of this noble estate. He had only recently discovered the very close link that existed between the Bingleys of Netherfield and Mr and Mrs Darcy. Someone at the Tates' dinner party had mentioned that Jonathan Bingley was the favourite nephew and godson of the Darcys, to which Mrs Tate had added that there could be no more intimate friendship than that which existed between their two families. He already knew that Jonathan Bingley valued Mr Darcy's opinion and deferred to him on many matters.

They entered the main park and crossed the bridge spanning a clear stream that widened naturally into a lake some short distance from the house. Colin Elliott, like others before him, found the prospect enchanting. A tall, distinguished-looking man rode up the path from the woods and Fitzwilliam called to him as he brought the curricle to a halt.

"Why, Darcy, how fortunate we are to meet you here. I was bringing Mr Colin Elliott to call on you. He is the new Member of Parliament from Hertfordshire."

Mr Darcy approached them and all three gentlemen alighted and greeted one another. Colin Elliott was not surprised at the warmth of the feeling evident between Fitzwilliam and his cousin. Clearly they had a close and intimate association.

Darcy greeted him cordially and invited them to follow him up to the house for refreshments.

"Have you been fishing, Darcy?" Fitzwilliam asked, as one of the servants followed close behind with rod and tackle.

I wish I had been," said Darcy. "That's not my catch in the bag, I'm afraid. I've been with Grantham, my manager, looking over some of the cottages in the valley. We are making some improvements to the houses of my tenants and adding some rooms to the parish school at Kympton," he explained and as they walked towards the house, he invited Mr Elliott to return and fish in his trout stream, whenever he felt inclined. The invitation was accepted with alacrity. Elliott was a keen fisherman.

They reached the house and walked up the steps to find Mrs Darcy waiting for them. She had seen them from her favourite window and had come down to meet them. Colin Elliott was immediately struck by her charming, friendly manner and handsome appearance. He had heard she was a beauty in her youth, and he certainly did not doubt it; indeed she was still an exceedingly fine-looking woman. They made a remarkably handsome couple, he thought.

As the mistress of this very impressive estate, one might have expected her to be more imposing—reserved perhaps? Instead, she greeted him with an open friendliness and in their continuing conversation struck him as a witty and intelligent woman, hospitable and eager to put him at ease, as she ordered tea and offered to show him around the house herself.

After they had taken tea, Fitzwilliam engaged his cousin in a long discussion, leaving Elizabeth to take Mr Elliott through some of the main rooms of the house. She explained that recently several areas had been refurbished, but her husband was very particular that nothing should be done that would change the essential character of the house and its environs.

Colin Elliott was most impressed, not only with the handsome proportions of the rooms and the elegance and good taste that marked all the furniture and accessories that adorned them, but equally, he admired the restraint with which Mrs Darcy explained the significance of a picture or the provenance of an objet d'Art, with never a hint of boastfulness or vanity. He had heard both Colonel Fitzwilliam and his wife Caroline speak very highly of Mr and Mrs Darcy; from his very first encounter, he could vouch for the veracity of their judgment.

Elizabeth took Mr Elliott through the music room and the formal drawing rooms up to the long gallery, which held some of the greatest treasures of Pemberley House.

At the far end of the gallery, among a group of family portraits, including the unmistakable likenesses of the Darcy children, was a striking portrait of an exquisitely beautiful young woman surrounded by four exceedingly attractive children, a boy and three girls, one remarkably like her mother.

The resemblance to Mrs Bradshaw was so striking that Colin Elliott stopped right in front of the picture and stared at it with great concentration, before turning around as if he wished to ask a question.

Elizabeth, who had been waiting for him a few feet away, anticipated his enquiry.

"That lady is Amelia-Jane Bingley, my nephew Jonathan's first wife. She was very beautiful. The picture was commissioned by my sister and brother-in-law and used to hang in the library at Ashford Park, but after her death, my sister Jane found it too painful to have on daily view and it was transferred to Pemberley. Besides, it used to upset the two young ones, Teresa and Cathy," she explained.

Colin Elliott was still gazing at the portrait.

"The resemblance to Mrs Bradshaw is amazing," he said at last.

"Ah yes," said Elizabeth, understanding his drift. "Even as a little girl Anne-Marie was very like her mother, who was very beautiful, as you can see. But there, I am happy to say, the resemblance ends."

"Indeed?" he sounded puzzled. He looked at her directly, an obvious question in his eyes unspoken, because he was reluctant to offend, even unwittingly.

Elizabeth sensed his reluctance and having never been other than honest herself and recalling her conversation with Jane regarding Mr Elliott's interest in Anne-Marie, she decided that frankness was called for.

"Oh yes, there is almost nothing of her mother in Anne-Marie, except her remarkable good looks. Even so, you may have noticed she wears little or no adornment, whereas Amelia-Jane loved expensive jewellery."

Colin Elliott indicated that it was something he had noticed. Indeed in the portrait, both mother and daughter wore exquisite ornaments of diamonds and pearls.

Elizabeth went on, "I do not say this with any malice, Mr Elliott. Amelia-Jane Collins was the youngest daughter of my dearest friend, Mrs Charlotte Collins, who now lives at Longbourn. You may have met?"

He indicated that they had.

"Well, Mrs Collins was widowed when her girls were still very young and she had to bring them up alone. The two older girls were well educated and disciplined by their mother, but Amelia-Jane had been somewhat over-indulged by her father from childhood." Elizabeth recalled that she had been Mr Collins's favourite child. "Unfortunately, unlike her sisters, she grew up with little or no interest in improving her mind or developing any artistic skills, beyond those required to adorn herself, move with ease in society, and please everyone she met.

"With the advantage of her looks, she was universally spoilt and flattered, until at the tender age of sixteen, she became engaged, after an amazingly brief courtship, to my nephew Jonathan, on the eve of his entry into Parliament. They were married and were declared to be blissfully happy, in which state they remained for some years, until boredom and the unhappy deaths of two sons, both before they were a year old, took their toll.

"The marriage crumbled despite the best efforts of Jonathan, his family and friends. Poor Amelia-Jane, with no real friends, she came to depend upon a pair of malevolent women, who convinced her to leave her husband and family and accompany them to Bath!"

By now, Elizabeth noticed that Colin Elliott was looking distinctly unhappy, but she persisted. "It was catastrophic! Amelia-Jane and her companions were all killed when their coach overturned somewhere near Maidenhead. Jonathan was left to cope with the scandal and opprobrium, while Anne-Marie, who was not then twenty-one, held their shattered family together and, I do believe, helped save her father's sanity."

Listening to her words, Colin Elliott was struck by the fact that in the space of twenty-four hours, he had heard the same story from two members of the family—Colonel Fitzwilliam and now Mrs Darcy. But, while each in their telling of it had clearly displayed their own personal attitude to the late Mrs Bingley, neither had had anything but good to say of Anne-Marie. Indeed, both had confirmed her strength of character and judgment.

He could not stop himself, as he looked back at the picture and said, "I can quite easily believe that. I have thought for sometime now that Mrs Bradshaw is one of the strongest, most single-minded women of my acquaintance. I would sincerely have wished she could have met my late mother."

Elizabeth smiled and nodded as they walked towards the stairs, and stopping once again to look at the picture, he said, "She is also one of the loveliest women I have ever met, yet she seems completely unconscious of her beauty."

Elizabeth said nothing but thought how her sister Jane would have given anything to have been present at that moment. Thinking the subject closed, she moved towards the stairs, when he spoke again. "Mrs Darcy, forgive me asking and I give you my word this is not out of idle curiosity, but did Mrs Bradshaw know...I mean was she old enough to understand at the time...?" his voice trailed off as the awkwardness of his question trammelled up his speech.

Surprised by his question and yet, determined to be open with him, Elizabeth replied, "Oh yes, she not only understood, she was the only member of the family who, knowing the danger her mother was in, tried desperately to avert what was about to happen. Both Jonathan and his sister Mrs Wilson can attest to the truth of this. And when it did happen, she was the only one, in the midst of the tragedy, who could console her father and sisters.

"Charles, her brother, was quite hopeless. Desolated by his mother's death, he blamed his father, quite unfairly, and was totally incapable of consoling anyone. Anne-Marie, later with Anna Faulkner's help, held them together. Her courage and compassion were quite astonishing in such a young woman."

Colin Elliott shook his head as if in bewilderment. In fact, he was agreeing with her. "Though I have no personal knowledge of these circumstances, I have long admired those qualities of selflessness and courage in her," he said.

Elizabeth thought, for one moment, that he was about to say something more, but just then they heard from below the sound of a vehicle coming up the drive and, looking out, they saw Mr Darcy and Fitzwilliam walking down to meet it.

As it approached the house, Elizabeth recognised the occupants.

"Look, it's Caroline and Anne-Marie," she exclaimed, and noticed how Colin Elliott's countenance coloured deeply. For a few moments, he looked very shy and would not meet her eyes, but then he seemed to force himself to speak.

"Mrs Darcy, please let me say how much I appreciate what you have told me today. I am grateful that you trusted me to know the details of what is surely an intimate family matter."

Elizabeth smiled.

"It is indeed an intimate family matter, Mr Elliott, and I do trust you to respect the confidence I have placed in you. But, I know you are acquainted with my nephew and his family and it is not inappropriate that you should learn the true circumstances of his first wife's death from one of us, rather than hear of it through rumour and gossip."

Assuring her that he would never have paid any heed to such sources, he thanked her again for trusting him, as he followed her down the stairs.

By the time they reached the main hall, the two ladies had been admitted to the saloon and were about to be seated. They entered the handsome room with its pleasing view of the park and the wooded hills beyond, where Caroline was busy explaining to her husband and Mr Darcy how they had visited Kympton and spent a most instructive morning with Emily Courtney at the parish school.

"Tomorrow, we are to visit the hospital at Littleford," said Caroline, and Anne-Marie, who had her back to the door, had removed her hat, and was attempting to fix a lock of her hair that was slipping down her neck, added, "We asked Emily if Mr Elliott could come, too; he was keen to visit the hospital and Emily was quite agreeable. We shall have to send word to him tonight," she said as Elizabeth and Mr Elliott entered the room.

Darcy, smiling broadly, aware that they had already heard her words, said lightly, "Well, here's the man himself, Anne-Marie; you can give him the good news."

Anne-Marie swung round and on seeing Mr Elliott standing there with Elizabeth, her face and neck became covered with a deep blush, and moments later, she asked to be excused and left the room. Elizabeth accompanied her as she went upstairs, asking permission to sit quietly for a few minutes. Though she did not press her at all, Lizzie was in no doubt that Anne-Marie was well aware of Colin Elliott's interest in her. They returned some fifteen minutes later to join the others for refreshments, which had been brought in and laid upon the table by the windows. After a while, Elizabeth noticed that Mr Elliott, who had been talking avidly to Caroline, had moved to seat himself beside Anne-Marie. Plans were being made to visit the hospital on the morrow and, before they left, an invitation was issued and gladly accepted for the entire party to dine at Pemberley on the Saturday.

"I should very much like you to meet our daughter Cassandra and her husband Dr Richard Gardiner," said Mr Darcy. "Richard has an abiding interest in improving the health of our communities. He has worked untiringly to establish and improve the hospitals at Littleford and Matlock and runs his own research laboratory."

Darcy was plainly very proud of the achievements of his son-in-law, and Mr Elliott looked most impressed. "Then he will certainly have much to tell that is of interest to us; both Mrs Bradshaw and I are hoping to do the same for our community in Hertfordshire with the hospital for children at Bell's Field. I look forward to meeting Dr Gardiner," he said.

Anne-Marie, glad to be back on a safe subject, agreed at once that Richard Gardiner, with his experience, would be an excellent source of advice. Fitzwilliam was sure there would be no other subject discussed on the night.

"Darcy, I suggest we retire to the billiard room after dinner," he said, as they parted in great good humour, looking forward very much to their next visit to Pemberley.

~❦~

The visit to Littleford hospital was a most salutary experience. It opened their eyes to so many significant matters that Anne-Marie had to borrow notepaper and pencil to take notes for future reference. Emily Courtney, who'd had charge of administering the hospital for several years, was able to explain all the possible problems they might encounter along the way and more besides. She introduced them, too, to Dr Henry Forrester, who gave them plenty of sound advice on the types of childhood ailments and diseases that would need to be attended to and the need to have an isolation room for children with contagious diseases. "It is essential if you are to avert an epidemic in the village, which can, if not diagnosed in time, cost the lives of very young children," he warned.

Time and again, Colin Elliott found himself surprised by the number of matters that had been overlooked and needed attention—licenses to practice, a willing apothecary to dispense medicines, competent nurses, sanitary officers, and above all, a good, hardworking doctor.

When they dined at Pemberley and met Dr Richard Gardiner and his wife Cassandra, the subject of a doctor for the hospital came up again. Richard was adamant that they must appoint a young man.

"He must not only be fit, with a strong constitution, and patient with sick children, who are notoriously fractious when away from home," he said, "but he should be young enough to be open to the new ideas that are coming thick and fast. Dr Faulkner is dedicated and competent, but he is elderly and may not be able to cope, though he will be a useful locum. Be warned; demand for services will double overnight, once the clinic is established," he explained. "The poor, Mr Elliott, especially those with many children, cannot afford to attend a doctor's consulting rooms. But establish a free clinic and they will come. Believe me, your hospital will save lives just as it did here."

Richard Gardiner made several worthwhile suggestions, while Colin Elliott and Anne-Marie listened carefully, taking note of his valuable advice. Mr Elliott was obviously impressed by Dr Gardiner's knowledge and experience, yet Cassandra sitting beside her mother and watching them from across the drawing room, detected something more in the air.

"I think he is in love with her, Mama," she whispered. "He keeps talking of doctors and hospitals, but he cannot tear his eyes away from her, even when Richard is speaking."

Elizabeth smiled, "Yes, I had noticed that, but then, my dear Cassy, even your handsome husband cannot compete with Anne-Marie's looks. She is looking particularly well tonight," she said and Cassy agreed.

"Indeed, she is; that brilliant blue suits her well. Could it be a serious attachment, Mama? Will they marry, do you think?"

Elizabeth was noncommittal. "I do not know, my dear; I am not the confidante of either party. But one thing is clear to anyone who has eyes to see, he is in love with her, and if people see them together often, it is going to be the talk of the county."

"Do you think he will ask her?"

"Probably, but how soon, I cannot tell. He seems a very proper young man and it is possible he will want to ask her father's permission first," said Elizabeth.

Later, Elizabeth and Caroline played the piano and Fitzwilliam was easily persuaded to join his wife in a song, as the party went late into the night. Neither Colin Elliott nor Anne-Marie volunteered to perform and, though they were seen talking earnestly as they sat together taking coffee, he did not propose.

Colin Elliott had been very tempted that night. The atmosphere of gracious living that Pemberley afforded them, together with good food and music, all enhanced his mood of romantic anticipation, especially with Mrs Bradshaw looking particularly appealing. Yet, something held him back and he decided to wait until they had returned to Hertfordshire. Elizabeth had read him correctly; he intended to approach Mr Bingley first. The letter he had written regarding the role Anne-Marie might play in the administration of the hospital at Bell's Field would afford him a convenient opening, he decided. Clearly, the family at Pemberley would have to wait a while longer to discover the answer to their question.

Later that night, Elizabeth revealed to her husband the gist of her conversation with Mr Elliott and her conviction that the gentleman was showing a clear partiality for Anne-Marie. Darcy had listened while she spoke, and when she asked, "What is your opinion? Do you think I was right to reveal the circumstances of Amelia-Jane's death or do you believe I was indiscreet?" he answered in his usual measured way, "That is hardly likely, Lizzie, my dear. That you chose to speak openly and honestly is to my mind a virtue. I believe you had no alternative; there was nothing to be gained by dissembling and trying to conceal the facts; he was bound to have discovered them anyway. There are enough people who make a living by spreading rumour and gossip, who would have seen fit to apprise him of the circumstances, no sooner had his connection with the Bingleys become common knowledge among the denizens of Hertfordshire. You, my dear, have forestalled them."

Elizabeth was pleased to have his approval.

"That was certainly my intention. I thought it also important to indicate that we were proud of Anne-Marie, not allowing her to be in any way tarnished by her mother's foolhardy escapade, tragic though it was in its consequences. But I admit, I have been apprehensive that my words may have discomposed him and caused him to change his mind regarding Anne-Marie." Darcy smiled; he was very proud of his wife's perspicacity.

"I can see no reason for that, my love; you were absolutely right to be frank and open with him. If I were Mr Colin Elliott, I would rather know the truth about the background of the lady I was hoping to marry than be surprised by any unpleasant revelations later."

Elizabeth's eyes sparkled; even though it was very late, all thought of sleep had fled. "Thank you, my dear, you are very kind. You have completely restored my belief in my judgment. Now let me put your powers of prediction to the test. Do you believe he intends to propose?"

"Lizzie dearest, I make no claim to any such powers, but I have eyes to see and I have no doubt he does. Fitzwilliam and I noted that Elliott hardly moved from Anne-Marie's side all evening. I am convinced he is in love and very likely to propose to her as soon as they are back in Hertfordshire."

"Cassy and I were surprised that he has not done so already," she said, prompting a typical reply from her husband, "Ah yes, no doubt you ladies would have him surrendering to the romantic ambience of the evening, eh? But, I believe he is a rather cautious man, who wishes to do the right thing and probably means to apply to her father first."

"And do you believe Jonathan will consent?" she asked.

"He has no reason not to do so; from what I hear of him, Elliott is a fine, principled young fellow, with excellent prospects," he replied.

She pressed him further. "And Anne-Marie, will she accept him, do you think?"

This time, he was more circumspect in his answer.

"That, my dear, is quite another matter. As you well know, Lizzie, I am not a good student of the minds of women in general and even with those with whom I am most intimate, I may sometimes blunder. Furthermore, the young lady is very good at keeping her feelings to herself. On that question, we shall have to wait and see."

Elizabeth laughed softly. She had asked the question more to test his mood than to obtain a definite answer. She knew her husband well and was content to find him in such a relaxed and amenable frame of mind.

Neither of them had any doubt that Colin Elliott had shown a strong partiality for Anne-Marie and knowing how deeply hurt she had been in her first marriage, they hoped sincerely she would be given another chance at happiness.

❧

After what, she was able to pronounce with confidence, was a very useful and enjoyable stay in Derbyshire, Anne-Marie returned to Netherfield Park to find her father alone. "Teresa and Cathy are gone to Ashford Park to spend a few weeks with your grandparents and thereafter to Pemberley, I believe," he said.

"And Anna?" she asked.

"My dear wife has been called away to her sister in Hampshire, who I believe is unwell," he explained. "Not again?" Anne-Marie was sceptical; Sarah Martyn was one of those women, whose indispositions tended to arouse more amusement than sympathy, so frequent and unaccountable had they become. She was married to a farmer in Hampshire, whose skills in animal husbandry were obviously of a higher order than those expected of a husband. While his mother-in-law assured everyone that Mr Martyn was an excellent farmer, she could never assure them of his success as a husband and father with the same degree of confidence. Apart from siring several children, who were also prone to innumerable ailments, he appeared quite incapable of caring satisfactorily for any of them or, indeed, his long-suffering wife. Her only recourse in such emergencies was to send urgent requests for help and consolation to her mother and sister.

Since her marriage to Jonathan Bingley, Anna had tried assiduously to avoid having to rush to her sister's bedside at regular intervals, but on this occasion, their mother, Mrs Faulkner, being unwell herself, there had been no help for it. Anna had to go.

"Whatever is it this time?" asked Anne-Marie, who was disappointed to find Anna away. She had wanted very much to confide in her. There were several matters she had wished to discuss.

Her father showed a little more patience. "I cannot be certain, but I gather from Dr Faulkner that this time, it has more to do with the mind than the body. In short, I believe Mrs Martyn suffers from depression."

Anne-Marie was unconvinced. "I am sure it is just another device to get poor Anna to rush to Hampshire and hold her hand. She has probably quarrelled with Mr Martyn or one of her children and wants a shoulder to weep on."

As she chattered on, Jonathan rose and went over to his desk, taking out a letter, which he unfolded as he stood before her.

Anne-Marie stopped talking and, looking up from perusing the letter in his hand, her father said, in a fairly matter-of-fact voice, "My dear, I have received this letter from Mr Elliott."

The words were scarcely out of his mouth, when she went crimson with embarrassment and ran from the room. Jonathan Bingley stood still for fully five minutes, before realization dawned. He had clearly made some sort of *faux pas*, giving her the impression that the letter contained a proposal of marriage from Mr Elliott. Unprepared for such an eventuality, Anne-Marie had been embarrassed and upset and fled the room.

Oh dear, what have I done? Jonathan mused, putting down the letter.

All he had set out to do was to inform Anne-Marie of Colin Elliott's proposition that she be persuaded to take up the management of the children's hospital at Bell's Field.

Folding the letter and putting it away in his pocket, Jonathan set off to find his daughter. Approaching her bedroom, he knocked and went in to find her sitting by the window, looking out on a bleak scene, with a fine spring drizzle obscuring her view of the park.

Jonathan was apologetic. "Anne-Marie, my dear, I am sorry, I should have said . . ." he began, but she did not let him finish. Tearful and sad at having upset her father, she protested, "No Papa, it is I who should be sorry; it was stupid and childish of me to have run away. I do apologise, sincerely." He put his arms around her and suddenly, weakening, she was in tears.

When she was calmer, he persuaded her to return to his study.

"First, let me reassure you, there is nothing whatever to be alarmed about in Mr Elliott's letter. Here, read it yourself," he said, taking it from his pocket and putting it in her hands.

On reading it, Anne-Marie's face became pale; she was mortified and embarrassed at having misunderstood the writer's intention and behaved in such a juvenile manner. She bit her lip and looked ashamed as she handed it back to her father. "Papa, I am truly sorry, I feel such a fool. I cannot think why I thought as I did and behaved as I did," she said, and he smiled.

"Do you not? Perhaps it will become clear later. Well, now you know what he has suggested, what have you to say? Would you like to have charge of the children's hospital you have worked so hard to establish?" he asked.

Her eyes were shining and not from her tears.

"Papa, nothing will make me happier. But is it what you would wish?"

"My dear child, it is not my wish that matters, but, of course I would like to see you do it and I know you will do it well. The whole scheme is not mine; oh, I know I purchased the site and helped in other ways and will continue to do so, but it was your brainchild and, together with Mr Elliott, you have worked to establish it. When it is completed, you must do whatever will bring you satisfaction," he said.

"And Mr Elliott suggests that I am able and qualified enough to do it?" She sounded a little unsure, but her father had no such qualms. "Indeed, he does." Jonathan picked up the letter. "He writes,"

"I cannot think of any other person better suited by qualification, experience and temperament to perform this important duty to our community, not to speak of her enthusiasm for the task."

"Clearly he appreciates your dedication and experience," he said and read on,

"Trained as she is in the best traditions of nursing care, should she accept, it will enhance the credentials of the children's hospital and curtail quite considerably the Council's capacity to criticise."

"Now that is an excellent recommendation from the local Member of Parliament, even if he is a Tory!" said Jonathan, and Anne-Marie had to agree. Still blushing, she said, "Mr Elliott has been very generous with his praise, Papa."

"He speaks only the truth, my dear. You are well qualified for the position," said her father. She smiled and embraced him, then said, "Papa, Mr Elliott is not such a diehard Tory, is he?" and Jonathan, realising the point of her question, said in a reassuring voice, "Indeed no, in fact I am beginning to believe he is almost a Liberal."

At this, they both looked at each other and broke into laughter, becoming engrossed in the recollection of a variety of matters upon which Mr Elliott's views and actions would surely have him marked out as a Reformist at least!

So wholly occupied were they with this fascinating exercise, they failed to notice that an express had just been delivered to the door.

Mrs Perrot collected it and brought it in. She looked excited as she said, "It's from Mrs Bingley, sir," and she lingered as Jonathan opened it up, and Anne-Marie peered over his shoulder to read.

Glancing over it very quickly, he said, "Thank God, she's coming home tomorrow. Mrs Perrot, would you tell Mr Bowles we shall need the carriage to meet Mrs Bingley at Meryton tomorrow around midday."

"Certainly, sir," said Mrs Perrot, glad to have her mistress home, "and I think we might have a celebratory dinner to welcome her back?"

"Most definitely, Mrs Perrot," he replied.

Anna Bingley was so happy to be home, she wept as they turned into the lane leading to Netherfield Park. With Jonathan, Anne-Marie, the baby and his nurse, they were quite a crowd. Anna could not wait for the journey to end. Her visit to Hampshire had left her physically and mentally exhausted. Never had she been happier to see the welcoming façade of Netherfield House, looming as it was through the rain; it could well have been a beacon signalling that she was home at last.

Mrs Perrot and the staff welcomed her and did their best to make a celebration of it. Anna did her best, too. Bathed and rested, she dressed slowly for dinner, savouring every moment of her homecoming to a comfortable, orderly, and loving household, the very opposite of the Martyn's chaotic farm. So utterly tired was she, Jonathan urged her to retire early, but she was reluctant to disappoint the staff and especially the cook, who had prepared all her favourite dishes to welcome her back. But in the end, having thanked them all, she excused herself and went upstairs to bed. When her husband followed her an hour or so later, he expected to find her sound asleep and was alarmed to hear her sobbing. At her side immediately, he was anxious and concerned.

"Anna, my dearest, what is wrong? Are you unwell?" he asked, attempting to discover the cause of her distress, but she shook her head and hid her face in her pillow, weeping as he had never seen her do before, inconsolably. He felt helpless and unhappy, unable to do anything to ease her anguish.

Anne-Marie, on her way to bed, looked in to say goodnight as she often did, but her father waved her away, indicating that something was amiss. Seeing her worried expression, he went later to reassure her that Anna was not ill, only tired and distressed.

She had given him no further explanation and, after an hour or more, Anna fell asleep. Clearly, something had caused her grief and it had to have happened while she was in Hampshire with her sister Sarah.

Jonathan slept only fitfully, troubled by the vision of his wife's tears, his own anxiety exacerbated by the fact that he had not been able to comfort her or share her pain. Ignorance of its cause angered and grieved him.

Towards dawn, he awoke with a start and found her gone from their bed. A light in his dressing room attracted his eye and he went over to the door and there, on the couch, was Anna. She looked up as he entered, and he went to her at once and held her close. This time, she did not weep and he was able to take her back into the bedroom, where it was warmer, and sit her down.

"Now, Anna, I think I am owed an explanation. What has distressed you, my darling? You must tell me. Has someone said or done something to cause this pain? Did anything untoward happen in Hampshire? Your sister is not recovered from her illness? Is someone in trouble? One of the children is ill? No?" She was shaking her head; it was none of those things.

"What is it then, Anna? I must know; I cannot bear to see you so miserable," he pleaded.

Then, as if a dam had broken inside her, she began to speak. It was an unhappy story, one whose truth she had suspected for many years, yet she had colluded with her sister to hide it, never openly questioning the accepted version, that Sarah was happily married to her farmer and enjoyed having five or six boisterous children, from whose clutches she rarely, if ever, escaped.

As Jonathan listened, in astonishment and disbelief, she told him, "Sarah is desperately unhappy; in spite of having five children by Mr Martyn, she hardly knows him, she fears him, and at times she hates him. He is often so engrossed in the welfare of his farm animals that he fails to take any notice of her existence for most of the day, until he sits down to a meal or climbs into bed," she said bitterly. "Poor Sarah, she used to long to be married and she thought, when Mr Martyn asked permission to propose to her, that he must have loved her dearly; well, she knows now that he loves all of his cows and sheep more."

As Jonathan stared, uncomprehending, she added, "If one of them were to fall sick, he would spend all night with the creature, but when Sarah was ill, he claimed her coughing was disturbing him and went downstairs to sleep. Jonathan, it is pathetic; she is alone and so deeply unhappy, I felt guilty leaving her, even though I hated every day I had to spend in that house. He has no sympathy for her, does not even see the need to make an effort to understand her feelings. This time, he simply handed her over to me and went."

"Went? Went where?" asked Jonathan in bewilderment.

"To the Spring markets with the pigs. He said, quite rudely, that if they did not sell their produce, they would have no money and, when I asked if one of his men could not go in his stead, he snapped that he would not trust them with his pigs or his money."

Jonathan shook his head. "Oh, my dear, I can see why you seemed so relieved to be home and yet you were so exhausted; it must have been hell," he said, and she nodded, "Yes, and for poor Sarah, it is hell; Jonathan, a loveless marriage to a selfish, unfeeling man, with no escape—for what will she do with five young children? It's quite hopeless."

Jonathan had very little knowledge of Sarah's husband. Martyn, whom he had met twice since their wedding, had seemed a good-natured oaf, with a hearty laugh and a big appetite. The family used to make jokes about how much food he could eat and still put his hand up for more. He had no illusions about Martyn's pretensions to being a gentleman, despite the broad acres he owned in a very fertile and salubrious part of Hampshire, yet nothing had prepared him for revelations such as these. If it were not Anna who was detailing them, he would have found it difficult to believe, but as she was so sensible and not given to alarmist talk, he did not doubt her word.

When she went on, she told how the children were for the most part undisciplined and the house, as a consequence of their depredations and Sarah's general malaise, reduced to an untidy mess.

"The cook, who is the only servant who has stayed with them above a year, spends all her waking hours attending to the master's pernickety demands for food at any hour of the day when he returns from the farm, and the chambermaid is so exhausted fetching and carrying she has no time to change the sheets on the children's beds. It's too terrible for words and I am so depressed because I can see no way out for her or for any of them."

"And Sarah, was this the cause of her illness?" he asked, and she nodded.

"I am sure it was, though her husband believed it was lack of exercise. She is grown fat and he tells her she eats too much and should exercise more. But Sarah is sick not just in her body, but deep in her mind. Poor Sarah, I do not think I could have lived a day longer in that house, which is why I sent you an express and left before I began to lose my own mind. Oh, Jonathan, whatever is to become of them?"

He had no immediate answers for her. Unfortunately, the type of desolate union that Sarah and her farmer had was not uncommon. Anna, whose life had been singularly blessed when she had married Jonathan Bingley, was feeling deep pangs of guilt as she confronted the truth of her sister's marriage.

"I am very shocked and saddened to hear this, my dear. I understand completely how difficult it must have been for you to leave your sister in such a situation," he said and, promising to think of some way to help Sarah, he consoled her and persuaded her to stay a while longer in bed. "You will not be expected downstairs early today, my love. Mrs Perrot will be told that you are tired from your journey and do not wish to be disturbed," he said as he tucked the bedclothes in around her.

❧

It was close to midday when, with a gentle knock on the door, Anne-Marie came in to see her. She looked very anxious and concerned that Anna had not eaten any breakfast. The nurse in her was quite censorious, "You must have some breakfast, Anna. I've brought you something, just a bit of porridge and fruit; it will do you good," she said and began to bustle around the room. "Mrs Perrot will bring you some tea in a minute."

Anna did not have the heart to refuse her and ate a morsel or two. When the tea arrived, she was more eager, knowing it would help clear her head, which ached from lack of sleep and too much weeping. After the maid had removed the breakfast tray, Anna rose and Anne-Marie asked, "Would you like me to go?"

Anna shook her head. "No, please stay and tell me about your visit to Derbyshire. How are they all? Did you visit Pemberley?"

Anne-Marie told her everything, excitedly retelling her meetings with the Tates, the Darcys, their daughter Cassy, and Dr Gardiner, her husband.

"Mr Elliott was there, with the Tates. He seemed to get on exceedingly well with Mr and Mrs Darcy and Dr Gardiner. Papa thinks he is not really a Tory at all, more a Liberal or at least a Reformist, he says."

She could not keep the excitement out of her voice and Anna, looking across at her, said, "Anne-Marie, I think we are going to have a talk about Mr Elliott fairly soon, are we not?" at which, she gave a shy smile and remembered that she had some very urgent business with Mrs Perrot and was gone, leaving Anna smiling to herself for the first time in many days.

Anne-Marie and Colin Elliott, she wondered at the possibility. He was at least in his midthirties, possibly ten years older than Anne-Marie. She was intrigued by the fact that there had been no trace of it a month ago and yet suddenly, out of Derbyshire, had come this new shyness . . .

Anna determined she would talk to Anne-Marie, but before that she would see Jonathan and discover what he knew of this business. Of one thing she was certain, she would not let Anne-Marie make another barren marriage like her last. Her visit to her sister had only served to strengthen her resolve in this regard.

Jonathan returned from Longbourn, where he had found Charlotte Collins unwell with what looked and sounded like a bad bout of quinsy.

Her throat was swollen and she had almost lost her voice. Having ascertained that Dr Faulkner had been called, he had left urging her to call on him if they needed help.

"I shall send Mr Bowles round this afternoon, Mrs Collins; please instruct him if there is anything you need," he had said, as he left.

Returning to Netherfield, he went upstairs and was delighted to discover that his wife had successfully overcome her depression and was, together with Anne-Marie, looking over the children's clothes closets for garments that may be donated to charity. Jonathan told them of Charlotte's illness, revealing his concern that Mrs Collins ought to rest; he thought she was more likely to struggle on, putting her health in greater danger through neglect.

"I believe she needs someone with her to ensure that she takes her medicine and rests when she should. Harriet Greene is good, but she is also very busy with the school and, though she may be a good companion, she is not a nurse," he said.

"I am," said Anne-Marie. "I could go over and look after Mrs Collins. Anna is too exhausted after nursing Mrs Martyn."

She would brook no argument. In less than an hour Anne-Marie was packed and ready, complete with a medicine kit, waiting for Mr Bowles to have the carriage brought round. At Anna's suggestion, her maid Jenny Dawkins went with her.

Left on their own, Jonathan and his wife went upstairs to spend a few hours together. Their warm and loving relationship had sustained them and brought them great happiness. While they enjoyed the company of their friends and family and dearly loved their children, they were never happier than when they were alone together. Each had brought the other truer, deeper happiness than they had known before.

Later, they talked of the matters that had troubled them yesterday.

Jonathan had had an idea. "Anna, my dear, I have had what I think is a rather useful idea, that may help get your sister out of her prison in Hampshire, albeit only for a short time. But, it would be better than nothing and may help improve her spirits." Anna rolled over and looked up at him, instantly interested, wondering what he was about to suggest.

Jonathan explained, "We know your Aunt Collins is in need of some care and company. You are in no fit state to go to her and I need you here anyway. Anne-Marie cannot stay forever and your mother has been unwell, so who do we appeal to?"

Anna looked disbelieving. "Surely not Sarah?"

"Why not? She is not ill, physically, and a change of scene would do her a great deal of good. She could take the coach; we might even send Bowles to meet her and, if she wanted to bring one of the children, it could be arranged…do you not think this is a good idea, my love?" Though not entirely convinced, Anna appreciated the possibilities and, turning to her husband, embraced him warmly.

"Oh, Jonathan, I think that would be a great relief to her; I know Sarah would love to come; she hardly ever gets out of the house only because Mr Martyn will not move. I know, also, that there is the little matter of my aunt's will; Sarah has often wondered if Aunt Collins will leave her anything."

Jonathan laughed. "Well, this may be a way to ensure she is not overlooked," he said, "Mrs Collins is unlikely to forget her niece if she comes all the way from Hampshire to attend on her."

Anna agreed that it was a very good idea and was enthusiastic about having found some way to free poor Sarah from her self-imposed life sentence of service to Mr Martyn and his farm. She promised to write to her sister straightaway. It made her feel a little less guilty about leaving her miserable sister and returning to Netherfield to enjoy the pleasures of her own marriage.

In the quiet hours that followed, they made love again and talked, inevitably, of Anne-Marie. Their own love rendered them more keenly sensitive to the sorrow of others. It was typical that the closer they drew to one another and the deeper their own happiness, the more likely they were to seek the means of alleviating another's distress. Furthermore, Anna wanted her husband to pay attention to a matter that had begun to concern her, in recent times.

"Dearest, I have a strong premonition that you will soon be hearing from Mr Elliott," she said. He looked at her quizzically for a moment, before asking, "Elliott? Why? Does he want me to bother the Council about the hospital again?" Anna shook her head and smiled. "I doubt it is the Council he wishes to talk about," she said.

"What then? Things appear to be going along well at Bell's Field; in fact I have already written him to say that Anne-Marie is happy to manage the place when it is completed. It was all his idea and she was agreeable, so I daresay he will be pleased."

Anna sat up and looked at him. "I am certain he will be very pleased indeed, especially since he seems to be on the verge of proposing to her."

At her words, Jonathan sat bolt upright and stared, "Whatever gave you that idea?" Anna could not contain her laughter.

"Do you really mean you are the last to know? I have had a letter from Caroline Fitzwilliam and she writes as if all of Derbyshire knows. Apparently, at the same time that Anne-Marie was staying with them at the farm, Colin Elliott had been invited to stay with the Tates at Matlock and, of course, they kept meeting at dinner parties and soirées and then, they were all asked to Pemberley, and on each occasion, Caroline says, it became increasingly obvious to her and a few others in the party that Mr Elliott was in love with Anne-Marie. Caroline claims that she was quite sure he would declare himself at Pemberley, but she admits to being disappointed that he did not appear to have done so."

Jonathan looked bewildered. His wife, surprised he had not even suspected it, asked, "Did you not think there may have been some partiality on his part?"

"No, not at all. Well, I admit I had noticed that the fellow is extraordinarily gracious and pays her some attention, but I had not thought to take it seriously, because it was clear to me that Anne-Marie was quite averse to even considering marriage after her experience with Bradshaw and, since I know her too well to believe she would trifle with a man's feelings, I did not think she would give him any encouragement. Do you believe she has?" he asked.

"I cannot tell with any certainty, but did you not notice how easily she colours when he is mentioned?" Anna replied.

"Oh, yes indeed, but that is the way of most young women. Tell me, my love, seriously, what do you think of the possibility?"

Anna was unwilling to speculate, unaware of Anne-Marie's inclinations. She did say, however, that she prayed their decision would be based only upon their own deepest feelings for each other.

"Anne-Marie has suffered far too much already. If she ever decides to wed again, it must only be because she loves him. It is too great a sacrifice to give one's life to another without the warmth and comfort of his love." Her voice was softer as she went on. "Indeed, despite all that marriage may bring in the way of social advantage, wealth, and security, there is nothing in it for a woman, unless she is also loved," she said, prompting him to ask, "And if she is loved?"

She knew the answer he wanted and gave it to him gladly, knowing how well it would please him.

"Why then," she said, "she has everything she needs in the world."

~❦~

Meanwhile, Anne-Marie, having arrived at Longbourn and attended upon the grateful Mrs Collins, went to her room to deal with her correspondence. Several notes and letters had arrived while she was away in Derbyshire; chief among them was one from her Aunt Emma Wilson. In her reply, Anne-Marie was less guarded than with any one else. Theirs was a close friendship, founded upon trust and love. Anne-Marie wrote of the pleasures of her visit to Derbyshire, the delights of the Fitzwilliams' farm at Matlock, the elegance of Pemberley, and her meetings with the Tates and Colin Elliott.

She continued,

I was surprised to find Mr Elliott visiting the Tates; but it is indeed difficult to believe how easily I am able to converse with him now. I think, dear Aunt, that when I first knew him, I was reluctant to say very much, unless I was speaking up for the hospital, because I felt somewhat inadequate and concerned that he would think me unlearned and ignorant.

Mr Elliott, as you would know, is a man of education and culture; Papa says he did extremely well at Cambridge and has a remarkable knowledge of literature and music.

I must confess I have only a nodding acquaintance with both, except that I read many of your books, when I stayed at Standish Park last Winter. Were it not for you, I may never have discovered the work of the Brontë sisters, especially Emily, whose Wuthering Heights *has fascinated me since. It is a most absorbing story.*

As for music, though I love to listen, I never did learn to read and play it. I do most sincerely regret that I did not. When we attended a soirée at the Fitzwilliams', we heard some exquisite music and Mr Elliott asked if I could play; I was both mortified and sad to admit that I had never found the time to learn seriously.

He has kindly invited us to attend a performance of Mr Handel's great oratorio The Messiah *next month and I am looking forward to it very much. Anna has promised to explain it to me before the performance. Papa says it is never too late to learn to appreciate fine music. I do hope he is right...*

Mrs Wilson, needless to say, was quite fascinated with the extraordinary interest her niece was revealing in matters cultural. She had always been too busy before. She kept her counsel, however, and said nothing, not wishing to embarrass Anne-Marie in any way. Her own observations had led her to believe that there was probably a good reason for it and she was prepared to wait, knowing that they were to see Mr Elliott after Easter. There would be an opportunity then, she thought, to observe if there had been any change in him.

⁓

Easter came and went without much fuss that year, except in the Parliament at Westminster. Colin Elliott had not realised that politics could become so tribalised and childish, with so little concern for the people that Members were elected to represent.

Disillusioned with his party, which was indulging in another round of bickering, he was ready for a change, when James Wilson, alerted by a letter from Colonel Fitzwilliam, had invited him to spend a few days at Standish Park. There, together with the charming Mrs Wilson and their talented children, he had spent an almost idyllic week, during which James Wilson used every persuasive argument to help him decide that his place was with the other side of politics.

It was during his stay that Mrs Wilson received a letter from her niece Anne-Marie, in which Mr Elliott figured rather prominently again. She gave a most interesting account of their attendance at the performance of Mr Handel's *Messiah*. When Emma mentioned this to Mr Elliott, in casual conversation after dinner, his report of her niece's appreciation of the great oratorio was quite remarkable.

"Indeed, it was a rare pleasure for me to see how totally she was absorbed in the music. Mrs Bingley, who is herself a teacher and a performer of great skill and sensitivity, agreed that she had rarely seen anyone so enchanted by it," he declared and there was no mistaking the enthusiasm in his voice, even as he added, "One must, of course, allow for the power of Mr Handel's music to captivate the listener."

Emma nodded her agreement, reminding him that King George himself had been one such. She was convinced that Mr Elliott was quite clearly captivated, and not just by the music of Mr Handel!

Having almost given Wilson his word that he would, at the very least, sit on the cross benches and work with the Reform Group, Elliott decided that he needed to see Anne-Marie and discover her mind on the subject before committing to it himself. He had entered a curious period in his life, in which her opinions seemed to carry a great deal of weight in his decisions, requiring him to find an occasion to discuss every significant matter with her. And so, in early May, he returned to Hertfordshire.

On reaching Netherfield House, he learned that the family had gone north to Pemberley for the wedding of Dr Frank Grantley and Amy Fitzwilliam and were expected to remain there for at least a fortnight.

"Are they all gone?" he asked. "Yes, sir, all, except Mrs Bradshaw, who volunteered to stay behind with Mrs Collins, who was poorly and unable to travel to the wedding," replied Mrs Perrot.

"And is Mrs Bradshaw staying at Longbourn then?" he asked, a little too eagerly to deceive Mrs Perrot, who noted the look of relief upon his face when she answered, "Yes, sir, she has been there above a week now."

The distance between Longbourn and Netherfield was a mere three miles. Colin Elliott's horses trotted along at a brisk pace, and he arrived just as the ladies were sitting down to afternoon tea. Anne-Marie and Charlotte were enjoying some excellent fruitcake made by Lucy Sutton, and the maid had just brought in the tea tray, when he walked, unannounced, into the room. They had lately dispensed with some of the old formalities at Longbourn.

Mr Elliott was greeted warmly by both ladies, who simultaneously invited him to join them and asked the maid to bring in another cup.

He thanked them and sat down at the table by the fire, noticing as he did, how very well Mrs Bradshaw looked, her usually pale cheeks glowing in the firelight, her dark eyes bright as she smiled and handed him his tea. Mrs Collins, knowing he was recently in Derbyshire, was eager to ask all about her daughter Rebecca Tate and her dear friends Mrs Darcy and Jane Bingley. Seeing how easy it was to please her with all the information she wished for, Colin Elliott was happy to oblige.

Anne-Marie warmed towards him, noting how much effort he put into detailing stories of people, places, and events for her grandmother, answering her questions without a trace of impatience. It confirmed her judgment that he was a genuinely kind man, who unlike many young men of today, appeared to be in no great hurry to finish his conversation. His attention to her grandmother who, she had to admit, could be quite pernickety at times, gained for him rather more than mere approval, almost her affection, she thought.

～✤～

In the last week or two, which she had spent mostly at Longbourn, Anne-Marie had found herself thinking more and more of Mr Elliott. Not only as she had first done, as a useful ally, whose position and influence she had appreciated in her quest to gain approval for the children's hospital, but to a far greater extent, as a valued friend. She had even caught herself, when alone, contemplating her own feelings for him. She could no longer deny, even to herself, that her attitude to him had changed since they had first met.

Anne-Marie was conscious of his interest in her, in everything she did and said. He solicited her opinion on several subjects, would pay special attention to her wishes, listened attentively to her views, and appeared to take them seriously. Frequently, he would discuss an issue and indicate later that he had changed his mind as a consequence of their discussion. Unfailingly, he was agreeable and appreciative of their time together. He told her so often, and Anne-Marie could not fail to respond to such appreciation.

There had been other occasions; when they had both dined at Pemberley, she had twice glanced across the table and found him looking at her with an expression that could only signify a keener interest. Though they had been separated by too many people to converse, she had been conscious of his eyes upon her.

Anne-Marie was not vain enough to believe he was in love with her and had certainly not, as yet, permitted herself to imagine what it might feel like to be in love with him. Not until reading Emily Brontë's stirring tale of passion and tragedy, *Wuthering Heights*, some months ago, had she thought seriously about being in love with any man. She had never pretended to be in love with Mr Bradshaw and, while she enjoyed his company very much and appreciated his friendliness towards her, she told herself she was definitely not in love with Mr Elliott either, certainly not in the manner of Heathcliff and Catherine. Their passion excited her, but she had never known its like.

Anne-Marie knew women could feel deeply and love passionately, too. She believed that it must feel very special and was not unaware of examples in their own circle. There had always been stories told of the great love affair of her Aunt Lizzie and Mr Darcy, of course, and seeing daily the love that sustained her father and Anna, and having experienced at Standish Park the strength and felicity of the Wilsons' marriage, she had wondered if such happiness would ever come her way. Following her experience with Mr Bradshaw, who had dispensed with the need for love in marriage, she'd had little hope.

She did not see Colin Elliott in that light, but could not deny, when she came to think about him, that she was probably finding more genuine pleasure in his company than that of any other man she had known.

His own behaviour had appeared to indicate that the feeling was mutual. So absorbed was she in her thoughts that she did not notice he had stood up when Mrs Collins's maid came to take her mistress out for her usual walk, and was in fact standing in front of her.

Startled, she apologised, thinking he was preparing to leave, but he was only offering her his arm, so they may follow Mrs Collins into the garden.

"Would you like to take a turn in the garden, too, Mrs Bradshaw?" he asked. "I noticed a very fine laurel as I drove into the park; it appears to be still in bloom, which is unusual at this time of year," he said and Anne-Marie, who had by now found her voice, explained,

"Oh yes indeed, the daphne; it was put in by my grandmother when she first came to Longbourn. She is very proud of it and tends it herself. Do you know much about gardens?" she asked, intrigued by his interest.

"I have always been interested in the art of landscaping and enhancing the natural environment. My mother was an enthusiast and the garden at Hoxton Park is mostly her work," he replied, adding, "But, I must confess, I found the grounds at Pemberley quite splendid. I have never seen any place as beautiful before."

Anne-Marie smiled. "I think that is a very understandable response. My father says he knows of no one who can resist the grace and beauty of Pemberley; it is the work of several generations, but my Aunt Lizzie tells me that Mr Darcy's mother, Lady Anne Darcy, was chiefly responsible for the present design of the park," she said, as she took his arm and went out into the garden, which was bathed in the light of the setting sun.

They talked as they walked, because he had plenty of news from Westminster and Standish Park, all of which she was very keen to hear. It was the last piece of information, he was keenest to impart.

"Mrs Bradshaw, I have been thinking very deeply these past few months about my future." His words alerted her to the possibility that he was on the verge of some declaration and she sought desperately to forestall it. She was not ready for this!

"Indeed? And is it to do with your work in the Parliament?" she asked quickly and was astonished to hear him say, "Yes it is and how very perceptive of you to have reached that conclusion. I had not thought it was that obvious. Have you been listening to my constant grumbling about the Tories?" he asked, "Did you realise I was growing increasingly impatient with them?"

So relieved was she that he had not brought her out into the garden to propose, she immediately confessed to having noticed just such a trend in his conversation of late and added, "I do believe my father has mentioned it, too, Mr Elliott. He thinks you are wasted on the Tories."

Colin Elliott laughed, appearing pleased at this information and declared firmly that he had been engaged all year in a process of self-examination to ascertain once and for all if he could credibly continue as a member of the Tory Party.

"As each day and each week passes, I see more of the pernicious influence of the forces of indifference and exploitation, which dominate the Tory Party, and no place for me amongst them," he said.

Anne-Marie responded with a question, "And in all this, has there been one issue or a particular matter of importance, which has brought you to this conclusion?"

He replied with a degree of earnestness that surprised her and left no doubt of his sincerity. "Indeed there has been just such an issue, Mrs Bradshaw," he said, "one on which I am confident of your support." Seeing her puzzled expression, he explained, "You will see that my disillusionment is not the consequence of some idle whim, when I tell you that the chief matter of contention has been the issue of the climbing boys. Are you familiar with the matter of the little chimney sweeps?" he asked.

When she agreed it was an important issue, he continued, "You will be aware, I am sure, that Lord Ashley, the Earl of Shaftesbury, has for years struggled in the Parliament to put a stop to this vile exploitation of young children. Each time he convinces the Commons, the bill gets sent to the Lords, where it is cut about and rendered useless. It seems impossible to make some of these men understand the need for a country that claims to be a leader of the civilised world to protect innocent children from abuse."

Anne-Marie moved towards a seat beside the fragrant bush of daphne. "I know you are not alone in your concern, Mr Elliott; my aunt, Mrs Wilson, has told me of Mr Wilson's determination to support Lord Ashley, even if he has to cross the floor to do so. It is a matter of conscience for him, she says."

Elliott was delighted to discover that she was herself well informed on the subject, but he added more fuel to the fire of her concern with a detailed report of the intransigent resistance to reform of those who saw no reason to legislate to protect the children. They had remained unmoved by the fact, that the practice of sending children as young as four or six years old up narrow chimneys to clean them, and even to extinguish fires, had resulted in several deaths by suffocation. "I could not believe that Shaftesbury's bill, which raised the age of employment to sixteen and which he had fought so hard to get passed, was being undermined by recalcitrant judges, magistrates, and even the police, whose job it is to uphold the law!"

Anne-Marie seemed stunned. "It seems incredible. Do they not have children of their own?" she asked.

"Oh they do, but their little poppets are safely ensconced in nurseries with nurses and governesses to care for them; a far cry from the little chimney sweeps, who are mostly got from among the orphans in the poor houses and apprenticed at four or six years old to master sweeps who will then abuse them in this dastardly way."

By this time, his companion was quite overcome and tears had begun to well in her eyes, as she considered the fate of the little "climbing boys." When he saw how she was affected, Colin Elliott stopped abruptly.

"My dear Mrs Bradshaw, I have upset you. I am sorry...I did not intend that you should be so grieved; please forgive me," but Anne-Marie shook her head, reassuring him.

"Please do not apologise, Mr Elliott; I have heard of the suffering of these children before, from my Aunt, but I was reminded again, by your most eloquent words, of the dreadful brutality of our society. I cannot believe that we, who insist upon the right of grown men and women to be free and safe from persecution, do not extend the same right to defenceless children . . ."

As her voice trailed off and she caught her breath, he proffered a large handkerchief, which she accepted and used gratefully. "Your uncle, Mr Wilson, has declared his intention to cross the floor to pass stronger laws, which Shaftesbury has promised to introduce, and I have given him my word that I shall do likewise," he said.

"Do you believe it will pass?" she asked and he sounded confident as he replied, "Once we have lobbied the Members and spoken both within and outside the Parliament, only men with hearts of stone will be able to oppose the measure."

"And should you help pass the bill, do you suppose you will be in trouble with your party?" she asked, quietly.

He looked at her as he spoke and she caught the glint of rebellion in his eyes as he said, "What if I am? Am I not to be permitted to have a conscience? I no longer regard it as my party, anyway. It sides consistently with the forces of reaction, the same men who are opposed to giving working people the vote, who voted against the Factory Act which afforded protection to women and children in workplaces, and would have us support the slave owners in the Southern United States! How can I remain part of such a group?"

Anne-Marie could not fail to hear the outrage in his voice, nor could she underestimate the courage required to take the next step.

"Are you determined then to sit on the cross benches," she asked and he nodded gravely as he answered, "I am and I shall support the Reformists whenever I see fit."

"Would the Tories not place obstacles in your way?" she asked, anxious that he may be putting in jeopardy a promising political career.

"They almost certainly will," he replied, "but I should feel I have at least done as my conscience demands, not just followed the dictates of the Tory Party."

Anne-Marie turned to him and said, in a voice which implied both admiration and sincerity, "You are to be congratulated on your stand, Mr Elliott; there are not too many who will do as you have done. My uncle, Mr Wilson, is one, of course, but he has less to lose, being almost at the end of his term, while you are just at the beginning of your career and may find your path blocked by those who resent your intervention. But you have made an honourable and completely justifiable choice; the opposite position is, in my opinion, indefensible."

Delighted by her response, he moved on impulse to take her hand as it lay in her lap and kissed it, saying, "God bless you, Mrs Bradshaw, I thank you. I am overjoyed to hear you say that. It is of no use to me to continue as a Member of Parliament, or even of a government, unless I was achieving some improvement to the lives of those who have no voice in Parliament."

Anne-Marie, surprised and touched as much by his gesture as his words, gave him praise in full measure. "I believe you can be proud of what you are doing, Mr Elliott; the voiceless have in you a most eloquent spokesman," she said and then rose, as if to indicate that it was probably time to return to the house. Her grandmother had gone indoors a while ago.

As they walked, he asked lightly, almost in jest, "And if I were to seek a change, in which direction do you suppose I might move? Would you care to hazard a guess?"

She smiled, relieved that their conversation had proceeded so well, despite her earlier anxiety about his intentions. "Well, Papa says you are almost a Liberal and certainly a Reformist," she said, in an almost playful fashion, smiling as she spoke.

If by speaking lightly, she had meant to discourage him, her smile had the very opposite effect. So delighted was Elliott that he almost broke his resolution and declared his feelings there and then. But, he restrained himself and held back, determined to wait until he had spoken with her father. This he felt he could not do until he had first resolved the question of his political loyalties. Colin Elliott did not want Mr Bingley, a dedicated Reformist, to think he was courting his political approval in order to more easily obtain permission to marry his daughter.

Consequently, their conversation proceeded upon a more relaxed and light-hearted path, as they discussed matters of mutual interest, of which they were discovering more each time they met. After they returned to the house, Mrs Collins thanked Mr Elliott and then invited him to dine with them on the following day—Sunday, an invitation that was accepted with obvious pleasure.

That night, Anne-Marie was surprised and not a little annoyed with herself, when she found that she was experiencing a distinct feeling of disappointment, on account of the fact that in spite of walking together and talking quite intimately for over half an hour, Mr Elliott had not said anything that she might construe as a hint of his feelings for her.

While she had been very relieved that he had not made a declaration of love, she had wondered whether he might have shown some warmth of feeling towards her.

She was sure she had detected some degree of affection and concern in his manner and attitude, yet he had said nothing. She was not, of course, to know that Colin Elliott had struggled valiantly to restrain his ardour and suppress his desire to speak of his affection for her. He had determined not to do so, until he had her father's permission.

For her part, Anne-Marie was becoming increasingly less certain of her own ability to comprehend her feelings for him. She had, for instance, felt a great surge of pleasure when he had complimented her upon looking so well; he was seeing her after a month or more and he professed that he had never seen her looking better. He had asked, with a smile, whether it was the very fine spell of Spring weather that had suited her so well, or was there perhaps another reason?

Anne-Marie surprised and suddenly rather shy, had mumbled something about the freshness of the air and thanked him for his compliment, but she could not hide her obvious pleasure. For a singularly beautiful young woman, she was unaccustomed to flattery and admiration, never having sought it and, indeed, for many years having actively shunned the company of those who indulged in it. That Mr Elliott's thoughts, charmingly expressed, had pleased her was in itself quite extraordinary.

Then, there was the matter of his decision to leave the Tory Party and perhaps support the Reform Group. His espousal of principles of compassion and fairness had delighted her and she had made no attempt to conceal her joy, even as she urged him to consider the matter carefully, in his own interest. She knew too, that her father, Mr Wilson, and her Aunt Emma would be overjoyed, a fact that increased her own pleasure immensely. That he had chosen to confide in her, declaring his intention to abandon the party his family had supported for generations, had made her feel some pride and satisfaction, knowing that not many men would choose to speak of such weighty matters to a woman, often not even if that woman were a wife.

Lastly, there was the moment he was preparing to leave, having accepted Mrs Collins's invitation to dinner on the Sunday with such alacrity, that Anne-Marie had to believe that he was looking forward to being in her company again. As they parted, having stood a while at the entrance, while he thanked her and recounted his pleasure in her company, he had kissed her hand and said how much he would be looking forward to seeing her again.

Anne-Marie had had her hand kissed by other men, yet she had felt, on this occasion, such a sensation of excitement like never before. For a moment, she had wished, foolishly, that he would not let go of her hand, but would hold it as they stood together by the door. Foolishly, because that would have been quite uncharacteristic of him and unlikely too for she knew him to be a proper, gentlemanly sort of man, who strove always to do the right thing.

And yet she, who had always regarded herself as proper, even prim, had wished, almost hoped, that he would forget decorum, abandon his gentlemanly behaviour, and hold her hand in his, just long enough for her to experience again the tumult of feelings that had swept over her like an unexpected wave, leaving her breathless.

Nothing in her marriage to Mr Bradshaw had aroused in her anything remotely resembling the bliss of first love. It was unlikely, therefore, that she would instantly recognise the emotion. But Anne-Marie was very much aware that she had felt the first stirrings of something completely new in her young life.

At Pemberley, meanwhile, the families had gathered for the wedding of two favourite children.

Amy Fitzwilliam, whose early life had been blighted by the sudden death of a beloved brother and cousin and had suffered with her parents the almost intolerable grief that had swamped them, had retained a sweetness of disposition and a genuine goodness that endeared her to everyone. Intelligent and pretty, she was a favourite with Elizabeth Darcy, who had once hoped to see her wed her own son Julian, but it was not to be.

Unlike Lady Catherine de Bourgh, Mrs Darcy had not felt the need to trumpet her personal preference to all and sundry, which was why very few people except those in her closest circle ever knew of her disappointment when young Julian Darcy had married Josie Tate.

Now, Amy was marrying their nephew, Frank Grantley, and there was no one happier than Elizabeth, for Frank, like his mother Georgiana, had a most amiable disposition with a natural dignity and intelligence, which she greatly admired.

Watching them as they walked out into the sunshine from the chapel at Pemberley, Elizabeth felt for Amy, who had borne her own unhappiness without rancour and, turning to her sister Jane, said, "I am so pleased for Amy; she deserves a good husband and I know Frank is the best of men and loves her dearly."

Jane smiled that subtle little smile that her sister knew so well; it was usually the prelude to a perceptive observation and this time was no exception.

"Lizzie, I know how you wished for Julian to marry her. Do you still feel the same? Are you not able to convince yourself that Josie would make him a good wife?" she asked, as if she had read her mind.

Elizabeth was startled into a laugh that masked her embarrassment.

"Why Jane, you sly thing, you must have caught me off my guard during the wedding. I confess I did shed a tear or two; Amy is a particular favourite of mine and, while I am sure Josie makes Julian very happy, she does not appear to have any interest in Pemberley or the community of which we are a part. With Julian so engrossed in his scientific studies, unless his wife takes a role in the work we do here, they will lose touch with the people and that would be a tragedy for them and for Pemberley. Darcy, like his father and his grandfather before him, has his heart here. If both Julian and his wife lose interest in the estate and its people, they will be no better than absentee landlords," she said.

Jane, shocked by the sentiments she had expressed, reacted immediately, "Lizzie, you cannot be serious!"

"Indeed, I am, Jane. I know it sounds ridiculous, but over the years since they were wed, I have made every effort to engage young Josie in the community life at Pemberley and have failed every time. Whether it is in the music festival or the harvest fair, the library, the hospital, or the school, none of these seems to hold her interest for long. I know she has written one or two pieces for the *Matlock Review*, but that is usually the limit of her interest in the community. Now Amy, on the other hand, works at the library, helps at the school and, since they've been engaged, she and Frank have both worked hard with the children's choir," she said, and her sister knew from the tone of her voice, that Elizabeth's concern was no small matter.

Yet, Jane tried to sound hopeful.

"Do you not think, Lizzie, that they are still rather young, I mean Julian and Josie, and they may well become more involved as they grow older? Perhaps, when they have had a few more children, they will understand the importance of the role that they will play at Pemberley, one day in the future."

Her sister shrugged her shoulders, "You may be right, Jane, I hope with all my heart that you are, because if it were not so, it will break Darcy's heart. Pemberley is the very centre of his life as it is of mine. I'm afraid it is never going to be the same with Julian and Josie. They both have far more absorbing interests outside of this community."

A sudden burst of music from the marquee on the lawn heralded the arrival of the wedded couple; it was time for Elizabeth to join her husband and greet the assembled guests.

Dr Grantley, the father of the groom, a distinguished dean of the church, a theologian of repute, and Mr Darcy's lifelong friend, had married the couple and now stood together with his wife Georgiana, the Darcys, and the Fitzwilliams at the entrance to Pemberley House, welcoming their guests to the wedding banquet.

Watching Georgiana as she graciously accepted the congratulations on behalf of her family, Elizabeth could not help remembering the rather gauche, shy girl she had first met at Lambton all those years ago. Today, and for many years since her marriage to Francis Grantley, she had been transformed into a handsome, self-composed woman with a wide range of interests and an exceptional musical talent. Elizabeth looked at Darcy, who was also watching his sister. Plainly, he was very proud of her.

It was a memorable wedding. Members of the family and friends had come from many parts of England and across the channel.

The Continis had travelled from Italy, whither they had fled from the English Winter. The Wilsons were there from Kent and the Bingleys from Ashford Park and Hertfordshire, although Jonathan and Anna had apologised for the absence of Anne-Marie, who had forgone the pleasure in order to keep her grandmother, Mrs Collins, company. Elizabeth was sorry her friend Charlotte was not well enough to travel.

Mr Gardiner was also too weak to attend and seeing her beloved aunt, alone without her husband, saddened Elizabeth. It was known among their closest friends, that he had not very long to live, despite the best efforts of his doctors. His heart had been weakened considerably.

When all their guests had been accommodated, plied with food and drink, of which there was an ample sufficiency, Elizabeth and Jane sought out Anna Bingley, to ask for news of Anne-Marie. She accompanied them to a quiet sitting room, where they were joined by their niece Emma Wilson, who had come in from the terrace.

"I've left James and Jonathan arguing furiously with Colonel Fitzwilliam about the Prime Minister's failure to understand the mood of the people," she said, explaining that, "James believes there is a danger of unrest to come, because there is so much discontent among the artisans and other working folk who pay their tithes and taxes but are denied the vote. He blames Lord Palmerston for procrastinating about the reforms which were promised to the people at the last election." Anna Bingley agreed. "Jonathan says the country is heartily sick of the Prime Minister's foreign adventures; he says Lord Russell has promised Parliamentary reform and is committed to it, but Palmerston is not. Jonathan believes the Whigs will lose the next election on this account."

Even Elizabeth and Jane, who were not usually interested enough to become involved in matters of politics, knew from their own husbands and from Caroline Fitzwilliam that there was much dissatisfaction with the government of Lord Palmerston.

"I understand," said Elizabeth, "that it is not only the matter of the franchise. Fitzwilliam has told Darcy that in the factory towns and outlying areas, many of the people are suffering considerable privation, with poor wages and terrible working conditions, no proper schools or hospitals for their children. They resent the expenditure of money on the Prime Minister's forays into Europe and elsewhere."

The women, who were all involved in charity work, were keenly aware of the increasing demand for help from destitute families and even the working poor, and talked a while of the problems they faced. It was, however, a domestic matter, far closer to home that engaged their attention, when Emma Wilson spoke in unusually grave tones. She had with her a letter, which she took from her reticule.

"I have thought long and hard about this and I feel I need your advice on this matter, which has troubled me for many days now, since I received this letter from Emily," she said.

"Emily?" said Jane and Lizzie together. Emily Courtney was their cousin and dear friend. They were all aware that she was very close to Emma, too, with whom she corresponded regularly, but that any letter from her should cause Emma concern seemed most unusual.

"Do you mean Mrs Courtney?" asked Anna.

"I do," Emma replied and continued, "and my anxiety flows from what she reveals about her daughter Eliza Harwood and Anne-Marie."

"Eliza Harwood? What could she have to do with Anne-Marie?" asked Anna, bewildered by this turn of events, adding, "Why, I doubt they have spoken since Mr Bradshaw's funeral!"

"That is precisely the point of Emily's letter," said Emma, and she proceeded to read out a few paragraphs.

"After a few items of family news, she writes . . ."

Dearest Emma,

Eliza, whose child is due within a month, fears that Anne-Marie, whom she once counted as her closest friend, will never see her again and her friendship is therefore lost to her forever. She is quite heartbroken believing she was responsible for persuading Anne-Marie to accept Mr Bradshaw's offer of marriage and now fears that she is blamed for all the unhappiness that followed.

Eliza judges herself very harshly in this matter and, while I have been with her this last fortnight since Mr Harwood is from home on business, I believe she has become seriously depressed. Indeed I am writing this because I honestly believe that she is so deeply melancholic, she may not survive this birth, if it turns out to be a very difficult one. Emma, I know Anne-Marie was very attached to Eliza and she loved her dearly. If there is anything you can do to help reconcile these two young women, you will be truly blessed.

From all I have heard on this subject, I do not believe that either Eliza or Anne-Marie knew very much about Mr Bradshaw, except that he was by reputation a good man and was a conscientious chaplain to the wounded men at the military hospital. Eliza has told me that Mr Harwood was a close friend of Mr Bradshaw and they served together in the war, yet even he claimed to know very little about him.

I do not doubt he was a good man, but Emma, I know as you do, that goodness alone does not suffice, where there is no love between partners in a marriage. Yet, where there is love, deeply felt, no suffering is too much to endure. When I lost my dear husband, Paul Antoine, and returned to live at Pemberley with Lizzie and Mr Darcy, who had themselves recently lost their son William, I was to learn from their example that only the strongest and most heartfelt emotions would endure through such an ordeal. It was the strength of their love that helped them survive and enabled them to help me cope with my own sorrow. This is why I understand that Anne-Marie may be bitter about her marriage to Mr Bradshaw. If there was no love between them, it would have been a mere charade and for a young woman like Anne-Marie, a most abhorrent one.

If she does still blame Eliza, it may help her to know that Eliza is sincerely sorry and wishes every day that she had never encouraged it. She claims it was only because she longed to see Anne-Marie securely settled, especially since the wretched business of her mother's death. She now realises that it was wrong to have persuaded her to marry Bradshaw, for no one can be happy in a marriage without genuine affection.

My dear Emma, I should not have troubled you, were I not certain of my daughter's remorse and her fervent wish to be reconciled with her friend.

If you can help in any way, I shall be most grateful.

At least two of the women listening had felt the need to reach for their handkerchiefs as she read, and when she concluded, even Anna, who had had very little knowledge of Eliza Harwood and whose loyalty and concern were entirely for Anne-Marie, had begun to feel some sympathy for the unfortunate young woman whose pain was so exposed.

Jane was the first to respond. "Poor dear Emily," she said, "it is a heart-rending letter. She must be very unhappy."

"Poor Eliza Harwood, it must be desolating enough to lose a dear friend but then to have to suffer such humiliation...to expose one's misery so...I wonder at her being able to do it," said Lizzie, whose own sense of dignity would not have let her do likewise.

Emma agreed. "Indeed, Lizzie, Emily entreats us to find a means of reconciling them, but however worthy that might be, I wonder how it might be achieved?"

Then turning to Anna, she asked, "What is your opinion, Anna? She has been with you at Netherfield a while; do you believe Anne-Marie may be ready to see Eliza Harwood?"

Anna's reluctance to give them an answer without speaking with Anne-Marie was entirely understandable. She was aware, even though they had never discussed the matter, that Anne-Marie was in a delicate state of transformation, moving slowly and with some trepidation, like a butterfly from the dark security of a chrysalis into the glare of sunlight. Anna had watched her as she flexed her wings and had begun to hope that a new, happier future may await her.

Recently, indeed in the last few weeks, she had seen signs of a deeper friendship developing between Anne-Marie and Colin Elliott. Anna had spoken of it to her husband, who, though he had not been very encouraging at first, had confessed that he would give anything to see his daughter happy again.

Yet, Anna did not feel she could reveal any of this to the others in her company; it belonged solely to Anne-Marie. If and when something came of it, they would be told by her father.

Her answer to Emma's question was, therefore, of necessity, ambivalent.

"I do not believe I can say for certain if she is sufficiently recovered from what was, for her, a totally demoralising experience. No woman can accept easily the fact that a man will marry her and expect all the privileges of a husband, without even a pretence of love. For a very young girl, as she was, this must have been a demeaning experience. Indeed, I know she felt used and suffered great humiliation, which added to her misery, even when it was all over. Anne-Marie, as you all know, is a deeply sincere person; she is very ashamed at what took place between herself and Mr Bradshaw, with her consent. Her refusal to see Eliza stems not from any blame she attaches to her, but from her own sense of personal mortification at ever having agreed to the marriage on such terms." Anna's voice shook with emotion.

Emma Wilson understood her reservations and both Lizzie and Jane admired her honesty and loyalty. Emma then asked, "Do you think, if I were to speak with her and let her see Emily's letter, it would help?"

"It may do, Anne-Marie is kind and soft-hearted. She will be moved, I am sure, by Emily's words. But I cannot be sure if she will want to proceed to meeting with Eliza," Anna replied.

"It can be very daunting to confront a person one has avoided for several months, especially if that person may have been responsible for causing some particular sorrow," said Elizabeth. "Even if Anne-Marie does not blame Eliza Harwood, there is no doubt that when she had to endure what must have been an intolerable marriage, Anne-Marie must have felt resentful of Eliza, who was quite content in hers."

Jane who had listened, often wiping tears from her eyes, spoke at last. "Poor Anne-Marie, I know she told no one, but Teresa told me how after Bradshaw's death, she would find her sister weeping, sobbing as though her heart was broken, and when young Tess, not realising the truth that lay behind her tears, tried to comfort her, she would burst out in a rage and beat her head against her pillow, weeping even more and crying out that she was not sorry, indeed she was glad he was dead! Tessie was very shocked," said Jane.

Emma knew of this, too. She had often held Anne-Marie in her arms during the weeks she had spent at Standish Park.

"No one knew then that it was her sense of shame and guilt that was destroying her mind. She was feeling guilty that she was glad Bradshaw was dead and she was free of a desolate marriage. Yet, in all those days, she never once blamed Eliza," she said.

"What is to be done?" asked Jane, whose gentle heart felt compassion for all the women involved and longed to help them. Before anyone could respond, there was the sound of laughter and cheering for the young couple, who had emerged from the house and were mingling with the guests in the rose garden. The ladies rose immediately and went downstairs to join them and help send the newlyweds off on their honeymoon.

After the guests had departed and the family had retired to their rooms for the night, Elizabeth told her husband of Emily's letter. Darcy was quite astonished to learn that the two young women had not written or spoken to one another since Bradshaw's death. "Do you mean, Lizzie, that Eliza Harwood has made no effort at all to communicate with her once dear friend in all this time?" he asked. Elizabeth replied that she believed this to be the case.

"Lizzie, my dear, I sometimes wonder at the timidity of our young people. Why would you, if you cared sufficiently about a friendship, let it degenerate and die, making no effort at all to keep it alive? Had you been placed in such a situation, would you not have written, even if you risked rejection by doing so?" he asked.

Elizabeth thought only for a moment, before acknowledging that she would have. "Would you?" she asked, then in an instant knew the answer, even before he spoke.

"Of course, and I did, as you well know, my love, when after my ill-judged and unpardonably presumptuous encounter with you at Hunsford parsonage, I contemplated the prospect of losing you altogether as a result of my arrogance. I was so utterly devastated by what I had brought upon myself that I resolved to write at once and explain my position. I did so, even though I risked your anger and rejection, because I had to; I could not let you continue to think ill of me.

"I had to try to correct the impression created by Wickham's lies and my own false pride and hope for your charity and understanding, if not your love."

Even after all these years, Elizabeth was moved by his recollection of the agony they had both endured as a result of Wickham's duplicity and Darcy's ill-fated, impetuous proposal. Yet, she replied lightly, "And indeed you did right, for you won both my forgiveness and my love," she said and when he smiled, remembering, she added, "But, I confess, my dear, I was never in my life more discomposed as I was by your letter. I doubted everything—Wickham's story, my own judgment—but not the truth of your words."

He was clearly pleased to hear her say what he had heard many times before. It had been a significant moment in their lives, when their future happiness had rested upon the soundness of their judgment.

"Do you then believe that Eliza Harwood should write to Anne-Marie?" she asked. Darcy, his countenance much softened, put his arms around her; they had sustained one another over many years with a love whose strength had helped overcome intolerable sorrow.

"Indeed I do, my dear; let Emily tell her daughter that a dear friend, like a dear wife, is worth some humility. She should write to her and be open with her as I was with you," he replied. Elizabeth promised to convey his advice.

It was ironic indeed that on this day, filled with the bright celebration of the marriage of Amy and Frank Grantley, they had ended with some sobering thoughts. It was not the first time Elizabeth and Darcy, whose love story had proceeded from an aggravating and hurtful beginning to a passionately happy conclusion, had been called upon to provide advice to younger members of the family. It was unlikely to be the last.

Elsewhere in the house, the Bingleys had retired to their rooms. Jane had decided not to trouble her husband with Emma's story, resolving to wait until they were back at Ashford Park. Anna was too troubled to keep it to herself. No sooner had they reached their bedroom than she had to tell her husband all about it.

Jonathan was at first sceptical about the prospect of reconciliation between Anne-Marie and Eliza Harwood.

"I cannot honestly say it is the right time to broach the subject of reconciliation between them," he said, "Anne-Marie has only recently recovered her spirits and is at present engrossed with the children's hospital; I would be most reluctant to distract her with reminders of a less than happy period in her past."

Anna could see that he was being protective of his daughter. "At least now, at Netherfield," he continued, "she knows she is needed and loved by us all; she has a place in the community, which she has earned for herself, not dependent upon a husband's status or position. Indeed, my dear Anna, I feel it would be a reckless thing to do, to rake up the past at this time."

"You do not agree with Emma then, that reconciliation would be in both their interests?" Anna asked quietly.

Jonathan was very firm in his response, "I certainly do, but only if it could be achieved without recriminations and disruption of her life."

"Would you object to letting Emma speak with her?"

"Of course not. Emma will have Anne-Marie's interest at heart as we have. But do you not see, my dearest, if we were to urge this reconciliation upon her, it may undo all the good work that has gone before."

Anna knew that there was no one better able to persuade him than his sister. "Why not let Emma tell her of Eliza's wish for reconciliation? Anne-Marie's own response would then reveal how she felt. You know Emma will be gentle and discreet. She will neither do nor say anything that will upset Anne-Marie. She loves her dearly."

Jonathan was moved by her appeal. "Your kindness does you credit, my love," he said. "Let me think on it a while. After all, we do not leave for Netherfield until the end of the week; there will be time enough, and I promise I will think seriously about it." Seeing her rather disappointed expression, he added, "I understand Emily's concern. Eliza is her daughter and, of course, she wants to ease her conscience, but I am responsible for Anne-Marie. She has already endured far too much pain and grievous humiliation for one so young. I cannot lightly agree to subject her to more strain, unless I am convinced she will not be further wounded by the exercise."

Anna knew how deeply he cared for his daughter and refrained from pressing the case any further, content that whatever decision he came to, Jonathan would do the right thing.

Meanwhile, Emma Wilson wrote to her cousin Emily Courtney.

My dearest Emily,

Your letter, which reached me the day before we left for Derbyshire to attend the wedding of Frank Grantley and Amy, has remained in my thoughts ever since. I cannot help feeling for you and Eliza a profound sympathy as I contemplate your unhappy situation. For Eliza, especially at this time, it is the very worst thing to suffer depression, and you must try hard to wean her from this most destructive mood. For yourself, think at least of the joy of awaiting and helping with the arrival of your grandchild and try to comfort her as best you can. However, remember you are not alone, for we have all suffered at one time or another, from Aunt Lizzie and Mr Darcy to you and I and Jonathan, everyone has known some profound sorrow, and we are all aware of your pain.

If Eliza suffers now because she fears she has lost the trust of her friend, she must be patient and wait for the right time, when the pain may be healed.

It is not a simple matter of urging reconciliation upon them, Emily; unless there is a genuine desire in both their hearts, it will be no more than a charade and no real good will come of it.

So do comfort Eliza and tell her I shall try my hardest; when we meet and at a time of her own choosing, Anne-Marie may agree to meet with Eliza and end the unhappy situation that exists between them. I do know this, that Anne-Marie, no matter what she feels, has never blamed Eliza for her unhappiness. She is far harsher upon herself and is filled with remorse that she ever accepted Mr Bradshaw's proposal.

Meanwhile, dearest Emily, you have our love and our prayers, God bless you,

Emma Wilson.

P.S. The wedding was most impressive, the service conducted by Dr Grantley very moving indeed, and Amy looked lovely, of course. They have gone first to London and later to Paris and Italy.

The letter was to be despatched on the morrow, and Emma hoped with all her heart that a way may be found to accomplish what Emily and she wished to do.

END OF PART TWO

THE LADIES OF LONGBOURN

Part Three

C OLIN ELLIOTT ARRIVED TO DINE at Longbourn on the Sunday, looking and feeling as if he had undergone something of a change. Usually a soberly dressed gentleman, he was attired rather less formally and appeared very much at ease. He had brought the ladies a basket of fruit and flowers from Hoxton Park, which was guaranteed to please them all.

While Mrs Collins and Harriet were engaged in admiring the excellent fruit, he contrived to pick out a rose in a soft peach tone, which exactly matched the colour of Anne-Marie's gown, ensuring, when he presented it to her, that she was seated at a little distance from the others, so as not to embarrass her with his attentions.

Anne-Marie was very touched by the gesture. When she left the room for a moment and returned with the rose pinned to her bodice, he was so obviously gratified and expressed his appreciation so openly, that she felt rather shy and wondered if she had been too bold. She was conscious, too, of his admiring glances throughout the evening and though flattering, they threw her into some confusion, and despite the undeniable pleasure she took from the experience, she almost wished it were not so.

Dinner was usually served at eight, and by half past seven, Anne-Marie was becoming restless. She had seated herself beside a long window looking out across the park and could see the drive as it came off the lane and turned in through the gates. She was alert and waited anxiously to hear the sound of the pony trap, which had been despatched to fetch Mrs Sutton, whom she had persuaded that morning to join them at dinner.

The feelings she had experienced the previous evening, on parting from Colin Elliott, had surprised her, and while she would not deny it had been a most agreeable encounter, in the bright light of the following day, she had felt somewhat apprehensive of becoming too deeply and too quickly involved in an association with him, despite the pleasure it brought.

If only Anna were here, she thought, she might have been able to confide in her, to seek some counsel; but Anna was miles and miles away in Derbyshire.

Seeing Lucy Sutton in church that morning, Anne-Marie had approached her and invited her to dine with them, hoping by increasing the number of guests to draw some attention away from herself. She knew Mr Elliott was a perfectly courteous gentleman and was unlikely to single her out for attention when there were other ladies around. She thought she had the ideal solution to her problem.

At first, Lucy Sutton had been reluctant to accept her invitation, especially at such short notice. She was nervous about leaving her two girls on their own, pointing out that since it was Sunday, her maid would be visiting her parents.

Anne-Marie had a suggestion. She would send one of the maids from Longbourn to sit with the children so Mrs Sutton could come to dinner. "Rosie will come to you, and you can come to us. I shall send the pony trap for you. When you return after dinner, Rosie will return to Longbourn. See, it is all quite simple," she had said, cheerfully, and Mrs Sutton, who rarely went out and was pleased to be invited, had accepted, albeit still with some show of reluctance. She was, however, not ungrateful.

"Thank you very much, Mrs Bradshaw; you are very kind. I do hope you will not think me fussy and stupid; it's just that I am very particular about leaving the children. They are unaccustomed to being on their own out here, unlike in town, where the neighbours are just a step away. You do understand?" she said, and Anne-Marie was most solicitous.

"Of course I do, Mrs Sutton, and I do appreciate your concern, but I am sure they will be happy with Rosie. She is a good, cheerful girl and will keep them occupied," she had said, reassuring her.

Sunday, at Pemberley, had been very quiet. A fine Spring morning had given way to a golden afternoon, unusually warm for the time of year, yet lightened by a gentle breeze from the rugged peaks to the North. The visitors who stayed overnight had been mainly family, some of whom left soon after breakfast. Others, like the Bingleys, rose late and breakfasted at leisure, planning to spend the day in the most undemanding of activities, expending a minimum of energy. The ladies had much to talk about after the wedding, while Darcy's steward had arranged a day's fishing for the gentlemen.

Caroline and Colonel Fitzwilliam had returned to their farm at Matlock and found waiting for them two letters, which were from different sources, but interestingly linked by reference to the same persons. Opening hers at once, eager to read it since she had recognised the perfectly rounded hand of her cousin Anne-Marie Bradshaw, Caroline saw it had been written only a day or two ago.

It was not particularly long, but was full of information.

Anne-Marie wrote . . .

My dear cousin Caroline, I had hoped to see you at Amy's wedding, but unfortunately, my dear grandmother has been unwell for a while now and cannot travel. I decided therefore, to stay with her at Longbourn while the rest of the family travelled to Derbyshire. I expect to stay until she is fully recovered.

The main reason for my letter, apart from wanting to know how you are and beg you to tell me all about the wedding, is to acquaint you with the news that I am to be in charge of the children's hospital at Bell's Field, when it is completed. This has come about as a result of a request from our local MP, Mr Colin Elliott, whom you met on his visit to Derbyshire, to Papa for permission to put my name up to the board.

While I do have a good deal of experience in nursing adults and am quite familiar with the workings of a military hospital, such as the one at Harwood Park, I would greatly appreciate your help in making a success of this one.

I am aware that you and Cousin Emily have both been involved with the hospital at Littleford and I wondered if you would have some advice

for me. Mr Elliott is very confident that I can do this well and so is Papa,
but like most men, they are not always aware of the hundreds of little
things that go to make a success of such a venture. If you are able to help in
any way, I should consider it a great favour.

I used to have a book written by Miss Nightingale herself shortly after
her return from the Crimea, when she reorganised the services in many of
our hospitals, but I fear I have left it behind at Harwood Park.

The letter concluded with a few remarks about the weather and a reference
to a visit to Longbourn by Mr Elliott, bringing with him a basket of early cher-
ries for Mrs Collins.

My grandmother was most appreciative indeed, of his thoughtful gift,

she wrote.

Caroline, smiling somewhat smugly, read it through a second time before
running upstairs to her husband, who had already read his letter, which lay
beside him. When she had told him of the detail in Anne-Marie's letter,
expressing great satisfaction at the news it had brought, he picked up James
Wilson's letter to him and handed it to her.

"It would seem that Mr Colin Elliott is creating a great deal of interest in
this family, of late. James Wilson's letter is all about him. He does not even
mention the draft Reform Bill, which he assured me was in preparation.

"This letter was written several days ago and yet he never mentioned it at
the wedding, wanting no doubt to keep the whole thing confidential until
Elliott decides which way he will leap."

Caroline had recognised James Wilson's fine copperplate handwriting and,
taking the letter in hand, began to read aloud . . .

My dear Fitzwilliam,

Since receiving your message, I have seen young Colin Elliott, the new
Tory MP.

I must thank you for your timely advice in alerting me to his situa-
tion. I find him very amenable and quite impatient to break with the old
guard in his party. Indeed, I had to restrain his enthusiasm somewhat, else

he might have bounded off to advise the party whip or some such official that he was about to cross the floor and ended up in a great deal of bother.

He is full of ideas and eager to demonstrate his concern for our cause, especially in matters of Parliamentary and electoral reform, and he has major concerns about education and health policy. He has hinted that he will support certain pieces of social legislation, even if it means crossing the floor. What is even better, as you know we have a vacancy in one of the new constituencies in South London, since Viscount —— has moved to the Lords; well, Elliott has as good as promised to support our candidate. We expect to have Jonathan Bingley here at the opening of the campaign, which should make for a very good show. Bingley has lost none of his eloquence in the years since he left the Commons.

Speaking of Bingley reminds me, my dear wife has asked that I pass on some very confidential information to your Caroline. She claims it may not be discreet to be heard discussing it, when they meet at the wedding. She has gathered that Mr Elliott has been a frequent visitor to Netherfield Park in recent months. She is quite certain that the attraction is more personal than political, since he seems to show a distinct partiality for the company of our niece, Mrs Bradshaw.

I have no more information on this matter, but I wonder, Fitzwilliam, whether Mr Elliott's Reformist zeal flows from the heart rather than the head. Perhaps I am being unfair. In his discussion with me on several issues, he seemed totally genuine and a very levelheaded fellow.

However, it is as well to remember that the most levelheaded of men may be overthrown by a woman, and Anne-Marie Bradshaw is a particularly beautiful woman.

Caroline Fitzwilliam gave a little shriek of delight and returning to sit beside her husband, declared, "There you are, Fitzy; I knew I was right about Colin Elliott and Anne-Marie. When they were up here at the Tates and later dined with us, he could not take his eyes off her. He followed her everywhere and, whenever the opportunity arose, would sit beside her and engage her in conversation. I must admit she appeared somewhat less interested than he was at the time, but I am certain she will not resist him for long. He is not only the handsomest parliamentarian in the House, since Jonathan Bingley left the Commons, but is also intelligent and well spoken; if he may be persuaded to leave the Tories and join the Reform Group, she could not ask for more, could she?"

Her enthusiasm for this romantic political scenario could not be dampened by her husband, who tried to point out that the biggest hurdle would probably be the wishes of the lady herself. "I have heard that she is unlikely to want to marry again; Bradshaw was not, I am told, the best of husbands and Anne-Marie has shown no inclination to try again," he warned, but his wife was not to be so easily discouraged.

"Oh, that is such a lot of nonsense, Fitzy. Everything will depend on Mr Elliott. It is he who must convince her. If Anne-Marie believes he loves her truly, she will marry him, mark my words."

Fitzwilliam knew her too well to try to argue with her, when she was so determined. Their own marriage had come about despite the quite considerable reservations of her parents, who had been concerned at the disparity in their ages. Yet Caroline, not yet sixteen and deeply in love, had won them over and made him a very happy man. Age had made little difference to her romantic outlook.

At Longbourn, well before Mr Elliott and Mrs Collins's nephew, Simon Lucas, arrived, Anne-Marie had despatched the young chambermaid Rosie in the pony trap, with strict instructions to keep the two Sutton children entertained, but not overly noisy or excited.

"John will call for you when he brings Mrs Sutton back from Longbourn," she reminded Rosie, as they drove away.

Anne-Marie had been keen to have Mrs Sutton attend. She was a quiet woman, with a good deal of common sense and, because of her own marital problems, one who could be relied upon not to gossip. She was, however, not always punctual and this evening, she was late.

The gentlemen arrived and were seated in the parlour and there was still no sign of her. Anne-Marie was anxious until at last, the crunch of wheels on the drive drew her to the window. Looking out, she saw the vehicle draw up at the front door and, when Lucy Sutton alighted, she sighed with relief.

Thereafter, the dinner party went exactly as planned, although Anne-Marie thought from time to time that Mrs Collins was looking askance at her nephew, Simon Lucas, who was paying a lot of attention to Lucy Sutton.

Mr Elliott seemed happy enough, having seated himself beside Anne-Marie at dinner and afterwards, except when he rose to help the other ladies with their chairs. Courteous to all the women in the room, but especially attentive to her and her grandmother, he was indeed an exemplary guest.

At dinner, Simon Lucas, who knew Mr Elliott only slightly but was in some degree of awe, owing to his being a member of the House of Commons, asked about India and why he had left it. He had his own theories, too. "Was it the terrible heat and flies?" he asked, adding that he once knew a chap who had gone mad with the heat and the insects.

Colin Elliott laughed and declared that there were many such stories about, but for the most part, they ought not be taken too seriously.

"The fellows who told them had often been drunk or under the influence of ganja, a most potent local weed, which the native Indians could inhale with only a somewhat soporific effect, but when Englishmen indulged, it would drive them crazy," he explained. "It was only a temporary condition, though, and there was not much harm done, except to a man's dignity, of course. The Indians had no respect for you at all, if you had made a fool of yourself," he said.

Simon Lucas pressed on, however, determined to know what particular horrors of the subcontinent had driven Mr Elliott back to England.

"Was it the natives during the Mutiny, then?" he asked and Anne-Marie knew he was moving onto sensitive ground. She was aware that Mr Elliott did not like to dwell upon the Mutiny and the dreadful deeds that were done by both sides of the conflict. She feared Mr Lucas might upset their guest with his questions. But she need not have worried, for Mr Elliott dealt with the matter very calmly, explaining that he had not been in India at all at the time of the Mutiny.

"No, Mr Lucas, to be quite honest, my objection was not to the Indian people, who mostly went about their own business. It was the poor administration and corrupt practices of the East India Company that decided me," and as Simon Lucas opened his mouth in astonishment, he went on, "Their treatment of their employees, both native Indians and British was quite appalling, and their exploitative practices were abhorrent to me. They had made no effort to understand local feelings until the Mutiny erupted and, when it did, they could do no more than call for the troops, and the rest is history," he said and, after this stirring little speech, it appeared that Simon Lucas had no more questions for a while.

The meal proceeded thereafter without further interruptions as everyone around the table appreciated the excellent food, thanked Mrs Collins, and sent their compliments to the cook.

This gave Colin Elliott an opportunity to address himself to a matter of crucial importance. With the advantage of an intimate dinner party, he had hoped that he would be able to discover whether a decision he had taken was the right one. Throughout the evening, Anne-Marie had been attentive and charming, quite the perfect hostess, in fact. When they moved to the drawing room, where a good fire provided a welcoming retreat, she was joined by Harriet Greene, who assisted with dispensing tea and coffee.

Mr Elliott noticed, with some satisfaction, that Anne-Marie had been exceedingly pleasant and even occasionally partial towards him. She had little to say to Simon Lucas, a fairly rough and ready sort of man; so it was really not surprising that she seemed to enjoy Mr Elliott's company and turned to him for conversation. They had discovered, over the past weeks, many subjects that engaged their minds and appeared to require constant discussion between them.

After they had taken coffee, Lucy Sutton, an accomplished performer at the pianoforte, was easily persuaded to entertain them with some music. While she was at the instrument, Colin Elliott, who had been seated beside Anne-Marie, leaned over to ask in a low voice if he might have an opportunity to speak with her in private. Anne-Marie would wonder later why she had not been more surprised by his request. Perhaps, she thought, she should have been and yet, it was almost as if she had been expecting his approach. Having signalled her willingness, she waited for the conclusion of one piece of music, rose quietly, and moved to cross the hall and enter the library, where Mr Elliott followed her.

The room had been Mr Bennet's favoured retreat; later Mary Bennet had made it her own with her piano in the alcove by the window. Since her death, Jonathan had had the piano moved out into the drawing room and refurbished the library, returning it to its original purpose. It was now an elegant, comfortable room, fitted out with some fine pieces of Regency furniture and holding many of the family's favourite books.

Colin Elliott had not been in the library at Longbourn before, and this occasion afforded him a chance to make conversation, commenting upon the charming room and the fine view of the garden from its windows. Anne-Marie was happy to accommodate him and sought to point out some items of interest that had belonged to Mr Bennet. But, as if aware that they may not have much time, Mr Elliott having begged her pardon for what might appear to be an impertinence, revealed that he had written her father a letter.

"Mrs Bradshaw, I have for some time been contemplating the manner in which I should set about this matter. Each time I have reached the same conclusion, that I must approach your father first and obtain his permission to speak with you."

Anne-Marie smiled. "Mr Elliott, why do you need my father's permission to speak with me? I have long achieved my majority and have no need at all of Papa's permission to speak with you or anyone else," she said, gently poking fun at him for his gravity and decorum.

It took him a few seconds to realise that he was being teased and, responding in like manner, he smiled and said, "Pardon me, my dear Mrs Bradshaw, by that, I did not in any way mean to imply that you were still under your father's guardianship. I am well aware that you are quite an independent woman and would not dream of suggesting otherwise. I was however, anxious to respect Mr Bingley's position, too, not wanting to give any offence."

Anne-Marie bowed slightly to indicate she had accepted his reason and then smiled to show she had not expected to be taken too seriously.

"And are you going to tell me the subject of your letter to Papa?" she asked in a quiet voice, "or must I wait patiently until he returns next week from Derbyshire?"

"No, indeed, that was my reason for asking to see you privately. I had hoped that this evening we would be the only members of Mrs Collins's party and had prepared myself to ask you to take a turn in the garden with me before dinner," he said, a little tentatively, and smiled before continuing. "Unhappily this was not to be, and I do not mean in any way to slight Mrs Sutton, but her presence here has introduced an obstacle I had not anticipated. I had, therefore, to take the liberty of requesting a private moment with you. I sincerely hope you will forgive my presumption," he said, and her smile allowed him to believe that he was already forgiven.

Anne-Marie was seated upon a chaise longue to the left of the fireplace in front of which he had been standing. Now, he approached closer, regarding her with an expression of some intensity, and began to speak.

"Dear Mrs Bradshaw," he said, "would you consider...may I have your permission..." he stopped, and then, suddenly, abandoning formality altogether, spoke in a headlong rush, quite uncharacteristic of his usual moderate manner.

"My dear Anne-Marie, I have discovered over the last few months that I love you deeply and cannot continue without knowing your true feelings. I have, therefore, written to your father to acquaint him with my intentions and seek his permission to ask you to marry me."

This time, she was surprised, for while she had had a very good idea that his thoughts were moving in this direction, she had not anticipated the fervour with which he had spoken nor how swiftly he had decided to approach her and declare his feelings.

Clearly he was aware of this, too, and said, "I do not expect you to give me an immediate answer, but I do want you to know and understand how ardently I love and respect you and how proud and happy you would make me, if you consented to be my wife. Should you so honour me, dearest Anne-Marie, I promise I would do everything, absolutely everything in my power, to ensure your happiness."

Anne-Marie was more than surprised; she was overwhelmed, not by the content but by the manner of his declaration. In an instant it had taken her mind back to the stilted little speech with which Mr Bradshaw had proposed marriage, offering her his hand and the security of his position and income. She recalled also, with some embarrassment, her own awkward response. Here in complete contrast was an unpretentious statement, an avowal of love, a promise not just of material security, but of all the happiness with which he had the power to endow her. It was spoken, too, with so much feeling, that she was genuinely moved.

Anne-Marie had never considered herself romantic, but she had longed to be told she was loved and found Colin Elliott's simple, passionate declaration irresistible. It reached and touched her heart, which responded directly to his words. Thanking him most sincerely, she asked if she might have some time to reply, a request that was immediately agreed to. She promised that it would not be very long before he would have his answer. She spoke gently, unwilling to offend or hurt his feelings.

"Pray do not misunderstand me, Mr Elliott. It is not because I do not believe you love me, nor do I doubt my own feelings; but only because I need some little time to discover if what we feel is as strong and as enduring as it needs to be for us to marry and be assured of happiness."

As she spoke, he had approached and was standing close beside her; his countenance reflecting the delight he felt at her words. When she stood up, he took her hands in his and, once more, Anne-Marie felt the stirring of emotions she had first experienced only the night before. She stood without moving away, letting him hold her. If they had been permitted a few more quiet moments together, it is entirely possible that he would have drawn her close and kissed her, as she had expected and in her heart, wanted him to do; but at that very moment, such a commotion erupted in the hall, as to cause them to rush out of the library in confusion and alarm.

They had heard a strange cry, followed by the sound of sobbing; in the hall were a couple of servants and Harriet Greene holding Rosie, who looking muddied and bedraggled, wept copiously. Stunned at her appearance and the fact she was here at all, Anne-Marie called out, "Rosie, Rosie, what on earth has happened? Why are you here?"

Simon Lucas and Mrs Sutton had both appeared in the hall, and the latter gave a sharp cry of horror as she rushed at the maid. "Rosie, what are you doing here? Where are my children?" she cried, in a voice filled with panic.

Anne-Marie felt fear grip her heart as never before. Rosie was incoherent; she stammered and stuttered and it was fully five agonising minutes before she could finally blurt out the terrible truth. The two Sutton children, Marigold and Lucinda, had been kidnapped, taken from their home by two men, one of whom was their own father.

"Oh, my God," said Anne-Marie softly, in a voice heard only by Colin Elliot who was at her side, "what have I done?"

Concerned, he tried to discover the cause of her distress, but she was immediately involved in helping Lucy Sutton, who had fainted into the arms of Harriet Greene. Poor Mrs Collins, left alone in the drawing room, had struggled out into the hall to be confronted with what seemed like mayhem. By the time Anne-Marie had explained to her grandmother that Mrs Sutton's daughters had been abducted by their father, Harriet Greene and the kitchen maid had carried Lucy Sutton to a couch in the parlour and were reviving her with smelling salts.

Rosie was still stumbling through her fearful tale of the two men who had forced their way into the house and, while she screamed and ranted, picked up the two girls and got back in their closed carriage. They had driven away, leaving her to walk a mile or more across the meadows to Longbourn to raise the alarm.

When Anne-Marie came out into the hall again, Colin Elliott approached her, but before he could offer to help, she spoke, her voice filled with the urgency of the moment. "Mr Elliott, I fear we have a most dreadful situation on our hands and with my father away, I have no one to ask but you, I am sorry . . ."

But he interrupted her, "Mrs Bradshaw, Anne-Marie, pray do not apologise. I am happy I was here, available to be of use. I shall gladly do whatever I can to help. However, we must first ascertain all the facts of the case. Your maid Rosie is still very shaken, but we must speak with her in private and discover the details of the incident."

He followed her into the parlour where Rosie sat, still sobbing, so ashamed she would not even look them in the face. "Oh, ma'am," she wailed as Anne-Marie approached, "I am so sorry, ma'am; I should have looked after the little ones better. I am sorry, I should not have opened the door when they knocked. I am sorry, ma'am; I have let you down, whatever will my mother say?"

It was Harriet Greene who took her in hand and comforted her with a cup of hot, sweet tea. When she had done with weeping, Rosie sat down and slowly, haltingly told the tale, while poor Lucy Sutton, who had recently been revived, broke down and wept again, as she learned how her children had been taken. They listened as Rosie told it . . .

Shortly before eight, after the children had finished their supper, there had been a knock on the door. When she called out, "Who is it?" a muffled reply had caused her to open it a mere crack to check who was calling. She had been pushed aside and two men had entered.

"They were both very big, ma'am, and I would not have known them at all, except that Miss Marigold and her sister called out to their father, "Papa, Papa," and ran to him. They seemed happy to see him, ma'am."

There was more weeping from Mrs Sutton and Harriet had to go to her again, as Rosie told how the children's father had picked them up in his arms and, when his companion in crime had tried to bully Rosie, he had shouted at him to "leave her alone and come along."

"Oh, ma'am, I am sorry I couldn't do nothing to stop them; I was so frightened. Mr Sutton, he took the children out and when I went to the door, he slammed it in my face. Then he came back in with a bag and ordered me to go upstairs and pack some of their clothes and things. I was so afraid, ma'am, I did not know what to do. I had never been upstairs before. It took time to find their things and he was shouting for me to bring 'em down quick, or he'd come up and teach me a lesson…oh, ma'am," and then she began to weep all over again.

Mrs Sutton, who had succeeded in sitting up, asked tearfully, "Did the children say anything at all?"

Rosie shook her head, "No, ma'am, I think they were struck dumb, like I was. Then as they were leaving I asked, where were they going and would they be back, and Mr Sutton just laughed. Oh, ma'am, I am so sorry . . ."

Rosie wept. She was feeling ashamed that she had not been able to stop them taking the girls away.

Anne-Marie put her arms around her. "Hush, Rosie, how could you have stopped them? It was not your fault."

"It was my fault," wailed Mrs Sutton from across the room. "I know I should never have left them alone to come here tonight. None of this would have happened if I had been home with them."

At this everyone fell silent and the only sound was that of Rosie's sobs. It was useless to contest the logic of her lament; Lucy Sutton was too deep in her grief to notice.

Amidst all this it was Anne-Marie who felt worst of all, knowing it was she who had invited Lucy Sutton to dinner and arranged to send Rosie to keep the children company.

"It's my fault; I am to blame," she whispered again to Colin Elliott, but when she had explained, he denied it firmly.

"You cannot take the blame, my dear Mrs Bradshaw, you could not have known what was about to happen. I believe they had it all planned and would have struck no matter who was at home with the children. Indeed, had Mrs Sutton been with them, what could she have done against two strong men? Had she tried to protect her children, it is more than likely, she would have been attacked and been injured herself. So please do not blame yourself, it will do no good," he said, standing up and preparing as if to leave.

Before he did, he spoke more generally, "This is a very serious matter; Mr Sutton has no right to abduct his daughters from their mother's custody. I shall have to inform the police and then I shall pay a visit to my friend Tillyard at the offices of the *Herald*."

"The police?" cried Mrs Sutton in some alarm. "That will make Mr Sutton very angry." There was abject fear in her voice.

Colin Elliott argued that her children may never be restored to her unless their abduction was reported to the police.

As he put on his coat and scarf, he said, "I shall have to hurry if I am to catch Tillyard." Promising to return as soon as he had some news for them, he urged them not to lose hope.

"Remember Sutton is their father; he will not harm the children. We shall do everything we can to find them," he said, and as Anne-Marie accompanied him into the hall, he kissed her hand, touched her cheek with great tenderness, and begged her once more not to blame herself for the calamity.

Then, he went out into the darkness and his waiting carriage.

Standing alone in the hall, Anne-Marie was moved by the calmness with which Elliott had taken the responsibility for dealing with the crisis. Not only had he comforted her and assured her of his willingness to help, he had also shown concern for Mrs Sutton and poor Rosie, who had both been desolated by what had occurred. It had been his idea to call on his friend Tillyard, whose investigative resources were much greater than any private citizen might command. She hoped with all her heart that they would be able to trace Mr Sutton and restore Lucy Sutton's children to her, else she knew she would never escape the censure of their mother's eyes.

"Oh, if only I had not persuaded her…if I had had the confidence to accept whatever that evening would bring, we would not now be facing possible disaster," she thought, knowing that nothing anyone could say would change that perception of her own guilt.

❧

None of the women at Longbourn could sleep that night, as they waited for Mr Elliott to return. Only he could bring them any news, good or bad. There was nothing they could do to improve the situation. Mrs Collins had been so upset by the news, she had begun to feel quite ill and when Harriet suggested that she may wish to retire to her room, she accepted gratefully and went upstairs.

Harriet returned later to keep Anne-Marie company and Rosie sat with them, still weeping intermittently, then drying her eyes and blowing her nose to relate some other detail she had recalled.

The women grasped at every bit of information and Harriet, methodical as usual, wrote it all down in a notebook. Rosie had been shivering from the cold when she arrived at Longbourn, having walked a mile or more across meadows in the dark. Yet at first, so afraid was she of being blamed for the children's disappearance, she had forgotten why she had been so cold.

Mercifully, no one, not even Mrs Sutton, who was most aggrieved, had had the heart to blame Rosie.

Suddenly, she remembered and spoke up, "I remember now," she said, "that's why I was so cold—he took my shawl to wrap around the little one. I was standing in the doorway calling out to them, asking where they were going, and I said, "Mind you don't go letting them catch cold. And the man, not Mr Sutton, the other one, he came back and ripped my shawl off me and put it around her. I didn't mind; poor little thing, I could see she was cold."

Harriet immediately asked for details of the shawl and wrote it all down. "The police will need to know about the shawl; it may help identify the children, if they had stopped at an inn for the night," she said.

Anne-Marie was very grateful for Harriet's calm, sensible presence. Poor Mrs Sutton began to weep again and Anne-Marie felt her head starting to throb; if only her father and Anna were home, she thought. Yet she knew they were not expected back until the end of the week, and even if she could send a message to Pemberley, they were two days' journey from Netherfield.

It was in the small hours of the morning they heard a vehicle returning, the horses racing along the road before turning into the drive leading to the house. Anne-Marie and Harriet were at the door as the carriage drew up and Mr Elliott alighted and was admitted to the hall.

As Anne-Marie went to him, Mrs Sutton ran towards them, pleading for news of her children. Colin Elliott did not present a picture of great optimism, but he did have some good news for them. He had been to the police and they had revealed that they had been warned of the presence in Meryton of a notorious villain.

"He comes from London and had been seen in the area for a week or more, with another man, whose identity was a mystery to the police. Obviously it was Mr Sutton; so they now have names and descriptions for both kidnappers and they are going to be looking for them," he said.

"Where will they look?" asked Anne-Marie.

"All possible places between Meryton and London," he replied.

"What about Mr Tillyard? Was he able to help?" she asked. Colin Elliott looked very pleased.

"Indeed he was, though I must confess I was unsure at first, but, as usual, Tillyard has come up trumps. He was very eager to help track down the men, because his reporters had received information about one of them. It would seem he is quite a blackguard, responsible for extortion and assaults all over the country. There is a reward out for his capture and two of Tillyard's men have been on his track, hoping to get some of the money themselves. When I explained what had happened with Mrs Sutton's children, Tillyard sent for them at once and ordered them to find the men. What they need is some information about Mr Sutton, his full name, last known address, a likeness if you have one, and anything else that may help identify him and the children."

Turning to Mrs Sutton, he spoke gently, conscious of her grief. "Mrs Sutton, may I make a suggestion? If you would take my carriage and go over to your house, perhaps with one of the ladies, and get some of this information together, I could take it to Tillyard in the morning."

Bravely, Lucy Sutton agreed to go, with Harriet Greene, who had volunteered to accompany her. "Thank you. Mr Elliott, I do hope you can find my little girls," she said, as they made ready to leave.

"I shall be trying my best, Mrs Sutton, and you may rest assured the police and Tillyard's men will all be working very hard," he said.

❧

While they were away, Anne-Marie stayed with Mr Elliott in the parlour, and in spite of the lateness of the hour, they set to work to compose a letter to her father, which Colin Elliott promised to take with him and despatch by express on the morrow. Sitting beside her as she wrote, he advised that she should tell Mr Bingley only sufficient detail to convince him of the seriousness of the situation and urge him to return.

"We do not wish to alarm or upset them, seeing they have a long journey before them," he said. "Besides, there is very little they can do until they get here." Then hesitating a moment, he added, "But wait, maybe there is a better way. Ask your father to go direct to his house in London; I will travel to town tomorrow myself and meet him there. Clearly Sutton and his partner plan to return to London with the children; they are unlikely to linger around these parts. It will be far better to concentrate our efforts in town," he said and she agreed.

She was sure he was right. She was immensely grateful for his help; his presence was a comfort to her in many ways. She had not the time to contemplate how it had happened but, in the midst of catastrophe, Anne-Marie had discovered love. Without her knowing it, it seemed to have crept up on her and settled quietly in her heart. Later she would recall that whenever she thought of it, she was filled with delight, even in the midst of fearful anxiety and dread. She had, as yet, told no one of her feelings and longed to tell the man who had inspired them, but decided that this was not the time to do so.

Mrs Sutton and Harriet Greene returned with various items that might help identify the children and their father, including a very clear likeness of Sutton in a sketch of the family by an itinerant artist at Brighton. That put Anne-Marie in mind of a drawing Anna had made of the two girls, which stood on the mantelpiece in her grandmother's room. It was a more recent likeness of the children and Mr Elliott assured them that it would all be very useful together with Harriet's notes. His hopeful demeanour went some way to allay their fears.

When he was ready to leave, Anne-Marie went to the door with him. She was, by now, quite exhausted and seeing her standing in the hall, apprehensive and vulnerable, he embraced her with a warmth that quite literally took her breath away. "I give you my word, Anne-Marie, they will be found. You must believe that," he said, and holding her close reminded her that he loved her dearly.

She was too overcome with confusion to say very much, except to thank him and beg him to take great care on his journey to London. Promising to send her word of any new developments, he went, leaving her struggling to understand an entirely new and quite bewildering array of feelings, such as she had never experienced before.

Harriet Greene came down to find Anne-Marie sitting alone at the foot of the stairs, "Mrs Bradshaw, you'll catch your death of cold," she said and urged her to get some sleep. Anne-Marie smiled and agreed that it was time for bed, but as for being cold, why, she thought, she had never felt warmer in her life. There was, however, no reason at all to tell Harriet, she decided as she went upstairs, clasping her happiness to her heart.

When Colin Elliott set off for London very early on the morrow, he had already arranged to send a man on ahead with an urgent letter from Tillyard to his two reporters, containing more information about their quarry.

He intended also to despatch the express letter to Jonathan Bingley at Pemberley and another to a friend at the Home Office, calling in a favour. Since the names of the two men involved in the abduction were known to him, he hoped to discover, by covert means if necessary, whether either of them had been before the police magistrates recently.

When he broke journey at an inn in the village of Barnet for refreshment, he thought seriously of writing to Anne-Marie, to tell her again that she must not worry, but realised it was more important to get to London as soon as possible. But, he could not bring himself to depart, without sending word to her; she had filled his thoughts as he travelled. He could still see her standing in the hall, pale and worried, though never weakening for a moment. In the end he sent her a private note, which was for her eyes alone, despatched his letters and went on his way.

⁓❦⁓

At Pemberley, meanwhile, the weather had deteriorated and an expedition to the Peaks had been cancelled. It seemed they would have to entertain themselves indoors, which in a house full of beautiful treasures and a well-stocked library presented no problem to most members of the party. Anna whose love of Art overwhelmed her every other interest, had decided to spend the morning in the long gallery, making sketches of some of Mr Darcy's fine works of art, while her husband and his host were engrossed in a game of chess. They were being observed by Bingley, who found it all too difficult and kept looking out at the leaden skies, hoping the sun would come out again, so he could ride out to the horse stud at Rushmore Farm. He had noticed a fine young colt during a visit last Summer and was keen to renew the acquaintance. Perhaps, he told Darcy and Jonathan, he might indulge in some speculation and buy it as a racing prospect.

"Bingley," said his friend censoriously, "you absolutely astonish me. Here you are, with little or no experience in trading in horseflesh, wanting to throw your money away on an untried colt. You are truly incorrigible."

Jonathan sagely advised his father to leave the colt at Rushmore at least until next Spring. "He'd be two years old then and you would have a much better notion of his worth," he said.

Elizabeth and Jane had retreated upstairs to their favourite room, over-looking the park, which was clothed in the fresh green of Spring. Engaged in the lightest of pastimes, they talked of their children, their grandchildren, and cousins. Jane, blessed with three beautiful daughters all content and happy, was looking forward to being a grandmother again when Sophie was brought to bed in the Autumn. Elizabeth admitted to being a little envious; her daughter-in-law Josie did not appear to want more children. "She claims she has her hands full with young Anthony," she said, in a voice in which Jane detected some deep disappointment.

"I cannot believe that. Lizzie; are you sure she is quite well?" asked Jane. "It may be that she is feeling poorly and cannot cope with another child, just yet. She and Julian are both very young; surely, there is no hurry."

"No, indeed, there is not. You are quite right," Elizabeth agreed as she moved to the window. "Besides, I am told that Julian is always very busy and often late coming home from his interminable scientific seminars and college meetings. I do have some concerns, however, about which I wish to talk with…" but Jane was never to discover what those concerns were, for Elizabeth had stopped speaking and peering out of the window, reached for her glasses.

"Now who could that be?" she asked and, as Jane came to join her at the window, "It's a man on…I recognise neither the man nor the horse…I wonder who he is…he's just coming over the bridge and up towards the house. Jane, look there's Bingley going to meet him. Does he know him?"

As they watched, they saw Bingley walk towards the entrance to meet the rider who dismounted and appeared to ask a question.

"Who can it be and what does he want?" said Elizabeth and, as she was about to suggest going downstairs, they saw Jonathan come out. Clearly he had seen the exchange between his father and the stranger and, whereas they had heard nothing, Jonathan was probably better informed, she thought.

They saw the man hand Jonathan a letter, which he opened as he ran up the steps, and when his mother and aunt came downstairs, they saw him standing in the hall reading it, with Mr Bingley beside him. "Good God!" they heard him exclaim, as he turned over the page, "I cannot believe this!" He had turned quite pale and both Jane and Elizabeth went to him at once.

"Jonathan, what is it, what has happened?" they asked almost together, fearful of the news he had received. "Who was that man and what news has he brought?"

Jonathan Bingley had always been a very steady character, calm and unruffled by crises, domestic or political. But there was no mistaking his demeanour on this occasion. He looked stunned. When he spoke, his voice was calm but his words struck fear into the hearts of the two women.

"Mrs Sutton's children have been kidnapped."

"What? When? By whom?" These questions were all flung at him simultaneously and Darcy, hearing the commotion in the hall, walked out to find them in turmoil, trying to make sense of the letter.

It took Jonathan some time to read again Anne-Marie's letter, to which Colin Elliott had attached a note written from Barnet, apprising him of the latest news and looking forward to their meeting in London.

"It looks as if the children's father is involved. He has made threats before, but I did not believe he would be so rash as to carry them out while they were housed on the estate," Jonathan explained, reading to the end of Anne-Marie's letter.

"Poor Anne-Marie, she must be at her wit's end," said Elizabeth.

"I must go directly to London," said Jonathan as he put the letters away.

Mr Darcy, realising the gravity of the situation, offered immediately to put a carriage and driver at his disposal. "It will mean Anna and the children can return to Hertfordshire immediately, where I have no doubt Anne-Marie would welcome her back," he said. "It must be dreadful for her, being on her own at such a time as this."

Jonathan agreed and went at once to find his wife. When she heard the news and had read Anne-Marie's letter, as well as the note from Colin Elliott, Anna Bingley was so shocked she had to sit down for several minutes before she felt sufficiently recovered to ask some pertinent questions about the condition of Anne-Marie and Mrs Sutton. Jonathan, armed only with the scant information in his daughter's letter, could not give her all the answers, but did provide sufficient facts to convince her she needed to return to Netherfield at once.

"Anne-Marie must be seriously worried and very short of comfort. If you and the children go directly to Hertfordshire, you may be able to afford her some consolation and support. I think, my dear, we must make arrangements to leave at once," he urged.

Anna agreed, "Oh yes, certainly, but what will you do in London? Do you intend to stay long at Grosvenor Street?"

"In view of Elliott's note, he is best placed to inform me of the situation. I shall probably stay in town for a few days, at least until the culprits are apprehended and the girls found," he said. "From what I have gathered, it seems Elliott has already done a great deal. As the local MP, he has called in the police, given them the evidence, and obtained the assistance of Tillyard at the *Herald*. I am amazed at how much he has accomplished in so short a time. He is now on his way to London."

Jonathan was genuinely grateful to Colin Elliott.

"It must have been a great relief to Anne-Marie that he was present," said Anna, as she gave instructions for the children to be made ready for the journey. She was sorry to miss the picnic to Dovedale, planned for a sunnier day, but she felt deeply for Anne-Marie and Mrs Sutton. Her husband was right; they had to return to Hertfordshire right away.

When they came downstairs, the carriage was waiting for them. They left with much sadness and promises that they would write. Having lovingly embraced his wife and children and settled them into Darcy's carriage, Jonathan bade farewell to his parents and Mr and Mrs Darcy, before setting off for London in his own vehicle.

Once clear of the Pemberley Estate, Jonathan took out a second letter he had received from Colin Elliott. It had reached him two days ago, but not having had time to fully consider its contents, he had said nothing of it to his wife. Now, he read it through once more; Mr Elliott specifically addressed him as Anne-Marie's father and asked permission to propose marriage to his daughter.

Jonathan was surprised by the request and the directness of Elliott's approach. Though he had, on a few occasions, noticed an apparent closeness between them and the ease with which they drew together in company, he had attributed this to their mutual interest in the children's hospital and other community matters. While he would not have been surprised that any man should show an interest in Anne-Marie, whose simplicity of dress and aversion to adornment could not hide her beauty, he was far less certain that she would encourage such an interest.

Yet Colin Elliott, being a man of some intelligence and dignity, would surely be unlikely to apply to him for permission to court her, unless he had received some encouragement. No doubt, he thought, it was a matter they would speak of when they met in London.

❧

Anne-Marie had begun to keep a diary while staying with the Wilsons at Standish Park following Mr Bradshaw's death. A rather solitary and private young person, she had found it useful to record her thoughts and feelings at what was a very trying and painful time in her life. Emma Wilson had encouraged it, explaining how through her own years of unhappiness, she had found some consolation in being able to express her feelings in private and urging Anne-Marie to use it to relieve herself of all the fears and anger which had accumulated over a year and a half of an unhappy, debilitating marriage. This she had done to good effect and, while she did not write every day, she had continued the practice after her return to Netherfield, even though there was now no reason to feel hurt or angry.

Indeed, the recent entries were less pessimistic, though no less introspective and thoughtful, expressing her hopes for the future. Much of it concerned her work with the hospital at Bell's Field, including an expression of her pleasure at being asked by Mr Elliott to manage the hospital when it was complete. She had been honoured to have him put her name up to the board and delighted when they agreed.

Her father and Anna had encouraged her to accept.

In the early hours of the following morning, unable to remain in bed, having been awake well before dawn, Anne-Marie rose and by candlelight, wrote in her diary . . .

How shall I recount this day just gone? I have not the words to describe fully the strange conjunction of events that have taken place, nor am I able easily to express my own feelings about them.

All I know is that I cannot recall another such day, not since Mama's death in the accident on the road at Maidenhead. I remember then suffering shock, guilt, and profound grief for my family and especially for Papa. Today, it has been the same, trying to comprehend how this awful thing has come about.

Poor Lucy Sutton, I know she must blame me, why would she not? I blame myself. Had I not persuaded her to come to dinner, leaving her children with Rosie for the evening, had I not been so selfish, thinking only of my own feelings, this dreadful abduction may never have taken place. Mr Elliott does not agree with me; he believes that Sutton would have done exactly the same, possibly attacking and injuring Lucy if she had stood in his way. I do not know what to think; I only know I feel deeply sorry for Lucy and pray that her girls may be found and restored to her soon else I shall never forgive myself.

Mr Elliott, God bless him, has gone to London to try to discover where the children may have been taken and lodged. As a Member of Parliament, he has contacts at the Home Office and in the Police, which he means to use to obtain more information. He has been exceedingly kind to all of us and, even as I write this, I am compelled to stop and review my thoughts about him, when I think what his intervention in our lives may mean.

Before tonight, Mr Elliott's association with me seemed to be concerned chiefly with the accomplishment of certain aims, which we both shared. While I cannot deny that I had become aware of a degree of interest and even partiality on his part, I did not anticipate the depth of feeling revealed in his words and actions tonight, when he, in the most ardent and yet gentlemanly way, declared his love and asked me to marry him.

I have not yet found the right words to tell him of my own feelings, but in this more intimate encounter, I have no doubt that he would have been able to draw some conclusions from my general demeanour. What could I do? I had once or twice thought it may come to this, but had not expected it would come so soon.

I felt no embarrassment or inhibitions... no sense of impropriety, even though I had permitted him a degree of closeness, which I had not thought I could ever have countenanced with any man.

What was it that let me, without any sense of outrage or immodesty, admit and if I may be totally honest, even welcome such intimacy? I do not know. I cannot explain it, except in terms of my own feelings, which I have yet to fully comprehend. Nor, in the light of his tender but totally honourable conduct throughout, have I any regrets that I did. Indeed, were I to be absolutely honest, I shall have to confess here, that never before in my life and certainly not in all the long months of marriage to Mr Bradshaw, have my innermost feelings been so deeply engaged, nor my thoughts so occupied by one person.

He has said he loves me and I believe him. I think I love him, too, but to accept his offer and marry him, I shall need to discover whether the feelings, that overwhelmed me last night, are only a passing passion or the awakening of true love, without which, marriage would be a cruel charade, and that is a game in which I want no part.

Anne-Marie locked away her diary and, noting there was now more light in the sky, completed her toilet, dressed, and went downstairs. She found herself alone at breakfast; Harriet had finished hers much earlier and Mrs Collins and Lucy Sutton had not yet left their rooms.

While she felt no hunger, Anne-Marie forced herself to eat. Her training as a nurse had taught her that an empty stomach was no preparation for a difficult day ahead. She was halfway through her tea, when the doorbell summoned the maid, who returned with a note for her. Recognising the handwriting—it was Mr Elliott's—Anne-Marie left the table and went into the parlour, which was empty. There, standing by the open window, she read it. Despatched from Barnet, where he had stopped for a meal, Colin Elliott had written two brief paragraphs, the first expressing with great tenderness his sadness at having to leave her so soon after he had first spoken of his love for her, with so little time to demonstrate the depth of his feelings. The second, begging her to take good care of herself and place her trust in him, promising he would not rest until Mrs Sutton's children were found and their kidnappers brought to book.

When he returned, he hoped she would have an answer for him, one that would increase his present happiness a hundredfold. It concluded with a most affectionate salutation, which caused her eyes to fill with tears and she had to rush upstairs to her room, where, having shut the door, she lay on her bed and read again the first love letter she had ever received.

Her face buried in her pillow, her eyes closed, Anne-Marie surrendered to the delight that filled her, as she contemplated the source of her joy. She knew she admired him and approved of his principles, his compassion and strength. She esteemed his sincere, upright character and enjoyed his sense of humour. Now, if he could, by a simple declaration of love for her, arouse such feelings as these, she thought, she must surely be in love with Colin Elliott. There could be no other explanation for this tumult of emotions. She wondered if her father had received Mr Elliott's letter and thought how he may respond. She hoped he would think as she did. She prayed he would not be set against them.

❧

Mr Elliott, on arriving in London, had gone directly to his apartment and immediately despatched a message to his friend at the Home Office. While awaiting a reply, he was visited by Thomson, one of Tillyard's men, bringing news that the fugitives had been seen at an inn quite close to London; there had, however, been only the two men, one recognisably Mr Sutton, with his ruddy face and beard, but no children with them.

"I think, Mr Elliott, sir, we're on to them, but I would not want them to find out until we have discovered the children," he said and Elliott was very puzzled.

"Where on earth could they be hiding them?" he asked. "It cannot be easy to hide two little girls, if you are travelling; they get hungry and need to be fed, for a start . . ."

"Indeed, sir," said Thomson, "and when they're tired and sleepy, they get crotchety, too. You couldn't keep them quiet. We are still making discreet inquiries, sir," he said and having accepted a quick drink, left assuring Elliott that they would soon find them. "We've got better sources than the police," he volunteered and Elliott hoped he was right. He was deeply concerned that the children had not been sighted, knowing how much it would mean to Anne-Marie and Mrs Sutton.

A note from Masters, his friend at the Home Office, arrived about an hour later, arranging a meeting at his club. Colin Elliott changed and dressed for dinner and went out to meet him. When Masters arrived, Elliott laid his cards on the table, giving him all the available facts including the latest from Thomson. He asked for information on both Sutton and his partner in crime; anything that would help track them down. Shocked by the story of the abduction of the children, Masters agreed to make inquiries and find out whatever he could.

"If you cannot find me at my apartment, try Mr Bingley's house at Grosvenor Street," Colin Elliott said.

Masters was curious. "Does Bingley have an interest in this matter?" he asked.

Colin Elliott was immediately alert; he had no right to give any information concerning Mr Bingley. "No, not directly, but his daughter does," he said. "Mrs Sutton, who is separated from her husband, is a friend of hers. Indeed, she was dining with Mrs Bradshaw at Longbourn when the children were abducted," he explained and urged Masters to be assiduous and discreet in his quest for information.

"If we are to restore these children to their mother, who is quite distracted with grief at the moment, we need to know where they have lodged them," he declared as they went to dinner.

Meanwhile, Jonathan Bingley had reached London. Weary and sore from travelling with very little time to rest, yet knowing there was no time to lose, he sent a servant with a note round to Colin Elliott's apartment, inviting him over to Grosvenor Street. It was late, but Mr Elliott, who had only just got in, went at once. The two men greeted each other cordially and, despite the fact that they both knew there were important matters to be settled between them, they took time to enquire after each other's health and exchange the usual pleasantries.

Over the time they had known one another, Jonathan had come to respect and value Elliott as a principled and hardworking MP and a fellow Reformist, despite his Tory antecedents. They shared many concerns and hopes for their nation's future and the improvement of their community. He had been particularly impressed with the expeditious way in which Colin Elliott had handled the negotiations with the Council and now, in this present peril, he appeared to have done everything that needed to be done with commendable speed. Jonathan was quick to commend him.

"I must say, Elliott, you have been exceedingly prompt in all the things you have done; it must have been a dreadful shock," he said, and Mr Elliott agreed. "It certainly was, sir; I was appalled, but it was the ladies who were most affected. Both Mrs Sutton and Mrs Bradshaw were absolutely distraught and I believe Mrs Collins was taken ill and had to be helped upstairs. I was very glad to be there and able to offer some assistance at once. I called in the police, who have been very thorough," he explained.

"What are they doing?" asked Jonathan.

"They were able to identify the men with some help from the maid's descriptions and, since then, they have been trying to track them down," he explained and Jonathan thought he sounded hopeful.

"Are they close to finding the children, do you think?"

"Unfortunately no, Mr Bingley." Colin Elliott sounded almost apologetic. "While the two men have been sighted on the road to London, the two children have not," he explained.

"What? How can that be? I thought Sutton wanted to take the children."

"That is what we deduced, sir, but while he may want them, he may not want to travel around with two young girls . . ."

"Why?" asked Jonathan, puzzled at this conundrum, but, this time a thought appeared to have struck Elliott, who did not answer him at once, taking time to do some thinking. "I wonder . . ." he said, and then added quickly, "By God, I should have thought of that, Mr Bingley. It is quite probable, in fact more than likely, that the children are still in the neighbourhood, or at least somewhere in Hertfordshire, concealed, left with some family he knows. The last thing he would want to do would be to drag them along to London. Where would he hide them? How would he explain their presence? It would present a mighty problem."

"You are probably quite right, Elliott; indeed, I am sure you are. But how shall we be certain?" asked Jonathan.

"There is but one way, sir. We must find Sutton or his henchman and confront them. Abduction is a crime; they could be hanged or transported if they are caught and charged," he said and Jonathan thought it was not a very practical scheme, even though Elliott did sound very determined.

"That could be dangerous," he warned. "Had you not better leave it to the police? They are better able to handle these men."

Colin Elliott agreed that it could indeed be a hazardous undertaking, but explained that the police, who were busy solving murders and robberies in London and its environs, were unlikely to spend much time and effort on what they would probably regard as a domestic matter, a squabble between estranged parents. They may well believe that Sutton has the right to take his children. "I have asked a friend in the Home Office to provide me with some information," he explained. "Depending on what he says, I shall decide whether to pursue the matter myself or leave it to the police."

Jonathan Bingley was very impressed with the decisive manner in which Elliott had acted. He had always had a problem with such situations, being loathe to become involved in confrontation himself. He envied Colin Elliott his sense of confidence and self-reliance. As Elliott prepared to leave, Jonathan said, "On another matter, Mr Elliott," and Colin Elliott swung around at once. "I have had your letter; you say you love Anne-Marie and wish to marry her?"

"With all my heart, sir," Elliott said earnestly.

"And have you any inkling of her feelings?"

"An inkling, yes, based chiefly upon my hopes, I think, but I am yet to know her mind, sir. I was hoping to discover how she would respond, but this terrible business has intervened. I expect I will know her feelings when I see her again," he replied.

"You have spoken with her, then?" asked Jonathan.

Colin Elliott smiled and looked a little sheepish. "I have, sir. I do apologise; I know I should have waited for your reply."

Jonathan shook his head and interrupted, "My dear fellow, you have no need to apologise. You are perfectly entitled to propose to my daughter. She is almost twenty-four years old and as you would know, a very independent young lady, with her own income. I made certain that she would not be dependent upon me, so I can hardly expect her to wait upon my approval, to decide if she is to accept or refuse you."

He was smiling and Colin Elliott indicated that while he was aware that Mrs Bradshaw was at liberty to marry whomever she chose, he had wanted to ensure that her father was made aware of his interest.

"I understand what you are saying, Mr Bingley, but it would give me very great pleasure, and I am sure Anne-Marie feels exactly the same, if you would give us your blessing," he said softly.

Jonathan was moved by his obvious sincerity.

"Of course you would have my blessing, if she accepts you. It is to your credit that you have sought my permission, but in truth you do not need it. May I ask, have you discussed your intentions with anyone else in the family?" he asked.

Mr Elliott was a little puzzled by the question.

"No, certainly not, sir," he assured him, but Jonathan continued, "Good, now, may I advise you to speak with my wife Anna first, yes, before you return to Anne-Marie for her response. Mr Elliott, Anne-Marie is my eldest daughter and, since her mother's death, she has been a source of comfort and support to her two young sisters and occasionally to me. She is very precious to us. But as you are aware, she was married for a very brief period. It was not, I regret to have to tell you, a happy experience for her. Indeed, it was quite the reverse."

Colin Elliott seemed troubled by his words and said quickly, "I am very sorry to hear that, sir. I had no idea. I learned only that she was widowed a year or so ago."

"She has not spoken of it to you?" Jonathan asked and Mr Elliott looked quite disconcerted. "No indeed, sir, I must protest; we have not discussed the subject of her marriage at all. Mrs Bradshaw has never intimated to me, by any means, that she was unhappy with her late husband," he declared, with so much fervour that Jonathan smiled, pleased to hear him leap to Anne-Marie's defence.

"That certainly bodes well," he thought, and said, "Well, in that case, I would advise that you see my wife and tell her what you have told me. Anne-Marie was seriously ill after Bradshaw's death and it was not because she was mourning his demise; my sister Mrs Wilson and Anna helped her through those dark days. I think you will learn something about her, which you may otherwise never know, by speaking with Mrs Bingley," he said gravely.

Colin Elliott, still somewhat perplexed, agreed to do as he asked.

"Thank you, sir," he said, holding out his hand, "I shall call on Mrs Bingley at Netherfield as soon as I return to Hertfordshire. Meanwhile, do I have your consent to my proposal?" he asked, still somewhat anxious.

Jonathan took his hand. "I see no reason at all to refuse my consent; so long as you do not expect me to campaign for the Tories at the next election," he quipped and Colin Elliott laughed out loud.

"You may rest assured that will not be necessary, Mr Bingley. I have already written to my party, or should I say my former party, informing them of my intention in the next session of Parliament, to move to the cross benches, from where I will support the Reform Group in their efforts to bring about the important changes we need to make."

"Have you now? That is excellent news." Jonathan was jubilant and shook his hand once more. "No doubt you have also informed my brother-in-law, Mr Wilson?" he asked and Elliott smiled broadly, as he replied, "I certainly have, sir. And I might say he was exceedingly pleased." He went out into the night, where a thin drizzle of rain was making puddles in the street, but did nothing to dampen Elliott's mood.

On returning to his apartment in Knightsbridge, he found a message from Masters, who asked to meet him at the White Hart, which was around the corner. Fortified against the cold and wet with a drink, Masters confirmed that Sutton's partner in crime was a returned convict, who was even now being hunted by the police. If he was caught, he would certainly be transported or worse, he said, and warned Elliott not to confront him.

"He's a thug and a bully, with a very bad reputation for battering his victims. Do watch your step and try not to cross him. If I were you, I'd let the police deal with him."

Elliott thanked his friend for the information and the warning, before they shook hands and parted.

⁓

Outside his apartment, Thomson was waiting for him, huddled in the doorway, trying to keep out of the rain, which was heavier now. Elliott took him indoors and, once he was gratefully installed in front of a good blaze with a drink in his hand, he revealed that Sutton's partner in crime had been arrested by the police for disorderly behaviour in a public house. Thomson had discovered that he was Baines, a convict in trouble again with the law, thereby confirming Masters's story.

"From what I hear, he's a nasty piece of work, sir, without much mercy for his victims. I'm told he has been evading the police for several months. Now, he's back in custody."

While this development may bode well for the general populace, since it took one dangerous villain out of society, it rather threw their own plans into disarray, since being inside, Baines could no longer lead them to Sutton and the children.

Elliott revealed to Thomson, his own belief that Sutton had probably not brought the children to London at all, but had lodged them with someone in Hertfordshire, intending to lie low for a while, before going back to get them. Thomson agreed. This would surely account for the fact that while there had been two sightings of the men, no one had seen two children with them, he said. "I'm afraid, sir, we seem to have travelled to London on a fool's errand; looks like it's going to be back to Hertfordshire and a bit more digging around Meryton and its environs."

Mr Elliott nodded; he was very tired and in need of sleep.

"Well, Mr Bingley agrees with me. I intend to return to Hertfordshire tomorrow. I shall leave early; perhaps we can meet up at Tillyard's office in the afternoon and decide on our next move."

Thomson agreed and took his leave, promising to "keep an eye open for anything useful" and at last, gratefully, Colin Elliott was able to get to bed.

When he awoke the following morning, he felt refreshed, even though he'd had only a few hours' sleep. The hope that the Sutton children may indeed still be in Hertfordshire, in Meryton even, had lifted his spirits. The weather had cleared and he was always pleased to be leaving the bustle of London. At least, he thought, looking for the girls may be easier in the country and it was quite likely they'd be safer. He left early, hoping to make the first part of his journey by midday. Despite his concern for Lucy Sutton's children, Colin Elliott was far more anxious about his meeting with Anna Bingley, wondering what was about to be revealed to him and hoping he would be able, soon afterwards, to see Anne-Marie again.

Advised by express letter from Jonathan, Anna was expecting Mr Elliott. She had a shrewd idea what his visit was about, too. When he arrived, she was kindness itself, making him welcome, plying him with refreshments and making sure he was comfortable and at ease.

Naturally, her first questions concerned the whereabouts of the Sutton children. "Poor Mrs Sutton has been desolated; she will neither eat nor sleep and Anne-Marie has been sharing the burden of her grief. Mrs Collins has not been too well either and Harriet Greene has been kept busy attending upon her. We have all been awaiting some news from London. Mr Bingley wrote to say you would have some news for us," she said and Colin Elliott told her all he knew. He was able to give her some little hope, but sadly, not the good news they had all been waiting to hear.

Mrs Bingley sighed and looked very worried as he tried to reassure her.

"We hope that it will not be long before they are found, Mrs Bingley," he said. "Meryton after all is not London. It is not easy to conceal persons for long here; especially not two small girls. Someone is bound to notice."

"I sincerely hope and pray you are right, Mr Elliott. It is not just poor Mrs Sutton who suffers while ever this dreadful business goes on. I am truly at a loss for words to say what I think of the villains who do this type of thing."

Colin Elliott realised she had been under great strain, especially with Mr Bingley away. He tried to reassure her, suggesting that with the police and Tillyard's men all looking for them, the children would surely be found.

She appeared to draw some comfort from his words and turning to him, changed the subject. Her voice was suddenly lighter, her expression less grave, and she smiled as she addressed him. "Mr Elliott, Mr Bingley says you wish to discuss a private matter with me. How can I help?" He was completely taken aback by the frankness of her approach.

Understanding his surprise she added, "I did not mean to discompose you, Mr Elliott. I received an express from my husband this morning, he expects to stay on in town for a day or two, and in it, he mentioned that you would be calling on me and that you had a private matter of some urgency to discuss with me."

She saw him relax visibly and invited him to take his time, for there was no hurry. If there was something that troubled him, she was happy to listen.

Colin Elliott was confused. "Mrs Bingley, believe me it is not a matter that has troubled me at all, indeed I am not even aware of its substance. It was Mr Bingley who suggested that I should speak with you about it."

"On what matter?" she asked, "Is it concerning the hospital?"

He shook his head; plainly Mr Bingley had not indicated clearly to his wife what they were to discuss. He felt a trifle put out, but took a deep breath and said, "Perhaps, I had better start at the beginning . . ." Anna agreed that might be a very sound idea.

And so, over the next half hour or so, he revealed to her, as he had to Mr Bingley, his love for Anne-Marie and his wish to marry her. He had written to Mr Bingley and asked Anne-Marie herself. Mr Bingley had given his consent, but had, at the same time, suggested that he talk to Mrs Bingley first. It was something to do with Mrs Bradshaw's first marriage, he said. Anna waited until he stopped to catch his breath and asked, "Has Anne-Marie given you her answer?" Colin Elliott looked concerned at her question, wondering whether Anne-Marie had spoken of his proposal to Mrs Bingley. Did she know more than he did? He wondered and was uneasy.

Anna was determined that she was not going to make things easier for him; she wanted to hear exactly what he had to say.

"I have asked Anne-Marie to marry me and she has asked for some time to consider my proposal," he explained.

"And did you tell her you loved her?" she asked, cautiously.

He smiled and answered without hesitation, "Of course, with all my heart. I told her much more besides and I am hopeful she believed me and will accept me," he said, then seeing her smile, he appealed to her, "Mrs Bingley, please, if you know of any reason why she may refuse me, some impediment that I know not of, I beg you to tell me." Anna's heart was moved by the sadness of his coun-tenance and the sincerity of his voice as he spoke.

She responded gently, "Mr Elliott, if you do love Anne-Marie dearly, as you have said you do, you have told her so and, in so doing, convinced her that you do love her, and if she believes that she loves you, too, I can see no reason why she will refuse you."

His spirits lifted instantly, she could see it in the straightening of his shoul-ders and the brightness of his expression. Speaking quite slowly and confiden-tially, she said, "Anne-Marie was married for about fifteen months, to a man, a clergyman whom she did not love and who must not have loved her, else he would not have agreed to the marriage on those terms. Quite clearly, he did not care greatly how she felt and when they were married, insisted upon his marital rights as her husband, despite a total lack of affection between them.

"Anne-Marie was absolutely miserable. Barely one-and-twenty, she had been persuaded to accept his offer by friends, whose good intentions were clearly misplaced, and she suffered terribly for her lack of judgment.

"Yet, her loyalty to her husband and her refusal to blame anyone else for her unhappy state prevented her from confiding in any of us. She said not a single word against him for all of that time, despite her anguish."

Anna was conscious of the disturbed expression upon Mr Elliott's counte-nance. Her next sentence brought a gasp of surprise.

"Then, one day, without warning, he collapsed and died in the vestry after Evensong." Anna paused before continuing; she could see he was deeply shocked.

"Anne-Marie's reaction to her husband's death was quite strange; at first she went through all the traditional rituals, the wife in deep mourning, a continua-tion of the charade that her marriage had been. But very soon, the mask began to slip; she began to feel free and genuinely happy and, of course, she was consumed with guilt about having such feelings. She suffered as I have seen no young woman suffer and it took a terrible toll upon her body and mind. She was very ill for several months, until my sister-in-law Mrs Wilson took her to stay at Standish Park. She remained with them until she recovered completely and was ready to return home. She came back to us last Spring, a healed and changed young woman."

Anna heard him say, "Thank God," under his breath as she went on. "So you understand why my husband thought you should speak with me first.

Anne-Marie is very precious to him, to all of us, and we would hate to see her hurt again. Mr Bingley probably thought it was best that you knew all about her first disastrous marriage and its painful consequences before you heard her answer. I agree that it was best that you knew what she has suffered; it is only a year or two ago and you may find she is still sensitive about it. I do know she has not forgotten it. You may need to be very gentle with her," she said.

Colin Elliott was shocked and deeply touched, not just by the troubling circumstances of the story he had just heard, but by the deep affection and care that her family had lavished upon young Mrs Bradshaw when she had needed them. It was the sort of affection he could never have found in his own family, where as a boy, he had often been left to his own devices and only his mother had cared whether he lived or died. After her death, he had had to fend for himself in what had been a rather cold, hard world of masculine disdain for tender feelings.

It served only to increase his regard for the Bingleys and their family, whose affectionate concern for one another he found endearing. As for Anne-Marie, it had made no change at all to his love for her and he was confident he could help her overcome any residual fears resulting from her unhappy marriage. He told Mrs Bingley so and, when they parted, Anna was sure he was right.

From the outset, she had liked Mr Elliott for his good sense and clear-sightedness. The excellence of his understanding was never in doubt and her husband Jonathan had already claimed him as a sincere and passionate Reformist. All this and a reputation for exemplary conduct had set him well apart. That he had fallen in love with Anne-Marie did not surprise Anna in the least, for of late her beauty had been greatly enhanced by the return of her qualities of enthusiasm and warmth, which they had missed for a while. They were traits naturally attractive to a young man like Colin Elliott.

"Thank you, Mrs Bingley, for your kindness and your good counsel. I am very grateful. I hope now to go to Longbourn and see Mrs Bradshaw," he said as he kissed her hand, preparing to leave.

It was midafternoon. They both knew that Mrs Collins, who was a creature of habit, always rested in her room upstairs at this time of day. He hoped this would allow him an opportunity to speak with Anne-Marie alone. Anna Bingley smiled and wished him success.

On a fine afternoon, with very little wind about and a cloudless sky over-head, Colin Elliott was glad of the shade afforded by the closed carriage in which he was riding. He felt some pity for a young man who passed him, riding furiously in the opposite direction, on the road between Netherfield and Longbourn. With only a battered hat for protection from the sun, he looked hot and tired, as though he had ridden a very long way.

Arriving at Longbourn, he slowed his horses down as they made their way up the road and into the drive, so as not to alarm or disturb the occupants of the house. Approaching the house, he was struck by the silence, as the old place basked in the afternoon sun. He recalled that he had arranged to meet Thomson at Tillyard's office later that day. Looking at his watch, he decided he had plenty of time to see Anne-Marie and obtain her answer.

Even though he felt reasonably confident of winning her affections, he could not avoid a feeling of uncertainty and trepidation that assailed him, as he alighted and walked to the entrance.

There was no one about. On such a soporific afternoon, even the servants were probably resting, he thought. He led the horses round to the side of the house, where he found the man who came regularly from Netherfield Park to help with the garden pruning a hedge. Gratefully surrendering the vehicle and horses into his care, Colin Elliott went around to the front door.

Anne-Marie had spent all morning trying to compose a letter to her aunt Emma Wilson. Ever since Sunday, when Mr Elliott had first declared his love for her, asked her to be his wife, and then raced off into the night because someone had kidnapped Lucy Sutton's children, her thoughts and feelings had been in turmoil. It was not that she had any doubts about the sincerity of his words or the strength of his feelings. It was her own diffidence that gave her concern.

She had wanted to confide in Anna, but it had not been possible to get away from Longbourn for any reasonable period of time. Though Mrs Collins was much recovered, there was the problem of Mrs Sutton and her missing children. If Anne-Marie had left her grandmother alone and Mrs Sutton arrived with bad news…there was no knowing what might happen.

Having struggled with a letter to her aunt and having written less than a paragraph, she determined that it would get done that very day. She needed to ask for some counsel and there was no other way. After Mrs Collins had retired to her room for her usual afternoon rest and Harriet had set off in the pony cart for Meryton, Anne-Marie had taken her writing materials, a rug and cushions and set off to sit in the shade of her favourite oak, on the far side of the house, out of sight of visitors.

It was there Colin Elliott found her, having drawn a blank at the house, in the kitchen garden and the shrubbery. She was deeply engrossed in her letter and did not hear him approach until a twig snapped underfoot and she looked up in some alarm. She was not expecting anyone; when she saw him, she could not believe her eyes.

"Mr Elliott! Why, you're back already…have they been found?" she cried, stumbling as she tried to get to her feet. Helping her up, he kept hold of her arm as he told her the news, grim and unsatisfactory though it was.

"I am sorry the news is not any better, Mrs Bradshaw," he said apologetically. "Unfortunately, it seems we raced off to London, believing the children had been removed from the neighbourhood, but they have not been seen with the two men, at all. We are now inclined to believe that they have been concealed here, possibly lodged with a person known to Mr Sutton. Perhaps he intends to return and take them away later, when the general alarm has died down."

Anne-Marie looked confused. Sensing her bewilderment, he took her hands in his, reassuring her, trying to convince her that they had not given up on finding the Sutton children. Then, before she could ask any more questions, he asked her if she had considered his proposal and did she have an answer for him. At first, it seemed to him that she was going to weep; her lovely face seemed to crumple under the wide-brimmed hat she wore to protect herself from the sun, and he was afraid she was going to refuse him. Indeed, he steeled himself for just such a response, determined to plead with her to reconsider.

At the very moment that he thought he had lost her, Colin Elliott knew how very dearly he loved her. But, she sat down again and indicated that he should sit beside her. He obeyed, sitting awkwardly in his travelling clothes and boots upon the rug she had thrown down on the grass. In his hands she placed the letter she had written to Emma Wilson, which lay beside all the torn and crumpled sheets of paper she had tossed away, testimony to the degree of difficulty she had encountered trying to express her feelings.

Colin Elliott looked at her, a little unsure. "Do you really want me to read this?" he asked, and she nodded. "Yes, please" she replied, indicating that was exactly what she wanted him to do. He unfolded the pages and began to read silently, and she watched him as he read. It was not an easy letter to read.

My dearest Aunt Emma, she wrote,

> *I had not expected to trouble you with this subject, not at any rate for many years. Marriage was not a matter in which I had an interest in anymore.*
>
> *Dear Aunt, you, more than anyone except perhaps Papa, know why this is such a difficult thing for me to deal with. However, no one, not even Papa or Anna, kind and well-intentioned though they are, can advise me, for they, unlike you and I, have not known the utter humiliation of discovering that one has quite deliberately married the very last person on earth with whom one could hope to find happiness. It was because you had shared the same pitiful fate and understood clearly what I had been through, that you were able to help me recover my lost esteem and restore my faith in my fellow human beings.*
>
> *Yet, dearest Aunt, I seem not to have been able to recover my belief in my own judgment and this time, I am so afraid of making another mistake, for if I do, I shall not merely destroy my own happiness, but I should be responsible for ruining the life of another as well; someone I hold very dear.*
>
> *Indeed, having known the bleak indignity of a loveless marriage, I would not wish to risk the happiness of someone who has been a good friend and seems to mean more to me every day. Unless I could be utterly certain of my own feelings, I would not wish to take this step and put his happiness in jeopardy. I think, you will have guessed that I speak of Mr Elliott, who has asked me to be his wife. I know that you and Mr Wilson like and respect him, as does Papa. Indeed there is not a single person I know, who does not.*

Even as he read her words, Colin Elliott glanced across at her, his eyes expressing both gratitude for her kind words and a plea for his case; but he said nothing and read on as she watched him in silence. Her words seemed to spill out across the paper, as if she had been unable to hold them back...her writing, usually neat and disciplined, seemed to be racing across the page trying to keep pace with her thoughts . . .

> *I want very much to say yes, because, if the truth were told, I have not met a better man, nor one for whom I have felt so much affection. And I know he is a good man, yet, I fear that if I make goodness alone my standard, I will be undone as I was before. You will recall that everyone agreed Mr Bradshaw was a good man! Of such appalling errors of judgment are barren marriages made, no matter how many children they may produce. Significantly, ours produced none.*
>
> *My dearest Aunt, if you understand my predicament, please write me as soon as you are able and tell me just one thing: if I were to accept Mr Elliott, as I truly want to do, how ever shall I ensure that the ghost of Mr Bradshaw will not hang around us and draw us to the same desolate fate?*

The letter was unfinished, the writer having been interrupted . . .

Colin Elliott put it down and turned to Anne-Marie, who had watched him read the letter and seen his changing countenance, as he struggled to understand and absorb the meaning of her words. He wondered if by speaking out he would help or hinder his cause.

Anne-Marie was silent; she had given him the letter precisely because she had known that she could never tell him in so many words of the doubts that assailed her, even as she acknowledged her love. Not even with Anna, whom she adored, could she have spoken openly and frankly as she could with Emma Wilson. Shared sorrow and shame at having made the kind of error that had led Emma to marry her first husband, a domineering, cruel young man, and allowed Anne-Marie to be persuaded by her friend that a man of good reputation could also be a good husband even though she felt no love for him, had forged a strong bond between them.

Recognising her fears and unwilling to break the fragile thread of understanding that linked them, Colin Elliott held out his hands to her and when she, without hesitation, put her hands in his, he clasped them together. Silent, unwilling, almost unable to speak, lest spoken words shatter the finely spun web of mutual affection, they waited several minutes, until at last unable to hold them back any longer, she let the tears that had been stinging her eyes, course down her cheeks.

For Elliott, this was an unbearable moment; he could no longer let her suffer alone and throwing his customary caution to the winds, took her in his arms and comforted her, assuring her of his understanding and love. Then, encouraged by her compliance and driven by longing, he kissed her.

Thereafter, it took him very little time to tell her of his meetings with her father and Anna, to inform her that they had both given him their blessing while Anna had told him of her unhappy marriage and urged him to be sensitive to her concerns. He wanted, he said, above all to pledge his love and through it render void her fears.

"If we are both certain it is right," he said, gently, "how can it be wrong? I have no doubts at all, my dearest, because we, neither of us, are seeking to marry for any reason other than love. I am asking you to marry me not because I claim to be a clever man or a rich one or even a particularly good man, for I am no better than many other decent men, but because I love you with all my heart and believe my life will be enriched if you agree to share it. For my part, I promise that I will do everything in my power to ensure your happiness."

She listened intently and when she finally spoke, said only that she asked for nothing more and, indeed, she hoped he would take her on the same terms.

"For I do not believe I have anything more valuable to offer you than my heartfelt love. Mr Elliott, Colin, I am truly sorry if in expressing my reservations I have hurt you. That was never my intention; I wished only to avoid, for us both, the misery of an unhappy marriage, because I care too much for you to take such a risk," she said, with a degree of warmth that left him in no doubt at all of her feelings. With many protestations of affection, new promises made and others renewed, they pledged their love to one another and prepared to return to the house, where she would write to her father and her Aunt Emma.

"I shall have to write another letter to my Aunt; there is no longer a reason to send this one," she said with a smile, as he helped collect her writing materials.

After a last affectionate embrace in the shelter of the trees, for they were both careful not to outrage Mrs Collins by exciting gossip among the servants, they were walking together towards the house, when the sound of a horse being ridden at great speed reached them and, as they watched, a young man on horseback turned into the drive. It was the same young man that Elliott had seen earlier in the day. "I wonder what he is doing here," said Colin Elliott. "I believe he is the man I saw riding furiously towards Netherfield, when I was on my way here to see you." Anne-Marie knew her father often sent express letters delivered overnight by hand, rather than trust the post; it was possible this could be one of them.

"It might be a message from Papa," she said and then, as if a thought had struck her, she turned to him, saying, "it may be news of Lucy's children," before she hastened towards the house, where the rider, having alighted from his horse, stood waiting for them. As they approached, he reached into his satchel and took out a small packet of papers, which he handed to Anne-Marie.

Back at Pemberley, Mr Darcy had not been idle. Angered and troubled by the news that Jonathan had received from Hertfordshire, he had felt the need to do something to help. After dinner on the day that Jonathan had left for London, while Anna and the children had set out to return to Netherfield, the conversation had been all about the kidnapping of Mrs Sutton's girls. Neither the Darcys nor Mr and Mrs Bingley knew Mrs Sutton, but they had heard of her unhappy situation from Jonathan and Anna.

Everyone was concerned for the two young girls, taken so rudely from their mother's home, and Jane wondered whether there was not something someone could do to restore them to their mother. "I cannot imagine how she must feel, Lizzie. It must be the very worst thing." Elizabeth agreed and pointed out that at least the children were with their father, who was unlikely to harm them in any way, although this was no consolation at all for their poor mother!

Mr Darcy had said very little at the time, but after the Bingleys had retired to bed, he raised the subject with his wife. Darcy had many contacts in London, in the fields of law and business, and he wondered whether a journey to London might not be useful.

Elizabeth did not favour the idea and asked, "Dearest, why need you go to London? Jonathan is already there and so is Mr Elliott; need you go as well? Might it not be better to wait and see what information they are able to glean from their own contacts, first?"

She was becoming more protective of her husband and preferred that he remain at Pemberley with her, for while he was still fit and strong, she had noticed that he tired more easily and was occasionally irritable after a long day away from home.

Furthermore, Elizabeth was well aware that following up any information on the activities of the kidnappers of the Sutton children might require Darcy to wander the back streets of East London—home to the indigent and criminal elements of the city. He would be far from the salubrious environs of Portman Square or Grosvenor Street and with the increasing incidence of crime in the cities she would be very concerned for his safety. Darcy was a little surprised by her response.

"Lizzie, my dear, it is not like you to dissuade me from going to the aid of someone in trouble, especially where a family and children are at risk," he said and she felt a little ashamed of her selfish desire to put his safety and her own peace of mind first. But with her Uncle Gardiner's recent illness, she had begun to worry more about her husband's health.

"Would you let me come with you to London?" she asked, adding, "At least that way, I would not worry as much. It is just that with my Uncle Gardiner so ill, I cannot help feeling anxious when you are away for long periods and I have no knowledge of your whereabouts."

When her husband shook his head, indicating he did not think this was a good idea, she continued, "I know you wish to help, and I love you for it, but will you not send one of the men first? Then, if there is a need, you could follow and maybe take Richard with you," she suggested. Darcy threw his head back and laughed out loud.

"And do you suppose Cassy would have no objection to that?" He was very touched by her concern and put his arms around her as he spoke.

"No doubt, the two of you will probably find any number of arguments to stop us going after these villains. My dear, do you fear that I am no longer capable of looking after myself and the footpads will get me?" he asked, teasing her gently.

Taking her cue from him, Elizabeth lightened her tone, "Indeed no, why I am quite sure you are well able to fend for yourself, but I do hear a great deal about the criminals and villains who roam the city streets and will not hesitate to strike you down, should you get in their way."

Darcy smiled, "Dear me," he said, in mock outrage, "villains and criminals! It does seem as if the world out there is a truly fearful place. Perhaps I should just send Richard? Or will our daughter be as anxious about her husband, as you are about me?" he teased, but then seeing she was quite genuinely concerned, he was keen to assuage her fears and said gently, "If it upsets you, my love, of course I shall not go, but I will send a couple of my men to meet Mr Bartholomew, who can make some enquiries for me. It will not be easy for this Sutton fellow to hide two young girls for very long. It's bound to come out."

Ever since the news had reached them, Elizabeth had been thinking that London was an unlikely place to take two little girls, if you wanted to conceal their presence.

"I find it difficult to believe that Sutton would have taken the girls to London," she said. "Why would he? Why not keep them hidden away in the country? Place them in a home with a large family and they would hardly be noticed. Wait until the hue and cry dies down before moving them away."

Darcy, who had been standing in front of the window looking out at the park, turned around in a trice. "Lizzie, my dear, you are a genius! Why have I not thought of this before? It is far more likely. Indeed, it is quite probable that they are even now in the neighbourhood with someone he can trust or pay to keep quiet. I shall send Hobbs to Hertfordshire, let him stay at a public house in the area and make some discreet inquiries." He was full of enthusiasm for the idea.

"Thank you, my dear, that was an excellent idea," he said. Elizabeth glowed, not just from his praise, which she enjoyed, but from knowing that he was no longer likely to insist upon travelling down to London. The very next morning, a man was despatched posthaste to Hertfordshire, with instructions to frequent the public houses in the Meryton area and make discreet inquiries. He was also to watch out for any sign of the two Sutton children in the neighbourhood.

Meanwhile, Colin Elliott and his helpers had been in London and, having drawn a blank there, had reached a similar conclusion. They had no idea, however, where to look next. Returning to Hertfordshire, hoping to find more information but finding very little, they felt thwarted and annoyed. The two Sutton children, it seemed, had disappeared without trace. Until an express received at Pemberley brought astonishing news.

Mr Darcy's man, Hobbs, had taken a room at a small local inn outside Meryton and in the bar, on the second night of his stay, he had found himself in the company of two young men probably in their thirties, he thought. They were both drinking quite heavily and talking volubly. He had guessed they were ex-militia, from their manner, as well as their language, which was colourful and loud.

Introducing himself as a visitor to the area, Hobbs had discovered that their name was Wickham, Philip and George, two brothers. And, he'd gathered they were not happy. Their main complaint appeared to be that their mother, recently widowed, had apparently taken to letting rooms in their house to itinerant travellers. Her sons had returned from Eastbourn to find their rooms let to a man from London, an ex-soldier named Sutton. This man, they grumbled, had two little children, girls who were constantly weeping and whining, so no one could get any sleep.

"We had to doss down on the sofas in the living room," grumbled the younger of the two, Philip, while his brother pointed out that his mother was kept awake as well, since her room was just next door to theirs.

"When we told her to send them packing, she claimed she needed the money. Sutton was paying her well." Hobbs, suspecting he had a good source of information, had bought them more drinks and loosened their tongues to the point at which they were telling him everything. Mrs Wickham, he learned, had been paid in advance for two weeks—she had insisted upon it, especially since Sutton was going back to London, ostensibly to arrange accommodation for his children.

He had claimed his wife was very ill and could not care for them, but Mrs W. had not been taken in, they said. "Mama winked and grinned when she told us about it, and it was plain she did not believe a word of it. But as long as he pays well, she is not complaining," said Philip.

"But we are!" his brother had claimed, adding that he'd like to discover what Sutton was up to in the area. "He could be a smuggler and we may get a reward for handing him over to the police," he'd suggested.

Hobbs, who was fairly certain the two girls referred to were the abducted Sutton children, had dissuaded them from going to the police, but was asking Mr Darcy for instructions.

Darcy thought long and hard before despatching careful instructions to Hobbs and an express to Jonathan with the details of what Hobbs had discovered, urging him to go to the police at once.

"This is not the sort of matter that you and Mr Elliott can deal with on your own; I strongly advise you to take this information to the police," he wrote, careful to ensure that his nephew knew of the grave risks involved.

When Darcy told his wife of the information he had received from Hobbs, Elizabeth could not believe it; nor could Jane. Their wayward sister Lydia Wickham, recently widowed when her husband's body had finally succumbed to the forces of nature, after a lifetime of self-indulgence and dissipation, was once again involved in a stupid scheme that was bound to end in disaster or disgrace or both!

"She was probably trying to make some extra money, without giving any thought to the consequences," said Elizabeth, who knew well that Lydia's extravagant habits could not be sustained on the meagre annuity she received after Wickham's death. She was always applying to her sisters for money to pay a variety of bills. When Darcy had revealed to her the contents of Hobbs's message, she had been shocked and ashamed.

"Oh no, not Lydia again! Darcy, I am so weary of carrying the shame of her impropriety. Is there never to be an end to this?" she had cried and he had comforted her, as he had always done on these occasions, reassuring her that he was quite indifferent to the antics of the Wickhams, especially now that Mr Wickham had departed the stage. Indeed, he declared, it was probably an advantage that the woman concerned was Lydia, because she was at least predictable in her attitude to money and was probably open to negotiation.

"She has probably agreed to keep the children there, for a fee, and it is quite possible that, if Mrs Sutton or someone on her behalf offers her more, she will let them return to their mother. All I need do now is send a message to Jonathan, so he can alert the police. They will then wait for Sutton to return and nab him," he said with a degree of satisfaction.

Elizabeth and Jane had long since ceased to be surprised by their sister's behaviour. Quite incorrigible, mainly as a result of special treatment in her youth by an indulgent mother and an indifferent father, Lydia was a law unto herself. But neither of her sisters would fail to be ashamed at the vulgarity and coarseness of her conduct.

Since the death of her unlamented husband, Lydia's bizarre activities appeared to have increased. Both Jane and Lizzie were grateful to be living at sufficient distance from her, as to prevent her visiting them on one pretext or the other, as she did constantly with the unfortunate Mrs Collins.

Time and again, on family occasions, chiefly weddings and funerals, Lydia would appear dressed in her best, which was usually more striking than tasteful, and proceed to embarrass her family, who had to observe her absurd behaviour.

"She does not have to do anything, Lizzie," Jane had once said. "Just her being there makes me all nervous, as though something calamitous could happen at any moment!" Elizabeth knew exactly how she felt, but on this occasion, if Darcy was to be believed, it seemed Lydia might be, albeit unwittingly, instrumental in assisting the recovery of Mrs Sutton's children. Indeed, she may actually do some good, without intending to, of course. Elizabeth prayed that her husband was right.

Mr Darcy's letter to Jonathan was despatched early and in it he advised him to take immediate steps to alert the police and request their help.

I must stress, Jonathan, that you should not attempt to confront this man under any circumstances without assistance from the police. My information is that he is both unpredictable and likely to resort to violence in a crisis. Sutton is an unknown quantity; he appears respectable but is known to be truculent and easily roused. Please advise your friend Mr Elliott that he, too, must avoid dealing with him on his own. The man may be desperate, and in that state, he is not to be trusted . . .

The rest of the letter detailed the information received from Hobbs and wished them luck in their efforts to recover the children and apprehend the miscreants.

It was this letter that Jonathan had enclosed within a note to his wife at Netherfield, urging her to acquaint Colin Elliott with Mr Darcy's advice without delay.

~⚬~

Cassandra and her husband Richard Gardiner called on her parents and aunt at Pemberley with the news that they were travelling to Cambridge, having received an urgent request from her brother Julian.

"He is concerned that Josie is unwell and will not see a doctor in Cambridge. He has begged Richard to come and take a look at her," Cassy had said, and Elizabeth was most concerned. For a few years their lives had returned to normal, when Julian and Josie had returned to live at Pemberley with their young son, Anthony. But, sadly, Julian was restless; nothing could keep him from his beloved laboratory at Cambridge, where scientific studies were engaging some of the best brains in the nation. Josie went with him and so did their son, to the chagrin of his grandparents, who loved the child dearly. Elizabeth was worried and so was Jane, who'd had no idea that Josie was unwell. Cassy, wise and practical, was keen to let her mother know the truth.

"You see, Mama, it is not easy for Richard to go at this time. Mr Gardiner grows weaker every day and Mrs Gardiner needs Richard when things get difficult. But you know how Richard is; he will not refuse a call for help, whether it is from a patient or a member of the family, and he truly believes this one is quite genuine."

"What did Julian say?" asked her mother.

"Not very much, except that Josie has not been herself lately; he believes she is ill but will not see a doctor. They both trust Richard and wish he would come to Cambridge and take a look at her. That was all, but reading between the lines, you could tell there was more to it. Julian is not the type to cry wolf, is he?" she said.

"He certainly is not," said Elizabeth, "which is why I am most concerned. Cassy, my darling, will you promise to send me word and tell me how things are and if there is anything your father or I could do to help?"

Cassandra promised. "Of course, I will, Mama," she said, but begged her mother not to worry unduly. "Richard believes it may be a condition of the mind. He knows how very disappointed Josie has been at having her manuscript rejected. She would give anything to have her little volume published and, indeed, I believe if it were not for the spate of women writers appearing recently, producing popular novels, she may well have been more successful. But no one wants to publish a learned documentary on the conditions of the rural poor, when they can produce cheap novelettes. Poor Josie has been unlucky and it is understandable that she is depressed," she explained.

"If only they would settle at Pemberley; it is their home," Elizabeth mused. "There is so much to occupy her, she would have far less time to be depressed."

Cassandra was more understanding than her mother.

"I know also that Josie has been concerned that Julian and she are not here to play their part at Pemberley. She has told me that she feels she is letting you and

Papa down. I have reassured her that I am happy to help with the work at Pemberley; I enjoy it and Richard does not mind, but I know Josie is not convinced. She believes she is not doing the right thing, yet her loyalty is to her husband."

"As indeed it should be," said Jane.

Elizabeth had voiced her own disappointment, and that of her husband, that their son had shown very little interest in managing the family properties, content to leave it to his father, his manager, and stewards. Not even the gift of one of the Welsh estates, on the occasion of their wedding, had engendered much enthusiasm, apart from a short trip to Bristol. Elizabeth, Jane, and Cassandra all knew that Darcy had been bitterly disappointed, especially when his son and heir had decided, at very short notice, to return to work at Cambridge.

"Perhaps, if they were to have another child?" suggested Jane a little tentatively, but Cassy was doubtful.

"Josie has declared that she could not cope with another child just now. Anthony, who is three, is a lively little boy and she has her hands full keeping up with him," she explained, and then, seeing Richard and her father approaching, begged her mother to keep these details from him.

"It would only upset Papa and I should hate to do that."

Cassandra was her father's favourite and they had an excellent understanding. They shared a deep love of Pemberley and spoke frankly together of many things. Yet, she was just as eager as her mother to protect him from undue anxiety or hurt. As it happened, Darcy was deep in conversation with his son-in-law, for whom he had great affection and respect, about his work on a new method of preventing infection in hospitals. Darcy, having financed Richard's initial research in antisepsis, was exceedingly proud of the work he had done. He was fast becoming an authority on the subject.

Fond farewells over, Cassy and her husband left, hoping to arrive in Cambridge early on the following day. Darcy, having heard a version of the news from Richard, was glad he was not leaving for London; clearly, Elizabeth would be anxious and needed him at Pemberley.

❧

At Longbourn, when Colin Elliott and Anne-Marie read the letters that had arrived from Netherfield, they took some time to understand the situation and its implications.

There was Mr Darcy's letter to Jonathan Bingley and Jonathan's note to his wife Anna, both of which had been passed on to Anne-Marie, with advice for Mr Elliott.

Then, there was a short note from Anna. She had sent the letters ahead by the same man who had delivered them to Netherfield, she said, to save precious time. She would follow, with Mr Bowles, as soon as she had been able to organise her household and they would pick up Mrs Sutton on the way, she explained. She urged Anne-Marie to advise Mr Elliott to pay heed to the warnings contained in Mr Darcy's letter.

"It is quite clear that Sutton is not to be trifled with; he seems to be an unreliable and violent man," she cautioned. As they read on, taking in all the details, they began to realise that they faced a particularly perilous situation.

If Mrs Sutton's children had been lodged with Mrs Wickham, at her house on the outskirts of Meryton, Sutton could quite easily call and collect them without anyone being any the wiser.

"And they may never be restored to their mother again," said Anne-Marie, her voice breaking with emotion at the thought.

Colin Elliott sought to reassure her, "He must be stopped, but we have very little time," he said. "I should go at once."

Anne-Marie had no wish to see him go into a situation fraught with danger,

"But both Mr Darcy and Papa have warned against confronting him," she protested. "If this man is as desperate as he seems, would it not be wise to call in the police?"

Colin Elliott explained gently, that if this were done, it was almost a certainty that the police would arrest and charge Mrs Wickham as well, as an accessory to the crime, because she had harboured the children since they were kidnapped. Sensitive to the feelings of her father and his family, he asked whether that would not cause consternation and, once the family connection were known and written about in the press, would not Mr and Mrs Bingley also suffer severe embarrassment? he asked.

She had to admit this was true. "If on the other hand, it were possible to persuade Mrs Wickham to release the children on the promise of some financial inducement, perhaps, she could be kept out of the public eye and the hands of the police," he said.

Anne-Marie was delighted by his sensitivity and concern for her family's reputation, but equally she knew it would not be easy to persuade Lydia Wickham to part with the children. She had probably accepted money from Sutton and would surely fear his anger.

There was, however, still another question. "Even if you do succeed in persuading Mrs Wickham, do you believe the children will come away with you? Having already been removed from their home once, they may refuse to move," she said, and this time Colin Elliott agreed that she was quite right. Indeed, it was something he had overlooked.

"Shall I come with you?" she asked, to which he replied at once, "Certainly not, my dear Anne-Marie, I would not let you put yourself in any danger and your father would never forgive me. No, let me think, there must be a way . . ." He paused and in a moment said, "Ah, I have it. I shall go to Tillyard's office as arranged and ask him to accompany me. When Mrs Bingley arrives with Mr Bowles and Mrs Sutton, send Bowles and Mrs Sutton to join us at the inn in Meryton. Once we are there, we shall call on Mrs Wickham with Mrs Sutton, and I have no doubt the children will come away with their mother. Now, what can be simpler?"

Anne-Marie agreed, it seemed like a good scheme. "Mrs Wickham will not be able to refuse to release them to their own mother, especially if it is sweetened with cash to compensate her for the loss of Sutton's money."

"Exactly. I am inclined to believe it will work," he said, but she was still concerned about what Sutton might do.

"What if he should turn up, fly into a rage, and attack you?" she asked.

Colin Elliott assured her that they would take great care. "We have no information that he is here in Meryton. He was last seen hiding from the police in London after his partner in crime, Baines, was arrested. I doubt he will show his face here, for a while." He rose to leave, reluctantly. "Now, my darling, I must go, else it will be too late and we may lose our way amidst the back lanes of Meryton." Urging her to remember all his instructions, he moved to the entrance.

Anne-Marie held on to his hand as they waited for his carriage to be brought round. "You will take great care, will you not, Colin? I shall wait anxiously for news," she said, and he sought to assuage her fears. "Dearest Anne-Marie, I am no warrior; I have never been a soldier and will not choose to confront or attack any man, if I can help it. I promise I shall take care and, when we return with Mrs Sutton's children, we shall have one thing more to celebrate on this lovely day."

As he kissed her hand and went to enter the carriage, the pony cart turned into the drive. It was Harriet Greene returning and Anne-Marie was very glad to see her. "Harriet, thank God you've come," she cried and spent the next few minutes trying unsuccessfully to give Harriet all the news of the afternoon. She was almost incoherent but finally, Harriet managed to get the gist of the story and expressed feelings of shock and revulsion.

Harriet Greene, who had been with Mrs Collins for several years, was almost a member of the family. Anne-Marie knew she could trust her and confidently told her the whole sorry tale. When she mentioned Lydia Wickham, Harriet shook her head.

"Not her again, ma'am; each time I hope she will learn a lesson, but she never does. Mr Elliott is right, ma'am, if you call in the police, it will be in the papers and around the county in no time at all. Mr Elliott seems a very steady young man, ma'am, he will not take any risks I am sure," she said, and then decided it was time to go upstairs to Mrs Collins. "I had better go tell Mrs Collins something of it, else she will feel she has missed out on all the excitement," she said.

While Harriet was upstairs, Anne-Marie paced the floor, watching the light fade from the sky, gradually bringing the long Summer twilight—that magical time that seems made for lovers. Yet, here she was alone, afraid and wondering if the man she loved was safe from harm. It was an excruciating agony, having discovered only today that she loved him enough to marry him. She could not escape the irony of it. She came back into the middle of the room, and ran her fingers along the old ivory keys of the pianoforte; Emma Wilson had told her that music had kept her sane in the midst of her deepest misery. How she wished she had learned to play proficiently.

When Anne-Marie returned to the window, night had fallen. It was quite dark outside and she heard the sounds of wheels and hooves on the gravel drive before she saw the carriage from Netherfield drive up to the entrance. Anne-Marie was relieved; Anna was here, and she knew everything would be much easier now. She was thankful that both her younger sisters, Teresa and Cathy, had left for Standish Park earlier in the week. They were to spend a part of the summer with the Wilsons, who usually kept them very happily occupied.

Anna Bingley alighted and came indoors. With her were Mr Bowles and an ashen-faced Lucy Sutton, desperate to discover if there had been any news of her daughters. Anne-Marie was glad to have Mr Bowles, who was always good at organising things. A widower in his middle years, he had been with the Bingleys for a very long time and she trusted him implicitly. Though she had wanted to confide in Anna and tell her of her engagement to Mr Elliott, Anne-Marie could find no time alone with her for private conversation in the midst of the crisis that had overtaken them. She did however explain carefully, and in detail, Mr Elliott's instructions to Mr Bowles and Mrs Sutton.

The latter was, at first, full of questions, but time was of the essence and Mr Bowles, who had to drive them to the inn at Meryton, persuaded her that it was in her interest to remain as quiet as possible. A kind but firm man, Bowles succeeded, where the ladies had failed, in convincing Mrs Sutton that calm and discreet behaviour ("no tears or tantrums, please, madam,") was the best way to secure the return of her girls. Having assured Anna that he would take good care of Mrs Sutton and promised them all that they would return with the children, he drove out of the park and set off on the road to Meryton.

When Colin Elliott reached Tillyard's office at the *Herald*, he found only Thomson present. Tillyard had had to go out on business and Jones, the other reporter, had been called home because his wife was sick, Thomson had said. That meant Elliott and Thomson would have to proceed alone. It was not a promising prospect, especially since neither man knew the way to Mrs Wickham's house. Worse, Thomson, who had arrived from London that afternoon, had received information that Sutton was on his way to Meryton by train! "He probably means to take the children away tonight, sir," he said. "No one would suspect it; he would be in and out of here before we could get to him and, once they were on the train, they'd be out of our reach."

Elliott was determined that it would not get that far. "We shall have to see that he does not succeed. He must not get to the children. You and I will have to persuade Mrs Wickham that it is in her interest to give them up. Tell her Sutton's a villain and if she helps him kidnap the children, she will go to jail herself," he said, with greater confidence than he felt. Leaving a hurried note for Tillyard, with some details of their destination and purpose, they left, going first to the inn at Meryton, where they were to meet Mr Bowles and Mrs Sutton.

To their great relief, Mr Bowles, when he arrived, had already succeeded in convincing Mrs Sutton of the need for remaining calm. He was also the only member of the party who knew where Mrs Wickham lived. When they reached the place, a large old house set in a rather unkempt and overgrown garden a mile or so outside Meryton, they were glad to note that there were no other vehicles about, suggesting that Sutton had not already arrived or if he had, he did not have a means of making a quick exit.

Bowles suggested that they conceal their vehicles farther up the lane, which led to a little spinney, before returning to the house on foot. Leaving Thomson on guard by the gate, Mr Bowles led the way in. Mrs Sutton was advised to remain concealed in the garden until it had been established that the children were within. If anyone approached, Thomson was to whistle to alert the others.

Mr Bowles, who was known to the Wickhams as Mr Bingley's steward, went to the front door and knocked smartly. Colin Elliott had observed that the bedrooms upstairs were in darkness, which must mean the children, if they were here, were downstairs, probably in the parlour. Since the blinds were drawn down, they could not see into the room, but the sound of voices carried to the door.

Lucy Sutton was convinced that she could hear her elder daughter's voice. "I know they're in there," she said in an agonised whisper, and they had to urge her to be quiet. Despite the sympathy they felt for her, her constant complaining was aggravating. In response to Mr Bowles's knock, the front door was opened and the maid, recognising him, called out to her mistress, "It's Mr Bowles ma'am, from Netherfield." Mrs Wickham sounded surprised, calling in a loud voice, "Mr Bowles? What on earth does he want at this hour? Is someone dead?"

Bowles meanwhile had stepped inside the door, taking Mr Elliott in with him, and asked to see Mrs Wickham. When she appeared, he greeted her politely and introduced Mr Elliott as "our new Member of Parliament." Colin Elliott was unpleasantly surprised by Mrs Wickham's appearance and coarse manner. "The new MP? Indeed? I suppose we should be honoured and what can we do for you, sir?" she asked in a rather saucy voice. Colin Elliott played his role perfectly.

He was, he explained politely, here on behalf of one of his constituents, a Mrs Lucy Sutton, whose two young daughters had been taken from their home, some days ago. Mrs Sutton was extremely distressed as no doubt Mrs Wickham may have been in the same situation, he suggested. At this point, Lydia Wickham laughed, loud and long. She had a particularly irritating laugh, he noticed.

"I think I'd have been grateful if someone had taken two of mine off my hands, sir. I had my hands full with five of them," she quipped.

Mr Elliott ignored her attempt at a joke and went on, "Well, Mrs Sutton has been desolated, ma'am; there has been a great search mounted for the children by the police and just today, information has been received that they are in fact here with you," he declared.

"With me?" she responded, indignant and quite brazen, her hand upon her heart, as if she was the aggrieved party. She would concede nothing until Mr Elliott said in a cold voice, "Mrs Wickham, I am sure I need not remind you that aiding and abetting an abduction is as heinous a crime as the deed itself and may well earn you a considerable term in jail or even transportation."

Lydia Wickham's face turned pale at his words; she certainly did not fancy jail or transportation to the other side of the world.

Elliott went on, "However, if you were to release the children to their mother now, the police, who have been on the trail of Mr Sutton, need not discover your part in his crime at all."

"I had no part in his crime, I tell you; I knew nothing of any abduction," she cried. "He told me the children's mother had gone away and would I keep them until he arranged accommodation for them. He paid well; I knew nothing of any crime, I swear." She sounded desperate and Colin Elliott almost believed her. For all her bravado, it was plain she did not want to be arrested and taken in for questioning by the police.

He pressed the advantage further. "If you help Mrs Sutton recover her children, we could arrange for you to receive a sum of money to compensate you for any loss.

"And what happens to me when Sutton gets here and finds the children gone? He will probably kill me; he told the innkeeper his wife was dead and he was going to take them to America," she said, babbling desperately, trying to save herself, careless of the truth, as usual.

Lucy Sutton who had crept round to the front door and heard her words, came forward and begged Mrs Wickham to let her have her children back. "Please, ma'am, you cannot let him take them away," she cried. "They're only little girls, and they're all I've got."

Whether it was her tears or the threat of jail or the lure of money, they would never know, but Lydia Wickham went meekly into the parlour and fetched the two children. On seeing their mother, the girls ran to her and they embraced and wept in the hallway.

Colin Elliott and Mr Bowles had moved farther into the house and were taking out the money they had intended to offer Mrs Wickham.

On seeing it, Lydia looked quite pleased and, when it was put in her outstretched hand, she whipped it away and out of sight inside her bodice.

The transaction over, they were about to leave when a long, drawn-out whistle was heard in the distance. The men looked at each other; it was Thomson warning them of the arrival of someone, possibly Sutton.

There was no going back into the house; they would have been trapped.

Racing out carrying the two children and dragging Mrs Sutton with them, they ran into the yard and the overgrown thicket at the bottom of the garden. Lucy Sutton and her daughters were hidden behind a barn, and warned to stay very quiet.

Mr Elliott and Bowles watched from the shelter of the shrubbery, so over-grown it could have concealed a regiment, as Sutton, looking somewhat the worse for drink, strode up to the house and banged upon the front door. When the maid opened the door, he forced it back and pushed his way inside. Within seconds, a great commotion had erupted with screams from the two women and a welter of rage and abuse from Sutton!

Mr Bowles and Colin Elliott waited only seconds, before deciding to go in. As they approached the house, they saw to their horror, that Sutton had a thick, knobby stick, which he was threatening to use upon the hapless women, if they did not tell him where his children were. He was shouting at them as they cowered in fright and Elliott hesitated only momentarily before racing in. But Sutton was taller and heavier than he was and brought the stick down sharply. Had it found its mark, Colin Elliott would have had a broken skull or at least a very sore head.

Leaping out of range he strove to put a table between them, as Bowles came around the other way. Sutton, surprised, wheeled around and struck out again, this time catching Bowles across the shoulders and causing him to fall to the floor. With a gleeful shout and his stick raised high, Sutton stood over him and was about to attack the fallen man, as the two women screamed in terror, when through the open door came Thomson, Tillyard, Jones, and the entire local constabulary! They had him overpowered and manacled in minutes and, soon afterwards, he was on his way to the police cells, calling out vile threats and imprecations as he went.

A relieved Mr Elliott and a sore but unbowed Mr Bowles were left to collect Lucy Sutton and her children, reassure Lydia Wickham that she would not be implicated in Sutton's crime, and return triumphant to Longbourn.

Later, the story would be told of how Tillyard had returned to his office, found the note, and informed the police. Together with Jones, Tillyard had followed only to ensure that his friend had not "come to a sticky end," as he put it. Only Colin Elliott and Mr Bowles knew how very close they had been to disaster.

Their return to Longbourn, bringing with them Lucy Sutton and her two daughters, saved as it were from the clutches of a desperate father turned abductor, was a cause for some celebration. Even Charlotte Collins had remained downstairs to await the news.

When the two carriages rolled in and the children leapt out and ran into the hall, there was, literally, not a dry eye in the house. There were many questions to be answered and much to tell, but amidst the celebrations, there were two important announcements.

The first was not entirely unexpected; for it came as no surprise to Anna that sometime in the last few hours, before his journey to recover the Sutton children, Colin Elliott had proposed to Anne-Marie and had been accepted. If the pleasure had not shown upon her countenance, the pain of waiting for him to return, of not knowing how he was faring, had certainly taken its toll of Anne-Marie. Her anxiety and constant perambulation between her seat by the fire and the window overlooking the drive had soon indicated to Anna that some very tender feelings were involved.

If confirmation were needed that these emotions were deeply felt and reciprocated, it came when Mr Elliott stepped out of his carriage and walked in the door behind the Sutton children and received what could only be called a "rapturous welcome."

Anna watched, with some amusement, his own impulsive response, when he reached out for Anne-Marie and gathering her into his arms, held her close for several minutes. It was as if neither cared any longer to whom their true feelings were revealed. A short while later, when Mrs Sutton had taken her children upstairs to bed, the couple approached Anna and told her simply and frankly, that they were in love and had become engaged that afternoon.

Anna was delighted and congratulated them warmly, thinking as she did so of her husband, probably only halfway on his overnight journey to Netherfield. She longed to have him home, to share with her these intimate, happy moments, yet she was not sure how he would accept Anne-Marie's engagement to Mr Elliott.

Jonathan Bingley's only concern was his daughter's happiness and well-being. He would certainly want to be quite sure she was making the right decision this time. Anna, on the other hand, seeing the pair together, could have no doubts. Not only was she convinced they were in love, they appeared in every other way to be well suited. In both appearance and disposition, they were perfectly matched, she thought, recalling how different had been her view of Mr Bradshaw, when he had first come to Netherfield.

Not long afterwards there came another announcement. Harriet Greene had been attending to Mr Bowles, who had sustained a huge bruise across his shoulders from the glancing blow dealt him by the enraged Sutton. Cold compresses and herbal fomentations were recommended and applied with care and diligence until the patient appeared more comfortable. Her task completed, Harriet, having put away her medications, came to the parlour where they were all engaged in a discussion of the days' events.

Anna had just been congratulating one happy couple, when another pair appeared before her and Bowles declared that Miss Harriet Greene had kindly consented to be his wife and they would like to be married in the Autumn, "if that was alright with you and Mr Bingley, ma'am."

Anna, quite taken aback, for she had had no idea of Mr Bowles's interest in Harriet Greene, nevertheless congratulated them and so did the other lovers, whose felicity, now seemingly increasing by the hour, was sufficient to share with anyone who needed cheering up. It was in Anne-Marie's nature that she should feel the need to share her joy with as many of her family as possible. By this same token, Mrs Sutton and her unhappy children were all drawn into and enveloped by the warm glow of the family's contentment.

Meanwhile, Charlotte Collins, who had scarcely become accustomed to one engagement, for she had known in advance of Mr Bowles's proposal and Harriet's decision to accept him, was now called upon to celebrate with another happy couple, as Anne-Marie brought Mr Elliott to sit with her and tell her of their happiness. Seeing, in addition to all this gladness, Mrs Sutton and her daughters reunited had been almost more than her heart could bear and a short while later, Mrs Collins asked to be excused and retired to bed. The faithful Harriet disengaged herself from the group and took her mistress upstairs as Mr Bowles, Anna noted, cast an approving eye upon her. Anna knew him to be a thoroughly reliable person, a man whose life had been changed by the untimely death of his wife, leaving him childless and lonely and yet remarkably unembittered. He was one of her husband's most trusted stewards. If Harriet and he had found happiness together, Anna was prepared to wish them the very best. It was something more she would have to tell her husband, when he returned home on the morrow.

With some difficulty, the now acknowledged lovers dragged themselves apart. Anna and Anne-Marie returned to Netherfield House with Mr Bowles, while Colin Elliott, having been invited to dine at Netherfield Park on the morrow, finally left Longbourn and returned to his lodgings at Meryton.

It had been an extraordinary day, which had begun and ended in great personal happiness, yet at its dark heart had revealed that no one is immune from the tragic consequences of obsession.

꙳

That night Anne-Marie, too excited to sleep, rose and wrote to her favourite aunt.

> My dearest Aunt Emma,
>   I am so happy, I can no longer keep it from you; Mr Elliott has asked me to marry him and I have accepted him. This time, dear Aunt, I know I have made the right decision, because I have never known such terror as when he went in search of Lucy Sutton's children and we feared he may

*have to confront the brutal Mr Sutton, nor have I experienced such over-
whelming relief and joy, as I did when he walked in the door and gathered
me in his arms. As you well know, I am not a romantic female, a la the
femmes fragiles of the popular novellas that divert young ladies of today,
but I do feel deeply and I know that he excites in me the deepest feelings of
love. I have, during the past few months, learned to value him as a friend,
but only in the last week have I understood my own heart. I love him,
dearest Aunt, and I do believe him when he says he loves me and I long to
be his wife.*

*You are already surprised, are you not, that I have not once spoken of
his "goodness?" You may conclude from this omission that he is lacking in
goodness, perhaps? Let me say then that he is thoughtful and tender,
compassionate, kind and loving, like no other man I have known. Do you
think all these qualities may equal goodness? If they do, then please believe
him to be good; so good that he has helped me draw myself out of dread and
depression into the sunlight again. I had not thought I would ever shed the
shackles of my previous misery, but even as I write, I feel a lightness of
heart and mind as never before, for they are gone. Mr Elliott has cut them
away and given me my freedom again.*

*Dearest Aunt, I long to see you and hope with all my heart that some
time may be found for us to visit you at Standish Park together. He has an
immense regard for Mr Wilson and speaks highly of you all.*

*Meanwhile, let me thank you once more for your affection and care as
well as your wonderful example of fearless love. What would I have been
without them?*

*I remember, dearest Aunt, your sage counsel when you told me I must
marry only for the deepest love. When I asked you how I would know it,
you said, "When you realise your life would be unendurable without him,
you will know."*

I think, now, I do know.

*He loves me and says so with warmth and passion. Could I do other
than accept him? I think not, and I am sure you will agree.*

*When Papa returns tomorrow, Mr Elliott will see him again and tell
him of our engagement. For my part, I am quite fixed in my intention, so
I pray Papa will approve, else it will break both his heart and mine.*

Your loving niece,
Anne-Marie Bingley.

Having sealed the letter, Anne-Marie unlocked her diary, repository of her innermost thoughts. At times, when it had seemed there never would be any purpose to her life and again, when little specks of light had begun to illuminate her horizon, its pages had recorded her feelings. She recounted there, in some detail, the events of the last few days and, as was her habit, drew her conclusions.

Should I live to be a hundred, I doubt I will know a week as strange as this one has been. How is it possible that one might swing through so many emotions as I have in the course of two days? There I was, at one moment quietly content, if a little confused, contemplating my possible future, when suddenly the world around me seemed to explode into tiny fragments, some sharp and hurtful like shattered glass, others shining like stars!

The hurt we have all felt; with poor Lucy Sutton's two girls being kidnapped and then recovered from their crazed father, whose obsession with his wife leads him to kidnap his own children, in order to punish her. The cruelty and pain inflicted upon all of them and upon us, who have had to support Lucy through her agony, makes one question whether love alone, without good sense and sound judgment, is worth having.

Mr Sutton claims he is motivated by love of his family, but in truth, he seems driven by hate. He cannot see that the obsessive passion he manifests destroys those he claims to love. Poor Lucy on the other hand, though she undoubtedly loves her children, appears too weak and timorous to thwart him. Between them, it has to be said, the unfortunate children have not had a fair deal.

I cannot help recalling Papa's strength and determination to protect all of us from injury, when my poor mama's understanding and judgment failed her. How different was his response to that of Mr Sutton. How calm and gentle was his response to our terrible tragedy. Were it not for the untiring efforts of Mr Elliott and his friend Mr Tillyard, as well as our dear Mr Bowles, whose courage must be commended, the Sutton children may have been lost to their mother forever! God knows where he might have taken them.

I was so proud today of my Mr Elliott, whose offer of marriage I had only just accepted. It was a joy to see how swiftly and with what vigour and determination, he organised himself and his friends and proceeded to Meryton, returning some hours later, with Lucy Sutton and her children safe and Mr Sutton handed over to the local constabulary. Yet all accomplished with such modesty; no boastful claims or triumphant pronouncements of success. Indeed, had I not already accepted him, I should have done so without hesitation.

Still, I was so glad that I had said I would marry him. It will surely be a matter of jest between us, even though I know he loves me, and my thoughts have been completely absorbed with him. I had not thought it possible to be so much in love with anyone nor to be so loved.

Here indeed, is one of the few shining fragments of this shattered day.

Papa will be here around midday and I expect he will want a full account of what has transpired. Anna will be the one to tell him; she longs for his return. It is clear she misses him terribly when he is away.

My news will keep until later.

Her writing done, in the small hours of the morning, Anne-Marie fell asleep, with very little to disturb her hopes of future happiness.

Jonathan Bingley arrived the following day around mid-morning. Having travelled for many hours, he went directly upstairs, with only his wife for company. He had missed her sorely; the generosity and warmth of her love always brought him comfort.

Later, Anna told him of the dramatic events of the previous evening. He was exceedingly relieved that the Sutton children were safely back with their mother and quite diverted by the news that it was largely the result of Colin Elliott's efforts.

"Thank God, they're safe," he said and, when Anna revealed that Mr Elliott would be dining with them that evening, added, "Oh, good, I shall congratulate him on his success. He certainly seems a decisive and brave fellow; I'll give him that."

"You will probably find that Mr Elliott is to be congratulated upon yet another achievement, my dear," Anna said archly.

"Indeed? Why, what more has he done?"

"Perhaps, I should have let Anne-Marie tell you herself, but I know you wish to rest before dinner and it is best that you are informed before you meet Mr Elliott," she explained, then seeing his expression sharpen as he understood her drift, she added, "Yes, they are engaged. He has proposed and she has accepted him. I cannot remember when I have last seen her look so delighted."

Jonathan rose, and pulling on a robe, went over to the window. He was silent, thoughtful. Anne-Marie was very precious to him; he could not abide the thought of her being hurt again. His concern was to protect her from another disappointment. Looking out, he saw her in the distance, walking in the grounds, a basket on her arm, her step light, her air confident. It was plain that there was nothing troubling her, as she tripped around the rose garden.

"Had she told you she intended to accept him?" he asked.

Anna shook her head. "Not directly, but in so many ways, in her looks and smiles, the brightness of her voice, the way she spoke of him with pride and pleasure; I had no doubt she was in love with him. I think she may well have confided in me, if not for this drama with Mrs Sutton's children. That had us all terrified for days; we had no thought of anything else."

"And Elliott, did he come and see you as I suggested he should?"

"Yes, indeed, and I gave him the benefit of my knowledge of the circumstances of Anne-Marie's marriage to Bradshaw and its unhappy consequences. He was, I think, more grieved than shocked. He is a man of the world, at thirty-four or thirty-five, he must surely be well aware of these types of arrangements, which are more common in smart society than we would like to think," said Anna.

"Did he say anything significant? How did he respond to the information you provided?" Jonathan asked.

"He was very moved by my story of Anne-Marie's depression and appeared to have a sympathetic understanding of her feelings," she replied.

"He listened with interest, but in the end, none of it seemed to deter him from his quest for her hand. Indeed, he set off for Longbourn, almost immediately, to see her and I know now that he was with her, having just been accepted, when your letter, which I sent on to Longbourn, reached them."

Jonathan appeared calmer; he smiled and shook his head as she continued, "Afterwards, when he returned from Meryton with the Sutton children, there was no attempt at concealment at all; they were most joyfully reunited and informed me directly of their engagement."

"Well, my love, I shall see what they have to say to me. Perhaps, you could tell Anne-Marie I should like to see her before Elliott arrives for dinner," he said and was about to ring for a servant to prepare his bath, when she said, "Oh, I almost forgot, our Mr Bowles is engaged as well." Jonathan swung round, amazed. "Bowles engaged? To whom and since when?"

"To Harriet Greene, since last night; though I do believe they had spoken with Mrs Collins some days ago. Harriet is her trusted companion and Aunt Charlotte would have been very hurt, had they kept her in ignorance. They hope to marry in the Autumn and I think Bowles may wish to move to Longbourn, where he already does a great deal of work, so you may be looking for a new steward for Netherfield."

Jonathan, still shaking his head in disbelief, said, "Bowles engaged! Who would have thought it? But, he has been a widower for many years and was probably very lonely. It is a good match for Harriet Greene, too; he is a fine man. Ah well, it does look as if romance has been in the air in these parts," he said as he rang for his servant and Anna left the room, laughing.

She went downstairs and, finding Anne-Marie reading to young Nicholas in the parlour, told her that her father wished to see her before dinner.

Anne-Marie was eager to discover how he had received the news of her engagement to Mr Elliott, but apart from assuring her that she had little to fear, since he had a very good opinion of her Mr Elliott, Anna preferred to let father and daughter speak directly to one another on the subject. "Your Papa loves you dearly, Anne-Marie. His concern is only for your happiness. If you are certain that Mr Elliott will make you happy, I doubt he will raise any objections to your marriage. It is you and Mr Elliott who must convince him that you care deeply for each other," she said, leaving Anne-Marie, smiling, grateful for her counsel.

Like her Aunt Emma Wilson, Anna had provided an example to her, in her moments of greatest sorrow, of what genuine love could achieve. She could not fail to see the intensity of feeling between her father and his wife, and the happiness that flowed from it had engendered an atmosphere of warm affection that enveloped the entire household at Netherfield.

That evening, Anne-Marie dressed with more than usual care and came downstairs well before Mr Elliott was expected. She found her father in his study, reading one of the London newspapers, which was clearly not pleasing him. He looked somewhat exasperated. When she entered the room, however, he put aside his paper, rose, and came towards her.

As they embraced and greeted one another, she said, "You must be relieved, Papa, that Mrs Sutton's children are safe."

He sighed, "I am, indeed, very relieved and I understand it was due chiefly to the efforts of a certain gentleman of our acquaintance. What a fortunate fellow he must be. A crisis develops, which he is able to resolve with a little help from his friends and our Mr Bowles, I believe, and he proves himself to a certain young lady and her admiring family! Quite like the knights of old, eh? Except instead of slaying the villain, he hands him over to the local constabulary. Well done, Mr Elliott!"

He was smiling down at her as he spoke, and Anne-Marie knew then that he would not object to her engagement; his gentle, teasing words and manner gave her confidence.

Taking her cue from him, she laughed lightly and said, "Yes, Papa, it will make a very diverting tale to tell around the table at Christmas, I am sure. No doubt my dear brother will find it very droll indeed." He surprised her then by asking directly, "Do you wish to be married by Christmas, my dear?"

"We have not fixed upon a date, Papa. Mr Elliott wishes to discuss that with you this evening. If we did, would you have any objection?" He took both her hands in his, as he used to when she was a very little girl asking a serious question. "My dear Anne-Marie, why would I object? If I knew it would make you happy, that is all that matters. Elliott is an honourable and apparently brave young man, with excellent prospects. All I want you to tell me is that this time, he is the right man for you. Is he, Anne-Marie? Do you love him enough and will he make you truly happy?"

He looked at her, searching her face for any sign of uncertainty or hesitancy, but found none.

She met his eyes directly and answered him in a firm, though quiet, voice, "I believe he will, Papa. I know I made a bad mistake; it was my fault and I suffered for it. This time, I know it is right, because I feel it is right. I love him dearly and I want to be his wife. I know what marriage means and I long to be

married to him. When he was gone last evening to recover Mrs Sutton's children, I was so afraid; I knew that if anything should happen to him, I should
not care to go on living. Papa, I do love him." Her voice shook and he put his
arms around her to comfort her.

Jonathan was sorry; he had not intended to compel her to reveal her deepest
feelings, but now she had done so, her commitment was clear. He could not
doubt the strength of her feelings for Colin Elliott. All that remained was to
await the man himself.

"Very well, my love, you have my blessing," he said and she smiled, drying
her tears. "When he arrives, send Mr Elliott in to see me and we shall see what
he has to say for himself. I have already had a letter explaining his intentions
and asking for my consent, so there is not a great deal more to discuss, if you are
both certain of your feelings. That was my chief concern."

Anne-Marie hugged her father and flew out of the study and into the hall,
almost colliding with Mr Elliott, who had just arrived and was divesting himself
of his coat. From the look on her face, he could have judged that she was
ecstatic, but the tears in her eyes concerned him.

"Anne-Marie, dearest, is something wrong?" he asked softly.

She shook her head and said, "No, not at all; Papa is waiting for you in his study.
You should go to him at once," she declared and then ran up the stairs to her room,
where she had to splash plenty of cool water on her face to help compose herself.

Anna, dressed and ready for dinner, had heard Anne-Marie come upstairs
and go into her room. She knocked and on entering, found a young woman so
elated, she could hardly believe her eyes. Anne-Marie had always been calm and
collected, except on one memorable occasion, following the death of Mr
Bradshaw. This time, however, there was certainly no hysteria; only a height-
ened excitement that surprised even Anna, who could well understand the
exhilarating effect of newly discovered emotions, now openly acknowledged for
the first time. She went to her at once and, without a word, put her arms around
her and held her, feeling the racing of her heart. Anne-Marie tried to speak, but
Anna put a finger to her lips.

"You have no need to explain yourself to me. I know how you feel, I know
it is a most exalting feeling; treasure it and share it with your Mr Elliott," she
said, gently. Anne-Marie thanked her as they tidied her hair and clothes before
they went downstairs.

As if on cue, Mr Elliott and Mr Bingley came out of the study together and met them at the foot of the stairs and they went into the parlour.

"Well, Anne-Marie, Mr Elliott tells me you have accepted him and, in view of your words to me earlier today, I have given you both my blessing."

After they had exchanged the customary congratulations, Jonathan asked, "Anna, my dear, do you believe we could manage a wedding before Christmas?"

As Anne-Marie went swiftly to his side, Colin Elliott took her hand in his.

Anna had replied that she thought it could be arranged, but they would need to discuss numbers of guests and other matters.

"I think, Papa, Mr Elliott and I would like a quiet family wedding at Netherfield," said Anne-Marie, and Colin Elliott agreed immediately. Anna asked, "Where will you live, when you are married?"

Jonathan intervened to say, "They will live here, my dear, until Longbourn has been refurbished and made ready for them. I have told Mr Elliott what you already know, that I intend Anne-Marie to inherit Longbourn, the estate, not the school, which remains my wife's responsibility, of course; in fact the arrangements have all been written into my will," he explained. "Mr Elliott has an apartment in Knightsbridge and it would serve no useful purpose to purchase or lease another country house, while Longbourn is available. Mrs Collins will continue to live there as our guest and, with Mr Bowles and Miss Greene getting married, they can set the household up for you. You may wish to have some changes made; I shall ask Bowles to get in a builder next week to look at the place."

Anne-Marie's pleasure was almost impossible to express. "Why, Papa, that is very generous of you, but what about my sisters?"

Jonathan laughed, "Your sisters are still too young to be concerned about their inheritance, my dear. You can leave that to me. It is, however, imperative that you live within easy distance of the hospital at Bell's Field, if you are to manage it. When I last visited the site, I was informed it would be ready to furnish and staff in the New Year. Now, Mr Elliott tells me he had intended to look at leasing Ashdown House, which is vacant, but it is more than ten miles from Bell's Field, whereas Longbourn is a mere ten minutes in the curricle and a pleasant walk across the park on a fine day. Do you not agree?" he asked reasonably and they agreed, of course.

Colin Elliott and Anne-Marie were astonished at the speed with which Mr Bingley had made these decisions. Once having ascertained that they had declared their love and wanted to marry, he had moved swiftly to arrange matters to suit them. Elliott had been overwhelmed by his generosity.

When asked where they proposed to live, he had replied that he had a list of probable houses in the district, knowing Anne-Marie would not wish to settle too far from her family, Ashdown House and Purvis Lodge among them. His prospective father-in-law had intervened to say that it would not be necessary to incur such an expense, since his daughter was to inherit Longbourn anyway.

"You should both talk to Mrs Bingley first; she knows a great deal about such matters, advised us on all of the changes we made here," he had said.

"The rooms downstairs have been recently refurbished, but the bedrooms and private sitting room upstairs could do with some alterations to suit you. Meanwhile, you are very welcome to live here until Longbourn is ready." Colin Elliott had tried to point out that he had sufficient funds from the sale of some of his father's shares to lease a property, but Mr Bingley had urged him to save his money.

"If, as I believe you intend to do, you are to leave your party and support the Reform Group, you will need money to help you win the next election. Mark my words, Mr Elliott, the Tories will fight you all the way," he had said. "It is better that you live in the area and use your own funds. That way, you are not beholden to anyone and can be your own man in Parliament; it is what I have always done," he had advised.

Mr Bingley's farsightedness surprised even Colin Elliott, who had heard much about him from his Parliamentary colleagues. His reputation for probity and good sense was well known. Thanking him profusely, he had accepted the generous offer, on condition Anne-Marie agreed. She was equally pleased, knowing how much it meant to her father to have her settled close to Netherfield.

Now all that remained to be done was to consult Anna, whose artistic talent and impeccable taste were apparent in the refurbishment of Netherfield House, and make plans for Longbourn and their wedding, to which exceedingly pleasant tasks they soon addressed themselves. Letters were written to advise family and friends of their engagement and an announcement was placed in *The Times*.

As the Autumn session of Parliament drew to a close, they travelled down to London to attend the House of Commons and hear Colin Elliott give his final speech as a member of the Tory Party. The family was well represented. Anne-Marie, Anna, and Emma Wilson were seated in the special gallery for ladies, while James Wilson had found accommodation for Jonathan and Charles Bingley among the distinguished visitors.

Anne-Marie was tingling with excitement. She held tight to her aunt's hand as they waited for Elliott to rise to his feet. When he began to speak however, she became so engrossed, she leaned forward to see him better and take in every word.

Absorbed by his passionate argument for a fairer society, she was drawn inevitably to recollections and comparisons with the past. She could not help contrasting the images of Colin Elliott with those of Mr Bradshaw in church when he had insisted that she sat in the front pew, while he made his pompous little sermons, using the sacred word of God to pontificate upon human frailty, while she knew he never acknowledged his own. She recalled how painful it had been, how she had cringed then; how differently did she feel listening to Mr Elliott. Anne-Marie was so proud of him, she wished she could tell the whole world how she felt.

It was generally agreed that it was an excellent speech; neither too long nor too portentous and self-congratulatory, it was delivered more in sorrow than in anger, stressing his disappointment with the Tories and his own determination to work for reform and the improvement of the lot of the poor, even if it meant he would have fewer chances of preferment himself.

When he finished speaking there was loud applause and Anne-Marie almost cheered, except Emma Wilson had warned her it was not considered proper for visitors, especially ladies, to do so. From the men there was an enthusiastic "Hear, Hear!" as he was surrounded by his colleagues on the floor of the House.

Anne-Marie was near to bursting with impatience and pride, so full of love for him that she thought she would weep and make a fool of herself.

But she did not. When they went down into the lobbies, however, and met him coming out of the chamber, she could not resist going to him and planting a warm, congratulatory kiss on his cheek. Colin Elliott reddened and looked pleased; then taking her by the arm in a rather proprietary manner, he walked out with her to be cheered by the waiting crowd of supporters and the gentlemen of the press. This was not just the day of his declaration of independence from his party; it was also her day to affirm openly her love for him, for all to see.

As they stood on the steps together, she felt his arm tighten around her waist and his hand holding hers firmly, as he whispered his thanks, without turning his head. The colour rose in her cheeks and she longed to be with him alone. Yet, with a crowd watching them, they had to maintain very proper decorum. Any expression of affection had to be postponed for later.

The opportunity would not come for several hours, for they had all been invited to dine with the Wilsons at Grosvenor Street, at a celebration to mark James Wilson's twentieth year in Parliament, as well as a more recent event, for which he had received most of the credit.

The conversion of young Elliott, whose staunchly Tory antecedents had been so publicly overthrown that afternoon, was a matter of great satisfaction to James and Emma Wilson. Naturally, the function attracted many of their friends and colleagues, eager to congratulate James and meet the new Reformist recruit and his beautiful wife-to-be, whom most members had never seen before.

"I had no idea Jonathan Bingley had such a lovely daughter," said one MP.

"Clearly he has been hiding her from the likes of you," said another, while a third wondered whether Elliott's conversion to Reform politics had been assisted by the presence of the beautiful niece of his mentor and friend, James Wilson.

Overhearing the exchange, Lord Shaftesbury, a friend of the Wilsons, assured them that if Wilson and Bingley needed beautiful women to recruit new members to their cause, there'd be quite a crowd battering at the gates.

"All of the women in this family are not only handsome; they are intelligent and public spirited as well," he quipped, "a combination irresistible to any self-respecting Reformist, I am told."

Anne-Marie, on the advice of her Aunt Emma, renowned for her excellent taste, dressed for the dinner in a simple, elegant gown of lilac silk, but never stopped to think of the impression she was making on the gathering.

She could, however, barely conceal her pride in her Mr Elliott, as she watched him converse easily with men many years his senior in age and political experience; all clearly impressed with his principled stand and his fine speech.

There was even a Tory admirer present; himself a maverick in his party, Lord Shaftesbury, a personal friend of Jonathan Bingley and the Wilsons, took the time to congratulate Elliott and urge him to hold fast to his beliefs. He had himself tried, often without much success, to persuade his party of the need for reform. He was glad, he said, to see Elliott making a stand.

At long last, when the celebrations were over and most of the guests had departed, Colin Elliott and Anne-Marie retreated to Mr Wilson's study to say their farewells and in those few loving moments made up for their many hours apart. Reluctantly, he left her then; promising to return early the following day, when they would be journeying with the Wilsons to Standish Park, where they had been invited to spend a week or two. It was something they both looked forward to with much pleasure.

Anne-Marie knew all about the enchantment of Standish Park, where Anna had assured her, lovers were guaranteed to fall even deeper in love. "There is something almost magical, about the place" she had said, recalling the days when she and Jonathan had found so much delight and contentment there. Seeing the felicity of Emma and James, Anne-Marie had no reason to doubt it. She knew its many pleasures and looked forward to sharing them with Colin Elliott.

Since their engagement, she had been delighted to find many subjects upon which they agreed; the world of books and music, of which she knew she had a good deal to learn from him, was only just opening up to her. He was an interested and patient teacher and she looked forward to further discoveries in fields where she had not ventured before.

One more important matter remained to be settled, however, before she could face the future with serenity; even though it was a matter of which she had not been much aware in recent times.

After they'd been at Standish Park some two or three days, a carriage arrived bearing Emily Courtney and her daughter Eliza Harwood, once Anne-Marie's confidante and dearest friend. They had, however, not met one another since the funeral of Mr Bradshaw. Eliza had been spending some time with her parents in Derbyshire, following the sad loss of a child, stillborn before its time. Grief stricken and unable to cope alone, she had written to her mother, who had arrived and taken her home to Kympton.

During her time there, Eliza had expressed her desire to meet Anne-Marie and be reconciled with her. Her mother Emily, whose warm friendship with her cousin Emma had continued over many years, had written asking if it might be arranged. Emma Wilson having considered the request and discussed it with her mother, and her Aunt Lizzie had decided to do something about it. The invitation to Anne-Marie and Mr Elliott had gone out on the very day she had received news of their engagement. It was a clever piece of manipulation but, as Emma had explained to her husband, it had been done in a good cause.

"I know Anne-Marie will not begrudge Eliza the consolation of reconciliation with her, now she has found true happiness herself," she had said, as they sat together at breakfast and James, though a little wary of such contrivances, had agreed that she was probably right. He thought Anne-Marie was not the type of young woman who would bear a grudge.

"But, do you not think you ought to warn her that they are expected tomorrow? And what do you suppose Elliott will make of it all?" he had asked, practical and thoughtful, as ever.

Emma smiled and pressed his hand, gently, "Now, that's where I need your help, my dear," she had said, "Do you suppose you could find a reason to invite Colin Elliott to accompany you on your journey to Maidstone tomorrow?"

James laughed; he never failed to be surprised at the ingenious ways by which his wife could draw him into her plans. She made the endearing excuse that she did not want him to feel left out and he almost always acquiesced.

"Well, my dear, since you mention it, it may well be a good idea for him to come along. We are convening a branch of the Reform Group in the area, to press the government for a national public education policy. I know it is a subject Elliott is keenly interested in; he may benefit from attending and may even choose to follow our example in his own constituency. I shall ask him later today. I could do with the company on the journey there and back, anyway," he said and was rewarded by his wife with a warm embrace.

⁓⁀⁓

So it happened that when Emily Courtney and her daughter arrived at Standish Park the following day, the gentlemen had already left for Maidstone.

Aunt and niece were sitting together upstairs and Emma had only just told Anne-Marie that they were expecting visitors.

"From London?" she asked, surprised.

"No, from Derbyshire; Kympton to be exact," Emma replied.

"Let me guess, it's Aunt Emily and Mr Courtney. No?" Seeing her aunt shake her head, "Not Mr Courtney; it must be Aunt Emily and Jessica then?"

Emma smiled and hearing a carriage coming up the drive, she rose and moved to the window. Anne-Marie followed her and the speculation ended, as she saw the two women alight.

Emma noticed that Anne-Marie had become very pale.

She took her hands in hers, "Now, my dearest, you are not going to be upset, are you? Eliza has been very ill after losing her baby and Emily has been looking after her. They are here only for a few days, en route to Ramsgate, and they have come especially to see you."

"Me? Why me?" Anne-Marie seemed confused.

"Because, my love, Eliza blames herself for having persuaded you to accept Mr Bradshaw. She believes that you blame her, too, and wishes to be reconciled with you before your wedding to Mr Elliott. Surely, you cannot refuse?" Emma pleaded.

Anne-Marie was silent and bit her lip hard, as they went downstairs to meet the visitors, who had been shown into the saloon. They found the ladies looking very tired and drawn, after their long journey by rail and coach. When they rose to greet them, it was quite obvious that Eliza was still far from well. She was thin and pale and her eyes filled with tears, as she came forward with some trepidation, her hand outstretched, to greet them.

Despite her pain, Anne-Marie had never blamed Eliza for her own misfortune; it had been more a question of avoiding the memories of those dreadful two years, which meeting Eliza would surely stir up. Yet her tender heart was so moved, seeing her thus, she ignored her hand and embraced her. As both women wept, Emily and Emma exchanged glances and slipped out of the room, leaving them together.

Nothing in Anne-Marie's character would have permitted her to turn her face away from Eliza Harwood in her present condition. As for Eliza, she had long blamed herself for ever having encouraged her friend to accept Mr Bradshaw, realising now that no amount of rectitude and Christian morality could make up for the desolation of a marriage devoid of the warmth of love. That she had persuaded her dearest friend into such a bleak relationship had left her feeling guilty and miserable.

Long months of separation had taken their toll and it was a while before the two women could converse easily, as they had done when Eliza had been the young girl's confidante and best friend. They had grown apart and it would take time to bridge the divide. When Emma and Emily returned, however, they had recovered their composure and were talking more easily together. Later, it became clear they had overcome their inhibitions and though they may never be as close as they'd been before, they could at least be companions again. Emily could tell from her daughter's demeanour that she had made her peace with Anne-Marie and blessed Emma for affording her the opportunity to do so. "It will go a long way towards healing her spirit, Emma," she said. "She has been desolated all year, believing Anne-Marie was lost to her as a friend. I cannot tell you how grateful I am. God bless you, Emma."

❧

Writing later to her father and Anna, Anne-Marie took up most of her letter with poetic descriptions of the park and woodlands in their Autumn splendour and the many delightful activities they were involved in at Standish Park.

> *Each day, we are able to enjoy the beauty of this place in one way or another, walks in the woods or picnics by the river, followed by evenings filled with exquisite music and excellent company. I have not mentioned the library or the gallery, both of which hold such treasures that I am sure I would not usually see in a lifetime. Both Aunt Emma and Mr Elliott have been taking me in hand and teaching me to appreciate them and I am very grateful indeed.*

In the last two paragraphs, she mentioned the visit of Emily Courtney and her daughter Eliza Harwood.

> *You will be surprised, perhaps, to hear that Mrs Courtney and Eliza were here for a few days, on their way to Ramsgate, where Eliza is to spend the rest of the Summer. She is very poorly and needs to recover her health; Mr Harwood is to join them later.*

Dear Papa and Anna, I know you will be happy to learn that Eliza and I have talked over our unhappy memories and are now quite reconciled. Eliza was relieved to discover that I had never held her responsible for my own sorrow, and she was especially pleased to know, that being engaged to Mr Elliott, memories of my earlier mistake no longer troubled me and I looked forward to our marriage, confident of happiness. Aunt Emily was happy, too, and said she had heard very good reports of my Mr Elliott from Aunt Caroline, Colonel Fitzwilliam, and others. She said she was sure we would be happy together. Poor Eliza has been very ill and miserable; I hope I have done something to help her recover. It must be dreadful to lose a little baby and not even have had the joy of holding it in your arms for a little while. I could not imagine such sorrow!

Anne-Marie's compassion and genuine kindness had clearly triumphed over any lingering bitterness she may have carried in her heart.

Her father was not surprised. "I was sure my sister would not rest until she had brought about some reconciliation between those two young women," said Jonathan, as he handed the letter back to his wife. Anna smiled but said nothing. She had had no intimation of Emma's plans, but had always believed that her sister-in-law, being a compassionate and loving woman, would find some way to bring Eliza Harwood and Anne-Marie together, convinced that Anne-Marie would be the better for it.

~꒳~

Returning to Netherfield, Anne-Marie and Mr Elliott were plunged back into preparations for the wedding, now fixed for December. The bridesmaids, Teresa and Cathy, had to be measured for their gowns and trained for their roles, while the choir was rehearsed until they were singing like angels!

Mr Griffin, who was to perform the ceremony, which Teresa said, must have been for him, the next best thing to marrying Anne-Marie himself, wore a perpetual smile. He seemed so pleased and was so excited, that Anna feared he would forget his words in the order of service, when he saw the bride standing before him.

"Poor Mr Griffin, he has long given up hope, but I am sure he still has a corner of his heart filled with love for Anne-Marie," she said, as she helped

Teresa with her gown, warning her to say nothing to Cathy, who would surely giggle and spoil everything. Teresa promised, adding that she had no doubt everything would turn out well, since their grandmother was arriving from Ashford Park to supervise it all.

"Cathy would not dare giggle," she declared, "not in her presence."

Meanwhile, plans for Longbourn and the hospital were well advanced. Mrs Collins, who had been rather lonely since the death of her friend and companion Mary Bennet, looked forward to a house that no longer fell silent once the students went home. She had always been fond of Anne-Marie and welcomed her company at Longbourn. As for Mr Elliott, his unfailing courtesy and attention to herself had won him her esteem long before he became engaged to her granddaughter.

Harriet Greene and Mr Bowles were married and, after they returned from a visit to her family, he moved to live at Longbourn, replaced at Netherfield by a man who had served Jonathan when he had been a member of the House of Commons, a Mr Alfred Dobson.

Everything appeared to be moving smoothly, when something they could have neither foreseen nor prevented occurred. On a fine, calm, Autumn afternoon, news came by telegraph of the death of Mr Edward Gardiner. Jonathan and Anna Bingley left immediately for Derbyshire to attend the funeral. Mr Gardiner, uncle of Jane and Elizabeth, was a much loved and respected member of the family and Jonathan knew his death would cause great grief among their cousins. At Pemberley, the Darcys were desolated.

Mr Darcy's close friendship with Mr Gardiner over many years had been of immense value to him, broadening his outlook, drawing him out of the close, rather dull circle of the country gentry into which he had been born, into the more enterprising, cosmopolitan world of Commerce. It had compelled him to meet new people and confront ideas, which he had either ignored or knew nothing of in his youth. Mrs Gardiner, one of the finest ladies Darcy had known, was Lizzie's friend and confidante, while their son Richard Gardiner, who had married Cassy Darcy, was closer to Mr Darcy than his own son Julian.

The two couples had been intimate for many years. Having been instrumental in bringing their favourite niece and Mr Darcy together, the Gardiners held a special place in their hearts.

Though his death had been long expected after several bouts of heart disease, when it came, it had been a shock which left both Darcy and Elizabeth grief stricken. When Jonathan and Anna arrived at Pemberley, it was Cassandra Gardiner who greeted them and made arrangements for their stay.

"My father has gone to Oakleigh with Richard; Mama and Aunt Jane are with Caroline, who is inconsolable," she explained, as she accompanied them indoors and rang for refreshments. While her parents had gone to offer comfort to the Gardiners, Jonathan and Anna found it was Cassy, not Julian, who was in charge at Pemberley. When her husband Richard returned, he revealed that Julian's wife Josie was unwell and unable to travel from Cambridge for the funeral. "Julian is expected tomorrow; I believe he has already left Cambridge," Richard explained, adding that "Cassy knows everything that needed doing, anyway."

Mr Darcy, at Mrs Gardiner's request, had arranged for the funeral to take place at the church at Pemberley, so her husband may be laid to rest in the churchyard there, close to his friends and beside the two young boys, William Darcy and Edward Fitzwilliam, whom he had loved so dearly and whose untimely deaths had filled him with great sadness. It had been his dying wish.

Cassandra followed all her father's instructions minutely, knowing how much Mr Gardiner had meant to him. Cassy knew the people of the estate well, far better than Julian, who spent very little time at Pemberley. Anna, who offered to help, was astonished at Cassy's strength and capacity for hard work. Later, she took her place beside her husband as he supported his mother and stood with her parents, whose own grief was so heavy that Anna noticed for the first time that Mr Darcy looked weary and strained.

Jane and Elizabeth, both in deep mourning, could conceal their sorrow behind their veils, but Darcy's countenance showed the ravages of his grief at the loss of a dear friend.

Julian Darcy was late, arriving at the church when the funeral service had almost ended. Indeed, it was his father, who at the very last moment, had stepped in to read the lesson assigned to his son. He was clearly disappointed that Julian had not arrived in time and though he gave no overt indication of his feelings, Cassy knew he had been deeply hurt.

Darcy's heavy heart was due primarily to his deep personal loss, but he was anxious also about the future of the family business Mr Gardiner had developed and controlled for so long and in which he held a valuable partnership. Neither Richard nor Robert Gardiner appeared to have the inclination to fill their father's place.

As the funeral ended and the mourners began to leave, it was Cassy who took her father's arm and moved him away from the graveside, while Jonathan Bingley went swiftly to support his Aunt Lizzie and help her into the carriage that waited to take them back to Pemberley.

Those members of the family who had been close to the Gardiners stayed on after the funeral. To Mrs Gardiner and her two daughters, it was a heavy loss indeed; a loving husband and father who had helped and counselled his family, was gone. Jonathan and Anna stayed at Pemberley at the invitation of the Darcys, while Julian had to return forthwith to Cambridge.

After dinner, Mr Darcy, who had been silent during most of the meal, spoke with great feeling. "I shall miss him; even though I have known for several months that this was coming, the blow is a heavy one indeed."

He was standing beside the fireplace, as he spoke, looking into the flames, then turning to face them, "He has been my friend, my partner in business and, yes, in some ways, my mentor, for many years. He had so much experience, such sound judgment and was most generous with his time; I cannot imagine how we will get on without him," he said, his sombre tones reflecting his feelings.

Elizabeth moved to his side and said quietly, "And yet, he was totally without arrogance or false pride and treated everyone with respect and consideration. In spite of his long illness, he hardly ever complained; he was an example to us all."

She recalled how her father, Mr Bennet, had relied upon their Uncle Gardiner's sound advice in all matters concerning the welfare of their family. "And he was invariably right," she concluded.

Anna asked if Mrs Gardiner would stay on at Lambton, and Darcy assured her that she would. "She is devoted to the place; her husband bought it for her, because she had longed to return to the village in which she had been born and raised."

They spoke of Robert Gardiner and the possibility that he may succeed his father in the business, but Darcy was unsure.

"I know Mrs Gardiner is very fond of him, he is her youngest after all, but I do not believe Robert is seriously interested in the business," he said.

"He and his wife have many other pursuits, which take them away from Derbyshire for several months of the year. Robert has given no indication that he wishes to change that and I can only conclude that he is disinclined to take on the responsibility."

"No doubt Mr Gardiner would have made provision for the administration of the business in his will," said Jonathan, and they all agreed that the situation would be clearer once the will was read.

As the footmen brought in the candles and they rose to say goodnight, Elizabeth, taking her husband's arm, said, "Dear Jonathan, I think we are both very grateful to you and Anna for staying over with us at Pemberley tonight. Your uncle and I would have been very gloomy companions for one another, without you. Thank you."

—⁂—

The families were to meet once more that year, for a quiet wedding at Netherfield, at which Jonathan Bingley gave his favourite daughter to be married to Mr Colin Elliott, MP. This time, he had the fullest confidence that Anne-Marie's happiness was not in any doubt.

On the morning of her wedding, he had gone to her room and found her dressed in her elegant gown and jewellery, looking very beautiful indeed.

In the time they spent together, she had assured him of her heartfelt desire to marry Mr Elliott. "Papa, he is, without doubt the best man I have known, except for you, of course," she had declared and Jonathan had recalled the previous occasion on which she had said little, as she went to be married to Mr Bradshaw. It had been revealed later that she had cared little for him.

This time he was sure it was different. The glow that lit up her lovely face was evidence of her pleasure, as she contemplated marriage to Colin Elliott. Anna had also reassured him the previous night, when she had gone to Anne-Marie's room and found her sitting up in bed, bright-eyed and sleepless, quite unashamedly admitting her eagerness for the morrow.

"There she was," Anna had said, "sitting up in bed, smiling, unable to sleep, like a child waiting for a special treat! When I asked her if she was looking forward to her wedding day, she answered with disarming honesty, 'Oh Anna, I cannot wait for tomorrow, I love him so much.'"

From the usually restrained young woman she knew, this was a surprisingly passionate admission, which provided Anna with the reassurance she needed. She knew this marriage would bring Anne-Marie the intensity of feeling, that would wipe away all the residual indifference and dullness of the last.

Anna smiled as she told it, recalling her own experience, and her husband, unable to resist the inevitable question, asked if she had suffered similar feelings of impatience before their wedding day. His wife could not and, indeed, did not wish to deny it.

"I confess I did, but I was not as fortunate as Anne-Marie, for I had no one in whom to confide, no one who would understand my longing. Indeed, the waiting was made doubly difficult by my having to conceal my feelings, so as to avoid outraging my mother. She would no doubt have considered any eagerness on my part to be most unseemly," she said.

Her husband's voice was gentle. "And yet, it was you, my love, who chose to wait. I would have preferred that we were married sooner."

"Yes, because I wanted no one to accuse you of unseemly haste after Amelia-Jane's death. Waiting a while longer was a small price to pay," she replied, "even though it meant many days of aching loneliness, when you were away in London. I know I would have given anything to be with you." This frank admission brought such a fond response from him, as to make any further discussion of the issue unnecessary, except to express their hope that Anne-Marie and Mr Elliott would be as deeply happy in their marriage as they were themselves.

Despite the recent death of Mr Gardiner, many members of the family, except Mrs Gardiner and Mr Robert Gardiner and his wife, travelled to Hertfordshire to attend the wedding of Anne-Marie to Colin Elliott.

Jonathan Bingley was so well regarded and Anne-Marie so loved that everyone wanted to congratulate him and wish her happiness. Most of them knew well how much unhappiness she had borne without complaint until Bradshaw's death and how she had devoted her time before and since to helping the poor and sick, using her skills and influence to ease suffering and save lives.

She was, said Mr Bingley, her grandfather, to those of the party that had travelled together from Derbyshire, "an exceptional young woman, who deserved to be exceptionally happy." And there was no dissent from his opinion on this occasion.

Later, at the church and the wedding breakfast, no opportunity was missed to praise the handsome couple for their generosity and wish them a most felicitous marriage. Such universal agreement on the suitability of a marriage was rare indeed. If good wishes and fond hopes could ensure conjugal bliss, then this couple's felicity was guaranteed. Fortunately, they were both far too sensible to depend on such ephemeral gifts alone. Their happiness was more likely to grow out of the strength of their love and their mutual esteem. For the moment, however, no one who saw them together could doubt their delight in each other.

Two days later, they were to leave on their wedding journey to Europe. Anna went to her room to help Anne-Marie pack and found her still in her nightgown; her hair tumbled around her shoulders, tripping around the room in bare feet. When Anna, after a few moments of silence, asked, "Anne-Marie, my dear, is your packing all done?" She had danced over to her and said, "Yes, my dear Anna, I have everything I need, I think," which, considering her trunk lay half-empty beside her bed and her closet stood open, still full of clothes, was something of an exaggeration, Anna thought. Anna's indulgent smile gave little away, but once downstairs, she sought out her maid. "Jenny, please do go and help Miss Anne-Marie, I mean Mrs Elliott pack, will you, my dear? Else I fear she will never be ready when the carriage arrives," she said and Jenny Dawkin's knowing smile revealed that she was well aware of the situation.

Indeed, Rosie the chambermaid had just informed the entire kitchen staff that she had taken up their tea tray in the morning and, when she went to retrieve it an hour later, "it was almost untouched and the couple were still in bed!"

The giggles and laughter this revelation had aroused had been swiftly suppressed when Mrs Bingley appeared at the door. Her instructions were soon carried out to good effect.

Jenny and Rosie went upstairs and presently, Anne-Marie was packed, dressed, and ready when her husband came to escort her downstairs to the waiting carriage. This time the entire household appeared on the steps to wish them Godspeed. While it is neither necessary nor seemly to intrude upon the private passion of the newlywed pair to ascertain the extent of their happiness, one letter from Anne-Marie to her Aunt Emma Wilson, will suffice to prove their felicity. Written from London, where they spent a few days at Mr Elliott's apartment in Knightsbridge, it read,

My dearest Aunt,

What can I say? For in truth you know it already, far better than I do.

It was you who taught me what joy a good marriage with a loved and loving man can bring a woman. You who helped me believe that a woman can and must have the right to love and be loved, with sincerity and passion. You who made me understand that it was neither wrong nor wicked to want such love, and for that I thank you from the bottom of my heart.

Dear Aunt, it is difficult for me to say just how happy I am, indeed, to describe how I feel, for I fear that you, who know well what a low ebb I had reached, may well believe my language to be extreme. Because I had so little happiness in my previous marriage, you may think that any joy, however small, may seem like heaven!

Please believe me, dearest Aunt, when I say that there is no longer anything more I desire, no one I envy, no one whose good fortune I covet, no woman in the whole world with whom I will exchange one hour of my life, from now on.

This I owe primarily to my husband, but also to you, to my dear father and Anna. Without your love, I may well have given up my struggle and never found true happiness. I do love you all with all my heart,

God bless you,

Your loving and dearly loved niece,

Anne-Marie Elliott.

While in London, Mr and Mrs Elliott dined with her brother, who was now a firm friend of Mr Elliott, whose courageous defection from the Tory Party had won his admiration. Charles Bingley had sat in the gallery as Elliott made his speech in the Commons and confessed later that he had wanted to cheer loudly at several points but was reluctant to risk ejection by the ushers.

"I thought it was superb. Your denunciation of the inertia and lethargy affecting the Tory Party was absolutely timely. I could not have put it better myself!" he declared, at dinner, "and when you stated that you would in the next session of Parliament support Lord Russell's Reform Bill, you should have seen their faces!"

Colin Elliott laughed and confessed he had avoided looking at some of his former colleagues.

"I have come to despise many of them; they are such consummate hypocrites, Charles. They claim to represent the people in their constituencies, yet they vote down everything unless it props up the privileges of the wealthy. I doubt I could have lived with myself, had I continued to support them," he declared and his wife added proudly, "Papa says it was one of the finest speeches he has heard in the Commons."

Charles smiled, hearing the adulation in her voice; it was clear that his sister adored and admired her husband. He could scarcely believe that a short time ago she had been so miserable he had feared she may find life too dreary and difficult to bear. Anne-Marie saw his expression and understood his thoughts. She had herself marvelled at the way her life had changed in the course of a year.

With Mr Elliott and her father both preoccupied with political and social change, she had found herself drawn into the discussion of matters generally regarded as outside her scope. The examples of Emma Wilson, Becky Tate, and Caroline Fitzwilliam, and her own work as a nurse were proof that women's minds could be occupied with much more than the cut of a gown and the length of a sleeve or the interminable round of society gossip.

She heard her husband say, in reply to a question from Charles, "Nothing can stop the Reform Movement now; even if the Whigs were not to win the next election, I believe Gladstone's Liberals would take up the cause. His commitment is more genuine than that of Disraeli, whom I do not entirely trust."

"And you believe he will extend the franchise to working people?" Charles asked, to which Elliott replied, "I have no doubt he will. He has no alternative; there is no turning back."

"And when do you think women will get the vote?" asked Anne-Marie eagerly, excited by all this talk of reform.

At that, unhappily, they fell silent. Neither man seriously believed this would be soon. However, Colin Elliott was unwilling to dismiss her question. Keen to nurture her interest, he explained gently, "It will not come soon, my darling. There will have to be a prolonged struggle, I fear. Neither the government nor the opposition wants to be first in promising women the vote."

His wife sounded disappointed and bewildered. "Why? Surely it is an important part of reform that women have the right to vote. Do you support it?"

"Of course I do, my dearest, as do many sensible men in the Parliament. Most see it as inevitable, but those entrenched in power do not want a change. They have irrational fears of what it will do to society. They claim it will destroy the foundations of family life. It's rubbish, of course!"

Charles laughed out loud. "More likely they have very well-founded fears that it will shake the foundations of their own power," he declared and Elliott agreed.

"You are quite right, Charles; I regret that the conservatism of the Queen does little to help the cause."

Charles Bingley, realising how disappointing this must be to his sister, decided it was time to announce some good news. Changing the subject, he said rather brightly, "I have been thinking, for some time now, of moving back to Hertfordshire."

Anne-Marie was immediately interested. "What? Leave London, you mean?"

"Yes, do you suppose Papa and Anna will have a room for me at Netherfield House?" he quipped.

At this, there was much laughter and Anne-Marie said, "Charles, of course they will; they will be delighted. But, what on earth has prompted this decision?"

Before he could answer, Colin Elliott asked, "Does this mean you will give up your work at the practice in East London?" Charles nodded and; seeing the astonishment upon his brother-in-law's countenance; proceeded to explain.

"Oh, I know I shall miss it. I have learned so much here, especially the work I've done on the diseases of children and the problems caused by poverty, malnutrition, unsanitary conditions, all of that has been invaluable. But, they will not go to waste, because I am thinking of applying for a most important position in the country."

"Indeed? Where?" asked his friend.

"Well, I have it on the best authority," said Bingley, slowly and deliberately, "that an appointment is soon to be made to the new Children's Hospital at Bell's Field."

At this, Anne-Marie could not contain her joy; she rose and threw her arms around her brother's neck, to the general amusement of the staff.

"Charles! How wonderful! You want to work with us? Is it not the very best news, Colin?" she cried and there were tears in her eyes as she turned to her husband. She had dreamed of this, but had not dared to suggest it to her brother, fearing he would refuse or worse, accept and then regret turning his back on a career in London. With the big teaching hospitals growing in size and reputation, she had thought he would look to them for a position, rather than a small country hospital.

Now he had made his decision and she was overjoyed. A new children's hospital with her own staff and Charles as its chief physician; she could not ask for more. Her husband agreed, "This will solve all our problems," he said, congratulating his brother-in-law. "Charles, you have made a most generous choice, yet I am sure you will not regret it."

Charles Bingley admitted he had thought long and hard about it; it had been, he said, a difficult choice, but once he had decided, he was quite certain it was the right thing to do.

"I am well aware how much time and effort you have all invested in this venture; Papa, you and most of all, my dear sister, here. I know my father has long wanted to do something significant to improve the health services and education for the children of the estate and the surrounding district. Well, I cannot do much about their education, but I can help improve their health and their chances of survival. I have seen too many die or be scarred by preventable diseases. I wanted to join you and achieve something worthwhile for Netherfield."

His sister's eyes shone, "Oh, you will, Charles, you will. And your reward will be great satisfaction; I can promise you that," she said. "I cannot wait to tell Papa and Anna. I must write tonight, so it will be in the post first thing tomorrow morning." Both men smiled at her enthusiasm.

"I had intended to write myself, but I would not dream of spoiling your pleasure. I shall delay mine until Monday, by which time yours will have reached them," said Charles. "However, I am expected at Netherfield for Christmas, so when you return from Italy, I shall already be there, awaiting the grand opening of the hospital by the wife of our new Reformist MP."

Anne-Marie delayed not a moment, after returning to their apartment in Knightsbridge, before sitting down to write to her father and Anna. Her husband was mightily amused even as he indulged her, wondering what other bride of less than a week would be preparing, late at night, to pen a letter to her father about a hospital! But he knew how much it meant to her. She wrote,

> *Dearest Papa and Anna, this is but a short note, for it is late, but it brings you the most wonderful news! We have just returned from dining with Charles, who has told us he intends to resign at Christmas from his practice in East London and move back to Hertfordshire. He wishes to work at the children's hospital! Papa, is this not the best news in the world?*
>
> *I cannot tell you what a relief it is to know that we shall have in my dear brother such a good, dedicated physician in charge. He must stay at Netherfield House, of course, and when Mr Elliott and I move to live at Longbourn, he can have our suite of rooms. Oh dear, I must not run on so; I had best conclude as my husband has waited patiently for me to finish this, so it may be ready for the post tomorrow.*

As her letter trailed to its happy conclusion, her patient and loving husband claimed her attention. For Anne-Marie it was perhaps the best moment of her young life, combining the sweet success of a dream with the warmth of deep and genuine love.

On the following morning, the letter despatched to the post, they left on their journey to Europe, which was to take them first to Paris and thence to Italy, where they were to spend Christmas enjoying the hospitality of a family who had long been their friends.

Two generations of Continis had known the Darcys and through them the Bingleys, with whom they had become close friends. The invitation to Anne-Marie and her husband had come via her father, who had frequently travelled in Europe and stayed with them. For Anne-Marie, who had never left England, it was a whole new experience. Their generous, warm hospitality was almost as overwhelming as the art treasures and architecture of Florence and Rome. The Continis were keen to draw them into their family celebrations and make them feel at home.

～❦～

However, in the New Year, as the Winter deepened across the continent, they began to feel the nostalgic tug of the familiar and returned to England.

242

Snow, and more often slush and mud, covered the streets of London and most of its environs, drawing them back to the comfort of home and family at Netherfield Park. So keen had they been to be home, they had stayed but one night in London, where the attractions of the city were seriously eroded by the dreadful weather and the condition of the streets.

"At least," said Anne-Marie to her husband, as they left for Hertfordshire, "in the country, the roads may be equally poor, but the air is infinitely sweeter."

The cold discomfort of the journey from London was soon replaced by the warmth of the welcome they received at Netherfield. Though it was only early afternoon, it was dark when they arrived at the house and their greatest desire was for a hot bath and bed. Accompanying them up the stairs, Anna informed them that Mrs Perrot was in the throes of preparing a celebratory dinner to welcome them home.

"Charles," she said, "has gone down to Longbourn at the request of my Aunt Collins, who had been concerned that one of the maids has had a persistent cough, which had worsened despite several home remedies. He has taken the small carriage and should be back in time for dinner." Anna, urged the weary travellers to take time to rest and recover from what must have been an arduous journey.

It was a respite they welcomed. Travelling in Europe had been all very well when they were being conveyed from place to place in the splendid equipages of the Continis, who had insisted on showing them the splendours of ancient Italy, but traversing the continent by public coach in Winter was not for the fainthearted.

Anne-Marie was very tired and glad indeed to be home and in her own bedroom. Her husband was determined that she should enjoy a long and undisturbed rest.

So deep was the slumber into which Anne-Marie had fallen, she was not awakened when, around six o'clock, there was a loud knocking at the front door and much calling out and shouting in the yard.

Mr Elliott, aroused by the sounds, had looked but could see nothing out of the window, which was thoroughly frosted over. As the noise continued, he decided to go downstairs to investigate. He met Anna on the stairs; she too had been disturbed.

"Who on earth could it be?" he asked and was astonished when she said, "I thought I recognised the Rector's voice."

"Mr Griffin? What would he want at this hour? He cannot be here to summon us to Evensong, surely?"

Anna had only just managed to smile at his joke, for by this time one of the servants had come up from the kitchen and opened the door, letting in a blast of cold air that swept through the hall and caught her as she came downstairs, causing her to gasp.

Pulling her shawl more closely around her shoulders, Anna went forward as Mr Griffin and another man from the village scurried into the hall and the doors were shut again.

Both men looked exhausted, cold and wet with the sleet that had been falling all afternoon, and as they were ushered into the saloon, where they would at least be dry and warm in front of the fire, Anna ordered that they be provided with towels and hot drinks.

But it was quite clear that Mr Griffin was surprisingly unwilling to accept any refreshment, before he had revealed the reason for their visit. This was certainly no social or pastoral call. Both Griffin and his companion looked stunned and distressed as they tried to explain.

"My dear Mrs Bingley, it is very kind of you, but we cannot stay, there is no time to lose; we must find Dr Bingley and take him with us, it is absolutely essential." Mr Griffin was getting quite agitated.

The mention of Dr Bingley alerted Colin Elliott, "Dr Bingley has gone to Longbourn to see a patient," he explained and asked, "Why do you need him? Who is ill? What is wrong, Mr Griffin?"

Elliott's voice seemed to cut through Mr Griffin's agitation, as he addressed him directly, "Oh, Mr Elliott, I am so thankful to find you here. You must help us find Dr Bingley; he is needed at once," and he began to blather on again, but Mr Elliott cut him short, determined to discover the reason for his alarm. "Why man, tell me, why do you need the doctor? What has happened?"

Then, as if roused from an autistic torpor, the farmhand in whose cart the two men had travelled to Netherfield, spoke for the first time in sepulchral tones, "There's been an accident, sir, a terrible accident; there's been people killed for sure."

Anna gasped and the maids, who had come in with hot drinks and towels, cried out, as Colin Elliott grasped the man's arm and demanded to know, "What accident, man? Where?"

Only then did Mr Griffin, by now fortified with a hot toddy, find words to explain what had happened. Still shaking, he began the tale.

"It's the train, Mr Elliott, the train from London, which was due in at five and when it failed to arrive, those at the station thought it was late on account of the weather and snow on the tracks, but it turns out, it has come off the tracks, sir, as it came around the hill and gone down the embankment and into the creek below Sidley."

"Good God! What has been done to recover the passengers and crew?" Elliott asked, shocked and appalled by the news. The farmhand, now identified as Thomas, was most pessimistic.

"Nothing so far sir; the driver's dead for sure, the engine's gone head first down the bank, straight into Sidley's Creek, and she's taken the first two coaches with her."

Everyone gasped and for a full minute nobody said a word. As they stood aghast, a carriage was heard arriving and Charles Bingley raced indoors. Word had been received at Longbourn, from one of the tenants who had gone to meet his brother at the station. The news had only reached the station when some of the survivors, from the coaches that had slewed around and fallen over in a paddock beside the railway lines, had struggled along the line to raise the alarm. Among the walking wounded was his brother.

Charles, who having treated the maid with bronchitis, had been taking tea with Mrs Collins, had heard enough to alert him to the fact that they had a crisis on their hands. He had returned at once to get his things together and leave for the site of the accident. "I shall need some volunteers to help me with the wounded. We could set up a first aid post at the railway station. I have sent word to the police, and I gather they are already on their way. If only it was not such a wretched night!" he groaned.

Meanwhile, Jonathan Bingley, hearing the voices downstairs, had come to find out what was afoot. On learning of the accident, he gave orders for all assistance to be rendered and Mr Dobson was immediately assigned to travel with Charles to the site of the crash, where it was feared many people lay dead or wounded with nobody to attend upon them. Fortuitously, Dobson had served as a medical orderly at Scutari, working for Miss Nightingale in the Crimea, and was well experienced in tending the sick and wounded. Calm and sensible as well, clearly he would be an asset to Charles in dealing with the disaster that faced them.

As various people scurried to make preparations, Colin Elliott, anxious to assist, went upstairs to warn his wife, that he would not be back for dinner and quite possibly for several hours later. He found her still sound asleep. So tired had she been, so relieved to be home, that the multitude of voices downstairs had not disturbed her sleep. Gently, her husband awakened her and as she sat up, explained what had happened. In an instant, Anne-Marie was wide awake.

Seeing the look of horror on her face, Elliott tried to assuage her fears, "It may not be as bad as it seems, dearest, but I must go and do what I can. Charles is back and preparing to leave for the site of the accident with Mr Dobson."

She interrupted him, "I must go, too. Charles will need help; if people are wounded, they will have to be attended to at once or they will die in this weather. I have to go."

He tried to protest, to advise that she was too tired after her long journey, but she would not hear of it and as she sprang out of bed, said, "Colin, I am a trained nurse, I have cared for soldiers returned from the war with dreadful wounds. I know what has to be done. Dobson has been an orderly; he can certainly help, but I can work with Charles to save lives. I must go. Now, please find Jenny Dawkins; she knows where all my things are, from the hospital at Harwood."

As she said the words, a thought occurred to her and she raced out calling to her father, "Papa, the hospital at Bell's Field, may we not use it to shelter and treat the wounded?" she asked, and hearing her, Charles, who was in the hallway about to leave, turned at the door and came back in. "Anne-Marie, that is an excellent idea! It would give us exactly what we need—shelter from the cold and a clean, safe place to treat them within easy distance."

"There aren't any beds for adults, although there are pallets, pillows, and blankets. And it's bound to be cold," warned Anna, but neither Charles nor Anne-Marie were concerned.

"It cannot be colder than lying in Sidley's creek or out in the paddock. I think, Father, it would help save lives if we could use the building and keep the injured from dying of pneumonia as much as from their wounds," said Charles and Anne-Marie did not even have to add her plea to his.

Convinced they were right, Jonathan agreed immediately and gave Dobson the keys to the hospital, while others bustled around gathering together blankets, candles, and other similar necessities. The large carriage was brought round and presently, they set off, driving with some trepidation into the still falling sleet.

Poor Mrs Perrot had tears in her eyes as she saw them depart. Anna was unsure whether they were tears of sympathy for the victims or sorrow for the ruins of the celebratory dinner with which she had planned to welcome Mr and Mrs Elliott home.

On arriving at the bridge over Sidley's Creek, they were met by a scene of absolute devastation and panic. The engine and two of the front coaches had plunged into the frozen creek where they lay, half-submerged, crumpled wrecks, wrapped in an ominous silence, which suggested that most of the unfortunates within had perished. It was possible that a few, those who were young and strong enough, had clambered out but for the most part, there was neither sound nor movement to signify any hope of life. It was a hideous thought and Anne-Marie, feeling a cold knot of fear inside her, reached for her husband's reassuring hand, as they moved slowly down the embankment towards the wreck.

On the other side of the tracks, lying on its side, broken and buckled, was the rest of the train, twisted, pulled apart as if by a raging giant, its bits and pieces flung around the paddock like a child's toys. While some of it had been reduced to matchwood, other parts of the train were intact, and out of them hung injured passengers, in a variety of grotesque postures, while some had escaped by climbing out of the shattered windows. Many lay on the ground, forlorn, calling for help; yet others lay still, dead or dying.

Colin Elliott, gazing upon the harrowing scene, could not help himself, "Good God!" he exclaimed, "This is Hell!"

His wife tightened her grip on his hand; clearly he was unfamiliar with the scale of destruction and suffering that confronted them. She knew she would have to help him cope, by concentrating upon the practical things that had to be done immediately and they were legion!

Charles Bingley and Mr Dobson had set to work at once, attending upon those who lay on the grass or fallen beside the tracks, having been flung or clambered out of the shattered coaches. Some men from the villages around Sidley's Creek had heard of the accident and had come along to help; others had gathered out of idle curiosity.

Charles soon directed the local police onto them. "Tell them, officer, that they must either help us or go home to their families. Those who can help, I want strong men who can lift and carry to bring along flat boards to be used as litters; blankets and oil sheets to cover the wounded; and any form of transport, farm carts, anything that may be used to move these people to the hospital at Bell's Field, else many of them will die of exposure," he warned.

As the police moved in, there were a few predictable grumbles about town toffs ordering them about, but most of them realised the gravity of the situation and did as they were asked.

Some returned with carts and litters made from old doors, farm wagons, lanterns, and a load of firewood and kindling, with which they made a fire in the middle of the paddock, providing welcome warmth and light.

Charles Bingley moved quickly to assess the state of each of the survivors, while the police began their grim duty of trying to identify and remove the dead. Several of the victims were women and children, returning from an expedition to the city or from visiting relatives and, to her horror, Anne-Marie found that some had already succumbed to their injuries. Their wounds and the biting cold to which they had been exposed for more than an hour had taken their toll.

When Elliott had overcome the shock of seeing such mayhem, he went to assist Mr Dobson, who had a flask of brandy which he held to the lips of those who needed fortification, as they waited to be treated, many of whom grasped it gratefully. It was the only comfort available.

Anne-Marie, meanwhile, was working quickly to staunch the bleeding and bind up their injuries, while trying also to give hope to desperate mothers struggling to comfort their injured and terrified children. Paying scant attention to her own health, she moved from one to another, sometimes stopping to help and comfort, or calling urgently to her brother for attention to an injury that required his special skill.

Watching her work, Colin Elliott realised that, while he was well aware of her compassionate nature, he had known little of her skill and strength. With each passing moment, she grew in his esteem. In the intervening hours, Jonathan Bingley and his wife Anna had hastened first to Longbourn to acquaint Mrs Collins with the grave news and borrow the services of Mr Bowles and Harriet and thence to Haye Park to collect Dr Faulkner, Anna's father. Together, they proceeded to the new but not as yet open hospital at Bell's Field to prepare for the arrival of the wounded travellers.

Plans had been afoot to have Mrs Elliott, the wife of their newlywed local MP do the honours in the New Year, but Fate had forced an earlier opening. The emergency room and main ward were opened up; lamps lit; and pallets, pillows, and blankets laid out for the wounded, who were soon to arrive by a variety of means. Anna was glad her father had been able to attend. Dr Faulkner, though now advancing in years and not capable of rushing to an accident as he used to do when the railways first came to the area, was still a most reliable and experienced physician and, with so many injured, he would be of considerable help to Charles.

Back at Sidley's Creek, there was weeping, as the bodies of some adults and several children were taken from the water and the ruins of the coaches. Others, who were past care, lay in the open, clearly near death and as Elliott watched, amazed, Anne-Marie and her brother made them comfortable with a blanket, a drink of water, and a kind word, knowing there was little more they could do, as life ebbed from their bodies. Mr Griffin wandered among them, dispensing consolation with prayers and Holy Water, while Mr Dobson provided more down-to-earth comfort from his hip flask. Both men were doing their best; they would probably never know who was more effective in ministering to the distressed and dying at Sidley's Creek that night.

The wounded were being transported slowly; too slowly it seemed to Anne-Marie, who was eager to see them removed to a more sheltered place, from the wreck to the road above the creek and thence to the hospital at Bell's Field. She had ensured that their wounds were at least cleansed of mud and dirt and bound up, the bleeding staunched and their bodies wrapped in blankets to keep out the cold. Mr Dobson had taken charge of moving the injured, giving instructions to those men and women who had stayed to help, on the need to move them swiftly yet with great care. His experience in the Crimea was proving invaluable.

It took several hours to move everyone from the site of the accident to Bell's Field, even though the distance was not great and during all of this time, Anne-Marie and Charles never wavered or appeared to be tiring.

Working assiduously to get the injured ready for their difficult journey, warning them it may be painful as their bodies were jarred as the crude vehicles carried them along rutted roads, yet promising there would soon be shelter and relief, Anne-Marie had hardly ever looked up from her labours. Her husband, watched in astonishment and admiration as she completed her tasks, cleansed her hands and arms in ice-cold water and after the last of the injured had been moved, joined him and her brother in the carriage to travel to the hospital. There was still a great deal of work to be done.

Many of the injured travellers were in shock; some hardly knew what had happened to them or where they were. Most were not from the county, travelling through to the Midlands. So bruised and cut about were they, so shaken and terrified, they had forgotten everything but their present predicament.

At Bell's Field, Charles, with his experience acquired at hospitals in the city, gave clear instructions and assigned tasks to all the volunteers.

With Anna and Jenny Dawkins to help, Mr Bowles was to organise the accommodation at the hospital and the efficient Harriet was assigned the important task of obtaining information from each patient and making notes of their injuries and treatment. Charles and Anne-Marie set to work to deal with the major injuries, while Dr Faulkner treated the rest.

Colin Elliott, who had volunteered to do anything that was asked of him, was ordered to fetch and carry like any of the others, and many from the village were amazed to see their distinguished MP labouring alongside of them, his boots covered in dirt, his clothes stained with mud and worse. When a cart arrived from Longbourn with bread and hot soup, it was he, who together with the cook, dished out the meal and took it to the workers and those among the injured who could eat, a task he performed as conscientiously as if he were a hospital orderly.

Mrs Collins, unable to assist in person, had donated the food to sustain them. More brandy and hot coffee arrived from Netherfield House and was welcomed by those working without any heating through the night. Colin Elliott marvelled at the generosity of the small community. For years he had heard his father receive news of similar incidents, farm accidents, floods, coach overturns and ask only that he be informed of the progress of the rescue. He had, as a boy, accompanied his mother to see the wounded or attend a funeral at the local church, but never had he or his family been involved as he was now in the actual work of rescuing and treating the victims It was, for him, a new and salutary experience.

When they had finished their tasks and the cook was cleaning up, he went outside into the cold night. The sleet had stopped falling and the sky had cleared. The fresh, cool air was balm to his head, aching from the smell of carbolic soap and iodine. He could scarcely believe his eyes, when he saw the pale light of a wintry dawn in the sky. They had worked all night. Returning indoors, he sought his wife and found her with Anna and Harriet, tearing up sheets and rolling them into bandages. They would be used to replace those, put on at the crash site, which were now caked with blood and dirt.

Elliott was astonished. It did not seem possible, but she was still at work, looking as though she intended to continue through the day that was just beginning.

Sitting down beside her, he asked softly, "Are you not weary, my love? It is almost dawn. Should you not rest a while, even an hour or two, perhaps?"

He was clearly anxious that she should not become overtired and fall ill herself. Anne-Marie smiled and touched his arm gently, acknowledging and appreciating his concern; but she shook her head, "How can I? I feel no weariness, while these unfortunate people and all these children lie here in pain and in great danger of infection. When we have cleansed and treated their wounds and found some way to alleviate their pain, then perhaps I can rest for an hour or two. Look at Charles; he has not stopped since we arrived at Sidley's Creek, nor has Dobson, and he is much older than us. I must stay, as long as Charles needs my help," she said simply and he had no heart to argue with her, even though he knew she must be close to exhaustion.

❦

Colin Elliott had seen nothing like this; certainly not in England.

Once or twice in India, he had noted with admiration the dedication of missionaries and their native helpers, who worked round the clock without food or sleep to save lives during floods and other disasters, epidemics of typhoid or cholera that regularly ravaged the villages. But they, he had always told himself, were probably driven by religious zeal and the hope of obtaining conversions. Here he observed his wife, Dr Bingley, Anna, Harriet, and many others who seemed motivated only by compassion and a strong sense of service. It was as though they had grown up believing that it was their duty to help ease the suffering of others, even strangers, upon whom misfortune or catastrophe fell.

As he came to comprehend, it would prove to be an important stage in his own journey through life. Colin Elliott had grown up in a home in which success was measured by a yardstick that took no account of compassion and dedication to public service. Commercial achievement, successful business transactions, and promotion up the rungs of the political and social ladders had counted for more than philanthropic intentions.

Anne-Marie, sensitive and perspicacious, understood his predicament and sought to draw him in by asking for his help and advice. Encouraging him to participate in the work, she hoped he would understand what impelled her and the others in her family to act as they did. She knew, more than any of the others, that Colin Elliott needed to feel a part of the community they lived in, which he had been elected to represent and serve.

It was, however, the ever practical Mr Dobson, who found Mr Elliott the right task. Aware of the need for the hospital to maintain an accurate account of the supplies used that night to treat the victims of the accident, he suggested a useful exercise. "Mr Elliott, sir, if you could compile a comprehensive list of materials and medical supplies used from our stores tonight, it would help Mrs Elliott to ascertain what items need to be replenished before we open to the public," he explained. "Mrs Bowles has been making notes, sir, which may be useful to you," he prompted.

Colin Elliott, realising immediately, from his own experience in India, the value of accurate inventories, set to work with the help of Harriet's methodical notes to compile one. He was particularly glad of having something useful to do, even as he saw the others working to alleviate the suffering of the victims. Later, when Anne-Marie, having finished her work, came in search of her husband, she found him sitting at the matron's desk, working by lamplight, a ledger at his side, making an inventory of supplies. She felt no weariness, but it was clear to her that he was tired. It had been a very long day.

"Mr Bowles and Harriet will stay on to help Charles; I think we could go home now and get some rest," she said and this time, to her surprise, it was he who asked for a few more minutes to complete the task.

"I shall have it done very soon, my dear," he promised and his wife, pleased, nodded her approval.

The appearance of Mr Tillyard and his reporters on the scene meant the news of the accident and rescue of the survivors was soon all over the county. Not only was the story told of the terrifying train crash and the tragic loss of life, but so was the tale of the heroic efforts of the rescuers; of Dr Bingley, his sister Mrs Elliott, her husband their new MP, and of course, the innumerable and often anonymous helpers from the Netherfield and Longbourn estates.

The vital importance of the hospital at Bell's Field, opened before its time, but invaluable in saving the lives of many of the victims, was most eloquently proclaimed by both the *Herald* and the *Hertford Chronicle*. Their front pages told the story of the night-long struggle by dedicated men and women to save the lives of passengers, many of them women and children, who would probably have died without their prompt assistance.

The hero of the moment was, of course, Dr Bingley, regarded as a local lad who had done well in the city and returned to Hertfordshire to work at the new hospital. His untiring efforts had been recounted in homes and public houses all over the district. Sadly, he had not succeeded in saving all those who had been dragged from the wreckage of the train. Two more had succumbed overnight to severe injuries, while another man lay unconscious. But, more than twenty-five others, a few men, several women and children had been saved; their wounds cleansed, soothed with medication and bound up so they may heal. None of them had any doubt that they owed their lives to the dedication and skill of Dr Bingley and his sister. All expressed their profound gratitude.

Tillyard, who had campaigned for the establishment of the hospital, despite the intransigence of the local Council, now used his newspaper to say, with obvious satisfaction, "I told you so," and point the accusing finger at the men in the Council, who had done their utmost to thwart or delay their plans. Elated that he had been vindicated, he now claimed that the accident had proved there was a clear case for the expansion of the institution, from a children's hospital to a general facility for the entire community.

Graphic descriptions, written by his reporters, of the scene of the crash and the horrific injuries of the victims, together with accounts of the work of the volunteers, were provided for their readers, bolstered by strong editorial comment; Mr Tillyard was eloquent indeed.

"There can be no better demonstration of the need for a general hospital to serve this community; the hospital at Bell's Field, a private initiative of Mr Jonathan Bingley and his daughter Mrs Elliott, whose generosity is deeply appreciated by the people of the area, has amply proved the case for its existence in a single night.

"It is an indictment of the government's Health Board and the local authorities that the people of this county must depend upon private benefactors in such dire circumstances," he wrote, to the great satisfaction of Anne-Marie and all those who had helped in her campaign for the hospital.

Jonathan Bingley was immensely proud of both his elder children, yet as he said to his wife, it was no more than he would have expected of them.

"It is what they know they must do. What is far more impressive," he declared, "is the fact that their example has drawn Mr Elliott into becoming involved himself. I have had remarkable reports of his hard work, from doing menial jobs, fetching, carrying, and cleaning, to documenting hospital supplies. Bowles is full of praise for his efforts."

Anna agreed, "Never before have they had a Member of Parliament, who was prepared to turn up and help in a disaster," she observed.

Jonathan clearly regarded this as an achievement for which his daughter was responsible and when an opportunity arose in the days that followed, he told her so. "My dear Anne-Marie, I must congratulate you," he said, and then as she made to protest that it was not all her work, he added, "No, hear me out please, I do not mean to suggest that you were solely responsible for the efforts of the rescuers, although there is no doubt that without your hospital, their work may have been in vain and many more would surely have died of exposure. I know that your brother Charles, Dr Faulkner, and others played vital roles in this operation, but my congratulations go to another matter for which you alone are responsible." Perplexed, she looked at him, shaking her head.

"My observation of Mr Elliott has led me to conclude that you have completely converted him to our cause, which I think is a considerable achievement. I am told he worked as hard as any man, doing whatever was needed to help. Considering he does not come from a family with any tradition of community service, this is surely all your own work, my dear."

Anne-Marie was delighted. Her father's approval was always the highest accolade she sought for herself. That he had seen fit to praise the work of her husband was a special pleasure.

"Indeed, Papa, you have been well informed. He worked as hard as any of us and though exhausted, would not stop until the task he had undertaken was done. I think Mr Dobson will vouch for the truth of this," and as her father nodded, "I was very proud of him, Papa," she said, her eyes shining.

Anne-Marie's love for her husband would have survived whether or not he had proved himself as he had done on the night of the accident, but his actions had served to strengthen her feelings of esteem. Her father's recognition set the seal upon them.

The arrival from Meryton, some hours later, of both Colin Elliott and Charles Bingley, with the news that Tillyard's newspaper had started a public fund for the hospital at Bell's Field, climaxed a particularly satisfying day. Most of the remaining patients, now on their way to recovery, had been discharged from hospital and had, after many expressions of appreciation, set out for their homes in the Midlands.

Mr Dobson, meanwhile, had heard that the *Herald*, which had already acknowledged several small donations, had that day received a thousand pounds, from a donor who wished to remain anonymous. The person, a resident of the area, it was said, had asked that the money be used to provide services at the hospital to women as well as children. Charles Bingley was particularly excited by the prospect. Having made his decision to move to Hertfordshire, he could not wait to start work.

When the last of the patients had left, the hospital was cleaned and disinfected under the supervision of Dr Bingley and made ready for the formal opening. The hospital board, meeting to hear an account of the disaster, placed on record its appreciation of the work done by several members of the community, especially Dr Bingley and his sister Mrs Elliott. The date for the opening was fixed and no one around the table had to think twice about who should be invited to perform the task. Mrs Colin Elliott, the wife of their new MP, was the unanimous choice.

The board's record of meeting reads, *It was decided that in view of her dedication, her untiring efforts to establish this hospital and to pursue the very highest ideals of the nursing profession, Mrs Colin Elliott should be invited to open the hospital at Bell's Field.*

When the formal invitation arrived, Anne-Marie pointed out that it was probably unnecessary to open the hospital.

"It would never be more open than it was on that dreadful night, when the train from London rolled down the embankment into Sidley's Creek and the hospital opened its doors to the victims," she said, "One could wish that so many unfortunate people did not have to die, before the Council was convinced, but I am glad their change of heart has come at last."

For Colin Elliott, to whose mother's memory the hospital was dedicated, the compliment paid to his wife brought great satisfaction. Having watched her work tirelessly for the fulfilment of her dream of a children's hospital, he had come to love her generosity and compassion.

Anne-Marie was a beautiful woman with a naturally affectionate nature and when he had realised how deeply he cared for her, he knew it was her warmth and beauty that had drawn him to her with feelings no other woman had aroused in him. But her passionate concern for others, that he had learned to share, had changed his life.

Unlike many young county gentlemen brought up in a culture of self-indulgence, Colin Elliott had always wanted to do more with his life than achieve material and social success. His wife, whom he loved dearly, had shown him the way.

END OF PART THREE

An Epilogue

THE LADY DOROTHY ELLIOTT HOSPITAL for women and children was
opened by Mrs Colin Elliott, well in time to treat the victims of an
epidemic of whooping cough and influenza. In past years, these and
other diseases had carried away many young children and often one or more of
their older siblings. Infections, which could have been avoided with early detec-
tion and treatment, had led to grave complications before families, too poor to
pay and much too proud to beg, called in the apothecary or a physician.

"At least this Winter, death will not have to be accepted into the homes of
the poor with fatalistic resignation, since modern medical treatment will be
available to all children of this community," Mrs Elliott had declared in her
speech and her words had clearly touched many hearts, since public donations
for the hospital had continued to pour in.

The family was not surprised to discover that Charlotte Collins had been
the secret donor of one thousand pounds and though they were not supposed
to speak of it openly, they knew and blessed her for her generosity. Having
been saved from a life of penny-pinching poverty and loneliness by the
benevolence of Jonathan Bingley and the kindness of Mary Bennet,
Charlotte had seized the chance to assist the hospital and through it the
community in which she had lived happily and with dignity for many years.

The sum of one thousand pounds left to her by her uncle was, she considered, appropriate recompense.

Jonathan, Anna, and Anne-Marie all knew full well the value of such a sum of money from a woman of modest means and blessed her for it.

As Charles Bingley moved to live at Netherfield and established himself as a hardworking and skilled physician, his reputation and that of the hospital at Bell's Field grew and its effectiveness in the areas around Netherfield and Longbourn increased considerably. Even those who had initially harboured some distrust of doctors and hospitals, preferring the old ways of herbalists, folk remedies, and spells, began to appreciate the benefits they had brought into the community.

That more infants and young children survived the Winter was proof enough for most families. Anne-Marie, advised by her husband, whose political instincts were improving every day, determined that the community would get even more than improved health care for their children. At his suggestion, she would draw upon the people of the area for workers at the hospital; cooks, gardeners, labourers, even nurses were to be found in the district. Young women, attracted to nursing by the example of Miss Florence Nightingale and her band of probationer nurses, were provided with training in nursing and hygiene, while older women with some experience of caring for the soldiers after the war were pleased to be paid fair wages for their work.

None of this would guarantee success, of course, as her father gently pointed out. "You do know, my dear, that the success or failure of the hospital will be judged only by the beneficial effects it has upon the health and well-being of the community, especially its children. And this," he had warned, "will take many years to ascertain. Meanwhile, you must be prepared for the sceptics and critics to become quite vocal from time to time."

"Indeed, Papa, I do know it and I am prepared, but I also am aware that many of the women, especially the mothers of children, are deeply grateful for the services we provide. They express their gratitude quite openly," she had replied, confident of its success.

That the hospital was a vast improvement upon the harsh, rudimentary facilities available to the poor at the workhouse was acknowledged even by the Council, whose members had been shamed into acknowledging its value to the community.

To Jonathan Bingley it was a source of deep satisfaction. A benevolent and solicitous landlord, Mr Bingley had urged the Council to set up a clinic to treat the poor in the area, offering to donate the land if necessary. In the face of their opposition, he had despaired of it ever being accomplished until his daughter began her campaign for a children's hospital. He had also confided in Anna that he had once worried about Charles's future in the medical profession.

"I wondered if he would remain in London, looking to take advantage of a more lucrative practice, perhaps, or maybe return to Edinburgh. I never believed he would be satisfied with a position in a country hospital. It is hard work and not as financially rewarding," he had said, adding with a sardonic smile, "which goes to show, my dear, how very wrong one can be, even about one's own children."

His wife had replied that, with his example of public service, it was no surprise at all that both his elder children had chosen to serve as they did. "I am immensely proud of both of them, as you are, dearest, but I think we must not forget that Charles has had the advantage of his sister's remarkable example. Anne-Marie's strength of purpose, her resilience, and dedication have astonished me."

Jonathan agreed. It had given them both great pleasure to see her recover from the morbid malaise of her previous marriage and regain her zest for life. There had been fearful times when this had seemed almost an impossible goal.

For Anne-Marie, who with her husband had worked with tenacity and courage to regain her self-esteem and bring a dream to reality, there was the greatest fulfilment of all. For along the way, difficult as it had been, she had discovered love, passionately felt and honestly acknowledged. Having endured the dreariness of a loveless union with Mr Bradshaw, she had learned with Colin Elliott to give and accept his love in return.

Two events, both unexpected, though inevitable, affected the lives of the families at Longbourn and Netherfield at this time. Their general consequences, however, flowed well beyond Hertfordshire, changing the course of English political history, itself. The election of 1865 saw the rising politician Mr Gladstone move to contest a seat in South Lancashire, where he immediately threw his considerable influence behind the campaign to extend the vote to ordinary working men, while at Westminster, the death of Lord Palmerston brought Lord Russell to the leadership of his party.

Colin Elliott was reelected after an exhilarating campaign in which he was assisted not only by the gentlemen of the Reform League, but also by several members of his family. Caroline Fitzwilliam, despite her own family responsibilities, arrived to help Anne-Marie and Anna as they visited homes and addressed meetings in his support. Together with great national Reformists like Edmund Beales and Samuel Morley, Mr Elliott promised to press Russell and Gladstone to hasten the pace of reform. On one occasion, Caroline told a meeting of supporters that her husband had told her that "Lord Russell has had a Reform Bill in his back pocket for ten years, hoping to sneak it in, when Palmerston was not paying attention."

To which Colin Elliott had added that, there would be many members in the new Parliament eager to get that bill out of Lord Russell's back pocket and onto the statute book! "There will be those who will try to thwart us, be assured, it will not be easy. They will claim that if men like you have the vote, the sun will not rise and the corn will not ripen, but we shall persevere and in the end, the demands of the people, the momentum for change in the country will carry the day," he had declared amidst applause.

After the election, Anne-Marie, her father and sisters made frequent journeys to Westminster to hear him speak in the great debates that raged in the Commons over the next eighteen months.

Not in all that time, did she once countenance the possibility of failure.

The death that Autumn of Sir Henry Wilcox, a neighbouring landowner and prosperous textile manufacturer who owned many mills in the Midlands and Yorkshire, brought a completely unforeseen development.

It arrived in the form of a visit from Miss Laura Wilcox, who called on Anne-Marie with a proposal for the endowment of the parish school. She offered to finance it with money she had inherited from her deceased father's estate.

Anne-Marie's astonishment at her approach was tempered somewhat by the reaction of her husband and her brother, both of whom enthusiastically supported the idea. Not even the fact that Sir Henry Wilcox had been an uncompromising Tory, who had resisted all attempts to assist the poor or improve working conditions in the mills, seemed to concern them.

"What does it matter now? If Miss Wilcox wishes to use some of her father's ill-gotten gains to improve the lives of the children of the parish, she should be encouraged to do so," said Colin Elliott. He was supported by Charles Bingley, who pointed out that the children of the area, who had no proper schooling, needed and deserved a chance to be educated. Though convinced they were right, Anne-Marie wrote to her Aunt Emma Wilson at Standish Park for advice.

My dearest Aunt,

If there was one more thing we needed for the improvement of the estates of Netherfield and Longbourn, it was a good parish school. Because of times in the country being rather uncertain and constant talk of depression, we have had little hope of finding the necessary funds.

That was until one wet afternoon, when a Miss Laura Wilcox called to see me. I knew of her, but we had never met; not surprising since she and her father Sir Henry Wilcox, the "textile Tory" moved in very different circles to our family. Yet, she came to me with a proposal to endow the parish school at Netherfield, if it would agree to teach reading, writing, and numbers to all the children in the parish who may wish to attend, and not just the children of churchgoers.

She struck me as sincere and determined. She said she had worked in East London among the children of the poor for almost two years and has taught at the parish school of St Francis, where I recall you did some work, too.

I am inclined to trust her and both Mr Elliott and my brother, who knows Miss Wilcox from meeting her in London, are in favour of accepting her offer. For my part, I think it would be a great joy to be able to have a real school and teach the children to read, write, and count as well as sing hymns and listen to Bible stories, as they do now, but I should like to have your opinion, before I put the proposal to Papa.

I mentioned the offer to Mr Griffin the Rector this morning after church and he, the dear old thing, can only see the advantage of it for his precious choir! "If they can learn to read, Mrs Elliott, they will learn to sing even better," was all he could say. So, it seems all we need is Papa's approval.

Dear Aunt, is this really a stroke of good fortune? Or is it just too good to be true? I shall wait eagerly for your answer.

I trust you and my dear Uncle Wilson are well and look forward to seeing you when we are next in London.

Your loving niece,

Anne-Marie Elliott.

Emma Wilson's reply was predictable; she wrote,

My dearest Anne-Marie,

What excellent news! If, as you have described, Miss Wilcox is genuinely interested in endowing the parish school, your Uncle James and I believe you should grasp the opportunity for the sake of the children, who will undoubtedly benefit from the scheme.

We think it will be a great advantage to the district and will do equally as well as your children's hospital. Your uncle agrees that there is no greater need for the children today than health and schooling, and since the government, to its shame, still spends a mere pittance on their education, the children of the poor, who never learn to read and write, are denied a decent chance in life. Should you and Miss Wilcox succeed in getting this school started at Netherfield, you will be helping to change that.

Believe me, my dear, nothing can be more worthy of your attention. We wish you every success and look forward to hearing more about it soon.

God bless you,

Your loving Aunt,

Emma Wilson.

P.S. Mr Elliott dined with us at Grosvenor Street last week, in between the debates on Lord Russell's Reform Bill. I must say he sounded very optimistic about the chances for reform, now Lord Russell leads the Whigs.

My dear Anne-Marie, he told us also of your other piece of good news, though he made us promise to keep your secret for now. Congratulations to you both, my dearest niece. Words cannot express how happy we are, your uncle and I, for you. Your dear father must be overjoyed.

A child at Christmas! What a wonderful blessing!

EW.

Her aunt's delight was appropriate and timely. Anna and Jonathan Bingley had only just been informed of the news that the Elliotts were expecting their first child. It provided Jonathan with another reason to hasten the conclusion of the refurbishments undertaken at Longbourn, while Mrs Collins was away in Derbyshire, visiting her daughter Rebecca Tate and the Darcys at Pemberley. He was quite determined that all the work should be finished in order that the Elliott's may move to Longbourn, well in time for the arrival of his first grandchild.

No expense would be spared and Anna was urged to select and have made all the necessary accessories and accoutrements that a young family may require to live in comfort. Indeed, it was Anne-Marie, whose taste for simplicity had not changed, who had to counsel restraint and curb her father's generosity.

꒰꒱

The following week, Miss Laura Wilcox called again to press her case. She had hoped to enthuse them with the idea of providing free schooling to all the children of the parish and she had certainly succeeded. With the encouragement of her aunt, her husband and her brother, Anne-Marie agreed to approach her father. He, after some discussion with his wife and his lawyers, set aside his reservations about the Wilcoxes, whose record of greed and selfishness he deplored, and agreed to permit the endowment and extension of the little parish school at Netherfield.

"I agree only on condition that the parish council of Netherfield keeps control of the school and Anne-Marie or her representative is on the council at all times, with the power to disallow anything that goes against the spirit of this agreement," he had said.

Miss Wilcox had been delighted and gladly accepted Mr Bingley's conditions. Later both she and Anne-Marie worked together on the plans for the school, which was to open in the New Year, and so began the remarkable association between two families who had hitherto travelled on opposite sides of the road, which was to lead to the establishment of one of the best primary schools in the county.

Incidentally and not surprisingly, the choir at Netherfield Church was so much improved by the infusion of new talent, with healthier and better taught choristers, that their reputation and that of their rector and choir master soon spread far outside the limits of his parish. So much so, they were in demand to sing at weddings and other functions around the district, which they did very creditably.

By which means, Mr Griffin, who, sadly, having failed in his quest for love, had at least found a compensatory degree of fame and satisfaction. Justly proud of the reputation of his choir, he naturally attributed this success almost wholly to the inspiration and encouragement provided by their beloved patron, Mrs Colin Elliott.

Postscript

B Y THE AUTUMN OF 1865, Mr Colin Elliott had been invited by Mr Gladstone to join him and his party in their campaign for reform, arguing persuasively that "we cannot fail because the great social forces which move us onward, are all marshalled on our side."

With his popularity among the people rising every day, Mr Gladstone seemed to be moving inevitably towards victory, and several promising young Reformist parliamentarians were ready to support him.

Colin Elliott had revealed to his wife the solemn promise he had received, that the extension of the vote to working men would be delivered in the next Reform Bill. "He has given me his word, my love, and he was most insistent upon it, even though I cannot believe my support would be of great significance to his campaign," he had said modestly, but Anne-Marie was delighted, quite unsurprised that her husband had been courted by the popular Mr Gladstone. "You are too modest, dearest," she had replied. "It is a sign of the recognition you deserve. Clearly, Mr Gladstone knows you for a man of principle and values your support."

Later that same month, as the trees in the woods around Netherfield put on their Autumn colours, young Teresa Bingley returned from Standish Park, where she had spent most of the Summer. She was accompanied by her uncle, aunt, and their two young sons.

With them came also Mr Frederick Fairfax, the architect, who had been working on the Wilson's new conservatory all Summer. The gentleman was not unknown to them, having done some work for Mr Bingley at Netherfield a year or two ago. Anne-Marie remembered that he had seemed very taken with her sister at the time, but after he had left the area, having completed his work, the association had gone no further.

When the pair had met again in Kent, however, they had renewed their friendship and this time Teresa, grown up and very much the accomplished young lady, had proved irresistible to the amiable young architect with a talent for making pen-portraits. It appeared that Mr Fairfax, having ascertained the lady's own wishes, had come to Netherfield to ask her father's permission to marry her.

That his elder brother was happily married to Victoria, the daughter of Mr and Mrs Wilson, may well have counted in his favour with Mr Bingley.

His blessing obtained, the pair were engaged, and a wedding was planned for Spring.

To see her young sister happy afforded Anne-Marie great satisfaction and she remarked to Anna that there was little more she could ask for, except the safe delivery of her child. The move to Longbourn satisfactorily accomplished, her loyal maids Jenny Dawkins and Rosie went with her to her new home. With the new household now well organised by Mr Bowles and Harriet, Anne-Marie had very little to trouble her.

Barely a fortnight before Christmas, Mr Elliott was urgently summoned home from a meeting of his constituency council, because his wife had been brought to bed a week before her time and been delivered of a son. He returned to her side with great haste, so beset with anxiety that it took Anna much time and effort to reassure him that all was well.

The little boy, universally agreed to be the image of his grandfather, was named Jonathan Charles, and his parents, their friends complained, could no longer be counted upon to speak on any subject for longer than five minutes without introducing the topic of their son.

❧

Some weeks into the New Year, sitting at her desk in her room overlooking the grounds of Longbourn, while young Jonathan Elliott slept, Anne-Marie wrote in her diary.

"Nothing can compare with this, the deepest, sweetest joy I have ever known. So intense, so pervasive are these feelings, as to have wiped out all the bitter residue of the past. Indeed, so deeply do I love my dear Colin and our son, and with such fondness does he care for us, that no other cause, no matter how significant, will ever engage my feelings as passionately, again.

I am truly blessed to have such happiness, as I might once only have dreamed of."

There is no written record of Colin Elliott's feelings, for he kept no personal diary, but it has been said, by members of the household, that he frequently and openly demonstrated his love for his wife and son in the most tender and affectionate terms.

Furthermore, no one who knew him was left in any doubt, that the serious young MP, who rose to support Mr Gladstone on the floor of the House, who was imbued with a strong sense of social justice, was also a deeply happy and contented man. It was clear from his general disposition as from the pleasure he obviously felt, as he glanced towards his wife in the gallery, when she attended to hear him speak in the House of Commons.

While there may have been some speculation about the direction in which the political career of the young MP may proceed, dependent as such matters are upon many unpredictable factors, there was certainly none about the happiness of Mr and Mrs Colin Elliott, whose personal lives were clearly completely satisfactory.

Appendix

A list of the main characters in *The Ladies of Longbourn*:

Anne-Marie Bradshaw (née Bingley)—eldest daughter of Jonathan Bingley and his first wife, Amelia Jane Collins (deceased)

Rev. John Bradshaw—husband of Anne-Marie

Jonathan Bingley, son of Charles and Jane Bingley—now the master of Netherfield Park

Anna Bingley (née Faulkner)—second wife of Jonathan Bingley

Teresa and Cathy Bingley—daughters of Jonathan Bingley by his first wife

Dr Charles Bingley—son of Jonathan Bingley by his first wife

Nicholas and Simon Bingley—young sons of Jonathan and Anna Bingley

Colin Elliott—the new Member of Parliament for the Netherfield district

Mr Griffin—rector of Netherfield Church

Eliza Harwood—daughter of Emily Courtney and friend of Anne-Marie

Emma and James Wilson—sister and brother-in-law of Jonathan Bingley; (Victoria, Stephanie, Charles, and Colin Wilson—Emma's children)

Dr and Mrs John Faulkner—parents of Mrs Anna Bingley

Caroline Fitzwilliam (née Gardiner)—cousin of the Bennet girls, married Colonel Fitzwilliam

Dr Richard Gardiner and Cassandra—son-in-law and daughter of Mr and Mrs Darcy of Pemberley

Julian Darcy—son of Mr and Mrs Darcy of Pemberley, married Josie Tate, daughter of Anthony and Rebecca Tate of Matlock. (Rebecca, née Collins—daughter of Charlotte Collins)

And from the annals of *Pride and Prejudice*:

Fitzwilliam and Elizabeth Darcy of Pemberley

Charles and Jane Bingley—parents of Jonathan Bingley and Emma Wilson

Colonel Fitzwilliam—cousin of Mr Darcy (married Caroline Gardiner)

Charlotte Collins—wife of Mr Collins (deceased), grandmother of Anne-Marie

Mr and Mrs Edward Gardiner—uncle and aunt of Jane and Elizabeth Bennet, parents of Richard and Robert Gardiner, Emily Courtney, and Caroline Fitzwilliam

Acknowledgements

The author wishes to thank Ms Claudia Taylor, librarian, and the graphic artist, Ms Marissa O'Donnell, for their excellent work and Ms Jenny Scott of Langtoft, England, for her interest and help with obtaining information on local government in Hertfordshire in the nineteenth century.

Thanks, too, to Ben and Robert for help with the computer system and to Ms Natalie Collins for her work in organising the original production of this book.

A debt of gratitude is, of course, due also to that most loved of writers, Miss Jane Austen, chief source of inspiration for this series.

May 2000.

About the Author

A lifelong fan of Jane Austen, Rebecca Ann Collins first read *Pride and Prejudice* at the tender age of twelve. She fell in love with the characters and since then has devoted years of research and study to the life and works of her favorite author. As a teacher of literature and a librarian, she has gathered a wealth of information about Miss Austen and the period in which she lived and wrote, which became the basis of her books about the Pemberley families. The popularity of the Pemberley novels with Jane Austen fans has been her reward.

With a love of reading, music, art, and gardening, Ms Collins claims she is very comfortable in the period about which she writes, and feels great empathy with the characters she portrays. While she enjoys the convenience of modern life, she finds much to admire in the values and worldview of Jane Austen.

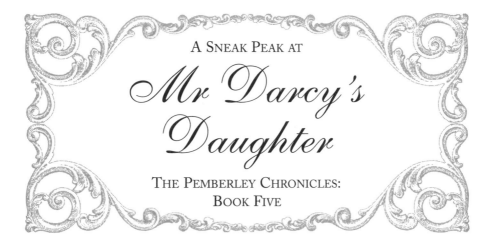

A SNEAK PEAK AT

Mr Darcy's
Daughter

THE PEMBERLEY CHRONICLES:
BOOK FIVE

THE INCLEMENT WEATHER INTO WHICH the Gardiners drove as they left the boundaries of Pemberley did nothing to improve Cassandra's apprehensive mood.

Travelling South through Leicestershire, they had hoped to reach Northhampton before nightfall, but the driving rain rendered that prospect more hazardous and less likely with every mile.

Forced to break journey at the small town of Market Harborough, they took rooms at the local hostelry, only to find Rebecca Tate and her maid Nelly ensconced next door. They had met at the top of the stairs, going down to dinner, and soon discovered that Julian Darcy had also written to his mother-in-law, though not, it appeared, in the same desperate terms that he had used in his letter to Richard Gardiner.

Rebecca apologised to Cassy for her non-attendance at their meeting on the previous afternoon, confessing that Julian's note had driven all else from her mind, leaving her time only to make hurried preparations for their journey to Cambridge.

"With Mr Tate already in London, I decided that Nelly and I would go to Cambridge on our own," she declared, adding, "I felt I could not wait one more day, when there may have been something I could do to help. Oh, my poor

Josie, I cannot imagine what has afflicted her. Why Cassy, you must remember what a bright, happy girl she used to be when she lived at home in Matlock. It must be the house—I am sure of it. It's cold and badly ventilated, quite unhealthy, especially in Winter. I said when they moved in, it was most unsuitable," she declared.

Both Richard and Cassy held their peace, not wishing to alarm her by revealing what they already knew. It was becoming clear to them that Julian had not been as candid with his mother-in-law as he had been with them. Cassy knew her husband would reveal nothing, nor would she.

At dinner, Richard enquired politely as to how Mrs Tate and her maid had travelled to Market Harborough from Matlock. It transpired that they were using one of the Tates' smaller vehicles. Mr Tate, they were told, had taken the carriage to London. Cassy was immensely relieved. It dispensed with the obligation for Richard to offer them seats in his carriage for the rest of the journey, which he would surely have done had they been travelling by coach. As it happened, they were well accommodated and, before retiring to their respective rooms, they agreed to leave for Cambridge after an early breakfast.

When they set out on the following morning, Cassy confessed to her husband, "I doubt if I could have concealed for much longer what we know of Josie's condition, if Becky Tate had been travelling with us to Cambridge."

He agreed. "It would certainly have been difficult to pretend that we knew no more than she does," he said.

The streets were wet as they drove into Cambridge.

The air was cold, and a sharp wind whipped the branches of the trees in the park and penetrated the carriage. Cassandra drew her wrap close around her, and yet she was cold and uncomfortable. The rain, though not as hard as before, was falling steadily as they approached the modest house that Julian and Josie rented in a quiet close not far from his college. It was not an unattractive dwelling, from an architectural point of view, but the garden appeared neglected, with sprouting bulbs and weeds competing for attention, and the house, with its blinds closed, seemed dark and unwelcoming. Once indoors, the aspect improved a little. Mrs Tate was at pains to explain how she had, on a previous visit, attempted to brighten up the parlour with new drapes and a few items of modern furniture, banishing an old horsehair sofa and two worn armchairs to the attic.

Julian met them in the hall, into which they were admitted by an anxious-looking young maidservant. While Mrs Tate insisted upon going upstairs to her daughter immediately, Richard and Cassy were ushered into the large but rather untidy parlour to the right of the hallway, where tea was to be taken.

Despite the best efforts of Mrs Tate, there was no disguising the general drabness of the room. Dark wood frames and striped wallpaper did little to help, while piles of books and journals lying on tables and strewn on the floor beside the chairs added clutter to a cheerless environment.

Only the fire burned brightly, keeping them warm, while the rain continued outside. How on earth, Cassy wondered, was anyone to recover from depression in surroundings such as these?

Writing later to her mother, she said:

Mama, everything is in such a state of disarray; it would drive me insane to live here. I cannot believe that Josie has been so ill as not to notice the disorderly condition of the house and the neglected garden. As for my poor brother, how anyone who has spent most of his life at Pemberley could possibly endure such wretched surroundings, not from poverty or privation, but by choice, I cannot imagine. Yet Julian does not appear to notice. His study, if it could be called that, so untidy and disorganised does it seem, is his chief retreat, when he is not with Josie or at work in his beloved laboratory.

By the time Mrs Tate came downstairs, tea had been served and the fire stoked up to a good blaze. Julian had insisted that they partake of tea and toasted muffins while he went upstairs to his wife. Once he had left the room, Cassandra turned expectantly to Mrs Tate, who was clearly eager to talk. "How is Josie?" she asked and Mrs Tate, speaking in a kind of stage whisper, loud enough for anyone to hear who cared to listen, said, "Very weak and pale, very weak, indeed, poor dear. It seems she has had little or no nourishment for days."

She sounded exceedingly anxious and puzzled. Becky Tate was the same age as Cassy, but despite her many talents, seemed much less able to cope with the situation that confronted them.

"Has Josie been refusing to take food as well as medication?" asked Richard, his brow furrowed by a frown. Mrs Tate nodded.

"It certainly seems so, Dr Gardiner; not that Josie would say anything, but I slipped out and asked her maid, when she removed the tea tray, if her mistress had not been eating well and she said, 'No, not at all well.' Indeed, it would appear she eats less than a child would at meals and then only to please her husband, who begs her to take some nourishment. In between times, she drinks only weak tea or barley water and, very occasionally, takes a small piece of fruit," she explained, while wearing a very bewildered expression.

Rebecca Tate was usually a sensible, practical sort of person, yet it was difficult for her to understand what had happened to her once bright and lively daughter.

Cassy noticed that Richard was shaking his head, and she could tell from his solemn countenance that he was worried, too.

"Refusing medication is bad enough—declining food is much more serious. It means that her body would be enfeebled by sheer lack of nourishment, and thereby, less able to cope with whatever it is that afflicts her," he said, unable to conceal his concern.

Shortly afterwards, Julian returned to say he had spoken with Josie and she was willing to see Richard now. Cassy thought it sounded as if she was granting him a privilege, which was strange! They went upstairs, all but Cassy who remained alone in the parlour, casting an eye upon the clutter that surrounded her.

Presently, the maid came to clear away the tea things and Cassy recognised her. It was Susan, one of the maids from the Tates' household, who had been Josie's personal maid and had moved with her to Pemberley after her marriage to Julian, and later to Cambridge.

Clearly delighted to see Cassandra, the girl curtseyed briefly, put the tray back on the table, wiped her hands on her apron, and became quite talkative.

"Miss Cassy—beg pardon, ma'am, I mean Mrs Gardiner—I am so very happy to see you, ma'am. Looking so well, too, if I may say so. Is your family well, ma'am, Miss Lizzie and Master Edward?" she asked, eager for information. Equally pleased to see her and remembering the poor girl must be homesick, so far from her family in Derbyshire, Cassy responded kindly, assuring the girl that her family was in excellent health, all but her dear father-in-law Mr Gardiner.

"Oh ma'am, I am sorry to hear that. It must be very hard for poor Mrs Gardiner, looking after the master alone," she said, and Cassy reassured her that Mr Gardiner was very well cared for and her aunt had many helpers.

"Both his daughters, Mrs Courtney and Mrs Fitzwilliam, are there often and Dr Gardiner and my son Mr Edward, who is now a physician himself, attend upon him every day. Indeed, Mr Edward is with his grandfather at this very moment, staying at Lambton until our return."

Susan expressed her relief. "Ah, that surely is a blessing, ma'am," she said and added in a woebegone sort of voice, "I wish I could say the same of my Miss Josie. She will see no doctors and take no medicine at all."

Alerted by her words, Cassy asked quickly, "Susan, do you mean Miss Josie—I mean Mrs Darcy—refuses to take any medication for her condition? Has not a doctor seen her at all?"

Susan's eyes widened, reflecting her alarm.

"No, ma'am, she will not see anyone, nor will she take any proper medicine. It is only with much coaxing that I can get her to take a spoonful of honey for her chest or some chamomile tea for her headaches, when they are really bad. She has had nothing more in weeks, ma'am. It really is a sad thing to see her wasting away."

Cassy was appalled. "And what about her food?" she asked. The maid rolled her eyes skywards and shook her head.

"That, too, ma'am. She will eat like a bird, and then only when the master pleads with her to do so. Poor Mr Julian, he is so worried about her, he forgets his hat or his scarf and has to rush back for them, else he will leave his tea until it is cold and gulp it down before rushing out the door. It's a wonder he can still work, ma'am."

Cassy agreed, though she said nothing to the girl, as she rose and walked about the room. It seemed things were a good deal worse than they had suspected. Hearing footsteps descending the stairs, Susan picked up the tea tray and left the room, leaving Cassy gazing out of the bay window that looked out on a forlorn old rosebush, so overgrown it had hardly any blooms. Yet, she recalled, the last time they had been here, it had been covered in roses and when she had opened the window, their sweet scent had filled the room.

Her brother entered the parlour and Cassy, turning to greet him, could see he was miserable. Several years her junior, Julian looked depressed and vulnerable as he stood there, his tousled hair and rumpled shirt, as much as his anxious expression, evidence of his anguish. Cassy went to him and took his hands in hers, trying to offer some reassurance, looking for the right words to assuage his pain. She was sure, she said, that Richard would be able to help Josie; after all, he had been their family doctor since she was a little girl.

"If only she would take some medicine and a little nourishment, I am sure she will begin to feel better," he said and then added helplessly, "but Cassy, she will take neither, no matter what I say!"

Cassy felt tears sting her eyes; she had always felt responsible for her young brother, especially because he had been born when everyone was still grieving for their beloved William. They had all treasured Julian, yet he did not appear to have grown into the role he was expected to play. There was a great deal to learn about running an estate, but Julian had shown little interest in it. Even as a boy, he had no talent for practical matters and relied upon their mother herself or the servants for advice on everything.

His sister knew, only too well, that the young man who would one day succeed her father as Master of Pemberley would need to be stronger and more determined than Julian was now.

Beset with domestic problems, he seemed even weaker and less likely than before to take up with confidence the onerous responsibilities of Pemberley, where he would influence the lives of many men, women, and children, who would depend upon his strength and judgment for their livelihoods and security.

Standing in the middle of that drab room, he looked so forlorn that she was moved to say, "Please try not to worry too much, Julian dear. Richard will do his very best. I know Josie trusts him and, when he has persuaded her to take some medication and good food, I have no doubt we will see her condition improve."

Julian did not appear convinced. "Oh Cassy, I do hope you are right. There have been times, awful frightening moments, when I have felt that she does not wish to recover at all."

His voice was so filled with despair that Cassy was shocked.

"Hush, Julian, you must never say that. Why on earth would your wife, who has everything to live for, feel so? She has you, her family, and young Anthony," but he interrupted her.

"Plainly, my dear sister, we are not enough to make her completely happy. Her life, she claims, is empty of purpose; she points out that I have a burning desire to find scientific ways of preventing diseases that kill people, but cannot understand her longing to have her work published. Cassy, I have offered to have it published at my expense, but she will not have it; she says that would not do: it would be no different to having it printed in her father's papers, and she must have it accepted by one of the reputable publishing houses. As you know, this has not occurred and she is bitterly disappointed."

Even as she listened, Cassandra could not help wondering whether this was really the entire story behind Josie's malaise.

"Julian, are you quite sure that is the only reason for her unhappiness? Is there no other cause?" she asked.

There was a long pause during which Cassy studied her brother's countenance as he struggled to find words to express what he was going to say; at last, with a huge effort, he spoke.

"Cassy, I wish I could truthfully say it was, but I cannot. I have tried to pretend otherwise, but I fear I must face the truth. I think, Cassy, my dear Josie no longer loves me."

He sounded so disconsolate, looked so melancholy, she was cut to the heart, just looking at him.

"Julian!" she cried, "what nonsense is this? Whatever makes you say such a thing? Josie has been ill and depressed, but to believe she does not love you, or has no desire to recover, what evidence have you of this outrageous claim?"

Before he could respond, if indeed he was going to make any response at all, Mrs Tate and Richard were heard coming downstairs and no further discussion of the subject was possible.

As they entered the room, talking together, Julian excused himself, claiming there were some papers he had to read before dinner, and went to his study, where he remained for the rest of the afternoon.

A short while later, Cassandra went up to Josie's room. She was very shocked to find Josie so pale and thin, as if after a long and debilitating illness. She was sitting up in bed, a knitted shawl around her thin shoulders, her hair, which had once been much admired for its colour and lustre, twisted into a tight plait. Cassandra could hardly recognise the lively young Josie Tate, who had married her brother a mere five years ago.

"Cassy," her voice was small and thin when she spoke, "it is very kind of you to come all this way to see me, and Richard, too. It is very good of him to come. Mama has told me how very ill Mr Gardiner is; I am so sorry to be so much trouble to you all."

Cassandra sat on the bed beside her and stroked her hand. It was frail and small like a child's. "Josie, my dear, you are not causing us any trouble, especially not if you promise to do as Richard advises and take some proper medication and some good, nourishing food. We shall soon have you fit and well again," she said, trying hard to sound cheerful.

Yet Josie, though she nodded and smiled a pale sort of half-smile, said nothing to show that she intended to be amenable. She let Cassy sit with her and hold her hand, but made no promises. Indeed, when Cassy left the room, she could not help feeling even more disturbed than when she had entered it, for she had elicited no positive response at all.

Cassandra's distress was particularly poignant, for it was to her that Julian had turned, having discovered almost by chance that he was in love with Josie Tate. She recalled his anxiety about meeting her father, the formidable Mr Anthony Tate, who had subsequently turned out to be a most reasonable man. He had also been concerned that Josie was not as yet nineteen and very much in awe of Mr and Mrs Darcy and the grandeur of Pemberley, of which he would, one day, be master.

Cassy recalled the occasion of her brother's twenty-first birthday celebrations and the ball at Pemberley, where there had been present several young women, some prettier and possibly more eligible than Josie; but Julian had preferred the lively and intelligent Miss Tate, with whom he could talk of travel and read poetry. Then it had seemed so simple; two young people in love—they had been so happy together. It was heartrending to see them now, Julian so dispirited and Josie so sad and withdrawn, she seemed almost not to be there at all.

Cassy had felt a good deal of sympathy for the pair. They had both been very young and, unlike her husband, Richard, who had been a great favourite with both her parents long before their engagement, Josie Tate had been a relative outsider at Pemberley. Indeed, in spite of the best endeavours of Mr and Mrs Darcy to draw her into their circle, Cassy had felt that Josie and, occasionally, even Julian had appeared as though they never felt quite at home there.

How else, she wondered, could one account for their preference for the rather dreary environment in which they chose to live, while their gracious apartments at Pemberley lay vacant for most of the year?

Though pressed by both Julian and Mrs Tate to stay to dinner, the Gardiners left and made their way to a hotel in the town, where Richard had stayed previously and was warmly welcomed. There, with some degree of privacy, they were able to talk over dinner.

Cassy was eager to discover her husband's opinion. At first, Richard was unusually silent and thoughtful and his wife was concerned lest he refused to discuss it at all. But by the time they had finished the main course, he began to relax and she realised that he had been silent because he was deeply concerned for his young brother-in-law and his wife. After a glass or two of wine and some excellent cheese, his mood was further lightened and he confessed that he had never before seen a case like it.

"Not in all these years have I had a patient quite like Josie. Young, intelligent, well educated, with a good husband and a beautiful son, it is the sort of situation most women would envy, yet she is sunk in a slough of despair, from which she appears not to want to be released. Each time I question her about her physical symptoms, she denies that she is unwell, yet she is so pale and listless, she seems a shadow of her former self.

"When I mention food, she pulls a face, as if it were something unpleasant and abhorrent to her. She will take neither medication nor nourishment. So what, my dear Cassy, am I to make of it? How shall I ever restore her body to health, and even more perplexing, by what means shall I free her mind from this dreadful despair?" He sounded unusually pessimistic.

Listening to him, Cassy found herself in a quandary. Should she tell him of her brother's rather irrational musings that Josie might not wish to be restored to health at all? While she did not wish to betray her brother's state of mind, on reflection she decided that if Richard was to treat Josie with any chance of success, he needed to know the truth.

When, with some degree of trepidation, she did tell him, he did not appear surprised. Indeed, he said, he had almost reached the same conclusion himself.

"It is difficult not to conclude that she is deliberately pursuing a grievous and most painful course, either to punish herself for some perceived guilt or to punish someone else—presumably her husband or her mother—I cannot, at the moment, tell which it is," he said and Cassy was quite confused.

"But why?" she cried. "What guilt could she possibly have to bear? As for the other possibility, why should she wish to punish the very people who love her?" and Richard had to hush her, for her voice had risen with exasperation as she spoke.

"Hush, dearest, it is not right that we should discuss this matter here; let us wait until we are upstairs," he said, and only when they had retired to their room, did they resume the conversation.

"Is it possible that poor Josie believes we do not care for her?" Cassy asked, still uncomprehending.

"It is possible," said Richard, "that Josie believes that the rest of her family, all of us, myself included, do not understand her. She may wish for praise, attention, whatever it is she feels she is not receiving, and this perverse, self-inflicted illness is her way of telling us all about it."

"But, Richard, Julian loves her dearly. He has told me so, only today," she protested.

He smiled. "Of course he does, but has he told her so? Does he, in all he says and does, demonstrate that love? I think not, my dear, for it is clear he is engrossed, for most of the time, in his work."

They talked late into the night before retiring to bed. The situation so depressed Cassy, she lay sleepless until the early hours of the morning. Only when Richard revealed that he had decided to seek the counsel of an eminent colleague on the morrow, did she finally fall asleep.

The following morning, Richard Gardiner set out to call on a distinguished scholar and physician at one of the colleges. Cassy, having finished breakfast, wrote to her mother as she had promised, recounting their journey and her impressions on arrival at her brother's house.

After some brief comments, she addressed the reason for their visit:

I wish I had better news for you, dear Mama, but I have not.

I cannot believe that Josie has deteriorated to this extent in so short a time. Indeed, to look at her, you would be hard put to recognise the lively young girl who was married to Julian five years ago, or the healthy young woman who used to run up and down the stairs at Pemberley or pursue little Anthony all over the lawns.

She is a mere shadow of the girl we knew and my poor brother is so unhappy, I cannot begin to tell you how sad he is. He talks despairingly of her not wishing to recover and seems to feel he is responsible.

Yet, Richard says he can find no physical sign of disease in her.

He is gone this morning to consult another physician, who is, I believe, an eminent scholar here at Cambridge, and Richard hopes he will have some advice for him. I pray he will and that Richard may succeed in helping both Josie and poor Julian, else I do not know what is to become of them.

I do not mean to alarm you and Papa, but I am so very fearful that things here are going very wrong and I do not know what we can do to help.

There is but one piece of good news—Mrs Tate is here, too, with her maid, Nelly, and no doubt will help relieve the burden upon Julian a little. I shall not delay this further, as I wish to catch the post.

I shall write again as soon as there is any news to hand.

Your loving daughter,

Cassy.

On his return some hours later, Richard sought out his wife, who, having despatched her letters to the post, had returned upstairs to their room. He found her disconsolate and sad, unable, she said, to erase from her mind the melancholy picture of Josie, wan and thin, and Julian, unhappy, despairing, convinced his wife no longer loved him. She had not revealed this piece of information to her husband earlier, reluctant to add to his burden of concern.

But now, unable to hold back, she told him, and when she did, he was most disturbed. This was something he had not expected of Julian, who was generally a logical and reasonable man, not given to irrational declarations.

"Are you quite sure, my love? Did Julian say in so many words?"

"'I fear, Cassy, that my dear Josie no longer loves me,'" she completed the sentence for him, quoting her brother's words.

Richard Gardiner, whose life had been filled with the affection of his parents, the love of his wife and children, and the esteem of friends and colleagues, could barely conceive of the wretched situation in which his unhappy brother-in-law apparently found himself.

"Poor Julian, struggling to cope with his work, which is both important and demanding, a wife sick with melancholy, and the belief that she no longer loves him. It is surely unendurable," he said softly, his voice betraying his distress. "Can you imagine, Cassy, how bereft he must feel?"

Cassy went to him at once and put her arms around him; neither could imagine such a situation in their own lives.

"I can, indeed, but what can we do to help him?" she asked, weeping.

Feeling a growing sense of helplessness, they clung together, saddened, aching, seeking solace from each other, as they faced the daunting prospect of trying to resolve problems whose causes lay hidden from them, finding their only comfort in the love they shared. Yet their own deep passion only compounded their concern about the state of Julian and Josie's lives.

Cassy, no less than her husband, was confounded by the situation that confronted her brother and his wife. Growing up at Pemberley, where the strength of her parents' love had sustained their family in the midst of tragedy, she had married Richard Gardiner, whose own parents had enjoyed a long and contented marriage. Consequently, she had scarcely any personal knowledge of the bitterness and grief that she had encountered with Julian and Josie.

Her own experience of marriage had taken her from eager young love to a deeply satisfying, mature, and passionate relationship with her husband and children. It permeated every aspect of her life and sharpened all her sensibilities; so much so, that strangers meeting them for the first time would become aware of the warmth and strength of their affection for one another.

To both Richard and Cassy, their marriage was a deep well of contentment. To put such a source of happiness in jeopardy, for any reason whatsoever, would have been utterly unthinkable. Sensing her anguish and understanding her need for reassurance, Richard was loving and consoling.

Later, he revealed that he had had a long and enlightening discussion with a colleague, a man for whom he had immense professional respect. This physician had healed many men after the terror and shock of war and was an acknowledged authority on the causes and treatment of acute trauma.

Where once priests and exorcists had held sway, scientific ideas were being applied to ease the curse of melancholia. Richard claimed he had learned much from their discussion and planned to talk to both Julian and his wife.

"Perhaps, if they can be convinced of the need to speak of their fears and anxieties to each other or to my colleague, who understands their situation, there may be a chance for some healing. At the moment, they are each locked in a prison of their own making, into which one will not permit the other entry," he explained.

Back at Pemberley, meanwhile, Elizabeth and Darcy had waited impatiently for news from Cambridge. When it came, in the form of Cassandra's letter, it brought little relief. Elizabeth, having read it twice over, could not make it out at all.

"What can be the matter?" she asked her husband, who, having reread their daughter's words, was at a loss to explain the circumstances, not having been privy to their problems.

His wife persisted, "Darcy, what has happened to poor Julian and Josie? They were so happy here last year—I had hoped they would return for the Summer."

Darcy tried to find a comforting explanation but could not. He too was baffled. His earlier simple prognosis, that Josie was probably bored, was being rapidly eroded by the realisation that she was possibly more seriously ill than any of them had imagined.

"My dear, I think we shall all have to wait until Richard and Cassy return to discover the real cause of the problem. Cassy would not have enough of the detail to give us any real understanding, but Richard would know, and I am sure he will explain it to us," he said.

Even as he spoke, he could see that Elizabeth was unconvinced; trying to reassure her, he was gentle and persuasive, understanding her grief. Losing her beloved William had been a dreadful blow and, though Julian could never replace him, he had brought some light and pleasure back into her life. Now, Julian was miserable and Lizzie suffered with him.

"There has to be some reason, Lizzie; if Richard can find no physical cause for Josie's affliction, there is bound to be another explanation. When he discovers it, he will also find the solution. Meanwhile, dearest, please do not upset yourself unduly or you will also become unwell," he said, anxious for her, using whatever means he could to alleviate her distress. Her happiness had been his concern throughout their long marriage.

Elizabeth smiled and took his hand; it was only a small gesture, but it meant she had accepted the comfort he offered and was glad of the relief. As on many previous occasions, his strength and devotion helped her cope with what might otherwise have been an unbearable burden of pain.

When Richard and Cassandra Gardiner returned to Julian's house the following afternoon, they found, to their astonishment, Mrs Tate and Josie sitting in the parlour in front of the fire. Their maid, Susan, beaming all over her face, had just brought in tea and scones, and while Josie was not exactly eating with relish, she was at least attempting to consume some part of what was on her plate.

A cheerful Mrs Tate informed them that Julian was expected at any moment, and they were to be joined at dinner by a visitor from London.

"A Mr Barrett, who is in Cambridge on business, called this morning and though Julian was unable to see him, being about to leave for his college, he has been asked to dine with us tonight," she explained, adding the information that she had not met him herself, but Julian and Josie knew Mr Barrett well.

"I myself would like very much to meet Mr Barrett, being in the business of writing, too, as you know," Mrs Tate said, prompting Cassy to ask if Mr Barrett was a writer.

At this, Josie, who had put down her plate, responded, surprising Cassy.

"No, but he does know a great many writers, being himself involved in the book trade. He stocks all the best volumes," she said.

It was the first time she had spoken, and both Richard and Cassy were astonished at the firmness and clarity of her voice, which only a day or two ago had sounded so weak and thin.

After the initial surprise, however, Cassy declared that she was delighted to see that Josie was feeling sufficiently well to venture downstairs again. Richard went further, pointing out that she was already looking much better, with more colour in her cheeks, and expressing his confidence that Josie would soon be on her way to recovery. Both of them congratulated Mrs Tate, giving her credit for having effected such a transformation in her daughter in so short a time.

Later, when Cassy left the room to go upstairs, she met Susan on the landing, carrying a gown, which she had pressed. The girl was so excited she could hardly contain herself, eager to tell Cassy of her mistress's recovery. "It's Miss Josie's gown for tonight, ma'am; it's ever so long since she got dressed up, I am to do her hair up, too, ma'am."

Cassy took the opportunity to ask if Josie had begun to take her medication again, and if Mrs Tate had persuaded her to do so. She was taken aback quite when Susan said emphatically, "Oh no, ma'am, it's not Mrs Tate; it's all on account of Mr Barrett." Then seeing the look of consternation on Cassy's face as she said "Mr Barrett," Susan added quickly, "The gentleman that's coming to dinner, ma'am. It's all his doing."

"Whatever do you mean, Susan?" asked Cassy, thinking the girl was babbling, as some silly young women are wont to do, but Susan insisted, "Indeed ma'am, when he was here last year, he was very taken with Miss Josie's writings, you know, ma'am, her poetry and such."

Cassy was unaware that her young sister-in-law wrote poetry, but let that pass, as she persevered, keen to learn more about the involvement of Mr Barrett.

"Was he?" Cassy was interested.

"Yes, ma'am, he sat with her and read some out loud, in the parlour; oh, it was lovely, ma'am. He has such a fine voice. Miss Josie was ever so pleased, because he said it was so good, it should be put in a book. Miss Josie could not stop talking about it for days and days, ma'am."

"And what happened after that?" Cassy asked, for it was plain the maid had more to tell and Cassy was keen to hear it.

"Nothing, ma'am," said Susan pulling a face. "Mr Barrett had to return to London and we heard no more of it. Miss Josie wrote him a letter to his office in London, I know she did, because I took it to the post, but I never heard if he replied, ma'am. But this morning, when he called on the master and was invited to return to dine tonight, the mistress was so pleased, she was up out of bed within an hour and wanted her clothes pressed and her hair washed and curled; she is coming down to dinner for the first time in weeks, ma'am." Susan was plainly excited by the prospect.

Cassy shook her head, still puzzled by the apparent speed with which Josie's recovery had been effected. Mrs Tate's maid, Nelly, appeared on the stairs and Susan's conversation seemed to dry up suddenly.

When Cassy returned to the parlour, Rebecca invited them to dinner.

"I am sure Julian will want you to stay," she said, smiling, and to her husband's surprise, Cassy accepted with some alacrity. She was very keen to meet Mr Barrett, whose appearance had caused so much activity and interest in the household.

Julian Darcy arrived home earlier than usual. So happy was he to find his wife downstairs taking tea, he rushed out again immediately, returning with a bunch of Spring flowers, which he presented to her. Mrs Tate, beaming with pleasure, summoned Susan to fetch a vase and arrange the flowers, which were then given pride of place on the centre table, which had been cleared of all its clutter.

Julian looked ecstatic, but Cassy could not help noticing that her brother's joy was not exactly matched by the response of his wife. Josie, she noted, had smiled and thanked her husband softly, but with no more enthusiasm or warmth than she would any stranger who may have brought her flowers.

Cassandra was beginning to wonder whether the malaise afflicting Josie and Julian was rather more deep-seated than any of them had believed. She said nothing to her husband though, not even when they went away to dress for dinner, and he expressed some surprise that she had so eagerly accepted the invitation to dine.

"I would not have thought you would want to return there tonight," he said, but she smiled and replied that she had been so very glad to see Josie downstairs and Julian was obviously so happy, it had seemed appropriate to join them and celebrate the occasion.

Richard nodded and said no more.

"You do not mind, do you, dearest?" she asked, and he said no, he did not. "For my part," he claimed, "it should afford me an opportunity to observe my patient without intruding upon her. It is possible that she has realised that it is in her power to change her situation. I sincerely hope that it is the beginning of her recovery."

❦

LOOK FOR *Mr Darcy's Daughter* IN NOVEMBER 2008